EVERYMAN,
I WILL GO WITH THEE,
AND BE THY GUIDE,
IN THY MOST NEED
TO GO BY THY SIDE

JONATHAN SWIFT

Gulliver's Travels

with an Introduction by
Pat Rogers

EVERYMAN'S LIBRARY

26

First included in Everyman's Library, 1940
Introduction, Bibliography, and Chronology © David Campbell
Publishers Ltd., 1991

ISBN 1-85715-026-0
A CIP catalogue record for this book is available from the
British Library

Published by David Campbell Publishers Ltd., 79 Berwick Street,
London W1V 3PF

Distributed by Random House (UK) Ltd.,
20 Vauxhall Bridge Road, London SW1V 2SA

GULLIVER'S TRAVELS

CONTENTS

———

PART ONE – A VOYAGE TO LILLIPUT

Chapter I
The author gives some account of himself and family.
His first inducements to travel. He is ship-wrecked,
and swims for his life; gets safe on shore in the
country of Lilliput; is made a prisoner, and carried

Chapter II
The Emperor of Lilliput, attended by several of the
nobility, come to see the author in his confinement.
The emperor's person and habit described. Learned
men appointed to teach the author their language.
He gains favour by his mild disposition. His pockets
are searched, and his sword and pistols taken from

Chapter III
The author diverts the emperor and his nobility of both
sexes in a very uncommon manner. The diversions of
the court of Lilliput described. The author hath his

ix

PART TWO – A VOYAGE TO BROBDINGNAG

Chapter I

A great storm described. The long boat sent to fetch water, the author goes with it to discover the country. He is left on shore, is seized by one of the

CONTENTS

natives, and carried to a farmer's house. His reception there, with several accidents that happened to
them. A description of the inhabitants

Chapter II

A description of the farmer's daughter. The author
carried to a market-town, and then to the metropolis. The particulars of his journey

Chapter III

The author sent for to court. The queen buys him of his
master the farmer, and presents him to the king. He
disputes with his majesty's great scholars. An apartment at court provided for the author. He is in high
favour with the queen. He stands up for the honour
of his own country. His quarrels with the queen's
dwarf

Chapter IV

The country described. A proposal for correcting
modern maps. The king's palace, and some account
of the metropolis. The author's way of travelling.
The chief temple described

Chapter V

Several adventures that happened to the author. The
execution of a criminal. The author shews his skill in
navigation

Chapter VI

Several contrivances of the author to please the king
and queen. He shews his skill in musick. The king
enquires into the state of Europe, which the author
relates to him. The king's observations thereon

Chapter VII

The author's love of his country. He makes a proposal
of much advantage to the king, which is rejected.
The king's great ignorance in politicks. The learning

CONTENTS

Chapter V
The author permitted to see the grand academy of
Lagado. The academy largely described. The arts
wherein the professors employ themselves .. ..

Chapter VI
A further account of the academy. The author proposeth some improvements, which are honourably
received .. ..

Chapter VII
The author leaves Lagado, arrives at Maldonada. No
ship ready. He takes a short voyage to Glubbdubdrib. His reception by the governor.. .. ..

Chapter VIII
A further account of Glubbdubdrib. Antient and
modern history corrected .. ..

Chapter IX
The author's return to Maldonada. Sails to the
kingdom of Luggnagg. The author confined. He is
sent for to court. The manner of his admittance. The
king's great lenity to his subjects .. .. ..

Chapter X
The Luggnuggians commended. A particular description of the Struldbrugs, with many conversations
between the author and some eminent persons upon
that subject .. ..

Chapter XI
The author leaves Luggnagg, and sails to Japan. From
thence he returns in a Dutch ship to Amsterdam,
and from Amsterdam to England .. .. ..

PART FOUR – A VOYAGE TO THE COUNTRY
OF THE HOUYHNHNMS

CONTENTS

Chapter VI

Chapter VII

Chapter VIII

Chapter IX

Chapter X

Chapter XI

Chapter XII

INTRODUCTION

One way of distinguishing between longer works of fiction is to identify the creative germ from which they evolved. *Madame Bovary* is an expanded poem, *Anna Karenina* an expanded pamphlet. *Wuthering Heights* is an amplified lyric, but *Mansfield Park* an amplified essay. *Werther* is an outsize letter, *Tom Jones* a mock-heroic satire drawn out to the length of a full-scale epic, Ford Madox Ford's *The Good Soldier* a short story that outgrew its strength. Proust's *A la recherche du temps perdu* is a wonderfully elaborated gossip column; *Tess of the D'Urbervilles* a swollen ballad, *Moby-Dick* a rhapsodic ode projected to an oceanic compass. Of course such a formula cannot tell the whole truth about novels: Proust's work, for instance, obviously goes far beyond mere gossip. But it is a useful way of catching the essence of a book, and defining its inner form. The seed from which novels are germinated can help to explain to us the leaves and the blossom they afterwards put on.

If we look at *Gulliver's Travels* in this light, there is no question where it belongs. For *Gulliver* is transparently a fairy story that escaped from the nursery, a children's folk tale that went deliberately wrong. Its plot is fabular and its events fabulous: Gulliver carried off in his box above Brobdingnag reminds us of Sindbad in the *Arabian Nights*, whilst the commonwealth of horses recalls Beatrix Potter as well as *Animal Farm*. The whole array of scenes in Lilliput, one might say, serves to infantilize politics, whilst in the second part it is Gulliver himself who becomes a toy or a piece of kindergarten equipment. But it is chiefly the traditional fairy story which insistently comes to the mind, as where Gulliver is caught by one of the reapers in the cornfield, at the start of his Tom Thumb existence in the land of giants.

Ever since it appeared in 1726, *Gulliver's Travels* has enjoyed a double life, as a light-hearted children's classic and as the morose and misanthropic vision of a gloomy dean. Some high-minded critics regret this state of affairs, believing that the existence of a truncated children's version demeans the 'serious' meaning of the work. On the contrary: the childlike quality of the story performs an important function, quite apart from constituting one of the book's main attractions to a wide body of readers. Three principal reasons can be given for this statement.

In the first place, Gulliver's adventures are based squarely on the fable. It happens that there were few literary works in earlier ages aimed specifically at children: juvenile reading as a recognizable category only came properly into being a generation after Swift died. Before then, one of the forms most widely read by the young was the fable – above all, the famous collection of Aesop's *Fables*, which ran through one popular edition after another in the seventeenth and eighteenth centuries. The form had been turned to social commentary in writers like La Fontaine, and was adapted to political purposes by Swift's close friend John Gay at this very moment in time – the first volume of Gay's *Fables* appeared in 1727, only months after *Gulliver*. Swift draws on the ancient tradition of the beast fable, which he used in some of his own most characteristic poems, including 'The Beasts' Confession to the Priest' (1732). By this time-honoured device Swift was able to dramatize his view on humanity in an accessible and familiar manner.

Second, it is clear that the author retained a very strong imaginative hold on the element of grotesque physical farce in his tale. This is most easily demonstrated from a letter which Swift wrote to his publisher, Benjamin Motte, when a new illustrated edition was being projected. During a visit to London in 1727, Swift had seen some crude engravings sold as a complement to the book, and in his letter to Motte, dated 28 December 1727, he points out the defects in these 'cuts' and indicates the form which a graphic treatment of the *Travels* ought to take:

As to having cuts in *Gulliver's Travels*; you will consider how much it will raise the price of the book; the world glutted itself with that book at first, and now it will go off but soberly, but I suppose will not be soon worn out ... The part of the little men will bear cuts much better than the great. I have not the book by me, but will speak by memory. Gulliver in his carriage to the metropolis, his extinguishing the fire. The ladies in their coaches driving about his table. His rising up out of his carriage when his is fastened to his house. His drawing the fleet. The troop upon his handkerchief. The army marching between his legs. His hat drawn by eight horses. Some of these seem to be the fittest to be represented, and perhaps two adventures may be sometimes put in one print.

It is difficult to do anything in the great men – because Gulliver makes so diminutive a figure, and he is but one in the whole kingdom. Among some cuts I bought in London, he is shown taken out of the bowl of cream, but the hand that holds him hides the whole body. He would appear best, wedged in the marrow bone up to the middle, or in the monkey's arms upon the roof, or left upon the ridge and the footman on the ladder going to relieve him or fighting with the rats on the farmer's bed, or in the spaniel's mouth, which being described as a small dog, he might look as large as a duck in one of ours; one of the best would I think be to see his chest just falling into the sea while three eagles are quarrelling with one another. Or the monkey hauling him out of his box.

Next, Swift points out that it is difficult to avoid the impression in illustrating Book II that Gulliver is tiny and the Brobdingnagians no more than ordinary lifesize:

Mr. Wotton the painter, who draws landscapes and horses, told Mr. Pope and me that the gravers did wrong in not making the big folks bear something large and enormous in their shapes, for as drawn by those gravers, they look only like common human creatures: Gulliver being alone and so little, cannot make the contrast appear. The Flying Island might be drawn as large as described in the book, and Gulliver drawing up into it, and some fellows with flappers. I know not what to do with the projectors. Nor what figure the Island of Ghosts would make, or any passage related in it because I do not well remember it. The Country of Horses, I think would furnish many. Gulliver brought to be compared with the yahoo, the family at dinner and he waiting. The grand council of horses assembled, sitting, one of them standing with a hoof extended as if he were speaking, the she-yahoo embracing Gulliver in the river, who turns away his head in disgust. The yahoos got into a tree to infest him under it. The yahoos drawing carriages, and driven by a horse with a whip in his hoof. I can think of no more; but Mr. Gay will advise you and carry you to Mr. Wotton, and some other skilful people.

It is obvious from what Swift writes that he had not lost his keen sense of physical misadventure and of what might be called the engaging surrealism of the narrative. It is a quality not far from that of oriental tales or fairy stories, with a blend of the magical and the exaggerated.

Third, there is considerable evidence that contemporary readers – including those who knew Swift best, and who could fathom best what he was up to – detected a quality of innocent fun in the book. Whatever deeper meanings we may, quite legitimately, read into the text, we ought not to ignore this element. Dr John Arbuthnot's comment, 'Gulliver is a happy man that at his age can write such a merry work,' is usually treated as either innocent in the bad sense or else ironic. In fact it is neither innocent nor precisely ironic: it is testimony to Swift's ability to convey his sharpest criticisms of the world in a mode that is predominantly comic, from start even to the very end (with Gulliver whinnying absurdly in his stable); and to choose a mode where even a strongly negative and hostile current of feeling is not allowed to destroy the fantasy, to eliminate the ridiculous, or to impede the energy of the narrative. *Gulliver*, of course, is not just a children's book; but its prevailing high spirits owe a great deal to the solid base it maintains in the juvenile adventure story.

*

We do not know very much about the inspiration and conception of the book, and we do not need to know very much, because its targets are broad enough to make themselves apparent to us, without detailed working notes compiled by the author in the throes of creation. It is not a work like *Ulysses* or *A la recherche du temps perdu*, where the labour of writing becomes almost a theme in the text. All we need to be aware of is the broad sequence of events and the stage which Swift's career had reached when he wrote *Gulliver*.

It is now generally agreed that the book was written from about 1720 to about 1725. It used to be thought that the origins of the work went back to the convivial and collaborative activities of the so-called Scriblerus Club, in which Swift had joined with Pope, Gay, Arbuthnot and a couple of others whilst he was living in London in 1713 and 1714. There are a few parallels between the satire on science in Book III and the Scriblerian projects of ridiculing the pseudo-learning of the day: only a few pamphlets were published at the time, but Pope later issued his *Art of Sinking in Poetry* in 1727 and the *Memoirs* of the arch-pedant Martin Scriblerus in 1741. But the links are tenuous, and it is likely that earlier commentators were misled by Swift's puzzling silence in the first years of his exile to Dublin, that is 1714–20, when he published nothing of substance. The truth seems to be that Swift, after four years of bustling importance at the side of the leading Tory ministers during Queen Anne's reign, fell into lassitude and near-despair as he watched the Hanoverian dynasty entrench itself from his enforced remoteness at St Patrick's cathedral. Only gradually did there return to him the literary oestrus which had gone into the creation of his exuberant early masterpieces – *A Tale of a Tub* and *The Battle of the Books* – and the corruscating journalism with which he had supported the Tory ministry of his friends Harley and Bolingbroke. Nor do we have any need to sentimentalize his private life and assume it was the competing affections of his two women friends, Stella and Vanessa, which distracted him from writing. In fact, it was largely public events which turned Swift back to sustained composition.

After 1720 Swift once more became prolific in both prose and verse. He never again suffered from any form of block, until his final collapse into senile dementia almost twenty years later, and the majority of his best poetry, as well as *Gulliver*, the *Drapier's Letters* and the *Modest Proposal*, are the products of those last two active decades. He was fifty-three in 1720, with his astonishing early satires now some way in the past, with his youthful hopes as a high-flying versifier dashed and little in the way of substantial poetic achievement to treasure, and with his worldly ambitions stunted by a Hanoverian court he despised and a Whig ministry who distrusted him. He probably adjusted quite soon to the realization that he would never be a bishop, but it would have been harder to come to terms with the fact that his immense potential as a writer had never properly been fulfilled.

Two things, principally, conspired to make him forget the narrow concerns of his deanery, which had shut out everything else for five years. In 1719 the English parliament passed the Declaratory Act, which confirmed the total dependency and colonial status of Ireland by removing the power of its House of Lords to alter legal decisions made in England. A year later, the Irish Lords had their role as a court of appeal removed by the London parliament. Swift's increasing resentment at the ways in which England treated Ireland – its people, its judicial system, its economy, its political institutions and even sometimes its Church – burst out in May 1720, with a pamphlet attacking English restrictions on free Irish trade. This work caused official outrage and attempts were made to prosecute the unnamed but not unidentifiable author. Swift seems to have relished both the political mischief and the notoriety. Three years later he was to return to the fray, when the imposition by Walpole's government of some unwanted coinage (a measure lining the pockets of the dishonest entrepreneur who supplied the coins, and of the court figures he had bribed to obtain his patent) created a national furore in Ireland. It was above all Swift, in the person of the humble Dublin tradesman writing the plainspoken *Drapier's Letters*, who unified the generally fissile Irish population into a coherent body of public opinion. It has seemed to many a paradox that Swift should have become the champion of liberties and the spokesman for his countrymen, since he regarded his situation as that of an exile and had little sympathy with the majority culture of downtrodden Catholics. But he was a man whose underlying humanity was often at odds with a surface streak of bigotry and even cruelty; the role he undertook as a tribune of the people suited many of his temperamental needs, despite the cold austerity of his deaconal self, and its rhetorical needs were precisely in line with his own unmatched powers as a writer of spare, concrete and vivid English prose. The Drapier became a national hero, and Swift once again felt the sense of power which his pen could bring him, whatever else went wrong with his life.

By this time *Gulliver* was well on towards completion. The first firm reference we have occurs in a letter to his friend

INTRODUCTION

Charles Ford in April 1721, mentioning an 'account of countries hitherto unknown'. On 1 January 1722, the exiled Jacobite politician Lord Bolingbroke (one of Swift's powerful allies in the heady days of Queen Anne) wrote to him, 'I long to see your travels', adding that he would undertake to find in two pages of Swift's *bagatelles* 'more good sense, useful knowledge, and true religion' than in nineteen out of twenty leading divines and philosophers of the age. Bolingbroke is not a reliable informant on true religion, but he was right to see that Swift's playful *bagatelles* concealed searing implications for the state of mankind. There are further references in the correspondence later in this same year, and then a revealing passage in Bolingbroke's letter of Christmas Day 1723, intended for Charles Ford but sent by error to Swift himself. But for the support of Stella, says Bolingbroke, Swift would himself have veered off into another world, like 'that country which he discovered not long ago, where horses and mules are the reasonable creatures, and men the beasts of burden'. This shows unmistakably that Book IV was already drafted in some form by this date. Swift replied on 18 January 1724, informing Bolingbroke that he had now 'left the country of horses, and am now in the flying island, where I shall not stay long'. He expected the *Travels* to be finished by the summer.

A month later, Swift reported to Ford that Bolingbroke had written again, and teased Swift about his 'Southern journey'. This is a more significant touch than has been realized. For it alludes more or less explicitly to the other great event of 1720, which had helped to draw Swift back into active authorship. This was the year of the South Sea Bubble, a major national trauma, a vast political scandal and a desperate blow to the emerging capitalist system. For conservative thinkers, as Swift and Bolingbroke were on such issues, the happenings of 1720, running over to 1721, had confirmed their worst fears of what Hanoverian rule and an entrenched Whig government would bring in their wake. They tended to share what had been called a 'politics of nostalgia', identifying the landed class as the natural guardians of the public weal, and mistrusting the new financial and administrative cadres which had grown up with the development of credit at a personal and public level.

For such thinkers, whom we may loosely identify with the Tory cause if not with any precise Tory parliamentary grouping, the creation of large banks and holding companies, the expansion of the national debt, and the growing influence of City interests in the running of the country all pointed to a political and moral loss of direction. Everyone had some opinion about the South Sea débâcle. Many had lost by it, not just get-rich-quick investors and financial innocents like John Gay, but also inoffensive annuitants who had been caught up in the crisis of confidence. Even Daniel Defoe, who had been as insistent as anyone on the merits of a South Sea trading company when he too had advised the ministers a decade back, was shocked by the amount of social upheaval which the Bubble caused. His *Journal of the Plague Year* (1722) is a fictional replay of the alternative calamity, with London ostensibly laid low by bubonic plague, but in a coded subtext shown as overwhelmed by the effects of the Bubble. His *Tour* of Britain is suffused with memories of this episode, seen as a national bankruptcy emotionally equivalent to the personal bankruptcy Defoe had himself endured and dreaded ever after.

Swift's perspective is a little different. He disliked the Bubble for several reasons; it symbolized the spreading effects of the City, it showed the dubious morality and efficacy of modern innovations in government, and it exposed the greed and innocence of the public. It also, no less balefully, brought to power Robert Walpole, who was to remain at the head of affairs until 1742, by which time Swift was incapable. Walpole became the target for much of the finest Augustan satire, in Gay's *Beggar's Opera* (1728) and in the work of Pope especially – indeed, Walpole and Pope have been termed the 'mighty opposites' of the age. But Swift returned to Walpole just as obsessively, and the writing of *Gulliver* may be regarded as marking the very juncture when Walpole seized the opening which the South Seas imbroglio had opened up for him. In Swift's terms, post-Bubble England gets the prime minister it deserves; the national developments which underlay the rise of Walpole are the subject matter of the *Travels*.

This applies especially to Book III. As we have seen, it was written last, and completed not long before Bolingbroke wrote to Swift about the 'Southern journey'. It is true that the experiments in the academy of Lagado can be traced to some of the pioneering scientific studies of the Royal Society, duly written up in their *Philosophical Transactions*. But these sections of the book contain a metaphor within a metaphor, it seems to me; for the underlying drift of this portion of the work is to assail a wider range of innovation. The most revelatory episode is the story of Lord Munodi, who has a good deal of Swift's former mentor, Robert Harley, about him (see III, iv). The allegory of the mill, with water elaborately driven uphill in defiance of Nature, stands for the new ways of doing things in politics as much as science. But the vehicle of this metaphor points unmistakably to the stagnation of the economy, and near-bankrupty, brought about by the financial and fiscal manipulations of the Bubble years. Moreover, those responsible are plainly named a 'club' of 'projectors', both ominous words in Swift's lexicon. The club is likely to be composed of factious self-appointed opportunists, whilst the projectors are the very people Swift sees everywhere and most distrusts; the promoters of the Bubble, whether commercial swindlers or government functionaries in their pay. They are the individuals who dreamt up absurd and implausible companies to fleece a gullible public during the wild optimism of the South Sea mania. They are rash speculators in other fields too – scientists or theologians – but their activity is significantly imaged in this book as a piece of preposterous and ill-managed *engineering*. The episode goes to show how closely Swift was attending to very recent developments, and to fix the effective subject matter of the *Travels* as extremely modern history. It is for this reason that we need to locate the writing precisely in the crucial period of 1720 to 1725.

Nonetheless, there are self-evidently some wider and more timeless concerns wrapped up in Swift's allegory. Before we look at these, we ought to conclude the story of composition and publication. The work was probably revised in 1725. By September of that year Swift was in a position to write to Pope of the *Travels* as complete and transcribed: this is the most famous and substantial comment he ever made on the work, and will be considered in detail shortly. Swift visited England for the first time since the débâcle of 1714 when he came to London in March 1726, spending five months in and around the capital in the company of Pope, Bolingbroke, Gay and others. Shortly before he left, negotiations began with the publisher concerning the dangerous manuscript Swift had brought with him from Ireland. A complex set of subterfuges were employed, but in brief it can be said that Gulliver's supposed cousin, 'Richard Sympson', surreptitiously conveyed the manuscript to the bookseller Motte (just possibly, I think, the name may have been chosen because the official who dealt with licensing regular publications with the Stationers' Company was called Simpson – or was when the printed text of the volume was registered in 1735). Motte replied with understandable enthusiasm, and the *Travels* were published on 28 October 1726. Swift naturally left no trace of his own identity on title page or elsewhere, but anonymity was the rule with him, and he would probably have suppressed his authorship even if the book had been less explosive in content. As it was, a number of small cuts and alterations were made, from fear of giving offence to those in power. Most of these were restored when Swift's collected works appeared, with some collusion on his part, in Dublin (1735). The Dublin text has been regarded as the best by most commentators, since it clearly benefited from the attentions of Charles Ford and possibly of Swift himself; even so, it still omitted the episode of the revolt by Lindalinians (Dubliners) at the end of III, iii, which was not incorporated into the received text until as late as 1899.

The book attained a great success when it was published, though it elicited some puzzled and some sceptical responses. The most famous comment is no doubt that of the Irish bishop who, as Swift told Pope, said that 'the book was full of improbable lies, and for his part, he hardly believed a word of it'. Swift's own correspondence for the next year or so is full of Gulliver-lingo, with the Dean professing not to understand references to Yahoos and flappers in the letters of his friends. The fullest description of the immediate reaction occurs in

Gay's letter of 17 November 1726. Gay reports to *Gulliver* that 'from the highest to the lowest it is universally read, from the cabinet council to the nursery'. There were continuations by others, ripostes, poetic tributes (including some charming trifles by Pope), and a veritable rage for Gulliver, not snuffed out until the following year. Then, as Swift wrote to Gay on 28 March 1728, 'The *Beggar's Opera* hath knocked down Gulliver, I hope to see Pope's Dulness [*The Dunciad*] knock down the *Beggar's Opera*, but not till it hath fully done its job.' Thus Swift sets out the line of descent of three masterpieces of Augustan satire, which each saw the light within a period of less than a year.

Here we can leave the story, postponing for subsequent discussion the controversies which soon came to rage around the work on moral and aesthetic grounds. We should just note briefly that there were further editions, including the one Motte had planned with 'cuts'; and that the Dublin edition of 1735, brought out by George Faulkner with some degree of connivance on Swift's part, introduced a large number of improvements. It was in this edition, too, that the letter from 'Cousin Sympson' was first printed at the head of the text. As mentioned earlier, the episode concerning the rebellion of the Lindalinians in Book III (probably an allegory of the affair of Wood's halfpence in 1724) was omitted: otherwise Faulkner provided his readers with the book as we now have it.

The structure of the work is crucial to its satiric effects. It is of course divided into four separate 'travels', each a distinct journey with a definite occasion, and described from the time of Gulliver's departure to the moment of his arrival home in England. This regular pattern of out/return, repeated four times, sets up a crucial narrative rhythm. Swift could not have achieved the same effects if he had allowed Gulliver to make one long peregrination, stopping along the way at the four parts of the world he visits, and only at the end coming back to London. For example, there are distinct advantages for the satire in the fact that Swift can show us Gulliver's more or less reluctant motives for leaving his home yet again. He can provide us with a different mode of isolating the hero each time: it has often been pointed out that his first adventures arise from mere accident, a shipwreck, whilst on the second occasion he is deserted by his comrades, on the third he is captured by pirates, and on the fourth his crew mutiny against him. This has been seen as painting a gradually darker picture of Gulliver's experiences as a castaway, and thus establishing a prevailing tone for the individual books right at their start.

However, a more important aspect of this device concerns the ending of each individual part. At the end of the first, second and fourth books we observe the difficulty with which Gulliver readjusts to his own surroundings – including his family – when he returns from his journey. This period of temporary maladjustment is seen at its funniest when Gulliver calls out to people he meets on the road to get out of his way in case he should trample them to death (II, viii). It is vital to Swift's purposes for us to have these episodes in our head when we reach Gulliver's final misanthropic state, after he has been obliged to leave his beloved land of the 'wise and virtuous' Houyhnhnms. We can connect these indications of Gulliver's excessive willingness to take over the standards of his host country with other aspects of his character. He boasts of his 'very faithful memory', which allows him to learn languages rapidly, one of the attributes of which he is most proud. To the reader this may suggest not so much an enviable talent as a surprising readiness to go native and an over-hasty absorption of the mind-set of others. Further, the patriotism of which Gulliver makes so much at times is an oddly limited one; it permits him to make an implausible 'panegyric' of his country to the King of Brobdingnag, echoing the most abject of current Whig paeans to the splendours of the nation. ('The next darling blessing, and privilege, we justly glory in as Englishmen, is liberty,' one such flourish began in the very year *Gulliver* was published.) But it does not breed any intelligent loyalty, it is not attached to individual leaders or institutions and it has none of the deep local piety which usually accompanies an abiding love of one's native soil – hence, perhaps, Gulliver's eagerness to be off and away whenever he spends any time in England.

The most obvious way in which Gulliver over-identifies with his new 'home', and the most comically energizing way, is found in Book II. Here Gulliver rapidly adapts his own sense of scale to the Brobdingnagian measure of things. Throughout this part, we find Gulliver describing what he sees not in terms of his familiar European scale but in the terms appropriate to one brought up according to the dimensions of Brobdingnag. Moreover, this process starts very soon after Gulliver has arrived in the land of the giants. Within a matter of weeks he is noticing that there was 'hardly a rivulet as small as the Thames at London Bridge'. Glumdalclith carried 'a little book in her pocket, not much larger than a Sanson's *Atlas*', that is the bulkiest tome known in Britain at that time. The court dwarf must be tiny indeed, for 'I verily think he was not full thirty foot high.' Gulliver had encountered whales 'so large that a man could hardly carry one upon his shoulders', a particularly happy inversion of semantic expectations. The tower of the temple disappoints Gulliver, 'for the height is not about three thousand foot, reckoning from the ground to the highest pinnacle'. The narrator instantly does his favourite proportion sum, dividing by twelve, to show that in relative terms this tower is less impressive than the steeple of Salisbury cathedral. Gulliver's well-established mathematical turn of mind betrays him into instant conversion sums and the effect is to make him an intellectual citizen of the host country.

Once again this technique is preparing us for later effects. When he meets the Struldbruggs in the next book, Gulliver mentions that the youngest was 'not above two hundred years old', despite the fact that he has only very recently come to learn of these pathetic immortals. More significantly, this tendency to over-adjust becomes apparent in the final book, when Gulliver immediately rejects the Yahoos and adopts a wholly Houyhnhnm-based view of the Land of the Horses. Perhaps the Houyhnhnms are indeed as admirable as Gulliver thinks (an issue we shall return to), but there can be little doubt that Gulliver's instant and wholesale conversion to their outlook suggests an extreme degree of suggestibility on his part. It is important to remember that the word 'gullible' did not yet exist, but the verb 'to gull' certainly did, and the hero is easily taken in by many of the inhabitants in all the countries he visits. If not deceived, he is certainly overimpressed. A man who can naturally see a thirty-foot human being as a true dwarf may well be expected to think himself into the condition of a horse when he meets some wise brutes.

The most obvious parallels in structure are those which take the form of contrast between Books I and II. For example, Gulliver is always liable to do inadvertent damage with his 'huge' clumsy body in Lilliput. When he arrives in Brobdingnag, his now 'tiny' body is constantly under threat of assault or destruction. He faces the possibility of being reaped in the cornfield, eaten, squashed and dashed to the ground from a height. He actually does suffer a number of humiliating physical mishaps: he is dropped into a bowl of cream, attacked by wasps, assailed by marauding frogs, carried by the monkey up to a rooftop and finally hauled away in his box by an eagle. All this serves to emphasize his vulnerability, and some critics, including Paul Fussell (see Bibliography, p. xxxviii), have seen this 'frailty' as an emblem of the damage to Gulliver's self-esteem which he incurs. But he gets over such adventures as being stuffed into a marrow-bone with his usual cheerful adaptability. The main underlying meaning of the device may be a little different.

Gulliver's apparent smallness makes the people of Brobdingnag, naturally applying their own giant scale to everything, look on him as a *splacknuck* (a small animal, possibly a rodent). The indignities to which the hero is subjected confirm his diminutive size, his impotence and his lack of value in the Brobdingnagian currency. The pride he had manifested in Lilliput now seems totally absurd; and this is one of many places where the significance of events in Brobdingnag only emerges when we make a comparison with what had happened in Lilliput. The local scientists relate him to such creatures as a fieldmouse; soon afterwards the King listens to Gulliver's first account of European wars and politics, remarking, 'how contemptible a thing was human grandeur, which could be mimicked by such diminutive insects as I: and yet, said he, I dare engage, these creatures have their titles and distinctions of honour, they contrive little nests and burrows, that they call houses and cities...' Once more we recall

Gulliver's absurd self-importance when he was granted the title of *nardac* in Lilliput.

All this is preparing for one of the climactic moments in the entire work, when the King launches his searing outburst against Gulliver after the traveller has given his complacent narrative of the beauties of European civilization. The famous peroration picks up the suggestions we have just been noting: 'I cannot but conclude the bulk of your natives to be the most pernicious race of little odious vermin that nature ever suffered to crawl upon the surface of the earth.' This would be a powerful tirade in any context; but it gains from the care Swift has taken to show Gulliver as being, effectively, vermin in the Brodingnagian order of things. Further on in the conversation, the King employs very similar language: 'He was amazed how so impotent and groveling as insect as I ... could entertain such inhuman ideas.' Yet again, it is noticeable that when Gulliver is rescued by the English seamen, he views them first as 'so many pigmies' and then, reverting even more closely to the earlier pattern of imagery, 'when I first got into the ship, and the sailors all stood about me, I thought they were the most little contemptible creatures I had ever beheld'. It is not just that Gulliver has, characteristically, adopted the viewpoint of the King of Brobdingnag. What has happened is that he has dissociated himself from the 'verminous' condition he now attributes to the rest of humanity – another premonition of the near-lunatic estrangement he feels from mankind at the end of Book IV. It should also be noted that the word 'insect' at this period could cover a wide variety of 'lesser' creatures, such as snails, earthworms, frogs and even tortoises.

In Book IV, the symbol of depravity is rather the simian figure of the Yahoo. Commentators have shown that Swift's choice of the filthy debased ape for his fable, along with the choice of the reasonable horse, can be related to several currents of thought. The Yahoo is loaded with some of the traditional attributes of sin in Christian theology; the animalistic had often been used to express the flight from God-given right-thinking and true 'humanity'. It has also been pointed out that many travel authors had recoiled in horror from the

'ape-like' characteristics of primitive peoples they had encountered. According to one view, Swift satirizes the ideal of a
'noble savage'; by showing unaccommodated man as living a
nasty, brutish and relatively short life, Book IV juxtaposes the
possibilities for a truly 'civilized' mode of living against the
bestial scramble for power, the greed and the selfishness of
people as they actually are. A spoilt idealist, Swift was quite
capable of such a proceeding, although it is not clear that he
was fully aware of a cult of noble savagery in a way that would
have been plausible two generations later, after the writings of
Enlightenment thinkers such as Rousseau and Diderot. It
seems more likely that he extends the Christian, and especially
Pauline, view of humanity as creatures subject to the insistent
call of the flesh. What matters for our present discussion is that
the simian Yahoos have loathsome qualities which make them
the successors of the verminous or insect-like beings whom we
have encountered in the earlier parts of the work.

Horses call up another set of ideas. Two trail-blazing studies
have enabled us to regain more of the meanings which an
educated contemporary of Swift might have discovered in the
final parable. Rosalie Colie (see Bibliography, p. xxxviii)
showed that Swift made explicit allusions to a recent philosophical controversy. The great English thinker of Swift's
youth, John Locke, had engaged in debate with the Bishop of
Worcester, Edward Stillingfleet, during the later 1690s. The
controversy was fairly technical, but it centred on the validity
of names as describing qualities or indicating essences in the
person or object named. At one point Locke argues, 'The
mind, in making its complex ideas of substances, only follows
nature, and puts no ideas together, which are not supposed to
have an union in nature; nobody joins the voice of a sheep,
with the shape of an horse, ... to be the complex ideas of any
real substance.' Swift does satirically yoke disparate attributes
together, such as the body of a horse with the speech of a
human being, and the shape of a human with the behaviour of
a monkey. At another point Locke expressed his doubts on
the identifying quality of a name by remarking, against
Stillingfleet's points, that he had known a horse called Peter,
and that others might be called James or John. Stillingfleet

blustered a little in response, but carried on with the same nomenclature, arguing that despite what Locke said a rational person could tell a horse or a 'drill' (baboon) from a man, whatever name was bestowed on it.

The relevance of this to Swift's thought is clear if we look at his most famous letter, one written to Pope in September 1725, just after he had finished revising *Gulliver*. Almost all commentators cite this letter, but it is necessary to do so yet once more because of the sharp shaft of light it throws on the issues at stake:

When you think of the world give it one lash the most at my request. I have ever hated all nations, professions, and communities and all my love is towards individuals; for instance, I hate the tribe of lawyers, but I love Counsellor such a one, Judge such a one, for so with physicians (I will not speak of my own trade) soldiers, English, Scotch, French; and the rest but principally I hate and detest that animal called man, although I heartily love John, Peter, Thomas and so forth. This is the system upon which I have governed myself many years (but do not tell) and so I shall go on till I have done with them. I have got material towards a treatise proving the falsity of the definition *animal rationale*; and to show it should be only *rationis capax*. Upon this great foundation of misanthropy (though not Timon's manner) the whole building of my travels is erected. And I never will have peace of mind till all honest men are of my opinion: by consequence you are to embrace it immediately, and procure that all who deserve my esteem may do so too. The matter is so clear that it will admit little dispute. Nay I will hold a hundred pounds that you and I agree in the point.

This is Swift's clearest statement on the themes which are caught up in *Gulliver*, and indeed writers seldom bequeath to posterity such helpful, if challenging, glosses on their own creative work. The reference to John, Peter and Thomas directly recalls the debate about the essence of humanity in the Locke–Stillingfleet controversy, and any reasonably well-read contemporary would see the drift of Swift's allusions to this fundamental debate about the nature of man.

But there is an even closer parallel from outside the text. This was pointed out by R. S. Crane in another seminal essay (see Bibliography, p. xxxviii). Crane showed that the logic textbooks which Swift had studied in his youth at Trinity College, Dublin, regularly employed man as the symbol of the rational (*homo est animal rationale*) and most commonly it was the horse which was the type of the irrational animal. Moreover, one of Swift's own mentors, Narcissus Marsh (who was Provost of the College when Swift was at Dublin), had written a textbook for the use of Trinity College students two years before Jonathan began his studies, which used exactly these forms of proposition in the basic course on logic. Even more appositely, if such a thing is possible, Marsh had given as examples of individuated human beings notional figures labelled John, Peter and Thomas. Looking back at Swift's letter, it is impossible to resist the conclusion that he had framed his *Travels* with this way of thinking in mind. To choose horses as the creatures of reason, and men-like Yahoos as the insensate brutes, was simply to reverse the normal philosophic definitions of the time.

There is another possible origin for certain of Swift's procedures which has not been so fully explored; it occurs in the *Essay on Ancient and Modern Learning* (1690), by Sir William Temple. This was the main contribution made to the long-running quarrel of Ancients and Moderns, or 'battle of the books', by Temple, a retired diplomat who was the author of high-minded and somewhat vacuous disquisitions on cultural and historical themes. Swift had been employed by Temple as his secretary and had edited his mentor's works after Temple died in 1699. This is how the relevant passage runs:

But what would we have, unless it be other natures and beings than God Almighty has given us? The height of our statures may be six or seven foot, and we would have it sixteen; the length of our age may reach to a hundred years, and we would have it a thousand. We are born to grovel upon the earth, and we would fain soar up to the skies ... The motion of the sun is plain and evident to some astronomers, and of the earth to others, yet we none of us know which of them moves, and meet with many seeming impossibilities in both, and beyond the fathom of human reason or comprehension. Nay, we do not know so much as know what motion is, nor how a stone moves from our hand, when we throw it across the street. Of all these that most ancient and divine writer [Job 11, 12] gives the best account in that short short satire, 'Vain man would fain be wise, when he is born like a wild ass's colt.'

Here there are hints for the Brobdingnagians (albeit slightly scaled down), the Struldbruggs and many of the traits of the Laputans. Swift's attitude on such broad issues of humanism and metaphysics was a conservative one; radical as he could be in his literary techniques, his political alliances and his psychological insights, he stands with Temple to the end of his days on the fundamentals of the good life.

It is less important to prove that one or other of these 'sources' underlay Swift's narrative than to see how he fictionalized some of the major philosophical issues of his time. This is the clearer since his basic ploy, the use of the beast fable, suited all the lines of thought we have just been considering.

*

From the start it has been the last part of the *Travels* which has occasioned the most intense and perplexed reactions. Swift's early biographer Lord Orrery asserted that 'in painting the Yahoos [Swift] becomes one himself'. In the most famous Victorian discussion, William Makepeace Thackeray declared that the fourth part was actually written in Yahoo language: 'a monster gibbering shrieks, and gnashing imprecations against mankind – tearing down all shreds of modesty, past all sense of manliness and shame; filthy in word, filthy in thought, furious, raging, obscene'. Twentieth-century critics have reacted against this view of the ending, and for some years a generation back it was fashionable to separate Swift the author very clearly from Gulliver the character. According to this reading, the alienation is all Gulliver's, and his refusal to see the absurdity of identifying with the horses should alert us to Swift's judgement on his gullible character. At this period the Houyhnhnms were often dismissed as cold and unfeeling, almost as much an object of satire as the Yahoos indeed. They were interpreted as caricatures of rationalistic thinking of the time, best represented by the deistic theologians. In recent years considerable inroads have been made in this reading; it can be shown that Swift's declared opinions on such matters as education chime in very closely with the upbringing of the young Houyhnhnms, and it is generally agreed that, even if Swift knew that human beings could never achieve the pure rationality of the horses, he would have been happier if such a thing had been possible.

Some of the most incisive modern accounts of the work are listed in the Bibliography which follows. An essay written as far back as 1943 by Joseph Horrell, 'What Gulliver Knew', remains trenchant and perceptive on such matters as the 'dull gravity' of the detail which Swift injects into his narrative, parodying the travel writers of his day as he names unwanted details of navigation and the like. A powerful essay by John Traugott, dating from 1961, analyses certain similarities between *Gulliver* and Thomas More's earlier picture of *Utopia*. Traugott concludes that 'at the end, in his passionate moments, Gulliver is very like the satirist'. He has found an ally in Claude Rawson, who has written one of the most influential modern essays on the work. For Rawson, in his study of 'Order and Cruelty', Swift's 'official' attitudes are constantly subverted by the anarchic and irresistible force of his imagination. He concludes: 'As the satire finally devolves from the third on to the first person, from world to gentle reader and back to the satirist, we could do worse than entertain the thought that Swift, in the place where all the ladders (and all the spirals) start, was and sensed that he was, in all rebellious recalcitrance, himself Yahoo.' It is a far more sophisticated account of the work than that of Orrery or Thackeray, but it arrives at a not wholly dissimilar point: the greatness of Swift's satire, and its capacity to disturb us, arise from his complicity in all the imaginative excesses of his characters. We cannot just safely leave Gulliver, as an object of derision, fraternizing with his horses in the stable. The effect of the entire work, *Gulliver's Travels*, is to involve us in the satire on mankind, and to make us realize that we are not, any more than Swift is, comfortably above the action. The bell tolls for us, as it does for Gulliver and his creator.

Pat Rogers

SELECT BIBLIOGRAPHY

BIOGRAPHY

EHRENPREIS, I., *Swift: The Man, his Works, and the Age*, 3 vols., Methuen, 1962–83. The fullest and richest account.

NOKES, D., *Jonathan Swift: A Hypocrite Reversed*, Oxford University Press, 1985.

DOWNIE, J. A. *Jonathan Swift: Political Writer*, Routledge, 1985.

REFERENCE

DONOGHUE, D., ed., *Jonathan Swift: A Critical Anthology*, Penguin, 1971.

WILLIAMS, K., ed., *Swift: The Critical Heritage*, Routledge, 1970. These two books permit study of the history of Swift's reputation.

PROBYN, C. T., ed., *Jonathan Swift: The Contemporary Background*, Manchester University Press, 1978. A valuable collection of documents and selections which place Swift's work, especially *Gulliver's Travels*, in context.

CRITICAL WORKS

(i) General studies

DONOGHUE, D., *Jonathan Swift: A Critical Introduction*, Cambridge University Press, 1969.

EHRENPREIS, I., *The Personality of Jonathan Swift, Vision Press,* Methuen, 1958.

FERGUSON, O. W., *Jonathan Swift and Ireland*, University of Illinois Press, Champaign, 1962.

(ii) Special studies

CARNOCHAN, W. B., *Lemuel Gulliver's Mirror for Man*, University of California Press, Berkeley, 1968.

RAWSON, C. J., *Gulliver and the Gentle Reader*, Routledge, 1974.

— *Order from Confusion Sprung*, Allen and Unwin, 1985. Contains some influential readings of Swift's methods.

(iii) Collections of essays

PROBYN, C., ed., *The Art of Jonathan Swift*, Vision Press, 1978.

RAWSON, C., ed., *The Character of Swift's Satire: A Revised Focus*, University of Delaware Press, Newark, 1983.

VICKERS, B., ed., *The World of Jonathan Swift*, Basil Blackwell, 1968.

GULLIVER'S TRAVELS

(iv) Anthologies of published criticism

BRADY, F., ed., *Twentieth Century Interpretations of Gulliver's Travels*, Prentice Hall, Englewood Cliffs, New Jersey, 1968.

GRAVIL, R., ed., *Swift: Gulliver's Travels*, Macmillan, 1974. Published in the 'Casebook' series.

TUVESON, E., ed., *Swift: A Collection of Critical Essays*, Prentice Hall, Englewood Cliffs, New Jersey, 1964. Published in the 'Twentieth Century Views' series.

(v) Articles

COLIE, R., 'Gulliver, the Locke-Stillingfleet Controversy and the Nature of Man', *History of Ideas Newsletter*, II, 1956, pp. 58–62.

CRANE, R. S., 'The Houyhnhnms, the Yahoos, and the History of Ideas', first published in 1962, excerpted in Brady, op. cit.

ELLIOTT, R. C., 'The Satirist Satirized', first published in 1960, excerpted in Brady, ibid.

HORRELL, J., 'What Gulliver Knew', first published in 1943, reprinted in Tuveson, op. cit.

FUSSELL, P., 'The Frailty of Lemuel Gulliver', first published in 1960, excerpted in Brady, op. cit.

NICOLSON, M. H., and MOHLER, N. M., 'The Scientific Background of Swift's *Voyage to Laputa*' first published in 1937, excerpted in Brady, ibid.

RAWSON, C., 'Order and Cruelty: A Reading of Swift', first published in 1970, reprinted in Gravil, op. cit.

TRAUGOTT, J., 'A Voyage to Nowhere with Thomas More and Jonathan Swift', first published in 1961, reprinted in Tuveson, op. cit.

A broad perspective on *Gulliver*, still useful though now sometimes hard to obtain, is CASE, A. E., *Four Essays on 'Gulliver's Travels'*, Princeton University Press, Princeton, New Jersey, 1945, reprinted Peter Smith, 1968, covering such matters as the text, the geographic basis and the political satire. On this last topic see also LOCK, F. P., *The Politics of Gulliver's Travels*, Oxford University Press, 1980.

CHRONOLOGY

DATE	AUTHOR'S LIFE	LITERARY CONTEXT
1660		
1662		
1667	Swift born in Dublin.	
1668		La Fontaine: *Fables* (3 books, to 1693).
1673–81	Studies at Kilkenny School (a contemporary of Congreve).	
1682–9	Studies at Trinity College, Dublin	Newton: *Principia* (1687).
1688–9		
1689	Moves to England as secretary to Sir William Temple; meets Esther Johnson ('Stella').	
1690		Locke: *An Essay Concerning Human Understanding.*
1692	MA from Oxford.	
1694		Congreve: *The Double Dealer.*
1695	Ordained priest; first clerical post in Northern Ireland.	
1697		Vanbrugh: *The Provok'd Wife.*
1699	Death of Temple.	
1700		Death of Dryden. Congreve: *The Way of the World.*
1701	*Contests and Dissensions.*	Defoe: *The True Born Englishman.*
1702	DD from Dublin.	Defoe: *The Shortest Way with Dissenters.*
1704	*A Tale of a Tub* and *Battle of the Books* published.	Newton: *Opticks.* Death of Locke.
1707		
1707–9	Intermittently in England on behalf of Irish Church.	Pope: *Pastorals* (1709).
1709–11		Steele and Addison: *The Tatler.*
1710	Begins *Journal to Stella*. Changes allegiance from Whigs to Tories. Begins series of essays in the *Examiner.*	

xl

HISTORICAL EVENTS

Restoration of Charles II.
Inception of Royal Society. Act of Uniformity.

Test Act (1673). Popish Plot (1678). Exclusion Crisis (1679–81)

Accession of James II. Monmouth Rebellion (1685).

'Glorious Revolution' ousts James II and brings William and Mary to the throne.
Bill of Rights. England enters the War of the Grand Alliance against France.

William III defeats the exiled James II at the Battle of the Boyne in Ireland.
Massacre at Glencoe.
Death of Mary II. Founding of the Bank of England.
Death of Purcell. Licensing Act expires.

Treaty of Ryswick ends War of the Grand Alliance.

Act of Settlement secures the Protestant succession in England.

Death of William III; Queen Anne succeeds. War of Spanish Succession.

Marlborough and Eugene of Savoy win Battle of Blenheim.

Union of parliaments of England and Scotland.
Allied victories at Oudenarde (1708) and Malplaquet (1709).

Sacheverell crisis precipitates fall of Whig ministry; Tories under Harley and Bolingbroke come to power.

DATE	AUTHOR'S LIFE	LITERARY CONTEXT
1711	Collection of works; *Conduct of the Allies*.	Pope: *Essays in Criticism*. Steele and Addison: *The Spectator* (to 1714).
1713	Appointed Dean of St Patrick's; friendship with Esther Vanhomrigh ('Vanessa').	
1714	Swift forms the Scriblerus Club, with Pope, Gay, Arbuthnot and others. Settles in Dublin.	Pope: *The Rape of the Lock*.
1715		
1716		
1717		
1719		Defoe: *Robinson Crusoe*.
1720	'Proposal for the Universal Use of Irish Manufactures.'	
1721		
1722		Defoe: *Moll Flanders* and *Journal of the Plague Year*.
1723	Vanessa dies.	
1724	*Drapier's Letters*.	
1724–6		Defoe: *Tour through the Whole Island of Great Britain*.
1726	Visits England; *Gulliver's Travels* published.	
1727	Last visit to England.	Gay: *Fables*.
1728	Death of Stella.	John Gay: *The Beggar's Opera*. Pope: *The Dunciad* (first version).
1729	*Modest Proposal*.	
1731	Composition of *Verses on the Death of Dr Swift* (published 1739).	Death of Defoe.
1732		Death of Gay.
1733		
1735	Collected works published by Faulkner in Dublin.	Death of Arbuthnot.
1737		
1739		Hume: *Treatise of Human Nature*.
1740		Richardson: *Pamela*.
1742	Declared of unsound mind.	Fielding: *Joseph Andrews*.

CHRONOLOGY

DATE	AUTHOR'S LIFE	LITERARY CONTEXT
1743		
1744		Death of Pope. Johnson: *Life of Savage.*
1745	Swift dies. Buried beside Stella in St Patrick's Cathedral Dublin.	

CHRONOLOGY

ADVERTISEMENT

Capt. Gulliver's letter to Mr. Sympson, prefixed to this volume, will make a long advertisement unnecessary. Those interpolations complained of by the captain, were made by a person since deceased, on whose judgment the publisher relyed to make any alterations that might be thought necessary. But, this person, not rightly comprehending the scheme of the author, nor able to imitate his plain simple style, thought fit, among many other alterations and insertions, to compliment the memory of her late Majesty, by saying, That she governed without a chief minister. We are assured, that the copy sent to the bookseller in London, was a transcript of the original, which original being in the possession of a very worthy gentleman in London, and a most intimate friend of the author's; after he had bought the book in sheets, and compared it with the originals, bound it up with blank leaves, and made those corrections, which the reader will find in our edition. For, the same gentleman did us the favour to let us transcribe his corrections.

A LETTER FROM CAPT. GULLIVER, TO HIS COUSIN
SYMPSON

I HOPE, you will be ready to own publickly, whenever you shall be called to it, that by your great and frequent urgency, you prevailed on me to publish a very loose and uncorrect account of my travels; with direction to hire some young gentlemen of either university to put them in order, and correct the style, as my Cousin Dampier did by my advice, in his book called, *A Voyage round the World.* But, I do not remember, I gave you power to consent, that any thing should be omitted, and much less that any thing should be inserted: therefore, as to the latter, I do here renounce every thing of that kind; particularly a paragraph about her Majesty the late Queen Anne, of most pious and glorious memory; although I did reverence and esteem her more than any of human species. But you, or your interpolator, ought to have considered, that as it was not my inclination, so was it not decent to praise any animal of our composition before my master Houyhnhnm: and besides, the fact was altogether false; for, to my knowledge, being in England during some part of her Majesty's reign, she did govern by a chief minister; nay, even by two successively; the first whereof was the Lord of Godolphin, and the second the Lord of Oxford; so that you have made me say the thing which was not. Likewise, in the account of the Academy of Projectors, and several passages of my discourse to my master Houyhnhnm, you have either omitted some material circumstances, or minced or changed them in such a manner, that I do hardly know mine own work. When I formerly hinted to you something of this in a letter, you were pleased to answer, that you were afraid of giving offence; that people in power were very watchful over the press; and apt not only to interpret, but to punish every thing which looked like an innuendo (as I think you called it.)   But pray, how could that which I spoke so many years ago, and at above five thousand leagues distance, in another reign, be applyed to any of the Yahoos, who now are said to govern the herd; especially at a time when I little thought on, or feared the unhappiness of living under them?   Have not I the most reason to complain, when I see these very Yahoos carried by Houyhnhnms in a vehicle, as if these were brutes, and those the rational creatures?   And, indeed, to avoid so monstrous and detestable a sight, was one principal motive of my retirement hither.

Thus much I thought proper to tell you in relation to your self, and to the trust I reposed in you.

I do in the next place complain of my own great want of judgment, in being prevailed upon by the intreaties and false reasonings of you and some others, very much against mine own opinion, to suffer my travels to be published. Pray bring to your mind how often I desired you to consider, when you insisted on the motive of publick good; that the Yahoos were a species of animals utterly incapable of amendment by precepts or examples; and so it hath proved; for instead of seeing a full stop put to all abuses and corruptions, at least in this little island, as I had reason to expect: behold, after above six months warning, I cannot learn that my book hath produced one single effect according to mine intentions: I desired you would let me know by a letter, when party and faction were extinguished; judges learned and upright; pleaders honest and modest, with some tincture of common sense; and Smithfield blazing with pyramids of law-books; the young nobility's education entirely changed; the physicians banished; the female Yahoos abounding in virtue, honour, truth and good sense: courts and levees of great ministers thoroughly weeded and swept; wit, merit and learning rewarded; all disgracers of the press in prose and verse, condemned to eat nothing but their own cotten, and quench their thirst with their own ink. These, and a thousand other reformations, I firmly counted upon by your encouragement; as indeed, they were plainly deducible from the precepts delivered in my book. And, it must be owned, that seven months were a sufficient time to correct every vice and folly to which Yahoos are subject; if their natures had been capable of the least disposition to virtue or wisdom: yet so far have you been from answering mine expectation in any of your letters, that on the contrary, you are loading our carrier every week with libels, and keys, and reflections, and memoirs, and second parts; wherein I see myself accused of reflecting upon great states-folk; of degrading human nature, (for so they have still the confidence to style it) and of abusing the female sex. I find likewise, that the writers of those bundles are not agreed among themselves; for some of them will not allow me to be author of mine own travels; and others make me author of books to which I am wholly a stranger.

I find likewise, that your printer hath been so careless as to confound the times, and mistake the dates of my several voyages and returns; neither assigning the true year, or the true month, or day of the month: and, I hear the original manuscript is all destroyed, since the publication of my book. Neither have I any copy left; however, I have sent you some corrections, which you may insert, if ever there should be a second edition: and yet I cannot stand to them, but shall leave that matter to my judicious and candid readers, to adjust it as they please.

I hear, some of our sea-Yahoos find fault with my sea-language, as not proper in many parts, nor now in use. I cannot help it. In my first voyages, while I was young, I was instructed by the oldest mariners, and learned to speak

as they did.   But, I have since found, that the sea-Yahoos
are apt, like the land ones, to become new fangled in their
words; which the latter change every year; insomuch, as
I remember upon each return to mine own country, their
old dialect was so altered, that I could hardly understand
the new.   And I observe, when any Yahoo comes from
London, out of curiosity, to visit me at mine own house,
we neither of us are able to deliver our conceptions in a
manner intelligible to the other.

If the censure of Yahoos could any way affect me, I
should have great reason to complain, that some of them
are so bold as to think my book of travels a meer fiction
out of mine own brain; and have gone so far as to drop
hints, that the Houyhnhnms, and Yahoos have no more
existence, than the inhabitants of Utopia.

Indeed I must confess, that as to the people of Lilliput,
Brobdingrag (for so the word should have been spelt, and
not erroneously Brobdingnag) and Laputa; I have never
yet heard of any Yahoo so presumptuous as to dispute their
being, or the facts I have related concerning them; because
the truth immediately strikes every reader with conviction.
And, is there less probability in my account of the Houyhnhnms or Yahoos, when it is manifest as to the latter,
there are so many thousands, even in this city, who only
differ from their brother brutes in Houyhnhnmland, because they use a sort of jabber, and do not go naked.   I
wrote for their amendment, and not their approbation.
The united praise of the whole race, would be of less consequence to me, than the neighing of those two degenerate
Houyhnhnms I keep in my stable; because, from these,
degenerate as they are, I still improve in some virtues, without any mixture of vice.

Do these miserable animals presume to think, that I am
so far degenerated, as to defend my veracity: Yahoo as I
am, it is well known through all Houyhnhnmland, that by

the instructions and example of my illustrious master, I was able in the compass of two years (although I confess with the utmost difficulty) to remove that infernal habit of lying, shuffling, deceiving, and equivocating, so deeply rooted in the very souls of all my species, especially the Europeans.

I have other complaints to make upon this vexatious occasion; but I forbear troubling myself or you any further. I must freely confess, that since my last return, some corruptions of my Yahoo nature have revived in me by conversing with a few of your species, and particularly those of mine own family, by an unavoidable necessity; else I should never have attempted so absurd a project as that of reforming the Yahoo race in this kingdom; but, I have now done with all such visionary schemes for ever.

April 2, 1727.

THE PUBLISHER TO THE READER

THE author of these travels, Mr. Lemuel Gulliver, is my antient and intimate friend; there is likewise some relation between us by the mother's side. About three years ago, Mr. Gulliver growing weary of the concourse of curious people coming to him at his house in Redriff, made a small purchase of land, with a convenient house, near Newark, in Nottinghamshire, his native county; where he now lives retired, yet in good esteem among his neighbours.

Although Mr. Gulliver were born in Nottinghamshire, where his father dwelt, yet I have heard him say, his family came from Oxfordshire; to confirm which, I have observed in the churchyard at Banbury, in that county, several tombs and monuments of the Gullivers.

Before he quitted Redriff, he left the custody of the following papers in my hands, with the liberty to dispose of them as I should think fit. I have carefully perused them three times: the style is very plain and simple; and the only fault I find is, that the author, after the manner of travellers, is a little too circumstantial. There is an air of truth apparent through the whole; and indeed the author was so distinguished for his veracity, that it became a sort of proverb among his neighbours at Redriff, when any one affirmed a thing, to say, it was as true as if Mr. Gulliver had spoke it.

By the advice of several worthy persons, to whom, with the author's permission, I communicated these papers, I now venture to send them into the world; hoping they may be, at least for some time, a better entertainment to our young noblemen, than the common scribbles of politicks and party.

8

This volume would have been at least twice as large, if I had not made bold to strike out innumerable passages relating to the winds and tides, as well as to the variations and bearings in the several voyages; together with the minute descriptions of the management of the ship in storms, in the style of sailors: likewise the account of the longitudes and latitudes; wherein I have reason to apprehend that Mr. Gulliver may be a little dissatisfied: but, I was resolved to fit the work, as much as possible to the general capacity of readers.   However, if my own ignorance in sea affairs shall have led me to commit some mistakes, I alone am answerable for them: and, if any traveller hath a curiosity to see the whole work at large, as it came from the hand of the author, I will be ready to gratify him.

As for any further particulars relating to the author, the reader will receive satisfaction from the first pages of the book.

RICHARD SYMPSON.

PART I
A VOYAGE TO LILLIPUT

CHAPTER I

The author giveth some account of himself and family; his first inducements to travel. He is shipwrecked, and swims for his life; gets safe on shore in the country of Lilliput; is made a prisoner, and carried up the country.

MY father had a small estate in Nottinghamshire; I was the third of five sons. He sent me to Emanuel-College in Cambridge, at fourteen years old, where I resided three years, and applied my self close to my studies: but the charge of maintaining me (although I had a very scanty allowance) being too great for a narrow fortune; I was bound apprentice to Mr. James Bates, an eminent surgeon in London, with whom I continued four years; and my father now and then sending me small sums of money, I laid them out in learning navigation, and other parts of the mathematicks, useful to those who intend to travel, as I always believed it would be some time or other my fortune to do. When I left Mr. Bates, I went down to my father, where, by the assistance of him and my Uncle John, and some other relations, I got forty pounds, and a promise of thirty pounds a year to maintain me at Leyden: there I studied physick two years and seven months, knowing it would be useful in long voyages.

Soon after my return from Leyden, I was recommended by my good master Mr. Bates, to be surgeon to the *Swallow*, Captain Abraham Pannell commander; with whom I continued three years and a half, making a voyage or two into the Levant, and some other parts. When I came back, I resolved to settle in London, to which Mr. Bates, my master, encouraged me; and by him I was recommended to several patients. I took part of a small house in the Old-Jury; and being advised to alter my condition, I married Mrs.

Mary Burton, second daughter to Mr. Edmond Burton, hosier, in Newgate-street, with whom I received four hundred pounds for a portion.

But, my good master Bates dying in two years after, and I having few friends, my business began to fail; for my conscience would not suffer me to imitate the bad practice of too many among my brethren. Having therefore consulted with my wife, and some of my acquaintance, I determined to go again to sea. I was surgeon successively in two ships, and made several voyages, for six years, to the East and West-Indies; by which I got some addition to my fortune. My hours of leisure I spent in reading the best authors, ancient and modern; being always provided with a good number of books; and when I was ashore, in observing the manners and dispositions of the people, as well as learning their language; wherein I had a great facility by the strength of my memory.

The last of these voyages not proving very fortunate, I grew weary of the sea, and intended to stay at home with my wife and family. I removed from the Old-Jury to Fetter-lane, and from thence to Wapping, hoping to get business among the sailors; but it would not turn to account. After three years expectation, that things would mend, I accepted an advantageous offer from Captain William Prichard, master of the *Antelope*, who was making a voyage to the South-Sea. We set sail from Bristol, May 4th, 1699, and our voyage at first was very prosperous.

It would not be proper for some reasons, to trouble the reader with the particulars of our adventures in those seas: let it suffice to inform him, that in our passage from thence to the East-Indies, we were driven by a violent storm to the north-west of Van Diemen's Land. By an observation, we found ourselves in the latitude of 30 degrees 2 minutes south. Twelve of our crew were dead by immoderate labour, and ill food; the rest were in a very weak condition.

On the fifth of November, which was the beginning of summer in those parts, the weather being very hazy, the seamen spyed a rock, within half a cable's length of the ship; but the wind was so strong, that we were driven directly upon it, and immediately split. Six of the crew, of whom I was one, having let down the boat into the sea, made a shift to get clear of the ship, and the rock. We rowed by my computation, about three leagues, until we were able to work no longer, being already spent with labour while we were in the ship: we therefore trusted ourselves to the mercy of the waves; and in about half an hour the boat was overset by a sudden flurry from the north. What became of my companions in the boat, as well as of those who escaped on the rock, or were left in the vessel, I cannot tell; but conclude they were all lost. For my own part, I swam as fortune directed me, and was pushed forward by wind and tide. I often let my legs drop; and could feel no bottom: but when I was almost gone, and able to struggle no longer, I found myself within my depth; and by this time the storm was much abated. The declivity was so small, that I walked near a mile before I got to the shore, which I conjectured was about eight o'clock in the evening. I then advanced forward near half a mile, but could not discover any sign of houses or inhabitants; at least I was in so weak a condition, that I did not observe them. I was extremely tired, and with that, and the heat of the weather, and about half a pint of brandy that I drank as I left the ship, I found myself much inclined to sleep. I lay down on the grass, which was very short and soft; where I slept sounder than ever I remember to have done in my life, and as I reckoned, above nine hours; for when I awaked, it was just day-light. I attempted to rise, but was not able to stir: for, as I happened to lie on my back, I found my arms and legs were strongly fastned on each side to the ground; and my hair, which was long and thick, tied down in the same manner. I likewise felt several slender ligatures across my body, from my arm-pits to my thighs. I could only look upwards; the sun began to grew hot, and the light offended mine eyes. I heard a confused noise about me, but in the posture I lay, could see nothing except the sky. In a little time I felt something alive moving on my left leg, which advancing gently forward over my breast, came almost up to my chin; when bending mine eyes downwards as much as I could, I perceived it to be a human creature not six inches high, with a bow and arrow in his hands, and a quiver at his back. · In the mean time, I felt at least forty more of the same kind (as I conjectured) following the first. I was in the utmost astonishment, and roared so loud, that they all run back in a fright; and some of them, as I was afterwards told, were hurt with the falls they got by leaping from my sides upon the ground. However, they soon returned; and one of them, who ventured so far as to get a full sight of my face, lifting up his hands and eyes by way of admiration, cryed out in a shrill, but distinct voice, 'Hekina degul': the others repeated the same words several times, but I then knew not what they meant. I lay all this while, as the reader may believe, in great uneasiness: at length, struggling to get loose, I had the fortune to break the strings, and wrench out the pegs that fastned my left arm to the ground: for, by lifting it up to my face, I discovered the methods they had taken to bind me; and, at the same time, with a violent pull, which gave me excessive pain, I a little loosened the strings that tied down my hair on the left side; so that I was just able to turn my head about two inches. But the creatures ran off a second time, before I could seize them; whereupon there was a great shout in a very shrill accent; and after it ceased, I heard one of them cry aloud, 'Tolgo Phonac'; when in an instant, I felt above an hundred arrows discharged on my left hand, which pricked me like so many needles; and besides, they shot another flight into the air, as we do bombs in Europe; whereof many, I suppose, fell on my body, (though I felt them not) and some on my face, which I immediately covered with my left hand. When this shower of arrows was over, I fell a groaning with grief and pain; and then striving again to get loose, they discharged another volley larger than the first; and some of them attempted with spears to stick me in the sides; but, by good luck, I had on me a buff jerkin, which they could not pierce. I thought it the most prudent method to lie still; and my design was to continue so until night, when my left hand being already loose, I could easily free my self: and, as for the inhabitants, I had reason to believe I might be a match for the greatest armies they could bring against me, if they were all of the same size with him that I saw. But fortune disposed otherwise of me. When the people observed I was quiet, they discharged no more arrows: but by the noise encreasing, I knew their numbers were greater; and about four yards from me over against my right ear, I heard a knocking for above an hour, like people at work; when turning my head that way, as well as the pegs and strings would permit me, I saw a stage erected about a foot and a half from the ground, capable of holding four of the inhabitants, with two or three ladders to mount it: from whence one of them, who seemed to be a person of quality, made me a long speech, whereof I understood not one syllable. But I should have mentioned, that before the principal person began his oration, he cryed out three times 'Langro dehul san': (these words and the former were afterwards repeated and explained to me.) Whereupon immediately about fifty of the inhabitants came, and cut the strings that fastened the left side of my head, which gave me the liberty of turning it to the right, and of observing the person and gesture of him who was to speak. He appeared to be of a middle age, and taller than any of the other three who attended him; whereof one was a page, who held up his train, and seemed to be somewhat longer than my middle finger; the other two stood one on each side to support him. He acted every part of an orator; and I could observe many periods of threatnings, and others of promises, pity, and kindness. I answered in a few words, but in the most submissive manner, lifting up my left hand and both mine eyes to the sun, as calling him for a witness; and being almost famished with hunger, having not eaten a morsel for some hours before I left the ship, I found the demands of nature so strong upon me, that I could not forbear shewing my impatience (perhaps against the strict rules of decency) by putting my finger frequently on my mouth, to signify that I wanted food. The Hurgo (for so they call a great lord, as I afterwards learnt) understood me very well: he descended from the stage, and commanded that several ladders should be applied to my sides, on which above an hundred of the inhabitants mounted and walked towards my mouth, laden with baskets full of meat, which had been provided, and sent thither by the king's orders upon the first intelligence he received of me. I observed there was the flesh of several animals, but could not distinguish them by the taste. There were shoulders, legs, and loins shaped like those of mutton, and very well dressed, but smaller than the wings of a lark. I eat them by two or three at a mouthful; and took three loaves at a time, about the bigness of musket-bullets. They supplyed me as fast as they could, shewing a thousand marks of wonder and astonishment at my bulk and appetite. I then made another sign that I wanted drink. They found by my eating that a small quantity would not suffice me; and being a most ingenious people, they slung up with great dexterity one of their largest hogsheads; then rolled it towards my hand, and beat out the top; I drank it off at a draught, which I might well do, for it hardly held half a pint, and

tasted like a small wine of Burgundy, but much more delicious. They brought me a second hogshead, which I
drank in the same manner, and made signs for more, but
they had none to give me. When I had performed these
wonders, they shouted for joy, and danced upon my breast,
repeating several times as they did at first, 'Hekinah degul.'
They made me a sign, that I should throw down the two
hogsheads, but first warned the people below to stand out
of the way, crying aloud, 'Borach mivola'; and when they
saw the vessels in the air, there was an universal shout of
'Hekinah degul.' I confess I was often tempted, while
they were passing backwards and forwards on my body, to
seize forty or fifty of the first that came in my reach, and
dash them against the ground. But the remembrance of
what I had felt, which probably might not be the worst
they could do; and the promise of honour I made them, for
so I interpreted my submissive behaviour, soon drove out
those imaginations. Besides, I now considered my self as
bound by the laws of hospitality to a people who had
treated me with so much expence and magnificence. However, in my thoughts I could not sufficiently wonder at the
intrepidity of these diminutive mortals, who durst venture
to mount and walk on my body, while one of my hands was
at liberty, without trembling at the very sight of so prodigious a creature as I must appear to them. After some
time, when they observed, that I made no more demands
for meat, there appeared before me a person of high rank
from his Imperial Majesty. His excellency having mounted
on the small of my right leg, advanced forwards up to my
face, with about a dozen of his retinue; and producing his
credentials under the signet royal, which he applied close
to mine eyes, spoke about ten minutes, without any signs
of anger, but with a kind of determinate resolution; often
pointing forwards, which, as I afterwards found was towards
the capital city, about half a mile distant, whither it was

agreed by his Majesty in council that I must be conveyed. I answered in few words, but to no purpose, and made a sign with my hand that was loose, putting it to the other, (but over his excellency's head, for fear of hurting him or his train) and then to my own head and body, to signify that I desired my liberty. It appeared that he understood me well enough; for he shook his head by way of disapprobation, and held his hand in a posture to shew that I must be carried as a prisoner. However, he made other signs to let me understand, that I should have meat and drink enough, and very good treatment. Whereupon I once more thought of attempting to break my bonds; but again, when I felt the smart of their arrows upon my face and hands, which were all in blisters, and many of the darts still sticking in them; and observing likewise, that the number of my enemies encreased; I gave tokens to let them know that they might do with me what they pleased. Upon this, the Hurgo and his train withdrew, with much civility and cheerful countenances. Soon after I heard a general shout, with frequent repetitions of the words, 'Peplom selan,' and I felt great numbers of the people on my left side relaxing the cords to such a degree, that I was able to turn upon my right, and to ease my self with making water; which I very plentifully did, to the great astonishment of the people, who conjecturing by my motions what I was going to do, immediately opened to the right and left on that side, to avoid the torrent which fell with such noise and violence from me. But before this, they had dawbed my face and both my hands with a sort of ointment very pleasant to the smell, which in a few minutes removed all the smart of their arrows. These circumstances, added to the refreshment I had received by their victuals and drink, which were very nourishing, disposed me to sleep. I slept about eight hours as I was afterwards assured; and it was no wonder; for the physicians, by the emperor's order, had mingled a sleeping potion in the hogsheads of wine.

It seems, that upon the first moment I was discovered sleeping on the ground after my landing, the emperor had early notice of it by an express; and determined in council, that I should be tyed in the manner I have related; (which was done in the night while I slept) that plenty of meat and drink should be sent me, and a machine prepared to carry me to the capital city.

This resolution perhaps may appear very bold and dangerous, and I am confident would not be imitated by any prince in Europe on the like occasion; however, in my opinion, it was extremely prudent as well as generous. For, supposing these people had endeavoured to kill me with their spears and arrows while I was asleep; I should certainly have awaked with the first sense of smart, which might so far have rouzed my rage and strength, as to enable me to break the strings wherewith I was tyed; after which, as they were not able to make resistance, so they could expect no mercy.

These people are most excellent mathematicians, and arrived to a great perfection in mechanicks, by the countenance and encouragement of the emperor, who is a renowned patron of learning. This prince hath several machines fixed on wheels, for the carriage of trees and other great weights. He often buildeth his largest men of war, whereof some are nine foot long, in the woods where the timber grows, and has them carried on these engines three or four hundred yards to the sea. Five hundred carpenters and engineers were immediately set at work to prepare the greatest engine they had. It was a frame of wood raised three inches from the ground, about seven foot long and four wide, moving upon twenty two wheels. The shout I heard, was upon the arrival of this engine, which, it seems, set out in four hours after my landing. It was brought

parallel to me as I lay. But the principal difficulty was to
raise and place me in this vehicle. Eighty poles, each of
one foot high, were erected for this purpose, and very strong
cords of the bigness of packthread were fastened by hooks
to many bandages, which the workmen had girt round my
neck, my hands, my body, and my legs. Nine hundred of
the strongest men were employed to draw up these cords
by many pullies fastened on the poles; and thus in less than
three hours, I was raised and slung into the engine, and
there tyed fast. All this I was told; for while the whole
operation was performing, I lay in a profound sleep, by the
force of that soporiferous medicine infused into my liquor.
Fifteen hundred of the emperor's largest horses, each about
four inches and a half high, were employed to draw me towards the metropolis, which, as I said, was half a mile distant.

About four hours after we began our journey, I awaked
by a very ridiculous accident; for the carriage being stopt
a while to adjust something that was out of order, two or
three of the young natives had the curiosity to see how I
looked when I was asleep; they climbed up into the engine,
and advancing very softly to my face, one of them, an
officer in the guards, put the sharp end of his half-pike a
good way up into my left nostril, which tickled my nose
like a straw, and made me sneeze violently: whereupon they
stole off unperceived; and it was three weeks before I knew
the cause of my awaking so suddenly. We made a long
march the remaining part of the day, and rested at night
with five hundred guards on each side of me, half with
torches, and half with bows and arrows, ready to shoot me
if I should offer to stir. The next morning at sunrise we
continued our march, and arrived within two hundred yards
of the city-gates about noon. The emperor, and all his
court, came out to meet us; but his great officers would by
no means suffer his Majesty to endanger his person by
mounting on my body.

At the place where the carriage stopt, there stood an ancient temple, esteemed to be the largest in the whole kingdom; which having been polluted some years before by an unnatural murder, was, according to the zeal of those people, looked upon as prophane, and therefore had been applied to common use, and all the ornaments and furniture carried away. In this edifice it was determined I should lodge. The great gate fronting to the north was about four feet high, and almost two feet wide, through which I could easily creep. On each side of the gate was a small window not above six inches from the ground: into that on the left side, the king's smiths conveyed fourscore and eleven chains, like those that hang to a lady's watch in Europe, and almost as large, which were locked to my left leg with six and thirty padlocks. Over against this temple, on the other side of the great highway, at twenty feet distance, there was a turret at least five feet high. Here the emperor ascended with many principal lords of his court, to have an opportunity of viewing me, as I was told, for I could not see them. It was reckoned that above an hundred thousand inhabitants came out of the town upon the same errand; and in spight of my guards, I believe there could not be fewer than ten thousand, at several times, who mounted upon my body by the help of ladders. But a proclamation was soon issued to forbid it, upon pain of death. When the workmen found it was impossible for me to break loose, they cut all the strings that bound me; whereupon I rose up with as melancholly a disposition as ever I had in my life. But the noise and astonishment of the people at seeing me rise and walk, are not to be expressed. The chains that held my left leg were about two yards long, and gave me not only the liberty of walking backwards and forwards in a semi-circle; but being fixed within four inches of the gate, allowed me to creep in, and lie at my full length in the temple.

CHAPTER II

The Emperor of Lilliput, attended by several of the nobility, comes to see the author in his confinement. The emperor's person and habit described. Learned men appointed to teach the author their language. He gains favour by his mild disposition. His pockets are searched, and his sword and pistols taken from him.

WHEN I found my self on my feet, I looked about me, and must confess I never beheld a more entertaining prospect. The country round appeared like a continued garden; and the inclosed fields, which were generally forty feet square, resembled so many beds of flowers. These fields were inter-mingled with woods of half a stang, and the tallest trees, as I could judge, appeared to be seven feet high. I viewed the town on my left hand, which looked like the painted scene of a city in a theatre.

I had been for some hours extremely pressed by the necessities of nature; which was no wonder, it being almost two days since I had last disburthened my self. I was under great difficulties between urgency and shame. The best expedient I could think on, was to creep into my house, which I accordingly did; and shutting the gate after me, I went as far as the length of my chain would suffer; and discharged my body of that uneasy load. But, this was the only time I was ever guilty of so uncleanly an action; for which I cannot but hope the candid reader will give some allowance, after he hath maturely and impartially considered my case, and the distress I was in. From this time my constant practice was, as soon as I rose, to perform that business in open air, at the full extent of my chain; and due care was taken every morning before company came, that the offensive matter should be carried off in wheel-barrows, by two servants appointed for that purpose.

I would not have dwelt so long upon a circumstance, that perhaps at first sight may appear not very momentous; if I had not thought it necessary to justify my character in point of cleanliness to the world; which I am told, some of my maligners have been pleased, upon this and other occasions, to call in question.

When this adventure was at an end, I came back out of my house, having occasion for fresh air. The emperor was already descended from the tower, and advancing on horseback towards me, which had like to have cost him dear; for the beast, although very well trained, yet wholly unused to such a sight, which appeared, as if a mountain moved before him, reared up on his hinder feet: but that prince, who is an excellent horseman, kept his seat, until his attendants ran in, and held the bridle, while his Majesty had time to dismount. When he alighted, he surveyed me round with great admiration, but kept beyond the length of my chains. He ordered his cooks and butlers, who were already prepared, to give me victuals and drink, which they pushed forward in a sort of vehicles upon wheels until I could reach them. I took these vehicles, and soon emptied them all; twenty of them were filled with meat, and ten with liquor; each of the former afforded me two or three good mouthfuls, and I emptied the liquor of ten vessels, which was contained in earthen vials, into one vehicle, drinking it off at a draught; and so I did with the rest. The empress, and young princes of the blood, of both sexes, attended by many ladies, sate at some distance in their chairs; but upon the accident that happened to the emperor's horse, they alighted, and came near his person; which I am now going to describe. He is taller by almost the breadth of my nail, than any of his court; which alone is enough to strike an awe into the beholders. His features are strong and masculine, with an Austrian lip, and arched nose, his complexion olive, his countenance erect, his body and limbs

well proportioned, all his motions graceful, and his deportment majestick.   He was then past his prime, being
twenty-eight years and three quarters old, of which he had
reigned about seven, in great felicity, and generally vic-
torious.   For the better convenience of beholding him, I
lay on my side, so that my face was parallel to his, and he
stood but three yards off: however, I have had him since
many times in my hand, and therefore cannot be deceived
in the description.   His dress was very plain and simple,
the fashion of it between the Asiatick and the European;
but he had on his head a light helmet of gold, adorned with
jewels, and a plume on the crest.   He held his sword drawn
in his hand, to defend himself, if I should happen to break
loose; it was almost three inches long, the hilt and scabbard
were gold enriched with diamonds.   His voice was shrill
but very clear and articulate, and I could distinctly hear
it when I stood up.   The ladies and courtiers were all most
magnificently clad, so that the spot they stood upon seemed
to resemble a petticoat spread on the ground, embroidered
with figures of gold and silver.   His Imperial Majesty spoke
often to me, and I returned answers, but neither of us
could understand a syllable.   There were several of his
priests and lawyers present (as I conjectured by their habits)
who were commanded to address themselves to me, and I
spoke to them in as many languages as I had the least
smattering of, which were High and Low-Dutch, Latin,
French, Spanish, Italian, and lingua franca; but all to no
purpose.   After about two hours the court retired, and I
was left with a strong guard, to prevent the impertinence,
and probably the malice of the rabble, who were very impatient to croud about me as near as they durst; and some
of them had the imprudence to shoot their arrows at me as
I sate on the ground by the door of my house; whereof one
very narrowly missed my left eye.   But the colonel ordered
six of the ringleaders to be seized, and thought no punish-

ment so proper as to deliver them bound into my hands, which some of his soldiers accordingly did, pushing them forwards with the but-ends of their pikes into my reach: I took them all in my right hand, put five of them into my coat-pocket; and as to the sixth, I made a countenance as if I would eat him alive. The poor man squalled terribly, and the colonel and his officers were in much pain, especially when they saw me take out my penknife: but I soon put them out of fear; for, looking mildly, and immediately cutting the strings he was bound with, I set him gently on the ground, and away he ran. I treated the rest in the same manner, taking them one by one out of my pocket; and I observed, both the soldiers and people were highly obliged at this mark of my clemency, which was represented very much to my advantage at court.

Towards night I got with some difficulty into my house, where I lay on the ground, and continued to do so about a fortnight; during which time the emperor gave orders to have a bed prepared for me. Six hundred beds of the common measure were brought in carriages, and worked up in my house; an hundred and fifty of their beds sown together made up the breadth and length, and these were four double, which however kept me but very indifferently from the hardness of the floor, that was of smooth stone. By the same computation they provided me with sheets, blankets, and coverlets, tolerable enough for one who had been so long enured to hardships as I.

As the news of my arrival spread through the kingdom, it brought prodigious numbers of rich, idle, and curious people to see me; so that the villages were almost emptied, and great neglect of tillage and household affairs must have ensued, if his Imperial Majesty had not provided by several proclamations and orders of State against this inconveniency. He directed that those, who had already beheld me, should return home, and not presume to come within fifty yards of my house, without licence from court; whereby the Secretaries of State got considerable fees.

In the mean time, the emperor held frequent councils to debate what course should be taken with me; and I was afterwards assured by a particular friend, a person of great quality, who was as much in the secret as any; that the court was under many difficulties concerning me. They apprehended my breaking loose; that my diet would be very expensive, and might cause a famine. Sometimes they determined to starve me, or at least to shoot me in the face and hands with poisoned arrows, which would soon dispatch me: but again they considered, that the stench of so large a carcase might produce a plague in the metropolis, and probably spread through the whole kingdom. In the midst of these consultations, several officers of the army went to the door of the great council-chamber; and two of them being admitted, gave an account of my behaviour to the six criminals above-mentioned; which made so favourable an impression in the breast of his Majesty, and the whole board, in my behalf, that an imperial commission was issued out, obliging all the villages nine hundred yards round the city, to deliver in every morning six beeves, forty sheep, and other victuals for my sustenance; together with a proportionable quantity of bread and wine, and other liquors: for the due payment of which his Majesty gave assignments upon his treasury. For this prince lives chiefly upon his own demesnes; seldom, except upon great occasions raising any subsidies upon his subjects, who are bound to attend him in his wars at their own expence. An establishment was also made of six hundred persons to be my domesticks, who had board-wages allowed for their maintenance, and tents built for them very conveniently on each side of my door. It was likewise ordered, that three hundred taylors should make me a suit of cloaths after the fashion of the country: that, six of his Majesty's greatest scholars should be employed to instruct me in their language: and lastly, that the emperor's horses, and those of the nobility, and troops of guards, should be exercised in my sight, to accustom themselves to me. All these orders were duly put in execution; and in about three weeks I made a great progress in learning their language; during which time, the emperor frequently honoured me with his visits, and was pleased to assist my masters in teaching me. We began already to converse together in some sort; and the first words I learnt, were to express my desire, that he would please to give me my liberty; which I every day repeated on my knees. His answer, as I could apprehend, was, that this must be a work of time, not to be thought on without the advice of his council; and that first I must 'Lumus kelmin pesso desmar lon emposo'; that is, 'Swear a peace with him and his kingdom.' However, that I should be used with all kindness; and he advised me to acquire by my patience and discreet behaviour, the good opinion of himself and his subjects. He desired I would not take it ill, if he gave orders to certain proper officers to search me; for probably I might carry about me several weapons, which must needs be dangerous things, if they answered the bulk of so prodigious a person. I said, his Majesty should be satisfied, for I was ready to strip my self, and turn up my pockets before him. This I delivered, part in words, and part in signs. He replied, that by the laws of the kingdom, I must be searched by two of his officers: that he knew this could not be done without my consent and assistance: that he had so good an opinion of my generosity and justice, as to trust their persons in my hands: that whatever they took from me should be returned when I left the country, or paid for at the rate which I would set upon them. I took up the two officers in my hands, put them first into my coat-pockets, and then into every other pocket about me, except my two fobs, and another secret pocket which I had no mind should be searched, wherein I had some little necessaries of no consequence to any but my self. In one of my fobs there was a silver watch, and in the other a small quantity of gold in a purse. These gentlemen, having pen, ink, and paper about them, made an exact inventory of every thing they saw; and when they had done, desired I would set them down, that they might deliver it to the emperor. This inventory I afterwards translated into English, and is word for word as follows.

'Imprimis, in the right coat-pocket of the great Man Mountain (for so I interpret the words "Quinbus Flestrin") after the strictest search, we found only one great piece of coarse cloth, large enough to be a foot-cloth for your Majesty's chief room of State. In the left pocket, we saw a huge silver chest, with a cover of the same metal, which we, the searchers, were not able to lift. We desired it should be opened; and one of us stepping into it, found himself up to the mid-leg in a sort of dust, some part whereof flying up to our faces, set us both a sneezing for several times together. In his right waistcoat-pocket, we found a prodigious bundle of white thin substances, folded one over another, about the bigness of three men, tied with a strong cable, and marked with black figures; which we humbly conceive to be writings; every letter almost half as large as the palm of our hands. In the left there was a sort of engine, from the back of which were extended twenty long poles, resembling the pallisado's before your Majesty's court; wherewith we conjecture the Man Mountain combs his head; for we did not always trouble him with questions, because we found it a great difficulty to make him understand us. In the large pocket on the right side of his middle cover, (so I translate the word "ransu-lo," by which they meant my breeches) we saw a hollow pillar of iron, about the length of a man, fastened to a strong piece of timber, larger than the pillar; and upon one side of the pillar were huge pieces of iron sticking out, cut into strange figures; which we know not what to make of. In the left pocket, another engine of the same kind. In the smaller pocket on the right side, were several round flat pieces of white and red metal, of different bulk: some of the white, which seemed to be silver, were so large and heavy, that my comrade and I could hardly lift them. In the left pocket were two black pillars irregularly shaped; we could not, without difficulty, reach the top of them as we stood at the bottom of his pocket: one of them was covered, and seemed all of a piece; but at the upper end of the other, there appeared a white round substance, about twice the bigness of our heads. Within each of these was inclosed a prodigious plate of steel; which, by our orders we obliged him to shew us, because we apprehended they might be dangerous engines. He took them out of their cases, and told us, that in his own country his practice was to shave his beard with one of these, and to cut his meat with the other. There were two pockets which we could not enter: these he called his fobs; they were two large slits cut into the top of his middle cover, but squeezed close by the pressure of his belly. Out of the right fob hung a great silver chain, with a wonderful kind of engine at the bottom. We directed him to draw out whatever was at the end of that chain; which appeared to be a globe, half silver, and half of some transparent metal: for on the transparent side we saw certain strange figures circularly drawn, and thought we could touch them, until we found our fingers stopped with that lucid substance. He put this engine to our ears, which made an incessant noise like that of a water-mill: and we conjecture it is either some unknown animal, or the god that he worships: but we are more inclined to the latter opinion, because he assured us, (if we understood him right, for he expressed himself very imperfectly) that he seldom did any thing without consulting it.   He called it his oracle, and said it pointed out the time for every action of his life.   From the left fob he took out a net almost large enough for a fisherman, but contrived to open and shut like a purse, and served him for the same use: we found therein several massy pieces of yellow metal, which if they be of real gold, must be of immense value.

'Having thus, in obedience to your Majesty's commands, diligently searched all his pockets, we observed a girdle about his waist made of the hyde of some prodigious animal; from which, on the left side, hung a sword of the length of five men; and on the right, a bag or pouch divided into two cells; each cell capable of holding three of your Majesty's subjects.   In one of these cells were several globes or balls of a most ponderous metal, about the bigness of our heads, and required a strong hand to lift them: the other cell contained a heap of certain black grains, but of no great bulk or weight, for we could hold above fifty of them in the palms of our hands.

'This is an exact inventory of what we found about the body of the Man Mountain; who used us with great civility, and due respect to your Majesty's commission.   Signed and sealed on the fourth day of the eighty ninth moon of your Majesty's auspicious reign.

'Clefren Frelock, Marsi Frelock.'

When this inventory was read over to the emperor, he directed me to deliver up the several particulars.   He first called for my scymiter, which I took out, scabbard and all. In the mean time he ordered three thousand of his choicest troops, who then attended him, to surround me at a distance, with their bows and arrows just ready to discharge: but I did not observe it; for mine eyes were wholly fixed upon his Majesty.   He then desired me to draw my scymiter, which, although it had got some rust by the sea water, was in most parts exceeding bright. I did so, and immediately all the troops gave a shout between terror and surprize; for the sun shone clear, and the reflection dazzled their eyes, as I waved the scymiter to and fro in my hand. His Majesty, who is a most magnanimous prince, was less daunted than I could expect; he ordered me to return it into the scabbard, and cast it on the ground as gently as I could, about six foot from the end of my chain. The next thing he demanded was one of the hollow iron pillars, by which he meant my pocket-pistols. I drew it out, and at his desire, as well as I could, expressed to him the use of it, and charging it only with powder, which by the closeness of my pouch, happened to escape wetting in the sea, (an inconvenience that all prudent mariners take special care to provide against) I first cautioned the emperor not to be afraid; and then I let it off in the air. The astonishment here was much greater than at the sight of my scymiter. Hundreds fell down as if they had been struck dead; and even the emperor, although he stood his ground, could not recover himself in some time. I delivered up both my pistols in the same manner as I had done my scymiter, and then my pouch of powder and bullets; begging him, that the former might be kept from fire; for it would kindle with the smallest spark, and blow up his imperial palace into the air. I likewise delivered up my watch, which the emperor was very curious to see; and commanded two of his tallest yeomen of the guards to bear it on a pole upon their shoulders, as dray-men in England do a barrel of ale. He was amazed at the continual noise it made, and the motion of the minute hand, which he could easily discern; for their sight is much more acute than ours: he asked the opinions of his learned men about him, which were various and remote, as the reader may well imagine without my repeating; although, indeed, I could not very perfectly understand them. I then gave up my silver and copper money,.

my purse with nine large pieces of gold, and some smaller ones; my knife and razor, my comb and silver snuff-box, my handkerchief and journal book. My scymiter, pistols and pouch, were conveyed in carriages to his Majesty's stores; but the rest of my goods were returned me.

I had, as I before observed, one private pocket which escaped their search, wherein there was a pair of spectacles (which I sometimes use for the weakness of mine eyes), a pocket perspective, and several other little conveniencies; which being of no consequence to the emperor, I did not think my self bound in honour to discover; and I apprehended they might be lost or spoiled if I ventured them out of my possession.

CHAPTER III

The author diverts the emperor and his nobility of both sexes, in a very uncommon manner. The diversions of the court of Lilliput described. The author hath his liberty granted him upon certain conditions.

My gentleness and good behaviour had gained so far on the emperor and his court, and indeed upon the army and people in general, that I began to conceive hopes of getting my liberty in a short time. I took all possible methods to cultivate this favourable disposition. The natives came by degrees to be less apprehensive of any danger from me. I would sometimes lie down, and let five or six of them dance on my hand. And at last the boys and girls would venture to come and play at hide and seek in my hair. I had now made a good progress in understanding and speaking their language. The emperor had a mind one day to entertain me with several of the country shows; wherein they exceed all nations I have known, both for dexterity and magnificence. I was diverted with none so much as that of the rope-dancers, performed upon a slender white thread, extended about two foot, and twelve inches from the ground. Upon which, I shall desire liberty, with the reader's patience, to enlarge a little.

This diversion is only practised by those persons, who are candidates for great employments, and high favour, at court. They are trained in this art from their youth, and are not always of noble birth, or liberal education. When a great office is vacant, either by death or disgrace, (which often happens) five or six of those candidates petition the emperor to entertain his Majesty and the court with a dance on the rope; and whoever jumps the highest without falling, succeeds in the office. Very often the chief ministers themselves are commanded to shew their skill, and to convince the emperor that they have not lost their faculty. Flimnap, the Treasurer, is allowed to cut a caper on the strait rope, at least an inch higher than any other lord in the whole empire. I have seen him do the summerset several times together, upon a trencher fixed on the rope, which is no thicker than a common packthread in England. My friend Reldresal, principal Secretary for Private Affairs, is, in my opinion, if I am not partial, the second after the Treasurer; the rest of the great officers are much upon a par.

These diversions are often attended with fatal accidents, whereof great numbers are on record. I my self have seen two or three candidates break a limb. But the danger is much greater, when the ministers themselves are commanded to shew their dexterity: for, by contending to excel themselves and their fellows, they strain so far, that there is hardly one of them who hath not received a fall; and some of them two or three. I was assured, that a year or two before my arrival, Flimnap would have infallibly broke his neck, if one of the king's cushions, that accidentally lay on the ground, had not weakned the force of his fall.

There is likewise another diversion, which is only shewn before the emperor and empress, and first minister, upon particular occasions. The emperor lays on a table three fine silken threads, of six inches long. One is blue, the other red, and the third green. These threads are proposed as prizes, for those persons whom the emperor hath a mind to distinguish by a peculiar mark of his favour. The ceremony is performed in his Majesty's great chamber of State; where the candidates are to undergo a tryal of dexterity very different from the former, and such as I have not observed the least resemblance of in any other country of the Old or the New World. The emperor holds a stick in his hands, both ends parallel to the horrison, while the candidates advancing one by one, sometimes leap over the stick, sometimes creep under it backwards and forwards several times, according as the stick is advanced or depressed. Sometimes the emperor holds one end of the stick, and his first minister the other; sometimes the minister hath it entirely to himself. Whoever performs his part with most agility, and holds out the longest in leaping and creeping, is rewarded with the blue-coloured silk; the red is given to the next, and the green to the third, which they all wear girt twice round about the middle; and you see few great persons about this court, who are not adorned with one of these girdles.

The horses of the army, and those of the royal stables, having been daily led before me, were no longer shy, but would come up to my very feet, without starting. The riders would leap them over my hand as I held it on the ground; and one of the emperor's huntsmen, upon a large courser, took my foot, shoe and all; which was indeed a prodigious leap. I had the good fortune to divert the emperor one day, after a very extraordinary manner. I desired he would order several sticks of two foot high, and the thickness of an ordinary cane, to be brought me; whereupon his Majesty commanded the master of his woods to give directions accordingly; and the next morning, six wood-men arrived with as many carriages, drawn by eight horses to each. I took nine of these sticks, and fixing them firmly in the ground in a quadrangular figure, two foot and a half square; I took four other sticks, and tyed them parallel at each corner, about two foot from the ground; then I fastned my handkerchief to the nine sticks that stood erected; and extended it on all sides, until it was as tight as the top of a drum; and the four parallel sticks rising about five inches higher than the handkerchief, served as ledges on each side. When I had finished my work, I desired the emperor to let a troop of his best horse, twenty four in number, come and exercise upon this plain. His Majesty approved of the proposal, and I took them up one by one in my hands, ready mounted and armed, with the proper officers to exercise them. As soon as they got into order, they divided into two parties, performed mock skirmishes, discharged blunt arrows, drew their swords, fled and pursued, attacked and retired; and in short discovered the best military discipline I ever beheld. The parallel sticks secured them and their horses from falling over the stage; and the emperor was so much delighted, that he ordered this entertainment to be repeated several days; and once was pleased to be lifted up, and give the word of command; and, with great difficulty, persuaded even the empress her self to let me hold her in her close chair, within two yards of the stage, from whence she was able to take a full view of the whole performance. It was my good fortune that no ill accident happened in these entertainments; only once a fiery horse that belonged to one of the captains, pawing with his hoof struck a hole in my handkerchief, and his foot slipping, he overthrew his rider and himself; but I immediately relieved them both: for, covering the hole with one hand, I set down the troop with the other, in the same manner as I took them up. The horse that fell was strained in the left shoulder, but the rider got no hurt; and I repaired my handkerchief as well as I could: however, I would not trust to the strength of it any more in such dangerous enterprizes.

About two or three days before I was set at liberty, as I was entertaining the court with these kinds of feats, there arrived an express to inform his Majesty, that some of his subjects riding near the place where I was first taken up, had seen a great black substance lying on the ground, very oddly shaped, extending its edges round as wide as his Majesty's bed-chamber, and rising up in the middle as high as a man: that it was no living creature, as they at first apprehended; for it lay on the grass without motion, and some of them had walked round it several times: that by mounting upon each others shoulders, they had got to the top, which was flat and even; and, stamping upon it, they found it was hollow within: that they humbly conceived it might be something belonging to the Man-Mountain; and if his Majesty pleased, they would undertake to bring it with only five horses.   I presently knew what they meant; and was glad at heart to receive this intelligence.   It seems, upon my first reaching the shore, after our shipwreck, I was in such confusion, that before I came to the place where I went to sleep, my hat, which I had fastened with a string to my head while I was rowing, and had stuck on all the time I was swimming, fell off after I came to land; the string, as I conjecture, breaking by some accident which I never observed, but thought my hat had been lost at sea. I intreated his Imperial Majesty to give orders it might be brought to me as soon as possible, describing to him the use and the nature of it: and the next day the waggoners arrived with it, but not in a very good condition; they had bored two holes in the brim, within an inch and a half of the edge, and fastened two hooks in the holes; these hooks were tied by a long cord to the harness, and thus my hat was dragged along for above half an English mile: but the ground in that country being extremely smooth and level, it received less damage than I expected.

Two days after this adventure, the emperor having ordered that part of his army, which quarters in and about his metropolis, to be in a readiness, took a fancy of diverting himself in a very singular manner. He desired I would stand like a Colossus, with my legs as far asunder as I conveniently could. He then commanded his general (who was an old experienced leader, and a great patron of mine) to draw up the troops in close order, and march them under me; the foot by twenty-four in a breast, and the horse by sixteen, with drums beating, colours flying, and pikes advanced. This body consisted of three thousand foot, and a thousand horse. His Majesty gave orders, upon pain of death, that every soldier in his march should observe the strictest decency, with regard to my person; which, however, could not prevent some of the younger officers from turning up their eyes as they passed under me. And, to confess the truth, my breeches were at that time in so ill a condition, that they afforded some opportunities for laughter and admiration.

I had sent so many memorials and petitions for my liberty, that his Majesty at length mentioned the matter first in the Cabinet, and then in a full council; where it was opposed by none, except Skyresh Bolgolam, who was pleased, without any provocation, to be my mortal enemy. But it was carried against him by the whole board, and confirmed by the emperor. That minister was Galbet, or Admiral of the Realm; very much in his master's confidence, and a person well versed in affairs, but of a morose and sour complection. However, he was at length persuaded to comply; but prevailed that the articles and conditions upon which I should be set free, and to which I must swear, should be drawn up by himself. These articles were brought to me by Skyresh Bolgolam in person, attended by two under secretaries, and several persons of distinction. After they were read, I was demanded to swear to the performance of them; first in the manner of my own country, and afterwards in the method prescribed by their laws; which was to hold my right foot in my left hand, to place the middle finger of my right hand on the crown of my head, and my thumb on the tip of my right ear. But, because the reader may perhaps be curious to have some idea of the style and manner of expression peculiar to that people, as well as to know the articles upon which I recovered my liberty; I have made a translation of the whole instrument, word for word, as near as I was able; which I here offer to the publick.

'Golbasto Momaren Evlame Gurdilo Shefin Mully Ully Gue, most mighty emperor of Lilliput, delight and terror of the universe, whose dominions extend five thousand *blustrugs*, (about twelve miles in circumference) to the extremities of the globe: monarch of all monarchs: taller than the sons of men; whose feet press down to the center, and whose head strikes against the sun: at whose nod the princes of the earth shake their knees; pleasant as the spring, comfortable as the summer, fruitful as autumn, dreadful as winter. His most sublime Majesty proposeth to the Man Mountain, lately arrived at our celestial dominions, the following articles, which by a solemn oath he shall be obliged to perform.

'First, the Man Mountain shall not depart from our dominions, without our licence under our great seal.

'Secondly, he shall not presume to come into our metropolis, without our express order; at which time, the inhabitants shall have two hours warning to keep within their doors.

'Thirdly, the said Man Mountain shall confine his walks to our principal high roads; and not offer to walk or lie down in a meadow, or field of corn.

'Fourthly, as he walks the said roads, he shall take the utmost care not to trample upon the bodies of any of our loving subjects, their horses, or carriages; nor take any of our said subjects into his hands, without their own consent.

'Fifthly, if an express require extraordinary dispatch; the Man Mountain shall be obliged to carry in his pocket the messenger and horse, a six days journey once in every moon, and return the said messenger back (if so required) safe to our imperial presence.

'Sixthly, he shall be our ally against our enemies in the island of Blefuscu, and do his utmost to destroy their fleet, which is now preparing to invade us.

Seventhly, that the said Man Mountain shall, at his times of leisure, be aiding and assisting to our workmen, in helping to raise certain great stones, towards covering the wall of the principal park, and other our royal buildings.

'Eighthly, that the said Man Mountain shall, in two moons time, deliver in an exact survey of the circumference of our dominions, by a computation of his own paces round the coast.

'Lastly, that upon his solemn oath to observe all the above articles, the said Man Mountain shall have a daily allowance of meat and drink, sufficient for the support of 1724 of our subjects; with free access to our royal person, and other marks of our favour. Given at our palace at Belfaborac the twelfth day of the ninty-first moon of our reign.'

I swore and subscribed to these articles with great chearfulness and content, although some of them were not so honourable as I could have wished; which proceeded wholly from the malice of Skyresh Bolgolam the High Admiral:

whereupon my chains were immediately unlocked, and I was at full liberty: the emperor himself, in person, did me the honour to be by at the whole ceremony. I made my acknowledgements, by prostrating my self at his Majesty's feet: but he commanded me to rise; and after many gracious expressions, which, to avoid the censure of vanity, I shall not repeat; he added, that he hoped I should prove a useful servant, and well deserve all the favours he had already conferred upon me, or might do for the future.

The reader may please to observe, that in the last article for the recovery of my liberty, the emperor stipulates to allow me a quantity of meat and drink, sufficient for the support of 1724 Lilliputians. Some time after, asking a friend at court how they came to fix on that determinate number; he told me, that his Majesty's mathematicians, having taken the height of my body by the help of a quadrant, and finding it to exceed theirs in the proportion of twelve to one, they concluded from the similarity of their bodies, that mine must contain at least 1724 of theirs, and consequently would require as much food as was necessary to support that number of Lilliputians. By which, the reader may conceive an idea of the ingenuity of that people, as well as the prudent and exact œconomy of so great a prince.

CHAPTER IV

Mildendo, the metropolis of Lilliput described, together with the emperor's palace. A conversation between the author and a principal secretary, concerning the affairs of that empire: the author's offers to serve the emperor in his wars.

THE first request I made after I had obtained my liberty, was, that I might have licence to see Mildendo, the metropolis; which the emperor easily granted me, but with a special charge to do no hurt, either to the inhabitants, or their houses. The people had notice by proclamation of my design to visit the town. The wall which encompassed it, is two feet and an half high, and at least eleven inches broad, so that a coach and horses may be driven very safely round it; and it is flanked with strong towers at ten feet distance. I stept over the great western gate, and passed very gently, and sideling through the two principal streets, only in my short waistcoat, for fear of damaging the roofs and eves of the houses with the skirts of my coat. I walked with the utmost circumspection, to avoid treading on any stragglers, who might remain in the streets, although the orders were very strict, that all people should keep in their houses, at their own peril. The garret windows, and tops of houses were so crowded with spectators, that I thought in all my travels I had not seen a more populous place. The city is an exact square, each side of the wall being five hundred foot long. The two great streets which run cross and divided it into four quarters, are five foot wide. The lanes and alleys which I could not enter, but only viewed them as I passed, are from twelve to eighteen inches. The town is capable of holding five hundred thousand souls. The houses are from three to five stories. The shops and markets well provided.

The emperor's palace is in the center of the city, where the two great streets meet. It is inclosed by a wall of two foot high, and twenty foot distant from the buildings. I had his Majesty's permission to step over this wall; and the space being so wide between that and the palace, I could easily view it on every side. The outward court is a square of forty foot, and includes two other courts: in the inmost are the royal apartments, which I was very desirous to see, but found it extremely difficult; for the great gates, from one square into another, were but eighteen inches high, and seven inches wide. Now the buildings of the outer court

*C 60

were at least five foot high; and it was impossible for me to stride over them, without infinite damage to the pile, although the walls were strongly built of hewen stone, and four inches thick. At the same time, the emperor had a great desire that I should see the magnificence of his palace: but this I was not able to do until three days after, which I spent in cutting down with my knife some of the largest trees in the royal park, about an hundred yards distant from the city. Of these trees I made two stools, each about three foot high, and strong enough to bear my weight. The people having received notice a second time, I went again through the city to the palace, with my two stools in my hands. When I came to the side of the outer court, I stood upon one stool, and took the other in my hand: this I lifted over the roof, and gently set it down on the space between the first and second court, which was eight foot wide. I then stept over the buildings very conveniently from one stool to the other, and drew up the first after me with a hooked stick. By this contrivance I got into the inmost court; and lying down upon my side, I applied my face to the windows of the middle stories, which were left open on purpose, and discovered the most splendid apartments that can be imagined. There I saw the empress, and the young princes in their several lodgings, with their chief attendants about them. Her Imperial Majesty was pleased to smile very graciously upon me, and gave me out of the window her hand to kiss.

But I shall not anticipate the reader with farther descriptions of this kind, because I reserve them for a greater work, which is now almost ready for the press; containing a general description of this empire, from its first erection, through a long series of princes, with a particular account of their wars and politicks, laws, learning, and religion; their plants and animals, their peculiar manners and customs, with other matters very curious and useful; my chief design at present being only to relate such events and transactions as happened to the publick, or, to my self, during a residence of about nine months in that empire.

One morning, about a fortnight after I had obtained my liberty; Reldresal, Principal Secretary (as they stile him) of Private Affairs, came to my house, attended only by one servant. He ordered his coach to wait at a distance, and desired I would give him an hour's audience; which I readily consented to, on account of his quality, and personal merits, as well as of the many good offices he had done me during my sollicitations at court. I offered to lie down, that he might the more conveniently reach my ear; but he chose rather to let me hold him in my hand during our conversation. He began with compliments on my liberty; said, he might pretend to some merit in it; but, however, added, that if it had not been for the present situation of things at court, perhaps I might not have obtained it so soon. For, said he, as flourishing a condition as we appear to be in to foreigners, we labour under two mighty evils; a violent faction at home, and the danger of an invasion by a most potent enemy from abroad. As to the first, you are to understand, that for above seventy moons past, there have been two struggling parties in this empire, under the names of Tramecksan, and Slamecksan, from the high and low heels on their shoes, by which they distinguish themselves.

It is alledged indeed, that the high heels are most agreeable to our ancient constitution: but however this be, his Majesty hath determined to make use of only low heels in the administration of the Government, and all offices in the gift of the Crown; as you cannot but observe; and particularly, that his Majesty's imperial heels are lower at least by a *drurr* than any of his court; (*drurr* is a measure about the fourteenth part of an inch.) The animosities between these two parties run so high, that they will neither eat nor drink, nor talk with each other. We compute the

Tramecksan, or high-heels, to exceed us in number; but the power is wholly on our side. We apprehend his Imperial Highness, the heir to the crown, to have some tendency towards the high-heels; at least we can plainly discover one of his heels higher than the other; which gives him a hobble in his gait. Now, in the midst of these intestine disquiets, we are threatened with an invasion from the island of Blefuscu, which is the other great empire of the universe, almost as large and powerful as this of his Majesty. For as to what we have heard you affirm, that there are other kingdoms and states in the world, inhabited by human creatures as large as your self, our philosophers are in much doubt; and would rather conjecture, that you dropt from the moon, or one of the stars; because it is certain, that an hundred mortals of your bulk, would, in a short time, destroy all the fruits and cattle of his Majesty's dominions. Besides, our histories of six thousand moons make no mention of any other regions, than the two great empires of Lilliput and Blefuscu. Which two mighty powers have, as I was going to tell you, been engaged in a most obstinate war for six and thirty moons past. It began upon the following occasion. It is allowed on all hands, that the primitive way of breaking eggs before we eat them, was upon the larger end: but his present Majesty's grand-father, while he was a boy, going to eat an egg, and breaking it according to the ancient practice, happened to cut one of his fingers. Whereupon the emperor his father, published an edict, commanding all his subjects, upon great penalties, to break the smaller end of their eggs. The people so highly resented this law, that our histories tell us, there have been six rebellions raised on that account; wherein one emperor lost his life, and another his crown. These civil commotions were constantly fomented by the monarchs of Blefuscu; and when they were quelled, the exiles always fled for refuge to that empire. It is computed, that eleven thousand persons have, at several times, suffered death, rather than submit to break their eggs at the smaller end. Many hundred large volumes have been published upon this controversy: but the books of the Big-Endians have been long forbidden, and the whole party rendered incapable by law of holding employments. During the course of these troubles, the emperors of Blefuscu did frequently expostulate by their ambassadors, accusing us of making a schism in religion, by offending against a fundamental doctrine of our great prophet Lustrog, in the fifty-fourth chapter of the *Brundrecal,* (which is their *Alcoran.*) This, however, is thought to be a meer strain upon the text: for the words are these; 'That all true believers shall break their eggs at the convenient end': and which is the convenient end, seems in my humble opinion, to be left to every man's conscience, or at least in the power of the chief magistrate to determine. Now the Big-Endian exiles have found so much credit in the Emperor of Blefuscu's court; and so much private assistance and encouragement from their party here at home, that a bloody war hath been carried on between the two empires for six and thirty moons with various success; during which time we have lost forty capital ships, and a much greater number of smaller vessels, together with thirty thousand of our best seamen and soldiers; and the damage received by the enemy is reckoned to be somewhat greater than ours. However, they have now equipped a numerous fleet, and are just preparing to make a descent upon us: and his Imperial Majesty, placing great confidence in your valour and strength, hath commanded me to lay this account of his affairs before you.

I desired the secretary to present my humble duty to the emperor, and to let him know, that I thought it would not become me, who was a foreigner, to interfere with parties; but I was ready, with the hazard of my life, to defend his person and state against all invaders.

CHAPTER V

The author by an extraordinary stratagem prevents an invasion.   A high title of honour is conferred upon him
Ambassadors arrive from the Emperor of Blefuscu, and sue
for peace.   The empress's apartment on fire by an accident;
the author instrumental in saving the rest of the palace.

THE empire of Blefuscu, is an island situated to the north
north-east side of Lilliput, from whence it is parted only
by a channel of eight hundred yards wide.   I had not yet
seen it, and upon this notice of an intended invasion, I
avoided appearing on that side of the coast, for fear of
being discovered by some of the enemies ships, who had
received no intelligence of me; all intercourse between the
two empires having been strictly forbidden during the war,
upon pain of death; and an embargo laid by our emperor
upon all vessels whatsoever.   I communicated to his
Majesty a project I had formed of seizing the enemies whole
fleet; which, as our scouts assured us, lay at anchor in the
harbour ready to sail with the first fair wind.   I consulted
the most experienced seamen, upon the depth of the channel, which they had often plummed; who told me, that in
the middle at high water it was seventy *glumgluffs* deep,
which is about six foot of European measure; and the rest
of it fifty *glumgluffs* at most.   I walked to the north-east
coast over against Blefuscu; where, lying down behind a
hillock, I took out my small pocket perspective glass, and
viewed the enemy's fleet at anchor, consisting of about fifty
men of war, and a great number of transports: I then came
back to my house, and gave order (for which I had a warrant) for a great quantity of the strongest cable and bars
of iron.   The cable was about as thick as packthread, and
the bars of the length and size of a knitting-needle.   I
trebled the cable to make it stronger; and for the same

reason I twisted three of the iron bars together, binding the extremities into a hook. Having thus fixed fifty hooks to as many cables, I went back to the north-east coast, and putting off my coat, shoes, and stockings, walked into the sea in my leathern jerken, about half an hour before high water. I waded with what haste I could, and swam in the middle about thirty yards until I felt the ground; I arrived to the fleet in less than half an hour. The enemy was so frighted when they saw me, that they leaped out of their ships, and swam to shore; where there could not be fewer than thirty thousand souls. I then took my tackling, and fastning a hook to the hole at the prow of each, I tyed all the cords together at the end. While I was thus employed, the enemy discharged several thousand arrows, many of which stuck in my hands and face; and besides the excessive smart, gave me much disturbance in my work. My greatest apprehension was for mine eyes, which I should have infallibly lost, if I had not suddenly thought of an expedient. I kept, among other little necessaries, a pair of spectacles in a private pocket, which, as I observed before, had escaped the emperor's searchers. These I took out, and fastned as strongly as I could upon my nose; and thus armed went on boldly with my work in spight of the enemy's arrows; many of which struck against the glasses of my spectacles, but without any other effect, further than a little to discompose them. I had now fastned all the hooks, and taking the knot in my hand, began to pull; but not a ship would stir, for they were all too fast held by their anchors; so that the boldest part of my enterprize remained. I therefore let go the cord, and leaving the hooks fixed to the ships, I resolutely cut with my knife the cables that fastned the anchors; receiving about two hundred shots in my face and hands: then I took up the knotted end of the cables to which my hooks were tyed; and with great ease drew fifty of the enemy's largest men of war after me.

The Blefuscudians, who had not the least imagination of what I intended, were at first confounded with astonishment. They had seen me cut the cables, and thought my design was only to let the ships run a-drift, or fall foul on each other: but when they perceived the whole fleet moving in order, and saw me pulling at the end; they set up such a scream of grief and despair, that it is almost impossible to describe or conceive. When I had got out of danger, I stopt a while to pick out the arrows that stuck in my hands and face, and rubbed on some of the same ointment that was given me at my first arrival, as I have formerly mentioned. I then took off my spectacles, and waiting about an hour until the tyde was a little fallen, I waded through the middle with my cargo, and arrived safe at the royal port of Lilliput.

The emperor and his whole court stood on the shore, expecting the issue of this great adventure. They saw the ships move forward in a large half moon, but could not discern me, who was up to my breast in water. When I advanced to the middle of the channel, they were yet more in pain because I was under water to my neck. The emperor concluded me to be drowned, and that the enemy's fleet was approaching in a hostile manner: but he was soon eased of his fears; for the channel growing shallower every step I made, I came in a short time within hearing; and holding up the end of the cable by which the fleet was fastned, I cryed in a loud voice, 'Long live the most puissant Emperor of Lilliput!' This great prince received me at my landing with all possible encomiums, and created me a Nardac upon the spot, which is the highest title of honour among them.

His Majesty desired I would take some other opportunity of bringing all the rest of his enemy's ships into his ports. And so unmeasurable is the ambition of princes, that he seemed to think of nothing less than reducing the whole empire of Blefuscu into a province, and governing it by a viceroy; of destroying the Big-Endian exiles, and compelling that people to break the smaller end of their eggs; by which he would remain sole monarch of the whole world. But I endeavoured to divert him from this design, by many arguments drawn from the topicks of policy as well as justice: and I plainly protested, that I would never be an instrument of bringing a free and brave people into slavery: and when the matter was debated in council, the wisest part of the ministry were of my opinion.

This open bold declaration of mine, was so opposite to the schemes and politicks of his Imperial Majesty, that he could never forgive me: he mentioned it in a very artful manner at council, where, I was told, that some of the wisest appeared, at least by their silence, to be of my opinion; but others, who were my secret enemies, could not forbear some expressions, which by a side-wind reflected on me. And from this time began an intrigue between his Majesty, and a junta of ministers maliciously bent against me, which broke out in less than two months, and had like to have ended in my utter destruction. Of so little weight are the greatest services to princes, when put into the balance with a refusal to gratify their passions.

About three weeks after this exploit, there arrived a solemn embassy from Blefuscu, with humble offers of a peace; which was soon concluded upon conditions very advantageous to our emperor; wherewith I shall not trouble the reader. There were six ambassadors, with a train of about five hundred persons; and their entry was very magnificent, suitable to the grandeur of their master, and the importance of their business. When their treaty was finished, wherein I did them several good offices by the credit I now had, or at least appeared to have at court; their excellencies, who were privately told how much I had been their friend, made me a visit in form. They began

with many compliments upon my valour and generosity;
invited me to that kingdom in the emperor their master's
name; and desired me to shew them some proofs of my
prodigious strength, of which they had heard so many
wonders; wherein I readily obliged them, but shall not
interrupt the reader with the particulars.

When I had for some time entertained their excellencies
to their infinite satisfaction and surprize, I desired they
would do me the honour to present my most humble
respects to the emperor their master, the renown of whose
virtues had so justly filled the whole world with admiration, and whose royal person I resolved to attend before I
returned to my own country. Accordingly, the next time
I had the honour to see our emperor, I desired his general
licence to wait on the Blefuscudian monarch, which he was
pleased to grant me, as I could plainly perceive, in a very
cold manner; but could not guess the reason, until I had a
whisper from a certain person, that Flimnap and Bolgolam
had represented my intercourse with those ambassadors,
as a mark of disaffection, from which I am sure my heart
was wholly free. And this was the first time I began to
conceive some imperfect idea of courts and ministers.

It is to be observed, that these ambassadors spoke to me
by an interpreter; the languages of both empires differing
as much from each other as any two in Europe, and each
nation priding itself upon the antiquity, beauty, and energy
of their own tongues, with an avowed contempt for that of
their neighbour: yet our emperor standing upon the advantage he had got by the seizure of their fleet, obliged them to
deliver their credentials, and make their speech in the Lilliputian tongue. And it must be confessed, that from the
great intercourse of trade and commerce between both
realms; from the continual reception of exiles, which is
mutual among them; and from the custom in each empire
to send their young nobility and richer gentry to the other,

in order to polish themselves by seeing the world, and understanding men and manners; there are few persons of distinction, or merchants, or seamen, who dwell in the maritime parts, but what can hold conversation in both tongues; as I found some weeks after, when I went to pay my respects to the Emperor of Blefuscu, which in the midst of great misfortunes, through the malice of my enemies, proved a very happy adventure to me, as I shall relate in its proper place.

The reader may remember, that when I signed those articles upon which I recovered my liberty, there were some which I disliked upon account of their being too servile, neither could any thing but an extreme necessity have forced me to submit. But being now a Nardac, of the highest rank in that empire, such offices were looked upon as below my dignity; and the emperor (to do him justice) never once mentioned them to me. However, it was not long before I had an opportunity of doing his Majesty, at least, as I then thought, a most signal service. I was alarmed at midnight with the cries of many hundred people at my door; by which being suddenly awaked, I was in some kind of terror. I heard the word 'burglum' repeated incessantly; several of the emperor's court making their way through the croud, intreated me to come immediately to the palace, where her Imperial Majesty's apartment was on fire, by the carelessness of a maid of honour, who fell asleep while she was reading a romance. I got up in an instant; and orders being given to clear the way before me; and it being likewise a moon-shine night, I made a shift to get to the palace without trampling on any of the people. I found they had already applied ladders to the walls of the apartment, and were well provided with buckets, but the water was at some distance. These buckets were about the size of a large thimble, and the poor people supplied me with them as fast as they could; but the flame was so violent, that they did little good. I might easily have stifled it with my coat, which I unfortunately left behind me for haste, and came away only in my leathern jerkin. The case seemed wholly desperate and deplorable; and this magnificent palace would have infallibly been burnt down to the ground, if, by a presence of mind, unusual to me, I had not suddenly thought of an expedient. I had the evening before drank plentifully of a most delicious wine, called *glimigrim*, (the Blefuscudians call it *flunec*, but ours is esteemed the better sort) which is very diuretick. By the luckiest chance in the world, I had not discharged myself of any part of it. The heat I had contracted by coming very near the flames, and by my labouring to quench them, made the wine begin to operate by urine; which I voided in such a quantity, and applied so well to the proper places, that in three minutes the fire was wholly extinguished; and the rest of that noble pile, which had cost so many ages in erecting, preserved from destruction.

It was now day-light, and I returned to my house, without waiting to congratulate with the emperor; because, although I had done a very eminent piece of service, yet I could not tell how his Majesty might resent the manner by which I had performed it: for, by the fundamental laws of the realm, it is capital in any person, of what quality soever, to make water within the precincts of the palace. But I was a little comforted by a message from his Majesty, that he would give orders to the grand justiciary for passing my pardon in form; which, however, I could not obtain. And, I was privately assured, that the empress conceiving the greatest abhorrence of what I had done, removed to the most distant side of the court, firmly resolved that those buildings should never be repaired for her use; and, in the presence of her chief confidents, could not forbear vowing revenge.

CHAPTER VI

Of the inhabitants of Lilliput; their learning, laws, and customs. The manner of educating their children. The author's
way of living in that country. His vindication of a great
lady.

ALTHOUGH I intend to leave the description of this empire
to a particular treatise, yet in the mean time I am content
to gratify the curious reader with some general ideas. As
the common size of the natives is somewhat under six
inches, so there is an exact proportion in all other animals,
as well as plants and trees: for instance, the tallest horses
and oxen are between four and five inches in height, the
sheep an inch and a half, more or less; their geese about
the bigness of a sparrow; and so the several gradations
downwards, until you come to the smallest, which, to my
sight, were almost invisible; but nature hath adapted the
eyes of the Lilliputians to all objects proper for their view:
they see with great exactness, but at no great distance.
And to shew the sharpness of their sight towards objects
that are near, I have been much pleased with observing a
cook pulling a lark, which was not so large as a common fly;
and a young girl threading an invisible needle with invisible
silk. Their tallest trees are about seven foot high; I mean
some of those in the great royal park, the tops whereof I
could but just reach with my fist clinched. The other
vegetables are in the same proportion: but this I leave to
the reader's imagination.

I shall say but little at present of their learning, which
for many ages hath flourished in all its branches among
them: but their manner of writing is very peculiar; being
neither from the left to the right, like the Europeans; nor
from the right to the left, like the Arabians; nor from
up to down, like the Chinese; nor from down to up, like the

Cascagians; but aslant from one corner of the paper to the other, like ladies in England.

They bury their dead with their heads directly downwards; because they hold an opinion, that in eleven thousand moons they are all to rise again; in which period, the earth (which they conceive to be flat) will turn upside down, and by this means they shall, at their resurrection, be found ready standing on their feet. The learned among them confess the absurdity of this doctrine; but the practice still continues, in compliance to the vulgar.

There are some laws and customs in this empire very peculiar; and if they were not so directly contrary to those of my own dear country, I should be tempted to say a little in their justification. It is only to be wished, that they were as well executed. The first I shall mention, relateth to informers. All crimes against the State, are punished here with the utmost severity; but if the person accused make his innocence plainly to appear upon his tryal, the accuser is immediately put to an ignominious death; and out of his goods or lands, the innocent person is quadruply recompensed for the loss of his time, for the danger he underwent, for the hardship of his imprisonment, and for all the charges he hath been at in making his defence. Or, if that fund be deficient, it is largely supplyed by the Crown. The emperor doth also confer on him some publick mark of his favour; and proclamation is made of his innocence through the whole city.

They look upon fraud as a greater crime than theft, and therefore seldom fail to punish it with death: for, they alledge, that care and vigilance, with a very common understanding, may preserve a man's goods from thieves; but honesty hath no fence against superior cunning: and since it is necessary that there should be a perpetual intercourse of buying and selling, and dealing upon credit; where fraud is permitted or connived at, or hath no law to punish it, the honest dealer is always undone, and the knave gets the advantage. I remember when I was once interceding with the king for a criminal who had wronged his master of a great sum of money, which he had received by order, and ran away with; and happening to tell his Majesty, by way of extenuation, that it was only a breach of trust; the emperor thought it monstrous in me to offer, as a defence, the greatest aggravation of the crime: and truly, I had little to say in return, farther than the common answer, that different nations had different customs; for, I confess, I was heartily ashamed.

Although we usually call reward and punishment, the two hinges upon which all government turns; yet I could never observe this maxim to be put in practice by any nation except that of Lilliput. Whoever can there bring sufficient proof, that he hath strictly observed the laws of his country for seventy-three moons, hath a claim to certain privileges, according to his quality and condition of life, with a proportionable sum of money out of a fund appropriated for that use: he likewise acquires the title of Snilpall, or Legal, which is added to his name, but doth not descend to his posterity. And these people thought it a prodigious defect of policy among us, when I told them that our laws were enforced only by penalties, without any mention of reward. It is upon this account that the image of justice, in their courts of judicature, is formed with six eyes, two before, as many behind, and on each side one, to signify circumspection; with a bag of gold open in her right hand, and a sword sheathed in her left, to shew she is more disposed to reward than to punish.

In chusing persons for all employments, they have more regard to good morals than to great abilities: for, since government is necessary to mankind, they believe that the common size of human understandings, is fitted to some station or other; and that Providence never intended to make the management of publick affairs a mystery, to be comprehended only by a few persons of sublime genius, of which there seldom are three born in an age: but, they suppose truth, justice, temperance, and the like, to be in every man's power; the practice of which virtues, assisted by experience and a good intention, would qualify any man for the service of his country, except where a course of study is required. But they thought the want of moral virtues was so far from being supplied by superior endowments of the mind, that employments could never be put into such dangerous hands as those of persons so qualified; and at least, that the mistakes committed by ignorance in a virtuous disposition, would never be of such fatal consequence to the publick weal, as the practices of a man, whose inclinations led him to be corrupt, and had great abilities to manage, to multiply, and defend his corruptions.

In like manner, the disbelief of a divine providence renders a man uncapable of holding any publick station: for, since kings avow themselves to be the deputies of Providence, the Lilliputians think nothing can be more absurd, than for a prince to employ such men as disown the authority under which he acteth.

In relating these and the following laws, I would only be understood to mean the original institutions, and not the most scandalous corruptions into which these people are fallen by the degenerate nature of man. For, as to that infamous practice of acquiring great employments by dancing on the ropes, or badges of favour and distinction by leaping over sticks, and creeping under them; the reader is to observe, that they were first introduced by the grandfather of the emperor now reigning; and grew to the present height, by the gradual increase of party and faction.

Ingratitude is among them a capital crime, as we read it to have been in some other countries: for they reason thus; that whoever makes ill returns to his benefactor, must needs be a common enemy to the rest of mankind, from whom they have received no obligation; and therefore such a man is not fit to live.

Their notions relating to the duties of parents and children differ extremely from ours. For, since the conjunction of male and female is founded upon the great law of nature, in order to propagate and continue the species; the Lilliputians will needs have it, that men and women are joined together like other animals, by the motives of concupiscence; and that their tenderness towards their young, proceedeth from the like natural principle: for which reason they will never allow, that a child is under any obligation to his father for begetting him, or to his mother for bringing him into the world; which, considering the miseries of human life, was neither a benefit in itself, nor intended so by his parents, whose thoughts in their love-encounters were otherwise employed. Upon these, and the like reasonings, their opinion is, that parents are the last of all others to be trusted with the education of their own children: and therefore they have in every town publick nurseries, where all parents, except cottagers and labourers, are obliged to send their infants of both sexes to be reared and educated when they come to the age of twenty moons; at which time they are supposed to have some rudiments of docility. These schools are of several kinds, suited to different qualities, and to both sexes. They have certain professors well skilled in preparing children for such a condition of life as befits the rank of their parents, and their own capacities as well as inclinations. I shall first say something of the male nurseries, and then of the female.

The nurseries for males of noble or eminent birth, are provided with grave and learned professors, and their several deputies. The clothes and food of the children are plain and simple. They are bred up in the principles of honour, justice, courage, modesty, clemency, religion, and love of their country: they are always employed in some business, except in the times of eating and sleeping, which are very short, and two hours for diversions, consisting of bodily exercises. They are dressed by men until four years of age, and then are obliged to dress themselves, although their quality be ever so great; and the women attendants, who are aged proportionably to ours at fifty, perform only the most menial offices. They are never suffered to converse with servants, but go together in small or greater numbers to take their diversions, and always in the presence of a professor, or one of his deputies; whereby they avoid those early bad impressions of folly and vice to which our children are subject. Their parents are suffered to see them only twice a year; the visit is not to last above an hour; they are allowed to kiss the child at meeting and parting; but a professor, who always standeth by on those occasions, will not suffer them to whisper, or use any fondling expressions, or bring any presents of toys, sweetmeats, and the like.

The pension from each family for the education and entertainment of a child, upon failure of due payment, is levyed by the emperor's officers.

The nurseries for children of ordinary gentlemen, merchants, traders, and handicrafts, are managed proportionably after the same manner; only those designed for trades, are put out apprentices at seven years old; whereas those of persons of quality continue in their exercises until fifteen, which answers to one and twenty with us: but the confinement is gradually lessened for the last three years.

In the female nurseries, the young girls of quality are educated much like the males, only they are dressed by orderly servants of their own sex, but always in the presence of a professor or deputy, until they come to dress themselves, which is at five years old. And if it be found, that these nurses ever presume to entertain the girls with rrightful or foolish stories, or the common follies practised by chamber-maids among us; they are publickly whipped thrice about the city, imprisoned for a year, and banished for life to the most desolate parts of the country. Thus, the young ladies there are as much ashamed of being cowards and fools, as the men; and despise all personal ornaments beyond decency and cleanliness; neither did I perceive any difference in their education, made by their difference of sex, only that the exercises of the females were not altogether so robust; and that some rules were given them relating to domestick life, and a smaller compass of learning was enjoined them: for, their maxim is, that among people of quality, a wife should be always a reasonable and agreeable companion, because she cannot always be young. When the girls are twelve years old, which among them is the marriageable age, their parents or guardians take them home, with great expressions of gratitude to the professors, and seldom without tears of the young lady and her companions.

In the nurseries of females of the meaner sort, the children are instructed in all kinds of works proper for their sex and their several degrees: those intended for apprentices are dismissed at seven years old, the rest are kept to eleven.

The meaner families who have children at these nurseries, are obliged, besides their annual pension, which is as low as possible, to return to the steward of the nursery a small monthly share of their gettings, to be a portion for the child; and therefore all parents are limited in their expences by the law. For the Lilliputians think nothing can be more unjust, than that people, in subservience to their own appetites, should bring children into the world, and leave the burthen of supporting them on the publick. As to persons of quality, they give security to appropriate a certain sum for each child, suitable to their condition;

and these funds are always managed with good husbandry, and the most exact justice.

The cottagers and labourers keep their children at home, their business being only to till and cultivate the earth; and therefore their education is of little consequence to the publick; but the old and diseased among them are supported by hospitals: for begging is a trade unknown in this empire.

And here it may perhaps divert the curious reader, to give some account of my domestick, and my manner of living in this country, during a residence of nine months and thirteen days. Having a head mechanically turned, and being likewise forced by necessity, I had made for my self a table and chair convenient enough, out of the largest trees in the royal park. Two hundred sempstresses were employed to make me shirts, and linnen for my bed and table, all of the strongest and coarsest kind they could get; which, however, they were forced to quilt together in several folds; for the thickest was some degrees finer than lawn. Their linnen is usually three inches wide, and three foot make a piece. The sempstresses took my measure as I lay on the ground, one standing at my neck, and another at my mid-leg, with a strong cord extended, that each held by the end, while the third measured the length of the cord with a rule of an inch long. Then they measured my right thumb, and desired no more; for by a mathematical computation, that twice round the thumb is once round the wrist, and so on to the neck and the waist; and by the help of my old shirt, which I displayed on the ground before them for a pattern, they fitted me exactly. Three hundred taylors were employed in the same manner to make me clothes; but they had another contrivance for taking my measure. I kneeled down, and they raised a ladder from the ground to my neck; upon this ladder one of them mounted, and let fall a plum-line from my collar to the floor, which just answered the length of my coat; but my waist and arms I measured my self. When my clothes were finished, which was done in my house, (for the largest of theirs would not have been able to hold them) they looked like the patch-work made by the ladies in England, only that mine were all of a colour.

I had three hundred cooks to dress my victuals, in little convenient huts built about my house, where they and their families lived, and prepared me two dishes a-piece. I took up twenty waiters in my hand, and placed them on the table; an hundred more attended below on the ground, some with dishes of meat, and some with barrels of wine, and other liquors, slung on their shoulders; all which the waiters above drew up as I wanted, in a very ingenious manner, by certain cords, as we draw the bucket up a well in Europe. A dish of their meat was a good mouthful, and a barrel of their liquor a reasonable draught. Their mutton yields to ours, but their beef is excellent. I have had a sirloin so large, that I have been forced to make three bits of it; but this is rare. My servants were astonished to see me eat it bones and all, as in our country we do the leg of a lark. Their geese and turkeys I usually eat at a mouthful, and I must confess they far exceed ours. Of their smaller fowl I could take up twenty or thirty at the end of my knife.

One day his Imperial Majesty being informed of my way of living, desired that himself, and his royal consort, with the young princes of the blood of both sexes, might have the happiness (as he was pleased to call it) of dining with me. They came accordingly, and I placed them upon chairs of state on my table, just over against me, with their guards about them. Flimnap the Lord High Treasurer attended there likewise, with his white staff; and I observed he often looked on me with a sour countenance, which I would not seem to regard, but eat more than usual, in honour to my dear country, as well as to fill the court with admiration. I have some private reasons to believe, that this visit from his Majesty gave Flimnap an opportunity of doing me ill offices to his master. That minister had always been my secret enemy, although he outwardly caressed me more than was usual to the moroseness of his nature. He represented to the emperor the low condition of his treasury; that he was forced to take up money at a great discount; that exchequer bills would not circulate under nine per cent. below par; that I had cost his Majesty above a million and a half of *sprugs*, (their greatest gold coin, about the bigness of a spangle;) and upon the whole, that it would be adviseable in the emperor to take the first fair occasion of dismissing me.

I am here obliged to vindicate the reputation of an excellent lady, who was an innocent sufferer upon my account. The treasurer took a fancy to be jealous of his wife, from the malice of some evil tongues, who informed him, that her Grace had taken a violent affection for my person; and the court-scandal ran for some time, that she once came privately to my lodging. This, I solemnly declare, to be a most infamous falshood, without any grounds, farther than that her Grace was pleased to treat me with all innocent marks of freedom and friendship. I own, she came often to my house, but always publickly, nor ever without three more in the coach, who were usually her sister and young daughter, and some particular acquaintance; but this was common to many other ladies of the court. And I still appeal to my servants round, whether they at any time saw a coach at my door without knowing what persons were in it. On those occasions, when a servant had given me notice, my custom was to go immediately to the door; and after paying my respects, to take up the coach and two horses very carefully in my hands, (for if there were six horses, the postillion always unharnassed four) and place them on a table, where I had fixed a moveable rim quite round, of five inches high, to prevent accidents. And I have often had four coaches and horses at once on my table full of company, while I sat in my chair leaning my face towards them; and when I was engaged with one sett, the coachmen would gently drive the others round my table. I have passed many an afternoon very agreeably in these conversations: but, I defy the treasurer, or his two informers, (I will name them, and let them make their best of it) Clustril and Drunlo, to prove that any person ever came to me incognito, except the secretary Reldresal, who was sent by express command of his Imperial Majesty, as I have before related. I should not have dwelt so long upon this particular, if it had not been a point wherein the reputation of a great lady is so nearly concerned; to say nothing of my own; although I had the honour to be a Nardac, which the treasurer himself is not; for all the world knows he is only a Clumglum, a title inferior by one degree, as that of a marquess is to a duke in England; yet I allow he preceded me in right of his post. These false informations, which I afterwards came to the knowledge of, by an accident not proper to mention, made the treasurer shew his lady for some time an ill countenance, and me a worse: for although he were at last undeceived and reconciled to her, yet I lost all credit with him; and found my interest decline very fast with the emperor himself, who was indeed too much governed by that favourite.

CHAPTER VII

The author being informed of a design to accuse him of high treason, maketh his escape to Blefuscu. His reception there.

BEFORE I proceed to give an account of my leaving this kingdom, it may be proper to inform the reader of a private intrigue, which had been for two months forming against me.

I had been hitherto all my life a stranger to courts, for which I was unqualified by the meanness of my condition. I had indeed heard and read enough of the dispositions of great princes and ministers; but never expected to have found such terrible effects of them in so remote a country, governed, as I thought, by very different maxims from those in Europe.

When I was just preparing to pay my attendance on the Emperor of Blefuscu; a considerable person at court (to whom I had been very serviceable at a time when he lay under the highest displeasure of his Imperial Majesty) came to my house very privately at night in a close chair, and without sending his name, desired admittance: the chairmen were dismissed; I put the chair, with his lordship in it, into my coat-pocket; and giving orders to a trusty servant to say I was indisposed and gone to sleep, I fastened the door of my house, placed the chair on the table, according to my usual custom, and sat down by it. After the common salutations were over, observing his lordship's countenance full of concern; and enquiring into the reason, he desired I would hear him with patience, in a matter that highly concerned my honour and my life. His speech was to the following effect, for I took notes of it as soon as he left me.

'You are to know,' said he, 'that several committees of council have been lately called in the most private manner on your account: and it is but two days since his Majesty came to a full resolution.

'You are very sensible that Skyris Bolgolam (Galbet, or High Admiral) hath been your mortal enemy almost ever since your arrival. His original reasons I know not; but his hatred is much encreased since your great success against Blefuscu, by which his glory, as admiral, is obscured. This lord, in conjunction with Flimnap the High Treasurer, whose enmity against you is notorious on account of his lady; Limtoc the general, Lalcon the chamberlain, and Balmuff the Grand Justiciary, have prepared articles of impeachment against you, for treason, and other capital crimes.'

This preface made me so impatient, being conscious of my own merits and innocence, that I was going to interrupt; when he intreated me to be silent; and thus proceeded.

'Out of gratitude for the favours you have done me, I procured information of the whole proceedings, and a copy of the articles, wherein I venture my head for your service.

Articles of impeachment against Quinbus Flestrin, (the Man-Mountain.)

ARTICLE I

Whereas, by a statute made in the reign of his Imperial Majesty Calin Dessar Plune, it is enacted, that whoever shall make water within the precincts of the royal palace, shall be liable to the pains and penalties of high treason: notwithstanding, the said Quinbus Flestrin, in open breach of the said law, under colour of extinguishing the fire kindled in the apartment of his Majesty's most dear imperial consort, did maliciously, traitorously, and devilishly, by discharge of his urine, put out the said fire kindled in the said apartment, lying and being within the precincts of the said royal palace; against the statute in that case provided, etc. against the duty, etc.

ARTICLE II

That, the said Quinbus Flestrin having brought the imperial fleet of Blefuscu into the royal port, and being afterwards commanded by his Imperial Majesty to seize all the other ships of the said empire of Blefuscu, and reduce that empire to a province, to be governed by a vice-roy from hence; and to destroy and put to death not only all

D 60

the Big-Endian exiles, but likewise all the people of that empire, who would not immediately forsake the Big-Endian heresy: he the said Flestrin, like a false traitor against his most auspicious, serene, Imperial Majesty, did petition to be excused from the said service, upon pretence of unwillingness to force the consciences, or destroy the liberties and lives of an innocent people.

Article III

That, whereas certain embassadors arrived from the court of Blefuscu to sue for peace in his Majesty's court: he the said Flestrin did, like a false traitor, aid, abet, comfort, and divert the said embassadors; although he knew them to be servants to a prince who was lately an open enemy to his Imperial Majesty, and in open war against his said Majesty.

Article IV

That, the said Quinbus Flestrin, contrary to the duty of a faithful subject, is now preparing to make a voyage to the court and empire of Blefuscu, for which he hath received only verbal licence from his Imperial Majesty; and under colour of the said licence, doth falsly and traitorously intend to take the said voyage, and thereby to aid, comfort, and abet the Emperor of Blefuscu, so late an enemy, and in open war with his Imperial Majesty aforesaid.

'There are some other articles, but these are the most important, of which I have read you an abstract.

'In the several debates upon this impeachment, it must be confessed, that his Majesty gave many marks of his great *lenity*; often urging the services you had done him, and endeavouring to extenuate your crimes. The treasurer and admiral insisted, that you should be put to the most painful and ignominious death, by setting fire on your house at night; and the general was to attend with twenty thousand men armed with poisoned arrows, to shoot you on the face and hands. Some of your servants were to have private orders to strew a poisonous juice on your shirts and sheets, which would soon make you tear your own flesh, and die in the utmost torture. The general came into the same opinion; so, that for a long time there was a majority against you. But his Majesty resolving, if possible, to spare your life, at last brought off the chamberlain.

'Upon this incident, Reldresal, Principal Secretary for Private Affairs, who always approved himself your true friend, was commanded by the emperor to deliver his opinion, which he accordingly did; and therein justified the good thoughts you have of him. He allowed your crimes to be great; but that still there was room for mercy, the most commendable virtue in a prince, and for which his Majesty was so justly celebrated. He said, the friendship between you and him was so well known to the world, that perhaps the most honourable board might think him partial: however, in obedience to the command he had received, he would freely offer his sentiments. That, if his Majesty, in consideration of your services, and pursuant to his own merciful disposition, would please to spare your life, and only give order to put out both your eyes; he humbly conceived, that by this expedient, justice might in some measure be satisfied, and all the world would applaud the lenity of the emperor, as well as the fair and generous proceedings of those who have the honour to be his counsellors. That, the loss of your eyes would be no impediment to your bodily strength, by which you might still be useful to his Majesty. That, blindness is an addition to courage, by concealing dangers from us. That, the fear you had for your eyes, was the greatest difficulty in bringing over the enemy's fleet; and it would be sufficient for you to see by the eyes of the ministers, since the greatest princes do no more.

'This proposal was received with the utmost disapprobation by the whole board. Bolgolam, the admiral, could not preserve his temper; but rising up in fury, said, he wondered how the secretary durst presume to give his opinion for preserving the life of a traytor: that, the services you had performed, were, by all true reasons of State, the great aggravation of your crimes: that you, who were able to extinguish the fire, by discharge of urine in her Majesty's apartment (which he mentioned with horror) might, at another time, raise an inundation by the same means, to drown the whole palace; and the same strength which enabled you to bring over the enemy's fleet, might serve, upon the first discontent, to carry it back: that, he had good reasons to think you were a Big-Endian in your heart; and as treason begins in the heart before it appears in overt-acts; so he accused you as a traytor on that account, and therefore insisted you should be put to death.

'The treasurer was of the same opinion; he shewed to what streights his Majesty's revenue was reduced by the charge of maintaining you, which would soon grow insupportable: that, the secretary's expedient of putting out your eyes, was so far from being a remedy against this evil, that it would probably encrease it; as it is manifest from the common practice of blinding some kind of fowl, after which they fed the faster, and grew sooner fat: that, his sacred Majesty, and the council, who are your judges, were in their own consciences fully convinced of your guilt; which was a sufficient argument to condemn you to death, without the *formal proofs required by the strict letter of the law*.

'But his Imperial Majesty, fully determined against capital punishment, was graciously pleased to say, that since the council thought the loss of your eyes too easy a censure, some other may be inflicted hereafter. And your friend the secretary humbly desiring to be heard again, in answer to what the treasurer had objected, concerning the great charge his Majesty was at in maintaining you; said, that his Excellency, who had the sole disposal of the emperor's revenue, might easily provide against this evil, by gradually lessening your establishment; by which, for want of sufficient food, you would grow weak and faint, and lose your appetite, and consequently decay and consume in a few months; neither would the stench of your carcass be then so dangerous, when it should become more than half diminished; and immediately upon your death, five or six thousand of his Majesty's subjects might, in two or three days, cut your flesh from your bones, take it away by cartloads, and bury it in distant parts to prevent infection; leaving the skeleton as a monument of admiration to posterity.

'Thus, by the great friendship of the secretary, the whole affair was compromised. It was strictly enjoined, that the project of starving you by degrees should be kept a secret; but the sentence of putting out your eyes was entered on the books; none dissenting except Bolgolam the admiral, who being a creature of the empress, was perpetually instigated by her Majesty to insist upon your death; she having born perpetual malice against you, on account of that infamous and illegal method you took to extinguish the fire in her apartment.

'In three days your friend the secretary will be directed to come to your house, and read before you the articles of impeachment; and then to signify the great *lenity* and favour of his Majesty and council; whereby you are only condemned to the loss of your eyes, which his Majesty doth not question you will gratefully and humbly submit to; and twenty of his Majesty's surgeons will attend, in order to see the operation well performed, by discharging very sharp pointed arrows into the balls of your eyes, as you lie on the ground.

'I leave to your prudence what measures you will take; and to avoid suspicion, I must immediately return in as private a manner as I came.'

His lordship did so, and I remained alone, under many doubts and perplexities of mind.

It was a custom introduced by this prince and his ministry, (very different, as I have been assured, from the practices of former times) that after the court had decreed any cruel execution, either to gratify the monarch's resentment, or the malice of a favourite; the emperor always made a speech to his whole council, expressing his *great lenity and tenderness, as qualities known and confessed by all the world.* This speech was immediately published through the kingdom; nor did any thing terrify the people so much as those encomiums on his Majesty's mercy; because it was observed, that the more these praises were enlarged and insisted on, the more *inhuman* was the punishment, and the *sufferer more innocent.* Yet, as to myself, I must confess, having never been designed for a courtier, either by my birth or education, I was so ill a judge of things, that I could not discover the *lenity* and favour of this sentence; but conceived it (perhaps erroneously) rather to be rigorous than gentle. I sometimes thought of standing my tryal; for although I could not deny the facts alledged in the several articles, yet I hoped they would admit of some extenuations. ˊBut, having in my life perused many State-tryals, which I ever observed to terminate as the judges thought fit to direct; I durst not rely on so dangerous a decision, in so critical a juncture, and against such powerful enemies. Once I was strongly bent upon resistance: for while I had liberty, the whole strength of that empire could hardly subdue me, and I might easily with stones pelt the metropolis to pieces: but I soon rejected that project with horror, by remembring the oath I had made to the emperor, the favours I received from him, and the high title of Nardac he conferred upon me. Neither had I so soon learned the gratitude of courtiers, to persuade myself, that his Majesty's *present severities acquitted me of all past obligations.*

At last I fixed upon a resolution, for which it is probable I may incur some censure, and not unjustly; for I confess I owe the preserving mine eyes, and consequently my liberty, to my own great rashness and want of experience: because, if I had then known the nature of princes and ministers, which I have since observed in many other courts, and their methods of treating criminals less obnoxious than myself; I should with great alacrity and readiness have submitted to so *easy* a punishment. But hurried on by the precipitancy of youth; and having his Imperial Majesty's licence to pay my attendance upon the Emperor of Blefuscu; I took this opportunity, before the three days were elapsed, to send a letter to my friend the secretary, signifying my resolution of setting out that morning for Blefuscu, pursuant to the leave I had got; and without waiting for an answer, I went to that side of the island where our fleet lay. I seized a large man of war, tied a cable to the prow, and lifting up the anchors, I stript myself, put my cloaths (together with my coverlet, which I carryed under my arm) into the vessel; and drawing it after me, between wading and swimming, arrived at the royal port of Blefuscu, where the people had long expected me: they lent me two guides to direct me to the capital city, which is of the same name; I held them in my hands until I came within two hundred yards of the gate; and desired them to signify my arrival to one of the secretaries, and let him know, I there waited his Majesty's commands. I had an answer in about an hour, that his Majesty, attended by the royal family, and great officers of the court, was coming out to receive me. I advanced a hundred yards; the emperor, and his train, alighted from their horses, the empress and ladies from their coaches; and I did not perceive they were in any fright or concern. I lay on the ground to kiss his Majesty's and the empress's hand. I told his Majesty, that I was come according to my promise, and with the licence of the emperor my master, to have the honour of seeing so mighty a monarch, and to offer him any service in my power, consistent with my duty to my own prince; not mentioning a word of my disgrace, because I had hitherto no regular information of it, and might suppose myself wholly ignorant of any such design; neither could I reasonably conceive, that the emperor would discover the secret while I was out of his power: wherein, however, it soon appeared I was deceived.

I shall not trouble the reader with the particular account of my reception at this court, which was suitable to the generosity of so great a prince; nor of the difficulties I was in for want of a house and bed, being forced to lye on the ground, wrapt up in my coverlet.

CHAPTER VIII

The author, by a lucky accident, finds means to leave Blefuscu; and, after some difficulties, returns safe to his native country.

THREE days after my arrival, walking out of curiosity to the north-east coast of the island; I observed, about half a league off, in the sea, somewhat that looked like a boat overturned: I pulled off my shoes and stockings, and wading two or three hundred yards, I found the object to approach nearer by force of the tide; and then plainly saw it to be a real boat, which I supposed might, by some tempest, have been driven from a ship. Whereupon I returned immediately towards the city, and desired his Imperial Majesty to lend me twenty of the tallest vessels he had left after the loss of his fleet, and three thousand seamen under the command of his vice-admiral. This fleet sailed round, while I went back the shortest way to the coast, where I first discovered the boat; I found the tide had driven it still nearer; the seamen were all provided with cordage, which I had beforehand twisted to a sufficient strength. When the ships came up, I stript myself, and waded until I came within an hundred yards of the boat; after which I was forced to swim until I got up to it. The seamen threw me the end of the cord, which I fastened to a hole in the forepart of the boat, and the other end to a man of war: but I found all my labour to little purpose; for being out of my depth, I was not able to work. In this necessity, I was forced to swim behind, and push the boat forwards as often as I could, with one of my hands; and the tide favouring me, I advanced so far, that I could just hold up my chin and feel the ground. I rested two or three minutes, and then gave the boat another shove, and so on, until the sea was no higher than my arm-pits. And now the most laborious part being over, I took out my other cables which were stowed in one of the ships, and fastening them first to the boat, and then to nine of the vessels which attended me; the wind being favourable, the seamen towed, and I shoved until we arrived within forty yards of the shore; and waiting until the tide was out, I got dry to the boat, and by the assistance of two thousand men, with ropes and engines, I made a shift to turn it on its bottom, and found it was but little damaged.

I shall not trouble the reader with the difficulties I was under by the help of certain paddles, which cost me ten days making, to get my boat to the royal port of Blefuscu;

*D 60

where a mighty concourse of people appeared upon my arrival, full of wonder at the sight of so prodigious a vessel. I told the emperor, that my good fortune had thrown this boat in my way, to carry me to some place from whence I might return into my native country; and begged his Majesty's orders for getting materials to fit it up; together with his licence to depart; which, after some kind expostulations, he was pleased to grant.

I did very much wonder, in all this time, not to have heard of any express relating to me from our emperor to the court of Blefuscu. But I was afterwards given privately to understand, that his Imperial Majesty never imagining I had the least notice of his designs, believed I was only gone to Blefuscu in performance of my promise, according to the licence he had given me, which was well known at our court; and would return in a few days when that ceremony was ended. But he was at last in pain at my long absence; and, after consulting with the treasurer, and the rest of that cabal; a person of quality was dispatched with the copy of the articles against me. This envoy had instructions to represent to the monarch of Blefuscu, the great lenity of his master, who was content to punish me no further than with the loss of mine eyes: that I had fled from justice, and if I did not return in two hours, I should be deprived of my title of Nardac, and declared a traitor. The envoy further added; that in order to maintain the peace and amity between both empires, his master expected, that his brother of Blefuscu would give orders to have me sent back to Lilliput, bound hand and foot, to be punished as a traitor.

The Emperor of Blefuscu having taken three days to consult, returned an answer consisting of many civilities and excuses. He said, that as for sending me bound, his brother knew it was impossible; that although I had deprived him of his fleet, yet he owed great obligations to me for many good offices I had done him in making the peace. That however, both their Majesties would soon be made easy; for I had found a prodigious vessel on the shore, able to carry me on the sea, which he had given order to fit up with my own assistance and direction; and he hoped in a few weeks both empires would be freed from so insupportable an incumbrance.

With this answer the envoy returned to Lilliput, and the monarch of Blefuscu related to me all that had passed; offering me at the same time (but under the strictest confidence) his gracious protection, if I would continue in his service; wherein although I believed him sincere, yet I resolved never more to put any confidence in princes or ministers, where I could possibly avoid it; and therefore, with all due acknowledgments for his favourable intentions, I humbly begged to be excused. I told him, that since fortune, whether good or evil, had thrown a vessel in my way; I was resolved to venture myself in the ocean, rather than be an occasion of difference between two such mighty monarchs. Neither did I find the emperor at all displeased; and I discovered by a certain accident, that he was very glad of my resolution, and so were most of his ministers.

These considerations moved me to hasten my departure somewhat sooner than I intended; to which the court, impatient to have me gone, very readily contributed. Five hundred workmen were employed to make two sails to my boat, according to my directions, by quilting thirteen fold of their strongest linnen together. I was at the pains of making ropes and cables, by twisting ten, twenty, or thirty of the thickest and strongest of theirs. A great stone that I happened to find, after a long search by the sea shore, served me for an anchor. I had the tallow of three hundred cows for greasing my boat, and other uses. I was at incredible pains in cutting down some of the largest timber trees for oars and masts, wherein I was, however, much assisted by his Majesty's ship-carpenters, who helped me in smoothing them, after I had done the rough work.

In about a month, when all was prepared, I sent to receive his Majesty's commands, and to take my leave. The emperor and royal family came out of the palace; I lay down on my face to kiss his hand, which he very graciously gave me; so did the empress, and young princes of the blood. His Majesty presented me with fifty purses of two hundred *sprugs* a-piece, together with his picture at full length, which I put immediately into one of my gloves, to keep it from being hurt. The ceremonies at my departure were too many to trouble the reader with at this time.

I stored the boat with the carcases of an hundred oxen, and three hundred sheep, with bread and drink proportionable, and as much meat ready dressed as four hundred cooks could provide. I took with me six cows and two bulls alive, with as many ewes and rams, intending to carry them into my own country, and propagate the breed. And to feed them on board, I had a good bundle of hay, and a bag of corn. I would gladly have taken a dozen of the natives; but this was a thing the emperor would by no means permit; and besides a diligent search into my pockets, his Majesty engaged my honour not to carry away any of his subjects, although with their own consent and desire.

Having thus prepared all things as well as I was able; I set sail on the twenty-fourth day of September 1701, at six in the morning; and when I had gone about four leagues to the northward, the wind being at south-east, at six in the evening, I descryed a small island about half a league to the north-west. I advanced forward, and cast anchor on the lee-side of the island, which seemed to be uninhabited. I then took some refreshment, and went to my rest. I slept well, and as I conjecture at least six hours; for I found the day broke in two hours after I awaked. It was a clear night; I eat my breakfast before the sun was up; and heaving anchor, the wind being favourable, I steered the same course that I had done the day before, wherein I was directed by my pocket-compass. My intention was to reach, if possible, one of those islands, which I had reason to believe lay to the north-east of Van Diemen's Land. I discovered nothing all that day; but upon the next, about three in the afternoon, when I had by my computation made twenty-four leagues from Blefuscu, I descryed a sail steering to the south-east; my course was due east. I hailed her, but could get no answer; yet I found I gained upon her, for the wind slackened. I made all the sail I could, and in half an hour she spyed me, then hung out her antient, and discharged a gun. It is not easy to express the joy I was in upon the unexpected hope of once more seeing my beloved country, and the dear pledges I left in it. The ship slackened her sails, and I came up with her between five and six in the evening, September 26; but my heart leapt within me to see her English colours. I put my cows and sheep into my coat-pockets, and got on board with all my little cargo of provisions. The vessel was an English merchant-man, returning from Japan by the North and South Seas; the captain, Mr. John Biddel of Deptford, a very civil man, and an excellent sailor. We were now in the latitude of 30 degrees south; there were about fifty men in the ship; and here I met an old comrade of mine, one Peter Williams, who gave me a good character to the captain. This gentleman treated me with kindness, and desired I would let him know what place I came from last, and whither I was bound; which I did in few words; but he thought I was raving, and that the dangers I underwent had disturbed my head; whereupon I took my black cattle and sheep out of my pocket, which after great astonishment, clearly convinced him of my veracity. I then shewed him the gold given me by the Emperor of Blefuscu, together with his Majesty's picture at full length, and some other rarities of that country. I gave him two purses of two hundred *sprugs* each, and promised, when we arrived in England, to make him a present of a cow and a sheep big with young.

I shall not trouble the reader with a particular account of this voyage; which was very prosperous for the most part. We arrived in the Downs on the 13th of April 1702. I had only one misfortune, that the rats on board carried away one of my sheep; I found her bones in a hole, picked clean from the flesh. The rest of my cattle I got safe on shore, and set them a grazing in a bowling-green at Greenwich, where the fineness of the grass made them feed very heartily, although I had always feared the contrary: neither could I possibly have preserved them in so long a voyage, if the captain had not allowed me some of his best bisket, which rubbed to powder, and mingled with water, was their constant food. The short time I continued in England, I made a considerable profit by shewing my cattle to many persons of quality, and others: and before I began my second voyage, I sold them for six hundred pounds. Since my last return, I find the breed is considerably increased, especially the sheep; which I hope will prove much to the advantage of the woollen manufacture, by the fineness of the fleeces.

I stayed but two months with my wife and family; for my insatiable desire of seeing foreign countries would suffer me to continue no longer. I left fifteen hundred pounds with my wife, and fixed her in a good house at Redriff. My remaining stock I carried with me, part in money, and part in goods, in hopes to improve my fortunes. My eldest uncle, John, had left me an estate in land, near Epping, of about thirty pounds a year; and I had a long lease of the Black-Bull in Fetter-lane, which yeilded me as much more: so, that I was not in any danger of leaving my family upon the parish. My son Johnny, named so after his uncle, was at the grammar-school, and a towardly child. My daughter Betty (who is now well married, and hath children) was then at her needle-work. I took leave of my wife, and boy and girl, with tears on both sides; and went on board the *Adventure*, a merchant-ship of three hundred tons, bound for Surat, Captain John Nicholas of Liverpool, commander. But my account of this voyage must be referred to the second part of my travels.

THE END OF THE FIRST PART

PART II
A VOYAGE TO BROBDINGNAG

CHAPTER I

HAVING been condemned by nature and fortune to an active and restless life; in ten months after my return, I again left my native country, and took shipping in the Downs on the 20th day of June 1702, in the *Adventure*, Capt. John Nicholas, a Cornish man, commander, bound for Surat. We had a very prosperous gale until we arrived at the Cape of Good-hope, where we landed for fresh water; but discovering a leak we unshipped our goods, and wintered there; for the captain falling sick of an ague, we could not leave the cape until the end of March. We then set sail, and had a good voyage until we passed the Streights of Madagascar; but having got northward of that island, and to about five degrees south-latitude, the winds, which in those seas are observed to blow a constant equal gale between the north and west, from the beginning of December to the beginning of May, on the 19th of April began to blow with much greater violence, and more westerly than usual; continuing so for twenty days together, during which time we were driven a little to the east of the Molucca Islands, and about three degrees northward of the line, as our captain found by an observation he took the 2d of May, at which time the wind ceased, and it was a perfect calm, whereat I was not a little rejoyced. But he being a man well experienced in the navigation of those seas, bid us all prepare against a storm, which accordingly happened the day following: for

85

a southern wind, called the southern monsoon, began to set in.

Finding it was like to overblow, we took in our sprit-sail, and stood by to hand the fore-sail; but making foul weather, we looked the guns were all fast, and handed the missen The ship lay very broad off, so we thought it better spooning before the sea, than trying or hulling. We reeft the fore-sail and set him, we hawled aft the fore-sheet; the helm was hard a-weather. The ship wore bravely. We belayed the fore down-hall; but the sail was split, and we hawled down the yard, and got the sail into the ship, and unbound all the things clear of it. It was a very fierce storm; the sea broke strange and dangerous. We hawled off upon the lanniard of the wipstaff, and helped the man at helm. We would not get down our top-mast, but let all stand, because she scudded before the sea very well, and we knew that the top-mast being aloft, the ship was the wholesomer, and made better way through the sea, seeing we had sea-room. When the storm was over, we set fore-sail and main-sail, and brought the ship too. Then we set the missen, main-top-sail and the foretop-sail. Our course was east north-east, the wind was at south-west. We got the star-board tack aboard, we cast off our weather-braces and lifts; we set in the lee-braces, and hawled forward by the weather-bowlings, and hawled them tight. and belayed them, and hawled over the missen tack to windward, and kept her full and by as near as she would lye.

During this storm, which was followed by a strong wind west-south-west, we were carried by my computation about five hundred leagues to the east, so that the oldest sailor on board could not tell in what part of the world we were. Our provisions held out well, our ship was staunch, and our crew all in good health; but we lay in the utmost distress for water. We thought it best to hold on the same course rather than turn more northerly, which might have brought us to the north-west parts of great Tartary, and into the frozen sea.

On the 16th day of June 1703, a boy on the top-mast discovered land. On the 17th we came in full view of a great island or continent, (for we knew not whether) on the south-side whereof was a small neck of land jutting out into the sea, and a creek too shallow to hold a ship of above one hundred tuns. We cast anchor within a league of this creek, and our captain sent a dozen of his men well armed in the long boat, with vessels for water, if any could be found. I desired his leave to go with them, that I might see the country, and make what discoveries I could. When we came to land we saw no river or spring, nor any sign of inhabitants. Our men therefore wandered on the shore to find out some fresh water near the sea, and I walked alone about a mile on the other side, where I observed the country all barren and rocky. I now began to be weary, and seeing nothing to entertain my curiosity, I returned gently down towards the creek; and the sea being full in my view, I saw our men already got into the boat, and rowing for life to the ship. I was going to halloo after them, although it had been to little purpose, when I observed a huge creature walking after them in the sea, as fast as he could: he waded not much deeper than his knees, and took prodigious strides: but our men had the start of him half a league, and the sea thereabouts being full of sharp pointed rocks, the monster was not able to overtake the boat. This I was afterwards told, for I durst not stay to see the issue of that adventure; but run as fast as I could the way I first went; and then climbed up a steep hill, which gave me some prospect of the country. I found it fully cultivated; but that which first surprized me was the length of the grass, which in those grounds that seemed to be kept for hay, was above twenty foot high.

I fell into a high road, for so I took it to be, although it served to the inhabitants only as a foot path through a field of barley. Here I walked on for some time, but could see little on either side, it being now near harvest, and the corn rising at least forty foot. I was an hour walking to the end of this field; which was fenced in with a hedge of at least one hundred and twenty foot high, and the trees so lofty that I could make no computation of their altitude. There was a stile to pass from this field into the next: it had four steps, and a stone to cross over when you came to the utmost. It was impossible for me to climb this stile, because every step was six foot high, and the upper stone above twenty. I was endeavouring to find some gap in the hedge; when I discovered one of the inhabitants in the next field advancing towards the stile, of the same size with him whom I saw in the sea pursuing our boat. He appeared as tall as an ordinary spire-steeple; and took about ten yards at every stride, as near as I could guess. I was struck with the utmost fear and astonishment, and ran to hide my self in the corn, from whence I saw him at the top of the stile, looking back into the next field on the right hand; and heard him call in a voice many degrees louder than a speaking trumpet; but the noise was so high in the air, that at first I certainly thought it was thunder. Whereupon seven monsters like himself came towards him with reaping-hooks in their hands, each hook about the largeness of six scythes. These people were not so well clad as the first, whose servants or labourers they seemed to be. For, upon some words he spoke, they went to reap the corn in the field where I lay. I kept from them at as great a distance as I could, but was forced to move with extreme difficulty; for the stalks of the corn were sometimes not above a foot distant, so that I could hardly squeeze my body betwixt them. However, I made a shift to go forward until I came to a part of the field where the corn had been laid by the rain and wind: here it was impossible for me to advance a

step; for the stalks were so interwoven that I could not
creep through, and the beards of the fallen ears so strong
and pointed, that they pierced through my cloaths into my
flesh.   At the same time I heard the reapers not above an
hundred yards behind me.   Being quite dispirited with
toil, and wholly overcome by grief and despair, I lay down
between two ridges, and heartily wished I might there end
my days.   I bemoaned my desolate widow, and fatherless
children: I lamented my own folly and wilfulness in
attempting a second voyage against the advice of all my
friends and relations.   In this terrible agitation of mind I
could not forbear thinking of Lilliput, whose inhabitants
looked upon me as the greatest prodigy that ever appeared
in the world; where I was able to draw an imperial fleet in
my hand, and perform those other actions which will be
recorded for ever in the chronicles of that empire, while
posterity shall hardly believe them, although attested by
millions.   I reflected what a mortification it must prove to
me to appear as inconsiderable in this nation, as one single
Lilliputian would be among us.   But, this I conceived was
to be the least of my misfortunes: for, as human creatures
are observed to be more savage and cruel in proportion to
their bulk; what could I expect but to be a morsel in the
mouth of the first among these enormous barbarians, who
should happen to seize me?   Undoubtedly philosophers
are in the right when they tell us, that nothing is great or
little, otherwise than by comparison: it might have pleased
fortune to let the Lilliputians find some nation, where the
people were as diminutive with respect to them as they were
to me.   And who knows but that even this prodigious race
of mortals might be equally overmatched in some distant
part of the world, whereof we have yet no discovery?

Scared and confounded as I was, I could not forbear
going on with these reflections; when one of the reapers
approaching within ten yards of the ridge where I lay,

made me apprehend, that with the next step I should be squashed to death under his foot, or cut in two with his reaping-hook.   And therefore when he was again about to move, I screamed as loud as fear could make me.   Whereupon the huge creature trod short, and looking round about under him for some time, at last espied me as I lay on the ground.   He considered a while with the caution of one who endeavours to lay hold on a small dangerous animal in such a manner that it shall not be able either to scratch or to bite him; as I my self have sometimes done with a weasel in England.   At length he ventured to take me up behind by the middle between his fore-finger and thumb, and brought me within three yards of his eyes, that he might behold my shape more perfectly.   I guessed his meaning; and my good fortune gave me so much presence of mind, that I resolved not to struggle in the least, as he held me in the air above sixty foot from the ground; although he grievously pinched my sides, for fear I should slip through his fingers.   All I ventured was to raise mine eyes towards the sun, and place my hands together in a supplicating posture, and to speak some words in an humble melancholy tone, suitable to the condition I then was in. For, I apprehended every moment that he would dash me against the ground, as we usually do any little hateful animal which we have a mind to destroy.   But my good star would have it, that he appeared pleased with my voice and gestures, and began to look upon me as a curiosity; much wondering to hear me pronounce articulate words, although he could not understand them.   In the mean time, I was not able to forbear groaning and shedding tears, and turning my head towards my sides; letting him know, as well as I could, how cruelly I was hurt by the pressure of his thumb and finger.   He seemed to apprehend my meaning; for, lifting up the lappet of his coat, he put me gently into it, and immediately ran along with me to his master, who was a substantial farmer, and the same person I had first seen in the field.

The farmer having (as I supposed by their talk) received such an account of me as his servant could give him, took a piece of a small straw, about the size of a walking staff, and therewith lifted up the lappets of my coat; which it seems he thought to be some kind of covering that nature had given me. He blew my hairs aside to take a better view of my face. He called his hinds about him, and asked them (as I afterwards learned) whether they had ever seen in the fields any little creature that resembled me. He then placed me softly on the ground upon all four; but I got immediately up, and walked slowly backwards and forwards, to let those people see I had no intent to run away. They all sate down in a circle about me, the better to observe my motions. I pulled off my hat, and made a low bow towards the farmer: I fell on my knees, and lifted up my hands and eyes, and spoke several words as loud as I could: I took a purse of gold out of my pocket, and humbly presented it to him. He received it on the palm of his hand, then applied it close to his eye, to see what it was, and afterwards turned it several times with the point of a pin, (which he took out of his sleeve,) but could make nothing of it. Whereupon I made a sign that he should place his hand on the ground: I then took the purse, and opening it, poured all the gold into his palm. There were six Spanish-pieces of four pistoles each, besides twenty or thirty smaller coins. I saw him wet the tip of his little finger upon his tongue, and take up one of my largest pieces, and then another; but he seemed to be wholly ignorant what they were. He made me a sign to put them again into my purse, and the purse again into my pocket; which after offering to him several times, I thought it best to do.

The farmer by this time was convinced I must be a

rational creature. He spoke often to me; but the sound of his voice pierced my ears like that of a water-mill; yet his words were articulate enough. I answered as loud as I could in several languages; and he often laid his ear within two yards of me, but all in vain, for we were wholly unintelligible to each other. He then sent his servants to their work, and taking his handkerchief out of his pocket, he doubled and spread it on his hand, which he placed flat on the ground with the palm upwards, making me a sign to step into it, as I could easily do, for it was not above a foot in thickness. I thought it my part to obey; and for fear of falling, laid my self at full length upon the handkerchief, with the remainder of which he lapped me up to the head for further security; and in this manner carried me home to his house. There he called his wife, and shewed me to her; but she screamed and ran back as women in England do at the sight of a toad or a spider. However, when she had a while seen my behaviour, and how well I observed the signs her husband made, she was soon reconciled, and by degrees grew extreamly tender of me.

It was about twelve at noon, and a servant brought in dinner. It was only one substantial dish of meat (fit for the plain condition of an husband-man) in a dish of about four and twenty foot diameter. The company were the farmer and wife, three children, and an old grandmother: when they were sat down, the farmer placed me at some distance from him on the table, which was thirty foot high from the floor. I was in a terrible fright, and kept as far as I could from the edge, for fear of falling. The wife minced a bit of meat, then crumbled some bread on a trencher, and placed it before me. I made her a low bow, took out my knife and fork, and fell to eat; which gave them exceeding delight. The mistress sent her maid for a small dram-cup, which held about two gallons; and filled it with drink: I took up the vessel with much difficulty in both

hands, and in a most respectful manner drank to her lady-
ship's health, expressing the words as loud as I could in
English; which made the company laugh so heartily, that
I was almost deafened with the noise.   This liquor tasted
like a small cyder, and was not unpleasant.   Then the
master made me a sign to come to his trencher side; but as
I walked on the table, being in great surprize all the time,
as the indulgent reader will easily conceive and excuse, I
happened to stumble against a crust, and fell flat on my face,
but received no hurt.   I got up immediately, and observing
the good people to be in much concern, I took my hat
(which I held under my arm out of good manners) and waving it over my head, made three huzza's, to shew I had got
no mischief by the fall.   But advancing forwards toward
my master (as I shall henceforth call him) his youngest son
who sate next him, an arch boy of about ten years old, took
me up by the legs, and held me so high in the air, that I
trembled every limb; but his father snatched me from him;
and at the same time gave him such a box on the left ear,
as would have felled an European troop of horse to the
earth; ordering him to be taken from the table.   But, being
afraid the boy might owe me a spight; and well remembring
how mischievous all children among us naturally are to
sparrows, rabbits, young kittens, and puppy-dogs; I fell
on my knees, and pointing to the boy, made my master
understand, as well as I could, that I desired his son
be pardoned.   The father complied, and the lad took his
seat again; whereupon I went to him and kissed his hand,
which my master took, and made him stroak me gently
with it.

In the midst of dinner my mistress's favourite cat leapt
into her lap.   I heard a noise behind me like that of a dozen
stocking-weavers at work; and turning my head, I found it
proceeded from the purring of this animal, who seemed to
be three times larger than an ox, as I computed by the

view of her head, and one of her paws, while her mistress
was feeding and stroaking her.   The fierceness of this creature's countenance altogether discomposed me; although I
stood at the further end of the table, above fifty foot off;
and although my mistress held her fast for fear she might
give a spring, and seize me in her talons.   But, it happened
there was no danger; for the cat took not the least notice
of me when my master placed me within three yards of her.
And as I have been always told, and found true by experience in my travels, that flying, or discovering fear before a
fierce animal, is a certain way to make it pursue or attack
you; so I resolved, in this dangerous juncture to shew no
manner of concern.   I walked with intrepidity five or six
times before the very head of the cat, and came within half
a yard of her; whereupon she drew herself back, as if she
were more afraid of me: I had less apprehension concerning
the dogs, whereof three or four came into the room, as it is
usual in farmers houses; one of which was a mastiff equal
in bulk to four elephants, and a grey-hound somewhat
taller than the mastiff, but not so large.

When dinner was almost done, the nurse came in with a
child of a year old in her arms; who immediately spyed me,
and began a squall that you might have heard from London-
bridge to Chelsea; after the usual oratory of infants, to get
me for a play-thing.   The mother out of pure indulgence
took me up, and put me towards the child, who presently
seized me by the middle, and got my head in his mouth,
where I roared so loud that the urchin was frighted, and let
me drop; and I should have infallibly broke my neck, if the
mother had not held her apron under me.   The nurse, to
quiet her babe, made use of a rattle, which was a kind of
hollow vessel filled with great stones, and fastned by a cable
to the child's waist: but all in vain, so that she was forced
to apply the last remedy by giving it suck.   I must confess
no object ever disgusted me so much as the sight of her

monstrous breast, which I cannot tell what to compare with, so as to give the curious reader an idea of its bulk, shape, and colour.   It stood prominent six foot, and could not be less than sixteen in circumference.   The nipple was about half the bigness of my head, and the hue both of that and the dug so varified with spots, pimples, and freckles, that nothing could appear more nauseous: for I had a near sight of her, she sitting down the more conveniently to give suck, and I standing on the table.   This made me reflect upon the fair skins of our English ladies, who appear so beautiful to us, only because they are of our own size, and their defects not to be seen, but through a magnifying glass, where we find by experiment, that the smoothest and whitest skins look rough and coarse, and ill coloured.

I remember when I was at Lilliput, the complexions of those diminutive people appeared to me the fairest in the world: and talking upon this subject with a person of learning there, who was an intimate friend of mine; he said, that my face appeared much fairer and smoother when he looked on me from the ground, than it did upon a nearer view when I took him up in my hand, and brought him close; which he confessed was at first a very shocking sight. He said, he could discover great holes in my skin; that the stumps of my beard were ten times stronger than the bristles of a boar; and my complexion made up of several colours altogether disagreeable: although I must beg leave to say for my self, that I am as fair as most of my sex and country, and very little sunburnt by all my travels.   On the other sides, discoursing of the ladies in that emperor's court, he used to tell me, one had freckles, another too wide a mouth, a third too large a nose; nothing of which I was able to distinguish.   I confess, this reflection was obvious enough; which, however, I could not forbear, lest the reader might think those vast creatures were actually deformed: for I must do them justice to say, they are a comely race of people; and particularly the features of my master's countenance, although he were but a farmer, when I beheld him from the height of sixty foot, appeared very well proportioned.

When dinner was done, my master went out to his labourers; and, as I could discover by his voice and gesture, gave his wife a strict charge to take care of me. I was very much tired and disposed to sleep, which my mistress perceiving, she put me on her own bed, and covered me with a clean white handkerchief, but larger and coarser than the main sail of a man of war.

I slept about two hours, and dreamed I was at home with my wife and children, which aggravated my sorrows when I awaked and found my self alone in a vast room, between two and three hundred foot wide, and above two hundred high; lying in a bed twenty yards wide. My mistress was gone about her houshold affairs, and had locked me in. The bed was eight yards from the floor. Some natural necessities required me to get down: I durst not presume to call, and if I had, it would have been in vain, with such a voice as mine, at so great a distance from the room where I lay, to the kitchen where the family kept. While I was under these circumstances, two rats crept up the curtains, and ran smelling backwards and forwards on the bed: one of them came up almost to my face; whereupon I rose in a fright, and drew out my hanger to defend my self. These horrible animals had the boldness to attack me on both sides, and one of them held his fore feet at my collar; but I had the good fortune to rip up his belly before he could do me any mischief. He fell down at my feet; and the other seeing the fate of his comrade, made his escape, but not without one good wound on the back, which I gave him as he fled, and made the blood run trickling from him. After this exploit, I walked gently to and fro on the bed, to recover my breath and loss of spirits. These creatures were of the size of a large mastiff, but infinitely more nimble and fierce; so that, if I had taken off my belt before I went to sleep, I must have infallibly been torn to pieces and devoured. I measured the tail of the dead rat, and found it to be two yards long, wanting an inch; but it went against my stomach to drag the carcass off the bed, where it lay still bleeding; I observed it had yet some life, but with a strong slash cross the neck, I thoroughly dispatched it.

Soon after, my mistress came into the room, who seeing me all bloody, ran and took me up in her hand. I pointed to the dead rat, smiling and making other signs to shew I was not hurt; whereat she was extremely rejoyced, calling the maid to take up the dead rat with a pair of tongs, and throw it out of the window. Then she set me on a table, where I shewed her my hanger all bloody, and wiping it on the lappet of my coat, returned it to the scabbard. I was pressed to do more than one thing, which another could not do for me; and therefore endeavoured to make my mistress understand, that I desired to be set down on the floor; which after she had done, my bashfulness would not suffer me to express my self farther than by pointing to the door, and bowing several times. The good woman with much difficulty at last perceived what I would be at; and taking me up again in her hand, walked into the garden, where she set me down. I went on one side about two hundred yards; and beckoning to her not to look or to follow me, I hid my self between two leaves of sorrel, and there discharged the necessities of nature.

I hope, the gentle reader will excuse me for dwelling on these, and the like particulars; which however insignificant they may appear to grovelling vulgar minds, yet will certainly help a philosopher to enlarge his thoughts and imagination, and apply them to the benefit of publick as well as private life; which was my sole design in presenting this, and other accounts of my travels to the world; wherein, I have been chiefly studious of truth, without affecting any ornaments of learning, or of style.   But, the whole scene of this voyage made so strong an impression on my mind, and is so deeply fixed in my memory, that in committing it to paper, I did not omit one material circumstance: however, upon a strict review, I blotted out several passages of less moment which were in my first copy, for fear of being censured as tedious and trifling, whereof travellers are often, perhaps not without justice, accused.

CHAPTER II

A description of the farmer's daughter.   The author carried to a market-town, and then to the metropolis.   The particulars of his journey.

MY mistress had a daughter of nine years old, a child of towardly parts for her age, very dexterous at her needle, and skilful in dressing her baby.   Her mother and she contrived to fit up the baby's cradle for me against night: the cradle was put into a small drawer of a cabinet, and the drawer placed upon a hanging shelf for fear of the rats. This was my bed all the time I stayed with those people, although made more convenient by degrees, as I began to learn their language, and make my wants known.   This young girl was so handy, that after I had once or twice pulled off my cloaths before her, she was able to dress and undress me, although I never gave her that trouble when she would let me do either my self.   She made me seven shirts, and some other linnen of as fine cloth as could be got, which indeed was coarser than sackcloth; and these she constantly washed for me with her own hands.   She was likewise my school-mistress to teach me the language: when

I pointed to any thing, she told me the name of it in her own tongue, so, that in a few days I was able to call for whatever I had a mind to. She was very good-natured, and not above forty foot high, being little for her age. She gave me the name of Grildrig, which the family took up, and afterwards the whole kingdom. The word imports what the Latins call *nanunculus*, the Italians *homunceletino*, and the English *mannikin*. To her I chiefly owe my preservation in that country: we never parted while I was there; I called her my Glumdalclitch, or little nurse: and I should be guilty of great ingratitude, if I omitted this honourable mention of her care and affection towards me, which I heartily wish it lay in my power to requite as she deserves, instead of being the innocent, but unhappy instrument of her disgrace, as I have too much reason to fear.

It now began to be known and talked of in the neighbourhood, that my master had found a strange animal in the field, about the bigness of a *splacknuck*, but exactly shaped in every part like a human creature; which it likewise imitated in all its actions; seemed to speak in a little language of its own, had already learned several words of theirs, went erect upon two legs, was tame and gentle, would come when it was called, do whatever it was bid, had the finest limbs in the world, and a complexion fairer than a nobleman's daughter of three years old. Another farmer who lived hard by, and was a particular friend of my master, came on a visit, on purpose, to enquire into the truth of this story. I was immediately produced, and placed upon a table; where I walked as I was commanded, drew my hanger, put it up again, made my reverence to my master's guest, asked him in his own language how he did, and told him he was welcome; just as my little nurse had instructed me. This man, who was old and dim-sighted, put on his spectacles to behold me better, at which I could not forbear laughing very heartily; for his eyes appeared like the full-moon shining into a chamber at two windows. Our people, who discovered the cause of my mirth, bore me company in laughing; at which the old fellow was fool enough to be angry and out of countenance. He had the character of a great miser; and to my misfortune he well deserved it, by the cursed advice he gave my master to shew me as a sight upon a market-day in the next town, which was half an hour's riding, about two and twenty miles from our house. I guessed there was some mischief contriving, when I observed my master and his friend whispering long together, sometimes pointing at me; and my fears made me fancy, that I overheard and understood some of their words. But, the next morning Glumdalclitch my little nurse told me the whole matter, which she had cunningly picked out from her mother. The poor girl laid me on her bosom, and fell a weeping with shame and grief. She apprehended some mischief would happen to me, from rude, vulgar folks, who might squeeze me to death, or break one of my limbs by taking me in their hands. She had also observed how modest I was in my nature, how nicely I regarded my honour; and what an indignity I should conceive, to be exposed for money as a publick spectacle to the meanest of the people. She said her papa and mamma had promised that Grildrig should be hers; but now she found they meant to serve her as they did last year, when they pretended to give her a lamb; and yet, as soon as it was fat, sold it to a butcher. For my own part, I may truly affirm, that I was less concerned than my nurse. I had a strong hope which never left me, that I should one day recover my liberty; and as to the ignominy of being carried about for a monster, I considered my self to be a perfect stranger in the country; and, that such a misfortune could never be charged upon me as a reproach if ever I should return to England; since the King of Great Britain himself, in my condition, must have undergone the same distress.

My master, pursuant to the advice of his friend, carried me in a box the next market-day to the neighbouring town; and took along with him his little daughter, my nurse, upon a pillion behind me.   The box was close on every side, with a little door for me to go in and out, and a few gimlet-holes to let in air.   The girl had been so careful to put the quilt of her baby's bed into it, for me to lye down on. However, I was terribly shaken and discomposed in this journey, although it were but of half an hour.   For the horse went about forty foot at every step; and trotted so high, that the agitation was equal to the rising and falling of a ship in a great storm, but much more frequent: our journey was somewhat further than from London to St. Albans.   My master alighted at an inn which he used to frequent; and after consulting a while with the inn-keeper, and making some necessary preparations, he hired the *grultrud*, or cryer, to give notice through the town, of a strange creature, to be seen at the sign of the Green Eagle, not so big as a *splacknuck*, (an animal in that country very finely shaped, about six foot long) and in every part of the body resembling an human creature; could speak several words, and perform an hundred diverting tricks.

I was placed upon a table in the largest room of the inn, which might be near three hundred foot square.   My little nurse stood on a low stool close to the table, to take care of me, and direct what I should do.   My master, to avoid a croud, would suffer only thirty people at a time to see me. I walked about on the table as the girl commanded; she asked me questions as far as she knew my understanding of the language reached, and I answered them as loud as I could.   I turned about several times to the company, paid my humble respects, said they were welcome; and used some other speeches I had been taught.   I took up a thimble filled with liquor, which Glumdalclitch had given me for a cup, and drank their health.   I drew out my hanger, and flourished with it after the manner of fencers in England. My nurse gave me part of a straw, which I exercised as a pike, having learned the art in my youth. I was that day shewn to twelve sets of company; and as often forced to go over again with the same fopperies, until I was half dead with weariness and vexation. For, those who had seen me, made such wonderful reports, that the people were ready to break down the doors to come in. My master for his own interest would not suffer any one to touch me, except my nurse; and, to prevent danger, benches were set round the table at such a distance, as put me out of every body's reach. However, an unlucky school-boy aimed a hazel nut directly at my head, which very narrowly missed me; otherwise, it came with so much violence, that it would have infallibly knocked out my brains; for it was almost as large as a small pumpion: but I had the satisfaction to see the young rogue well beaten, and turned out of the room.

My master gave publick notice, that he would shew me again the next market-day: and, in the mean time, he prepared a more convenient vehicle for me, which he had reason enough to do; for I was so tired with my first journey, and with entertaining company eight hours together, that I could hardly stand upon my legs, or speak a word. It was at least three days before I recovered my strength; and that I might have no rest at home, all the neighbouring gentlemen from an hundred miles round, hearing of my fame, came to see me at my master's own house. There could not be fewer than thirty persons with their wives and children; (for the country is very populous;) and my master demanded the rate of a full room whenever he shewed me at home, although it were only to a single family. So, that for some time, I had but little ease every day of the week, (except Wednesday, which is their sabbath) although I were not carried to the town

My master, finding how profitable I was like to be, resolved to carry me to the most considerable cities of the
kingdom. Having therefore provided himself with all
things necessary for a long journey, and settled his affairs
at home; he took leave of his wife; and upon the 17th of
August 1703, about two months after my arrival, we set
out for the metropolis, situated near the middle of that
empire, and about three thousand miles distance from our
house: my master made his daughter Glumdalclitch ride
behind him. She carried me on her lap in a box tied about
her waist. The girl had lined it on all sides with the softest
cloth she could get, well quilted underneath; furnished it
with her baby's bed, provided me with linnen and other
necessaries; and made every thing as convenient as she
could. We had no other company but a boy of the house,
who rode after us with the luggage.

My master's design was to shew me in all the towns by
the way, and to step out of the road for fifty or an hundred
miles, to any village or person of quality's house where he
might expect custom. We made easy journies of not above
seven or eight score miles a day: for Glumdalclitch, on purpose to spare me, complained she was tired with the trotting
of the horse. She often took me out of my box at my own
desire, to give me air, and shew me the country; but always
held me fast by leading-strings. We passed over five or
six rivers many degrees broader and deeper than the Nile
or the Ganges; and there was hardly a rivulet so small as
the Thames at London-bridge. We were ten weeks in our
journey; and I was shewn in eighteen large towns, besides
many villages and private families.

On the 26th day of October, we arrived at the metropolis,
called in their language 'Lorbrulgrud,' or 'Pride of the
Universe.' My master took a lodging in the principal street
of the city, not far from the royal palace; and put out bills
in the usual form; containing an exact description of my

person and parts.   He hired a large room between three and
four hundred foot wide.   He provided a table sixty foot in
diameter, upon which I was to act my part; and pallisadoed
it round three foot from the edge, and as many high, to
prevent my falling over.   I was shewn ten times a day to
the wonder and satisfaction of all people.   I could now
speak the language tolerably well; and perfectly understood every word that was spoken to me.   Besides, I had
learned their alphabet, and could make a shift to explain a
sentence here and there; for Glumdalclitch had been my
instructer while we were at home, and at leisure hours
during our journey.   She carried a little book in her pocket,
not much larger than a Sanson's Atlas; it was a common
treatise for the use of young girls, giving a short account of
their religion; out of this she taught me my letters, and
interpreted the words.

CHAPTER III

The author sent for to court.   The queen buys him of his
master the farmer, and presents him to the king.   He disputes with his Majesty's great scholars.   An apartment at
court provided for the author.   He is in high favour with
the queen.   He stands up for the honour of his own country.
His quarrels with the queen's dwarf.

THE frequent labours I underwent every day, made in a
few weeks a very considerable change in my health: the
more my master got by me, the more unsatiable he grew.
I had quite lost my stomach, and was almost reduced to a
skeleton.   The farmer observed it; and concluding I soon
must die, resolved to make as good a hand of me as he
could.   While he was thus reasoning and resolving with
himself; a *slardral*, or gentleman usher, came from court,

commanding my master to bring me immediately thither for the diversion of the queen and her ladies. Some of the latter had already been to see me; and reported strange things of my beauty, behaviour, and good sense. Her Majesty, and those who attended her, were beyond measure delighted with my demeanor. I fell on my knees, and begged the honour of kissing her imperial foot; but this gracious princess held out her little finger towards me, (after I was set on a table) which I embraced in both my arms, and put the tip of it, with the utmost respect, to my lip. She made me some general questions about my country and my travels, which I answered as distinctly, and in as few words as I could. She asked, whether I would be content to live at court. I bowed down to the board of the table, and humbly answered, that I was my master's slave; but, if I were at my own disposal, I should be proud to devote my life to her Majesty's service. She then asked my master, whether he were willing to sell me at a good price. He, who apprehended I could not live a month, was ready enough to part with me; and demanded a thousand pieces of gold; which were ordered him on the spot, each piece being about the bigness of eight hundred moydores: but, allowing for the proportion of all things between that country and Europe, and the high price of gold among them; was hardly so great a sum as a thousand guineas would be in England. I then said to the queen; since I was now her Majesty's most humble creature and vassal, I must beg the favour, that Glumdalclitch, who had always tended me with so much care and kindness, and understood to do it so well, might be admitted into her service, and continue to be my nurse and instructor. Her Majesty agreed to my petition; and easily got the farmer's consent, who was glad enough to have his daughter preferred at court: and the poor girl herself was not able to hide her joy. My late master withdrew, bidding me farewel, and saying he had left me in a good service; to which I replyed not a word, only making him a slight bow.

The queen observed my coldness; and when the farmer was gone out of the apartment, asked me the reason. I made bold to tell her Majesty, that I owed no other obligation to my late master, than his not dashing out the brains of a poor harmless creature found by chance in his field; which obligation was amply recompensed by the gain he had made in shewing me through half the kingdom, and the price he had now sold me for. That, the life I had since led, was laborious enough to kill an animal of ten times my strength. That, my health was much impaired by the continual drudgery of entertaining the rabble every hour of the day; and that, if my master had not thought my life in danger, her Majesty would not have got so cheap a bargain. But, as I was out of all fear of being ill treated under the protection of so great and good an empress, the ornament of nature, the darling of the world, the delight of her subjects, the phœnix of the creation; so, I hoped, my late master's apprehensions would appear to be groundless; for I already found my spirits to revive by the influence of her most august presence.

This was the sum of my speech, delivered with great improprieties and hesitation; the latter part was altogether framed in the style peculiar to that people, whereof I learned some phrases from Glumdalclitch, while she was carrying me to court.

The queen giving great allowance for my defectiveness in speaking, was however surprized at so much wit and good sense in so diminutive an animal. She took me in her own hand, and carried me to the king, who was then retired to his cabinet. His Majesty, a prince of much gravity, and austere countenance, not well observing my shape at first view, asked the queen after a cold manner, how long it was since she grew fond of a *splacknuck*; for such it seems he took me to be, as I lay upon my breast in her Majesty's right hand. But this princess, who hath an infinite deal of wit and humour, set me gently on my feet upon the scrutore; and commanded me to give his Majesty an account of my self, which I did in a very few words; and Glumdalclitch, who attended at the cabinet door, and could not endure I should be out of her sight, being admitted; confirmed all that had passed from my arrival at her father's house.

The king, although he be as learned a person as any in his dominions; had been educated in the study of philosophy, and particularly mathematicks; yet, when he observed my shape exactly, and saw me walk erect, before I began to speak, conceived I might be a piece of clockwork, (which is in that country arrived to a very great perfection) contrived by some ingenious artist. But, when he heard my voice, and found what I delivered to be regular and rational, he could not conceal his astonishment. He was by no means satisfied with the relation I gave him of the manner I came into his kingdom; but thought it a story concerted between Glumdalclitch and her father, who had taught me a sett of words to make me sell at a higher price. Upon this imagination, he put several other questions to me, and still received rational answers, no otherwise defective than by a foreign accent, and an imperfect knowledge in the language; with some rustick phrases which I had learned at the farmer's house, and did not suit the polite style of a court.

His Majesty sent for three great scholars who were then in their weekly waiting (according to the custom in that country.) These gentlemen, after they had a while examined my shape with much nicety, were of different opinions concerning me. They all agreed, that I could not be produced according to the regular laws of nature; · because I was not framed with a capacity of preserving my

*E 60

life, either by swiftness, or climbing of trees, or digging holes in the earth. They observed by my teeth, which they viewed with great exactness, that I was a carnivorous animal; yet most quadrupeds being an over-match for me; and field-mice, with some others, too nimble, they could not imagine how I should be able to support my self, unless I fed upon snails and other insects; which they offered by many learned arguments to evince, that I could not possibly do. One of them seemed to think, that I might be an embrio, or abortive birth. But this opinion was rejected by the other two, who observed my limbs to be perfect and finished; and that I had lived several years, as it was manifested from my beard; the stumps whereof they plainly discovered through a magnifying glass. They would not allow me to be a dwarf, because my littleness was beyond all degrees of comparison; for the queen's favourite dwarf, the smallest ever known in that kingdom, was near thirty foot high. After much debate, they concluded unanimously, that I was only *relplum scalcath*, which is interpreted literally *lusus naturæ;* a determination exactly agreeable to the modern philosophy of Europe: whose professors, disdaining the old evasion of occult causes, whereby the followers of Aristotle endeavour in vain to disguise their ignorance; have invented this wonderful solution of all difficulties, to the unspeakable advancement of human knowledge.

After this decisive conclusion, I entreated to be heard a word or two. I applied my self to the king, and assured his Majesty, that I came from a country which abounded with several millions of both sexes, and of my own stature; where the animals, trees, and houses, were all in proportion, and where, by consequence, I might be as able to defend my self, and to find sustenance, as any of his Majesty's subjects could do here; which I took for a full answer to those gentlemen's arguments. To this they only replied with a smile of contempt; saying, that the farmer had instructed me very well in my lesson The king, who had a much better understanding, dismissing his learned men, sent for the farmer, who by good fortune was not yet gone out of town: having therefore first examined him privately, and then confronted him with me and the young girl; his Majesty began to think, that what we told him might possibly be true. He desired the queen to order, that a particular care should be taken of me; and was of opinion, that Glumdalclitch should still continue in her office of tending me, because he observed we had a great affection for each other. A convenient apartment was provided for her at court; she had a sort of governess appointed to take care of her education, a maid to dress her, and two other servants for menial offices; but, the care of me was wholly appropriated to her self. The queen commanded her own cabinet-maker to contrive a box, that might serve me for a bed-chamber, after the model that Glumdalclitch and I should agree upon. This man was a most ingenious artist; and according to my directions, in three weeks finished for me a wooden chamber of sixteen foot square, and twelve high; with sash windows, a door, and two closets, like a London bed-chamber. The board that made the cieling was to be lifted up and down by two hinges, to put in a bed ready furnished by her Majesty's upholsterer; which Glumdalclitch took out every day to air, made it with her own hands, and letting it down at night, locked up the roof over me. A nice workman, who was famous for little curiosities, undertook to make me two chairs, with backs and frames, of a substance not unlike ivory; and two tables, with a cabinet to put my things in. The room was quilted on all sides, as well as the floor and the cieling, to prevent any accident from the carelessness of those who carried me; and to break the force of a jolt when I went in a coach. I desired a lock for my door to prevent rats and mice from coming in: the smith, after several attempts, made the smallest that was ever seen among them; for I have known a larger at the gate of a gentleman's house in England. I made a shift to keep the key in a pocket of my own, fearing Glumdalclitch might lose it. The queen likewise ordered the thinnest silks that could be gotten, to make me cloaths; not much thicker than an English blanket, very cumbersome until I was accustomed to them. They were after the fashion of the kingdom, partly resembling the Persian, and partly the Chinese; and are a very grave decent habit.

The queen became so fond of my company, that she could not dine without me. I had a table placed upon the same at which her Majesty eat, just at her left elbow; and a chair to sit on. Glumdalclitch stood upon a stool on the floor, near my table, to assist and take care of me. I had an entire set of silver dishes and plates, and other necessaries, which in proportion to those of the queen, were not much bigger than what I have seen in a London toy-shop, for the furniture of a baby-house: these, my little nurse kept in her pocket, in a silver box, and gave me at meals as I wanted them; always cleaning them her self. No person dined with the queen but the two princesses royal; the elder sixteen years old, and the younger at that time thirteen and a month. Her Majesty used to put a bit of meat upon one of my dishes, out of which I carved for my self; and her diversion was to see me eat in miniature. 'For the queen (who had indeed but a weak stomach) took up at one mouthful, as much as a dozen English farmers could eat at a meal, which to me was for some time a very nauseous sight. She would craunch the wing of a lark, bones and all, between her teeth, although it were nine times as large as that of a full grown turkey; and put a bit of bread in her mouth, as big as two twelve-penny loaves. She drank out of a golden cup, above a hogshead at a draught. Her knives were twice as long as a scythe set strait upon the handle. The spoons, forks, and other instruments, were all in the same proportion. I remember when Glumdalclitch carried me out of curiosity to see some of the tables at court, where ten or a dozen of these enormous knives and forks were lifted up together; I thought I had never until then beheld so terrible a sight.

It is the custom, that every Wednesday, (which as I have before observed, was their sabbath) the king and queen, with the royal issue of both sexes, dine together in the apartment of his Majesty; to whom I was now become a favourite; and, at these times my little chair and table were placed at his left hand before one of the salt-sellers. This prince took a pleasure in conversing with me; enquiring into the manners, religion, laws, government, and learning of Europe, wherein I gave him the best account I was able. His apprehension was so clear, and his judgment so exact, that he made very wise reflections and observations upon all I said. But, I confess, that after I had been a little too copious in talking of my own beloved country; of our trade, and wars by sea and land, of our schisms in religion, and parties in the State; the prejudices of his education prevailed so far, that he could not forbear taking me up in his right hand, and stroking me gently with the other; after an hearty fit of laughing, asked me whether I were a Whig or a Tory. Then turning to his first minister, who waited behind him with a white staff, near as tall as the main-mast of the *Royal Sovereign*; he observed, how contemptible a thing was human grandeur, which could be mimicked by such diminutive insects as I: 'And yet,' said he, 'I dare engage, those creatures have their titles and distinctions of honour; they contrive little nests and burrows, that they call houses and cities; they make a figure in dress and equipage; they love, they fight, they dispute, they cheat, they betray.' And thus he continued on, while my colour came and went several times, with indignation, to hear our

noble country, the mistress of arts and arms, the scourge
of France, the arbitress of Europe, the seat of virtue, piety,
honour, and truth, the pride and envy of the world, so
contemptuously treated.

But, as I was not in a condition to resent injuries, so,
upon mature thoughts, I began to doubt whether I were
injured or no. For, after having been accustomed several
months to the sight and converse of this people, and observed every object upon which I cast mine eyes, to be of
proportionable magnitude; the horror I had first conceived
from their bulk and aspect was so far worn off, that if I had
then beheld a company of English lords and ladies in their
finery and birth-day cloaths, acting their several parts in
the most courtly manner of strutting, and bowing, and
prating; to say the truth, I should have been strongly
tempted to laugh as much at them, as this king and his
grandees did at me. Neither indeed could I forbear smiling
at my self, when the queen used to place me upon her hand
towards a looking-glass, by which both our persons appeared
before me in full view together; and there could nothing be
more ridiculous than the comparison: so, that I really began
to imagine my self dwindled many degrees below my
usual size.

Nothing angred and mortified me so much as the queen's
dwarf, who being of the lowest stature that was ever in
that country, (for I verily think he was not full thirty foot
high) became so insolent at seeing a creature so much
beneath him, that he would always affect to swagger and
look big as he passed by me in the queen's antichamber,
while I was standing on some table talking with the lords
or ladies of the court; and he seldom failed of a smart word
or two upon my littleness; against which, I could only
revenge my self by calling him brother, challenging him to
wrestle; and such repartees as are usual in the mouths of
court pages. ' One day at dinner, this malicious little cubb

was so nettled with something I had said to him, that raising himself upon the frame of her Majesty's chair, he took me up by the middle, as I was sitting down, not thinking any harm, and let me drop into a large silver bowl of cream; and then ran away as fast as he could. I fell over head and ears, and if I had not been a good swimmer, it might have gone very hard with me; for Glumdalclitch in that instant happened to be at the other end of the room; and the queen was in such a fright, that she wanted presence of mind to assist me. But my little nurse ran to my relief; and took me out, after I had swallowed above a quart of cream. I was put to bed; however, I received no other damage than the loss of a suit of cloaths, which was utterly spoiled. The dwarf was soundly whipped, and as a further punishment, forced to drink up the bowl of cream, into which he had thrown me; neither was he ever restored to favour: for, soon after, the queen bestowed him to a lady of high quality; so, that I saw him no more, to my very great satisfaction; for I could not tell to what extremity such a malicious urchin might have carried his resentment.

He had before served me a scurvy trick, which set the queen a laughing, although at the same time she were heartily vexed, and would have immediately cashiered him, if I had not been so generous as to intercede. Her Majesty had taken a marrow-bone upon her plate; and after knocking out the marrow, placed the bone again in the dish erect as it stood before; the dwarf watching his opportunity, while Glumdalclitch was gone to the side-board, mounted the stool that she stood on to take care of me at meals; took me up in both hands, and squeezing my legs together, wedged them into the marrow-bone above my waist; where I stuck for some time, and made a very ridiculous figure. I believe it was near a minute before any one knew what was become of me; for, I thought it below me to cry out. But, as princes seldom get their meat hot, my legs were not scalded, only my stockings and breeches in a sad condition. The dwarf at my entreaty had no other punishment than a sound whipping.

I was frequently rallied by the queen upon account of my fearfulness; and she used to ask me whether the people of my country were as great cowards as my self. The occasion was this. The kingdom is much pestered with flies in summer; and these odious insects, each of them as big as a Dunstable lark, hardly gave me any rest while I sat at dinner, with their continual humming and buzzing about mine ears. They would sometimes alight upon my victuals, and leave their loathsome excrement or spawn behind, which to me was very visible, although not to the natives of that country, whose large opticks were not so acute as mine in viewing smaller objects. Sometimes they would fix upon my nose or forehead, where they stung me to the quick, smelling very offensively; and I could easily trace that viscous matter, which our naturalists tell us enables those creatures to walk with their feet upwards upon a cieling. I had much ado to defend my self against these detestable animals, and could not forbear starting when they came on my face. It was the common practice of the dwarf to catch a number of these insects in his hand, as school-boys do among us, and let them out suddenly under my nose, on purpose to frighten me, and divert the queen. My remedy was to cut them in pieces with my knife as they flew in the air; wherein my dexterity was much admired.

I remember one morning when Glumdalclitch had set me in my box upon a window, as she usually did in fair days to give me air, (for I durst not venture to let the box be hung on a nail out of the window, as we do with cages in England) after I had lifted up one of my sashes, and sat down at my table to eat a piece of sweet-cake for my breakfast; above twenty wasps, allured by the smell, came flying into the room, humming louder than the drones of as many bagpipes. Some of them seized my cake, and carried it piece-meal away; others flew about my head and face, confounding me with the noise, and putting me in the utmost terror of their stings. However, I had the courage to rise and draw my hanger, and attack them in the air. I dispatched four of them, but the rest got away, and I presently shut my window. These insects were as large as partridges; I took out their stings, found them an inch and a half long, and as sharp as needles. I carefully preserved them all, and having since shewn them with some other curiosities in several parts of Europe; upon my return to England I gave three of them to Gresham College, and kept the fourth for my self.

CHAPTER IV

The country described. A proposal for correcting modern maps. The king's palace, and some account of the metropolis. The author's way of travelling. The chief temple described.

I NOW intend to give the reader a short description of this country, as far as I travelled in it, which was not above two thousand miles round Lorbrulgrud the metropolis. For, the queen, whom I always attended, never went further when she accompanied the king in his progresses; and there staid until his Majesty returned from viewing his frontiers. The whole extent of this prince's dominions reached but six thousand miles in length, and from three to five in breadth. From whence I cannot but conclude, that our geographers of Europe are in a great error, by supposing nothing but sea between Japan and California: for, it was ever my opinion, that there must be a balance of earth to counterpoise the great continent of Tartary; and therefore they ought to correct their maps and charts, by joining this vast tract of land to the north-west parts of America; wherein I shall be ready to lend them my assistance.

The kingdom is a peninsula, terminated to the north-east by a ridge of mountains thirty miles high, which are altogether impassable by reason of the volcanoes upon the tops. Neither do the most learned know what sort of mortals inhabit beyond those mountains, or whether they be inhabited at all. On the three other sides it is bounded by the ocean. There is not one sea-port in the whole kingdom; and those parts of the coasts into which the rivers issue, are so full of pointed rocks, and the sea generally so rough, that there is no venturing with the smallest of their boats; so, that these people are wholly excluded from any commerce with the rest of the world. But the large rivers are full of vessels, and abound with excellent fish; for they seldom get any from the sea, because the sea-fish are of the same size with those in Europe, and consequently not worth catching; whereby it is manifest, that nature in the production of plants and animals of so extraordinary a bulk, is wholly confined to this continent; of which I leave the reasons to be determined by philosophers. However, now and then they take a whale that happens to be dashed against the rocks, which the common people feed on heartily. These whales I have known so large, that a man could hardly carry one upon his shoulders; and sometimes for curiosity they are brought in hampers to Lorbrulgrud: I saw one of them in a dish at the king's table, which passed for a rarity; but I did not observe he was fond of it; for I think indeed the bigness disgusted him, although I have seen one somewhat larger in Greenland.

The country is well inhabited, for it contains fifty one cities, near an hundred walled towns, and a great number of villages. To satisfy my curious reader, it may be sufficient to describe Lorbrulgrud. This city stands upon almost two equal parts on each side the river that passes through. It contains above eighty thousand houses. It is in length three *glonglungs* (which make about fifty four English miles) and two and a half in breadth, as I measured it my self in the royal map made by the king's order, which was laid on the ground on purpose for me, and extended an hundred feet; I paced the diameter and circumference several times bare-foot, and computing by the scale, measured it pretty exactly.

The king's palace is no regular edifice, but an heap of buildings about seven miles round: the chief rooms are generally two hundred and forty foot high, and broad and long in proportion. A coach was allowed to Glumdalclitch and me, wherein her governess frequently took her out to see the town, or go among the shops; and I was always of the party, carried in my box; although the girl at my own desire, would often take me out, and hold me in her hand, that I might more conveniently view the houses and the people as we passed along the streets. I reckoned our coach to be about a square of Westminster-hall, but not altogether so high; however, I cannot be very exact. One day the governess ordered our coach-man to stop at several shops; where the beggars watching their opportunity, crouded to the sides of the coach, and gave me the most horrible spectacles that ever an European eye beheld. There was a woman with a cancer in her breast, swelled to a monstrous size, full of holes, in two or three of which I could have easily crept, and covered my whole body. There was a fellow with a wen in his neck, larger than five wool-packs; and another with a couple of wooden legs, each about twenty foot high. But, the most hateful sight of all, was the lice crawling on their clothes: I could see distinctly the limbs of these vermin with my naked eye, much better than those of an European louse through a microscope; and their snouts with which they rooted like swine. They were the first I had ever beheld; and I should have been curious enough to dissect one of them, if I had proper instruments (which I unluckily left behind me in the ship) although indeed the sight was so nauseous, that it perfectly turned my stomach.

Beside the large box in which I was usually carried, the queen ordered a smaller one to be made for me, of about twelve foot square, and ten high, for the convenience of travelling; because the other was somewhat too large for Glumdalclitch's lap, and cumbersome in the coach; it was made by the same artist, whom I directed in the whole contrivance. This travelling closet was an exact square, with a window in the middle of three of the squares, and each window was latticed with iron wire on the outside, to prevent accidents in long journeys. On the fourth side, which had no window, two strong staples were fixed, through which, the person that carried me, when I had a mind to be on horseback, put in a leathern belt, and buckled it about his waist. This was always the office of some grave trusty servant, in whom I could confide, whether I attended the king and queen in their progresses, or were disposed to see the gardens, or pay a visit to some great lady or minister of State in the court, when Glumdalclitch happened to be out of order: for I soon began to be known and esteemed among the greatest officers, I suppose more upon account of their Majesties favour, than any merit of my own. In journeys, when I was weary of the coach, a servant on horseback would buckle my box, and place it on a cushion before him; and there I had a full prospect of the country on three sides from my three windows. I had in this closet a field-bed, and a hammock hung from the cieling, two chairs and a table, neatly screwed to the floor, to prevent being tossed about by the agitation of the horse or the coach. And having been long used to sea-voyages, these motions, although sometimes very violent, did not much discompose me.

Whenever I had a mind to see the town, it was always in my travelling-closet; which Glumdalclitch held in her lap, in a kind of open sedan, after the fashion of the country, born by four men, and attended by two others in the queen's livery. The people who had often heard of me, were very curious to croud about the sedan; and the girl was complaisant enough to make the bearers stop, and to take me in her hand, that I might be more conveniently seen.

I was very desirous to see the chief temple, and particularly the tower belonging to it, which is reckoned the highest in the kingdom. Accordingly one day my nurse carried me thither, but I may truly say I came back disappointed; for, the height is not above three thousand foot, reckoning from the ground to the highest pinnacle top; which allowing for the difference between the size of those people, and us in Europe, is no great matter for admiration, nor at all equal in proportion (if I rightly remember) to Salisbury steeple. But, not to detract from a nation, to which during my life I shall acknowledge myself extremely obliged; it must be allowed, that whatever this famous tower wants in height, is amply made up in beauty and strength. For, the walls are near an hundred foot thick, built of hewen stone, whereof each is about forty foot square, and adorned on all sides with statues of gods and emperors, cut in marble, larger than the life, placed in their several niches. I measured a little finger which had fallen down from one of these statues, and lay unperceived among some rubbish; and found it exactly four foot and an inch in length. Glumdalclitch wrapped it up in a handkerchief, and carried it home in her pocket, to keep among other trinkets, of which the girl was very fond, as children at her age usually are.

The king's kitchen is indeed a noble building, vaulted at top, and about six hundred foot high. The great oven is not so wide by ten paces as the cupola at St. Paul's: for I measured the latter on purpose after my return. But if I should describe the kitchen-grate, the prodigious pots and kettles, the joints of meat turning on the spits, with many other particulars; perhaps I should be hardly believed; at least, a severe critick would be apt to think I enlarged a little, as travellers are often suspected to do. To avoid which censure, I fear I have run too much into the other extreme; and that if this treatise should happen to be translated into the language of Brobdingnag, (which is the general name of that kingdom) and transmitted thither, the king and his people would have reason to complain, that I had done them an injury, by a false and diminutive representation.

His Majesty seldom keeps above six hundred horses in his stables: they are generally from fifty four to sixty foot high. But, when he goes abroad on solemn days, he is attended for State, by a militia guard of five hundred horse, which indeed I thought was the most splendid sight that could be ever beheld, until I saw part of his army in battalia; whereof I shall find another occasion to speak.

CHAPTER V

Several adventures that happened to the author. The execution of a criminal. The author shews his skill in navigation.

I SHOULD have lived happy enough in that country, if my littleness had not exposed me to several ridiculous and troublesome accidents; some of which I shall venture to relate. Glumdalclitch often carried me into the gardens of the court in my smaller box, and would sometimes take me out of it and hold me in her hand, or set me down to walk. I remember, before the dwarf left the queen, he followed us one day into those gardens; and my nurse having set me down, he and I being close together, near some dwarf apple-trees, I must need shew my wit by a silly allusion between him and the trees, which happens to hold in their language as it doth in ours. Whereupon, the malicious rogue watching his opportunity, when I was walking under one of them, shook it directly over my head, by which a dozen apples, each of them near as large as a Bristol barrel, came tumbling about my ears; one of them hit me on the back as I chanced to stoop, and knocked me down flat on my face, but I received no other hurt; and the dwarf was pardoned at my desire, because I had given the provocation.

Another day, Glumdalclitch left me on a smooth grass-plot to divert my self while she walked at some distance with her governess. In the mean time, there suddenly fell such a violent shower of hail, that I was immediately by the force of it struck to the ground: and, when I was down, the hail-stones gave me such cruel bangs all over my body, as if I had been pelted with tennis-balls; however, I made a shift to creep on all four, and shelter my self, by lying flat on my face on the lee-side of a border of lemmon thyme, but so bruised from head to foot, that I could not go abroad in ten days. Neither is this at all to be wondered at; because nature in that country observing the same proportion through all her operations, a hail-stone is near eighteen hundred times as large as one in Europe; which I can assert upon experience, having been so curious to weigh and measure them.

But, a more dangerous accident happened to me in the same garden, when my little nurse, believing she had put me in a secure place, which I often entreated her to do, that I might enjoy my own thoughts; and having left my box at home, to avoid the trouble of carrying it, went to another part of the gardens, with her governess, and some ladies of her acquaintance: while she was absent and out of hearing, a small white spaniel belonging to one of the chief gardeners, having got by accident into the garden, happened to range near the place where I lay.   The dog following the scent, came directly up, and taking me in his mouth, ran strait to his master, wagging his tail, and set me gently on the ground.   By good fortune, he had been so well taught, that I was carried between his teeth without the least hurt, or even tearing my cloaths.   But, the poor gardener, who knew me well, and had a great kindness for me, was in a terrible fright.   He gently took me up in both his hands, and asked me how I did; but I was so amazed and out of breath, that I could not speak a word.   In a few minutes I came to my self, and he carried me safe to my little nurse, who by this time had returned to the place where she left me, and was in cruel agonies when I did not appear, nor answer when she called; she severely reprimanded the gardener on account of his dog.   But, the thing was hushed up, and never known at court; for the girl was afraid of the queen's anger; and truly as to my self, I thought it would not be for my reputation that such a story should go about.

This accident absolutely determined Glumdalclitch never to trust me abroad for the future out of her sight.   I had been long afraid of this resolution; and therefore concealed from her some little unlucky adventures that happened in those times when I was left by myself.   Once a kite hovering over the garden, made a stoop at me, and if I had not resolutely drawn my hanger, and run under a thick espalier, he would have certainly carried me away in his talons.   Another time, walking to the top of a fresh mole-hill, I fell to my neck in the hole through which that animal had cast up the earth; and coined some lye not worth remembring, to excuse my self for spoiling my cloaths.   I likewise broke my right shin against the shell of a snail, which I happened to stumble over, as I was walking alone, and thinking on poor England.

I cannot tell whether I were more pleased or mortified to observe in those solitary walks, that the smaller birds did not appear to be at all afraid of me; but would hop about within a yard distance, looking for worms, and other food, with as much indifference and security as if no creature at all were near them. I remember, a thrush had the confidence to snatch out of my hand with his bill, a piece of cake that Glumdalclitch had just given me for my breakfast. When I attempted to catch any of these birds, they would boldly turn against me, endeavouring to pick my fingers, which I durst not venture within their reach; and then they would hop back unconcerned to hunt for worms or snails, as they did before. But, one day I took a thick cudgel, and threw it with all my strength so luckily at a linnet, that I knocked him down, and seizing him by the neck with both my hands, ran with him in triumph to my nurse. However, the bird, who had only been stunned, recovering himself, gave me so many boxes with his wings on both sides of my head and body, although I held him at arms length, and was out of the reach of his claws, that I was twenty times thinking to let him go. But I was soon relieved by one of our servants, who wrung off the bird's neck; and I had him the next day for dinner by the queen's command. This linnet, as near as I can remember, seemed to be somewhat larger than an English swan.

The maids of honour often invited Glumdalclitch to their apartments, and desired she would bring me along with her, on purpose to have the pleasure of seeing and touching me. They would often strip me naked from top to toe, and lay me at full length in their bosoms; wherewith I was much disgusted; because, to say the truth, a very offensive smell came from their skins; which I do not mention or intend to the disadvantage of those excellent ladies, for whom I have all manner of respect: but, I conceive, that my sense was more acute in proportion to my littleness; and that those illustrious persons were no more disagreeable to their lovers, or to each other, than people of the same quality are with us in England. And, after all, I found their natural smell was much more supportable than when they used perfumes, under which I immediately swooned away. I cannot forget, that an intimate friend of mine in Lilliput, took the freedom in a warm day, when I had used a good deal of exercise, to complain of a strong smell about me; although I am as little faulty that way as most of my sex: but, I suppose, his faculty of smelling was as nice with regard to me, as mine was to that of this people. Upon this point, I cannot forbear doing justice to the queen my mistress, and Glumdalclitch my nurse; whose persons were as sweet as those of any lady in England.

That which gave me most uneasiness among these maids of honour, when my nurse carried me to visit them, was to see them use me without any manner of ceremony, like a creature who had no sort of consequence. For, they would strip themselves to the skin, and put on their smocks in my presence, while I was placed on their toylet directly before their naked bodies: which, I am sure to me was very far from being a tempting sight, or from giving me any other motions than those of horror and disgust. Their skins appeared so coarse and uneaven, so variously coloured when I saw them near, with a mole here and there as broad as a trencher, and hairs hanging from it thicker than pack-threads; to say nothing further concerning the rest of their persons. Neither did they at all scruple while I was by, to discharge what they had drunk, to the quantity of at least two hogsheads, in a vessel that held above three tuns. The handsomest among these maids of honour, a pleasant frolicksome girl of sixteen, would sometimes set me astride upon one of her nipples; with many other tricks, wherein the reader will excuse me for not being over particular. But, I was so much displeased, that I intreated Glumdalclitch to contrive some excuse for not seeing that young lady any more.

One day, a young gentleman, who was nephew to my nurse's governess, came and pressed them both to see an execution. It was of a man who had murdered one of that gentleman's intimate acquaintance. Glumdalclitch was prevailed on to be of the company, very much against her inclination, for she was naturally tender hearted: and, as for my self, although I abhorred such kind of spectacles; yet, my curiosity tempted me to see something that I thought must be extraordinary. The malefactor was fixed in a chair upon a scaffold erected for the purpose; and his head cut off at one blow with a sword of about forty foot long. The veins and arteries spouted up such a prodigious quantity of blood, and so high in the air, that the great *jet d'eau* at Versailles was not equal for the time it lasted; and the head when it fell on the scaffold floor, gave such a bounce, as made me start, although I were at least an English mile distant.

The queen, who often used to hear me talk of my sea-voyages, and took all occasions to divert me when I was melancholy, asked me, whether I understood how to handle a sail or an oar; and whether a little exercise of rowing might not be convenient for my health. I answered, that I understood both very well. For, although my proper employment had been to be surgeon or doctor to the ship; yet often upon a pinch, I was forced to work like a common mariner. But, I could not see how this could be done in their country, where the smallest wherry was equal to a first rate man of war among us; and such a boat as I could manage, would never live in any of their rivers: her Majesty said, if I would contrive a boat, her own joyner should make it, and she would provide a place for me to sail in. The fellow was an ingenious workman, and by my instructions, in ten days finished a pleasure-boat with all its tackling, able conveniently to hold eight Europeans. When it was finished, the queen was so delighted, that she ran with it in her lap to the king, who ordered it to be put in a cistern full of water, with me in it, by way of tryal; where I could not manage my two sculls or little oars for want of room. But, the queen had before contrived another project. She ordered the joyner to make a wooden trough of three hundred foot long, fifty broad, and eight deep; which being well pitched to prevent leaking, was placed on the floor along the wall, in an outer room of the palace. It had a cock near the bottom, to let out the water when it began to grow stale; and two servants could easily fill it in half an hour. Here I often used to row for my diversion, as well as that of the queen and her ladies, who thought themselves agreeably entertained with my skill and agility. Sometimes I would put up my sail, and then my business was only to steer, while the ladies gave me a gale with their fans; and when they were weary, some of the pages would blow my sail forward with their breath, while I shewed my art by steering starboard or larboard as I pleased. When I had done, Glumdalclitch always carried back my boat into her closet, and hung it on a nail to dry.

In this exercise I once met an accident which had like to have cost me my life. For, one of the pages having put my boat into the trough; the governess who attended Glumdalclitch, very officiously lifted me up to place me in the boat; but I happened to slip through her fingers, and should have infallibly fallen down forty foot upon the floor, if by the luckiest chance in the world, I had not been stopped by a corking-pin that stuck in the good gentlewoman's stomacher; the head of the pin passed between my shirt and the waistband of my breeches; and thus I was held by the middle in the air, until Glumdalclitch ran to my relief.

Another time, one of the servants, whose office it was to fill my trough every third day with fresh water; was so careless to let a huge frog (not perceiving it) slip out of his pail. The frog lay concealed until I was put into my boat, but then seeing a resting place, climbed up, and made it lean so much on one side, that I was forced to balance it with all my weight on the other, to prevent overturning. When the frog was got in, it hopped at once half the length of the boat, and then over my head, backwards and forwards, dawbing my face and cloaths with its odious slime. The largeness of its features made it appear the most deformed animal than can be conceived. However, I desired Glumdalclitch to let me deal with it alone. I banged it a good while with one of my sculls, and at last forced it to leap out of the boat.

But, the greatest danger I ever underwent in that kingdom, was from a monkey, who belonged to one of the clerks of the kitchen. Glumdalclitch had locked me up in her closet, while she went somewhere upon business, or a visit. The weather being very warm, the closet window was left open, as well as the windows and the door of my bigger box, in which I usually lived, because of its largeness and conveniency. As I sat quietly meditating at my table, I heard something bounce in at the closet window, and skip about from one side to the other; whereat, although I were much alarmed, yet I ventured to look out, but not stirring from my seat; and then I saw this frolicksome animal, frisking and leaping up and down, until at last he came to my box, which he seemed to view with great pleasure and curiosity, peeping in at the door and every window. I retreated to the farther corner of my room, or box; but the monkey looking in at every side, put me into such a fright, that I wanted presence of mind to conceal my self under the bed, as I might easily have done. After some time spent in peeping, grinning, and chattering, he at last espyed me; and reaching one of his paws in at the door, as a cat doth when she plays with a mouse, although I often shifted place to avoid him; he at length seized the lappet of my coat (which being made of that country silk, was very thick and strong) and dragged me out. He took me up in his right fore-foot, and held me as a nurse doth a child she is going to suckle; just as I have seen the same sort of creature do with a kitten in Europe: and, when I offered to struggle, he squeezed me so hard, that I thought it more prudent to submit.   I have good reason to believe, that he took me for a young one of his own species, by his often stroaking my face very gently with his other paw.   In these diversions he was interrupted by a noise at the closet door, as if some body were opening it; whereupon he suddenly leaped up to the window at which he had come in, and thence upon the leads and gutters, walking upon three legs, and holding me in the fourth, until he clambered up to a roof that was next to ours.   I heard Glumdalclitch give a shriek at the moment he was carrying me out.   The poor girl was almost distracted: that quarter of the palace was all in an uproar; the servants ran for ladders; the monkey was seen by hundreds in the court, sitting upon the ridge of a building, holding me like a baby in one of his fore-paws, and feeding me with the other, by cramming into my mouth some victuals he had squeezed out of the bag on one side of his chaps, and patting me when I would not eat; whereat, many of the rabble below could not forbear laughing; neither do I think they justly ought to be blamed; for without question, the sight was ridiculous enough to every body but my self.   Some of the people threw up stones, hoping to drive the monkey down; but this was strictly forbidden, or else very probably my brains had been dashed out.

The ladders were now applied, and mounted by several men; which the monkey observing, and finding himself almost encompassed; not being able to make speed enough with his three legs, let me drop on a ridge-tyle, and made his escape. Here I sat for some time, five hundred yards from the ground, expecting every moment to be blown down by the wind, or to fall by my own giddiness, and come tumbling over and over from the ridge to the eves. But, an honest lad, one of my nurse's footmen, climbed up, and putting me into his breeches pocket, brought me down safe.

I was almost choaked with the filthy stuff the monkey had crammed down my throat; but, my dear little nurse picked it out of my mouth with a small needle; and then I fell a vomiting, which gave me great relief. Yet I was so weak and bruised in the sides with the squeezes given me by this odious animal, that I was forced to keep my bed a fortnight. The king, queen, and all the court, sent every day to enquire after my health; and her Majesty made me several visits during my sickness. The monkey was killed, and an order made, that no such animal should be kept about the palace.

When I attended the king after my recovery, to return him thanks for his favours, he was pleased to railly me a good deal upon this adventure. He asked me what my thoughts and speculations were while I lay in the monkey's paw; how I liked the victuals he gave me, his manner of feeding; and whether the fresh air on the roof had sharpened my stomach. He desired to know, what I would have done upon such an occasion in my own country. I told his Majesty, that in Europe we had no monkies, except such as were brought for curiosities from other places, and so small, that I could deal with a dozen of them together, if they presumed to attack me. And as for that monstrous animal with whom I was so lately engaged, (it was indeed as large as an elephant) if my fears had suffered me to think so far as to make use of my hanger (looking fiercely, and clapping my hand upon the hilt as I spoke) when he poked his paw into my chamber, perhaps I should have given him such a wound, as would have made him glad to withdraw it with more haste than he put it in. This I delivered in a firm tone, like a person who was jealous lest his courage should be called in question. However, my speech produced nothing else besides a loud laughter; which all the respect due to his Majesty from those about him, could not make them contain. This made me reflect, how vain an attempt it is for a man to endeavour doing himself honour among those who are out of all degree of equality or comparison with him. And yet, I have seen the moral of my own behaviour very frequent in England since my return; where a little contemptible varlet, without the least title to birth, person, wit, or common sense, shall presume to look with importance, and put himself upon a foot with the greatest persons of the kingdom.

I was every day furnishing the court with some ridiculous story; and Glumdalclitch, although she loved me to excess, yet was arch enough to inform the queen, whenever I committed any folly that she thought would be diverting to her Majesty. The girl who had been out of order, was carried by her governess to take the air about an hour's distance, or thirty miles from town. They alighted out of the coach near a small foot-path in a field; and Glumdalclitch setting down my travelling box, I went out of it to walk. There was a cow-dung in the path, and I must needs try my activity by attempting to leap over it. I took a run, but unfortunately jumped short, and found my self just in the middle up to my knees. I waded through with some difficulty, and one of the footmen wiped me as clean as he could with his handkerchief; for I was filthily bemired, and my nurse confined me to my box until we returned home; where the queen was soon informed of what had passed, and the footmen spread it about the court; so, that all the mirth, for some days, was at my expence.

CHAPTER VI

Several contrivances of the author to please the king and queen.
He shews his skill in musick. The king enquires into the
state of Europe, which the author relates to him. The
king's observations thereon.

I USED to attend the king's levee once or twice a week, and
had often seen him under the barber's hand, which indeed
was at first very terrible to behold. For, the razor was
almost twice as long as an ordinary scythe. His Majesty,
according to the custom of the country, was only shaved
twice a week. I once prevailed on the barber, to give me
some of the suds or lather, out of which I picked forty or
fifty of the strongest stumps of hair. I then took a piece
of fine wood, and cut it like the back of a comb, making
several holes in it at equal distance, with as small a needle
as I could get from Glumdalclitch. I fixed in the stumps
so artificially, scraping and sloping them with my knife
towards the points, that I made a very tolerable comb;
which was a seasonable supply, my own being so much
broken in the teeth, that it was almost useless: neither did
I know any artist in that country so nice and exact, as
would undertake to make me another.

And this puts me in mind of an amusement wherein I
spent many of my leisure hours. I desired the queen's
woman to save for me the combings of her Majesty's hair,
whereof in time I got a good quantity; and consulting with
my friend the cabinet-maker, who had received general
orders to do little jobbs for me; I directed him to make two
chair-frames, no larger than those I had in my box, and
then to bore little holes with a fine awl round those parts
where I designed the backs and seats; through these holes
I wove the strongest hairs I could pick out, just after
the manner of cane-chairs in England. When they were

finished, I made a present of them to her Majesty, who kept them in her cabinet, and used to shew them for curiosities; as indeed they were the wonder of every one who beheld them. The queen would have had me sit upon one of these chairs, but I absolutely refused to obey her; protesting I would rather dye a thousand deaths, than place a dishonourable part of my body on those precious hairs that once adorned her Majesty's head. Of these hairs (as I had always a mechanical genius) I likewise made a neat little purse about five foot long, with her Majesty's name decyphered in gold letters; which I gave to Glumdalclitch, by the queen's consent. To say the truth, it was more for shew than use, being not of strength to bear the weight of the larger coins; and therefore she kept nothing in it, but some little toys that girls are fond of.

The king, who delighted in musick, had frequent concerts at court, to which I was sometimes carried, and set in my box on a table to hear them: but, the noise was so great, that I could hardly distinguish the tunes. I am confident, that all the drums and trumpets of a royal army, beating and sounding together just at your ears, could not equal it. My practice was to have my box removed from the places where the performers sat, as far as I could; then to shut the doors and windows of it, and draw the window-curtains; after which I found their musick not disagreeable.

I had learned in my youth, to play a little upon the spinet; Glumdalclitch kept one in her chamber, and a master attended twice a week to teach her: I call it a spinet, because it somewhat resembled that instrument, and was played upon in the same manner. A fancy came into my head, that I would entertain the king and queen with an English tune upon this instrument. But this appeared extremely difficult: for, the spinet was near sixty foot long, each key being almost a foot wide; so that, with my arms extended, I could not reach to above five keys; and to press them down, required a good smart stroak with my fist, which would be too great a labour, and to no purpose. The method I contrived was this. I prepared two round sticks about the bigness of common cudgels; they were thicker at one end than the other; and I covered the thicker end with a piece of a mouse's skin, that by rapping on them, I might neither damage the tops of the keys, nor interrupt the sound. Before the spinet, a bench was placed about four foot below the keys, and I was put upon the bench. I ran sideling upon it that way and this, as fast as I could, banging the proper keys with my two sticks; and made a shift to play a jigg to the great satisfaction of both their Majesties: but, it was the most violent exercise I ever underwent, and yet I could not strike above sixteen keys, nor, consequently, play the bass and treble together, as other artists do; which was a great disadvantage to my performance.

The king, who, as I before observed, was a prince of excellent understanding, would frequently order, that I should be brought in my box, and set upon the table in his closet. He would then command me to bring one of my chairs out of the box, and sit down within three yards distance, upon the top of the cabinet; which brought me almost to a level with his face. In this manner I had several conversations with him. I one day took the freedom to tell his Majesty, that the contempt he discovered towards Europe, and the rest of the world, did not seem answerable to those excellent qualities of mind that he was master of. That, reason did not extend itself with the bulk of the body: on the contrary, we observed in our country, that the tallest persons were usually least provided with it. That, among other animals, bees and ants had the reputation of more industry, art, and sagacity, than many of the larger kinds. And that, as inconsiderable as he took me to be, I hoped I might live to do his Majesty some signal service. The king heard me with attention; and began to conceive a much better opinion of me, than he had ever before. He desired I would give him as exact an account of the government of England as I possibly could; because, as fond as princes commonly are of their own customs (for so he conjectured of other monarchs by my former discourses) he should be glad to hear of any thing that might deserve imitation.

Imagine with thy self, courteous reader, how often I then wished for the tongue of Demosthenes or Cicero, that might have enabled me to celebrate the praise of my own dear native country, in a style equal to its merits and felicity.

I began my discourse by informing his Majesty, that our dominions consisted of two islands, which composed three mighty kingdoms under one sovereign, besides our plantations in America. I dwelt long upon the fertility of our soil, and the temperature of our climate. I then spoke at large upon the constitution of an English Parliament, partly made up of an illustrious body called the House of Peers, persons of the noblest blood, and of the most ancient and ample patrimonies. I described that extraordinary care always taken of their education in arts and arms, to qualify them for being counsellors born to the king and kingdom; to have a share in the legislature, to be members of the highest court of judicature, from whence there could be no appeal; and to be champions always ready for the defence of their prince and country by their valour, conduct and fidelity. That, these were the ornament and bulwark of the kingdom; worthy followers of their most renowned ancestors, whose honour had been the reward of their virtue; from which their posterity were never once known to degenerate. To these were joined several holy persons, as part of that assembly, under the title of bishops; whose peculiar business it is, to take care of religion, and of those who instruct the people therein. These were searched and sought out through the whole nation, by the prince and wisest counsellors, among such of the priesthood, as were most deservedly distinguished by the sanctity of their lives, and the depth of their erudition; who were indeed, the spiritual fathers of the clergy and the people.

That, the other part of the Parliament consisted of an assembly called the House of Commons; who were all principal gentlemen, *freely* picked and culled out by the people themselves, for their great abilities, and love of their country, to represent the wisdom of the whole nation.   And, these two bodies make up the most august assembly in Europe; to whom, in conjunction with the prince, the whole legislature is committed.

I then descended to the Courts of Justice, over which the judges, those venerable sages and interpreters of the law, presided, for determining the disputed rights and properties of men, as well as for the punishment of vice, and protection of innocence.   I mentioned the prudent management of our Treasury; the valour and atchievements of our forces by sea and land.   I computed the number of our people, by reckoning how many millions there might be of each religious sect, or political party among us.   I did not omit even our sports and pastimes, or any other particular which I thought might redound to the honour of my country. And, I finished all with a brief historical account of affairs and events in England for about an hundred years past.

This conversation was not ended under five audiences, each of several hours; and the king heard the whole with great attention; frequently taking notes of what I spoke, as well as memorandums of what questions he intended to ask me.

When I had put an end to these long discourses, his Majesty in a sixth audience consulting his notes, proposed many doubts, queries, and objections upon every article. He asked, what methods were used to cultivate the minds and bodies of our young nobility; and in what kind of

business they commonly spent the first and teachable parts
of their lives. What course was taken to supply that
assembly, when any noble family became extinct. What
qualifications were necessary in those who are to be created
new lords: whether the humour of the prince, a sum of
money to a court-lady, or a Prime Minister; or a design of
strengthening a party opposite to the publick interest, ever
happened to be motives in those advancements. What
share of knowledge these lords had in the laws of their
country, and how they came by it, so as to enable them to
decide the properties of their fellow-subjects in the last
resort. Whether they were always so free from avarice,
partialities, or want; that a bribe, or some other sinister
view, could have no place among them. Whether those
holy lords I spoke of, were constantly promoted to that rank
upon account of their knowledge in religious matters, and
the sanctity of their lives, had never been compliers with
the times, while they were common priests; or slavish prostitute chaplains to some nobleman, whose opinions they
continued servilely to follow after they were admitted into
that assembly.

He then desired to know, what arts were practised in
electing those whom I called Commoners. Whether, a
stranger with a strong purse, might not influence the vulgar
voters to chuse him before their own landlords, or the most
considerable gentleman in the neighbourhood. How it
came to pass, that people were so violently bent upon
getting into this assembly, which I allowed to be a great
trouble and expence, often to the ruin of their families,
without any salary or pension: because this appeared such
an exalted strain of virtue and publick spirit, that his
Majesty seemed to doubt it might possibly not be always
sincere: and, he desired to know, whether such zealous
gentlemen could have any views of refunding themselves
for the charges and trouble they were at, by sacrificing the

publick good, to the designs of a weak and vicious prince, in conjunction with a corrupted ministry. He multiplied his questions, and sifted me thoroughly upon every part of this head; proposing numberless enquiries and objections, which I think it not prudent or convenient to repeat.

Upon what I said, in relation to our courts of justice, his Majesty desired to be satisfied in several points: and, this I was the better able to do, having been formerly almost ruined by a long suit in Chancery, which was decreed for me with costs. He asked, what time was usually spent in determining between right and wrong; and what degree of expence. Whether advocates and orators had liberty to plead in causes manifestly known to be unjust, vexa-- tious, or oppressive. Whether party in religion or politicks were observed to be of any weight in the scale of justice. Whether those pleading orators were persons educated in the general knowledge of equity; or only in provincial, national, and other local customs. Whether they, or their judges, had any part in penning those laws, which they assumed the liberty of interpreting and glossing upon at their pleasure. Whether they had ever at different times pleaded for and against the same cause, and cited precedents to prove contrary opinions. Whether they were a rich or a poor corporation. Whether they received any pecuniary reward for pleading or delivering their opinions. And particularly, whether they were ever admitted as members in the lower senate.

He fell next upon the management of our Treasury; and said, he thought my memory had failed me, because I computed our taxes at about five or six millions a year; and when I came to mention the issues, he found they sometimes amounted to more than double; for, the notes he had taken were very particular in this point; because he hoped, as he told me, that the knowledge of our conduct might be useful to him; and he could not be deceived in his calculations. But, if what I told him were true, he was still at a loss how a kingdom could run out of its estate like a private person. He asked me, who were our creditors? and, where we found money to pay them? He wondered to hear me talk of such chargeable and extensive wars; that, certainly we must be a quarrelsome people, or live among very bad neighbours; and that our generals must needs be richer than our kings. He asked, what business we had out of our own islands, unless upon the score of trade or treaty, or to defend the coasts with our fleet. Above all, he was amazed to hear me talk of a mercenary standing army in the midst of peace, and among a free people. He said, if we were governed by our own consent in the persons of our representatives, he could not imagine of whom we were afraid, or against whom we were to fight; and would hear my opinion, whether a private man's house might not better be defended by himself, his children, and family; than by half a dozen rascals picked up at a venture in the streets, for small wages, who might get an hundred times more by cutting their throats.

He laughed at my odd kind of arithmetick (as he was pleased to call it) in reckoning the numbers of our people by a computation drawn from the several sects among us in religion and politicks. He said, he knew no reason, why those who entertain opinions prejudicial to the publick, should be obliged to change, or should not be obliged to conceal them. And, as it was tyranny in any Government to require the first, so it was weakness not to enforce the second: for, a man may be allowed to keep poisons in his closet, but not to vend them about as cordials.

He observed, that among the diversions of our nobility and gentry, I had mentioned gaming. He desired to know at what age this entertainment was usually taken up, and when it was laid down. How much of their time it employed; whether it ever went so high as to affect their fortunes. Whether mean vicious people, by their dexterity in that art, might not arrive at great riches, and sometimes keep our very nobles in dependance, as well as habituate them to vile companions; wholly take them from the improvement of their minds, and force them by the losses they received, to learn and practise that infamous dexterity upon others.

He was perfectly astonished with the historical account I gave him of our affairs during the last century; protesting it was only a heap of conspiracies, rebellions, murders, massacres, revolutions, banishments; the very worst effects that avarice, faction, hypocrisy, perfidiousness, cruelty, rage, madness, hatred, envy, lust, malice, and ambition could produce.

His Majesty in another audience, was at the pains to recapitulate the sum of all I had spoken; compared the questions he made, with the answers I had given; then taking me into his hands, and stroaking me gently, delivered himself in these words, which I shall never forget, nor the manner he spoke them in. 'My little friend Grildrig; you have made a most admirable panegyrick upon your country. You have clearly proved that ignorance, idleness, and vice, are the proper ingredients for qualifying a legislator. That laws are best explained, interpreted, and applied by those whose interest and abilities lie in perverting, confounding, and eluding them. I observe among you, some lines of an institution, which in its original might have been tolerable; but these half erased, and the rest wholly blurred and blotted by corruptions. It doth not appear, from all you have said, how any one perfection is required towards the procurement of any one station among you; much less that men are ennobled on account of their virtue, that priests are advanced for their piety or learning, soldiers for their conduct or valour, judges for their integrity, senators for the love of their country, or counsellors for their wisdom. As for yourself (continued the king) who have spent the greatest part of your life in travelling; I am well disposed to hope you may hitherto have escaped many vices of your country. But, by what I have gathered from your own relation, and the answers I have with much pains wringed and extorted from you; I cannot but conclude the bulk of your natives, to be the most pernicious race of little odious vermin that nature ever suffered to crawl upon the surface of the earth.'

CHAPTER VII

The author's love of his country. He makes a proposal of much advantage to the king, which is rejected. The king's great ignorance in politicks. The learning of that country very imperfect and confined. Their laws, and military affairs, and parties in the State.

NOTHING but an extreme love of truth, could have hindered me from concealing this part of my story. It was in vain to discover my resentments, which were always turned into ridicule: and, I was forced to rest with patience, while my noble and most beloved country was so injuriously treated. I am heartily sorry as any of my readers can possibly be, that such an occasion was given: but this prince happened to be so curious and inquisitive into every particular, that it could not consist either with gratitude or good manners to refuse giving him what satisfaction I was able. Yet thus much I may be allowed to say in my own vindication; that I artfully eluded many of his questions; and gave to every point a more favourable turn by many degrees than the strictness of truth would allow. For, I have always born that laudable partiality to my own country, which Dionysius Hallicarnassensis with so much justice recommends to an historian. I would hide the frailties and deformities of my political mother, and place her virtues and beauties in the most advantageous light. This was my sincere endeavour in those many discourses I had with that monarch, although it unfortunately failed of success.

But, great allowances should be given to a king who lives wholly secluded from the rest of the world, and must therefore be altogether unacquainted with the manners and customs that most prevail in other nations: the want of which knowledge, will ever produce many *prejudices*, and a certain *narrowness of thinking*; from which we, and the politer countries of Europe are wholly exempted. And, it would be hard indeed, if so remote a prince's notions of virtue and vice were to be offered as a standard for all mankind.

To confirm what I have now said, and further to shew the miserable effects of a *confined education*; I shall here insert a passage which will hardly obtain belief. In hopes to ingratiate my self farther into his Majesty's favour, I told him of an invention discovered between three and four hundred years ago, to make a certain powder; into an heap of which the smallest spark of fire falling, would kindle the whole in a moment, although it were as big as a mountain; and make it all fly up in the air together, with a noise and agitation greater than thunder. That, a proper quantity of this powder rammed into an hollow tube of brass or iron, according to its bigness, would drive a ball of iron or lead with such violence and speed, as nothing was able to sustain its force. That, the largest balls thus discharged, would not only destroy whole ranks of an army at once; but batter the strongest walls to the ground; sink down ships with a thousand men in each, to the bottom of the sea; and when linked together by a chain, would cut through masts and rigging; divide hundreds of bodies in the middle, and lay all waste before them. That, we often put this powder

into large hollow balls of iron, and discharged them by an
engine into some city we were besieging; which would rip
up the pavement, tear the houses to pieces, burst and throw
splinters on every side, dashing out the brains of all who
came near.   That, I knew the ingredients very well, which
were cheap, and common; I understood the manner of com-
pounding them, and could direct his workmen how to make
those tubes of a size proportionable to all other things in
his Majesty's kingdom; and the largest need not be above
two hundred foot long; twenty or thirty of which tubes,
charged with the proper quantity of powder and balls,
would batter down the walls of the strongest town in his
dominions in a few hours; or destroy the whole metropolis,
if ever it should pretend to dispute his absolute commands.
This, I humbly offered to his Majesty, as a small tribute of
acknowledgment, in return of so many marks that I had
received of his royal favour and protection.

The king was struck with horror at the description I had
given of those terrible engines, and the proposal I had made.
He was amazed how so impotent and grovelling an insect
as I (these were his expressions) could entertain such inhuman ideas, and in so familiar a manner as to appear
wholly unmoved at all the scenes of blood and desolation,
which I had painted as the common effects of those de-
structive machines; whereof he said, some evil genius,
enemy to mankind, must have been the first contriver.   As
for himself, he protested, that although few things delighted him so much as new discoveries in art or in nature;
yet he would rather lose half his kingdom, than be privy to
such a secret; which he commanded me, as I valued my life,
never to mention any more.

A strange effect of *narrow principles* and *short views*! that
a prince possessed of every quality which procures veneration, love and esteem; of strong parts, great wisdom and
profound learning; endued with admirable talents for

government, and almost adored by his subjects; should from a *nice unnecessary scruple*, whereof in Europe we can have no conception, let slip an opportunity put into his hands, that would have made him absolute master of the lives, the liberties, and the fortunes of his people. Neither do I say this with the least intention to detract from the many virtues of that excellent king; whose character I am sensible will on this account be very much lessened in the opinion of an English reader: but, I take this defect among them to have risen from their ignorance; by not having hitherto reduced *politicks* into a *science*, as the more acute wits of Europe have done. For, I remember very well, in a discourse one day with the king; when I happened to say, there were several thousand books among us, written upon the *art of government*; it gave him (directly contrary to my intention) a very mean opinion of our understandings. He professed both to abominate and despise all *mystery, refinement*, and *intrigue*, either in a prince or a minister. He could not tell what I meant by *secrets of State*, where an enemy or some rival nation were not in the case. He confined the knowledge of governing within very *narrow bounds*; to common sense and reason, to justice and lenity, to the speedy determination of civil and criminal causes; with some other obvious topicks which are not worth considering. And, he gave it for his opinion; that whoever could make two ears of corn, or two blades of grass to grow upon a spot of ground where only one grew before; would deserve better of mankind, and do more essential service to his country, than the whole race of politicians put together.

The learning of this people is very defective; consisting only in morality, history, poetry and mathematicks; wherein they must be allowed to excel. But, the last of these is wholly applied to what may be useful in life; to the improvement of agriculture and all mechanical arts; so, that among us it would be little esteemed. And, as to ideas, entities, abstractions and transcendentals, I could never drive the least conception into their heads.

No law of that country must exceed in words the number of letters in their alphabet; which consists only of two and twenty. But indeed, few of them extend even to that length. They are expressed in the most plain and simple terms, wherein those people are not mercurial enough to discover above one interpretation. And, to write a comment upon any law, is a capital crime. As to the decision of civil causes, or proceedings against criminals, their precedents are so few, that they have little reason to boast of any extraordinary skill in either.

They have had the art of printing, as well as the Chinese, time out of mind. But their libraries are not very large; for that of the king's, which is reckoned the largest, doth not amount to above a thousand volumes; placed in a gallery of twelve hundred foot long; from whence I had liberty to borrow what books I pleased. The queen's joyner had contrived in one of Glumdalclitch's rooms a kind of wooden machine five and twenty foot high, formed like a standing ladder; the steps were each fifty foot long: it was indeed a moveable pair of stairs, the lowest end placed at ten foot distance from the wall of the chamber. The book I had a mind to read was put up leaning against the wall. I first mounted to the upper step of the ladder, and turning my face towards the book, began at the top of the page, and so walking to the right and left about eight or ten paces, according to the length of the lines, until I had gotten a little below the level of mine eyes; and then descending gradually until I came to the bottom: after which, I mounted again, and began the other page in the same manner, and so turned over the leaf, which I could easily do with both my hands, for it was as thick and stiff as a paste-board, and in the largest folios not above eighteen or twenty foot long.

Their style is clear, masculine, and smooth, but not florid; for they avoid nothing more than multiplying unnecessary words, or using various expressions. I have perused many of their books, especially those in history and morality. Among the latter I was much diverted with a little old treatise, which always lay in Glumdalclitch's bed-chamber, and belonged to her governess, a grave elderly gentlewoman, who dealt in writings of morality and devotion. The book treats of the weakness of human kind; and is in little esteem, except among women and the vulgar. However, I was curious to see what an author of that country could say upon such a subject. This writer went through all the usual topicks of European moralists; shewing how diminutive, contemptible, and helpless an animal was man in his own nature; how unable to defend himself from inclemencies of the air, or the fury of wild beasts; how much he was excelled by one creature in strength, by another in speed, by a third in foresight, by a fourth in industry. He added, that nature was degenerated in these latter declining ages of the world, and could now produce only small abortive births, in comparison of those in ancient times. He said, it was very reasonable to think, not only that the species of man were originally much larger, but also, that there must have been giants in former ages; which, as it is asserted by history and tradition, so it hath been confirmed by huge bones and sculls, casually dug up in several parts of the kingdom, far exceeding the common dwindled race of man in our days. He argued, that the very laws of nature absolutely required we should have been made in the beginning, of a size more large and robust, not so liable to destruction from every little accident of a tile falling from an house, or a stone cast from the hand of a boy, or of being drowned in a little brook. From this way of reasoning, the author drew several moral applications useful in the conduct of life, but needless here to repeat. For, my own part, I could not avoid reflecting, how universally this talent was spread of drawing lectures in morality, or indeed rather matter of discontent and repining, from the quarrels we raise with nature. And, I believe, upon a strict enquiry, those quarrels might be shewn as ill grounded among us, as they are among that people.

As to their military affairs; they boast that the king's army consists of an hundred and seventy six thousand foot, and thirty two thousand horse: if that may be called an army, which is made up of tradesmen in the several cities, and farmers in the country, whose commanders are only the nobility and gentry, without pay or reward. They are indeed perfect enough in their exercises; and under very good discipline, wherein I saw no great merit: for, how should it be otherwise, where every farmer is under the command of his own landlord, and every citizen under that of the principal men in his own city, chosen after the manner of Venice by *ballot*?

I have often seen the militia of Lorbrulgrud drawn out to exercise in a great field near the city, of twenty miles square. They were in all not above twenty five thousand foot, and six thousand horse; but, it was impossible for me to compute their number, considering the space of ground they took up. A cavalier mounted on a large steed might be about ninety foot high. I have seen this whole body of horse, upon the word of command, draw their swords at once, and brandish them in the air. Imagination can figure nothing so grand, so surprizing, and so astonishing. It looked as if ten thousand flashes of lightning were darting at the same time from every quarter of the sky.

I was curious to know how this prince, to whose dominions there is no access from any other country, came to think of armies, or to teach his people the practice of military discipline. But, I was soon informed, both by conversation, and reading their histories. For, in the course of many ages, they have been troubled with the same disease, to which the whole race of mankind is subject; the nobility often contending for power, the people for liberty, and the king for absolute dominion. All which, however happily tempered by the laws of that kingdom, have been sometimes violated by each of the three parties; and have more than once occasioned civil wars, the last whereof, was happily put an end to by this prince's grandfather in a general composition; and the militia then settled with common consent, hath been ever since kept in the strictest duty.

CHAPTER VIII

The king and queen make a progress to the frontiers. The author attends them. The manner in which he leaves the country very particularly related. He returns to England.

I HAD always a strong impulse that I should some time recover my liberty, although it were impossible to conjecture by what means, or to form any project with the least hope of succeeding. The ship in which I sailed was the first ever known to be driven within sight of that coast; and the king had given strict orders, that if at any time another appeared, it should be taken ashore, and with all its crew and passengers brought in a tumbril to Lorbrulgrud. He was strongly bent to get me a woman of my own size, by whom I might propagate the breed: but, I think, I should rather have died, than undergone the disgrace of leaving a posterity to be kept in cages like tame canary birds; and perhaps in time, sold about the kingdom to persons of quality for curiosities. I was indeed treated with much kindness; I was the favourite of a great king and queen, and the delight of the whole court; but it was upon such a foot as ill became the dignity of human kind. I could never forget those domestick pledges I had left behind me. I wanted to be among people with whom I could converse upon even terms; and walk about the streets and fields without fear of being trod to death like a frog or young puppy. But, my deliverance came sooner than I expected, and in a manner not very common: the whole story and circumstances of which I shall faithfully relate.

I had now been two years in this country; and, about the beginning of the third, Glumdalclitch and I attended the king and queen in a progress to the south coast of the kingdom. I was carried as usual in my travelling box, which, as I have already described, was a very convenient closet of twelve foot wide. I had ordered a hammock to be fixed by silken ropes from the four corners at the top; to break the jolts, when a servant carried me before him on horseback, as I sometimes desired; and would often sleep in my hammock while we were upon the road. On the roof of my closet, set not directly over the middle of the hammock, I ordered the joyner to cut out a hole of a foot square to give me air in hot weather as I slept; which hole I shut at pleasure with a board that drew backwards and forwards through a groove.

When we came to our journey's end, the king thought proper to pass a few days at a palace he hath near Flan-flasnic, a city within eighteen English miles of the sea-side. Glumdalclitch and I were much fatigued; I had gotten a small cold; but the poor girl was so ill as to be confined to her chamber. I longed to see the ocean, which must be the only scene of my escape, if ever it should happen. I pretended to be worse than I really was; and desired leave to take the fresh air of the sea, with a page whom I was very fond of, and who had sometimes been trusted with me. I shall never forget with what unwillingness Glumdalclitch consented; nor the strict charge she gave the page to be careful of me; bursting at the same time into a flood of tears, as if she had some foreboding of what was to happen.   The boy took me out in my box about half an hour's walk from the palace, towards the rocks on the sea-shore.   I ordered him to set me down; and lifting up one of my sashes, cast many a wistful melancholy look towards the sea.   I found myself not very well; and told the page that I had a mind to take a nap in my hammock, which I hoped would do me good.   I got in, and the boy shut the window close down, to keep out the cold.   I soon fell asleep: and all I can conjecture is, that while I slept, the page thinking no danger could happen, went among the rocks to look for birds eggs; having before observed him from my window searching about, and picking up one or two in the clefts.   Be that as it will; I found my self suddenly awaked with a violent pull upon the ring which was fastned at the top of my box, for the conveniency of carriage.   I felt the box raised very high in the air, and then born forward with prodigious speed.   The first jolt had like to have shaken me out of my hammock; but after-wards the motion was easy enough.   I called out several times as loud as I could raise my voice, but all to no purpose. I looked towards my windows, and could see nothing but the clouds and sky.   I heard a noise just over my head like the clapping of wings; and then began to perceive the woeful condition I was in; that some eagle had got the ring of my box in his beak, with an intent to let it fall on a rock, like a tortoise in a shell, and then pick out my body and devour it.   For, the sagacity and smell of this bird enabled him to discover his quarry at a great distance, although better concealed than I could be within a two inch board.

In a little time I observed the noise and flutter of wings to encrease very fast; and my box was tossed up and down like a sign-post in a windy day.   I heard several bangs or buffets, as I thought, given to the eagle (for such I am certain it must have been that held the ring of my box in his beak) and then all on a sudden felt my self falling perpendicularly down for above a minute; but with such incredible swiftness, that I almost lost my breath. My fall was stopped by a terrible squash, that sounded louder to mine ears than the cataract of Niagara; after which I was quite in the dark for another minute, and then my box began to rise so high, that I could see light from the tops of my windows. I now perceived, that I was fallen into the sea. My box, by the weight of my body, the goods that were in, and the broad plates of iron fixed for strength at the four corners of the top and bottom, floated about five foot deep in water. I did then, and do now suppose, that the eagle which flew away with my box, was pursued by two or three others, and forced to let me drop while he was defending himself against the rest, who hoped to share in the prey. The plates of iron fastned to the bottom of the box, (for those were the strongest) preserved the balance while it fell; and hindred it from being broken on the surface of the water. Every joint of it was well grooved, and the door did not move on hinges, but up and down like a sash; which kept my closet so tight, that very little water came in. I got with much difficulty out of my hammock, having first ventured to draw back the slip - board on the roof already mentioned, contrived on purpose to let in air; for want of which, I found myself almost stifled.

How often did I then wish my self with my dear Glumdalclitch, from whom one single hour had so far divided me! And, I may say with truth, that in the midst of my own misfortune, I could not forbear lamenting my poor nurse, the grief she would suffer for my loss, the displeasure of the queen, and the ruin of her fortune. Perhaps many travellers have not been under greater difficulties and distress than I was at this juncture; expecting every moment to see my box dashed in pieces, or at least overset by the first violent blast, or a rising wave. A breach in one single pane of glass would have been immediate death: nor could any thing have preserved the windows but the strong lattice wires placed on the outside against accidents in travelling. I saw the water ooze in at several crannies, although the leaks were not considerable; and I endeavoured to stop them as well as I could. I was not able to lift up the roof of my closet, which otherwise I certainly should have done, and sat on the top of it, where I might, at least, preserve my self from being shut up, as I may call it, in the hold. Or, if I escaped these dangers for a day or two, what could I expect but a miserable death of cold and hunger! I was four hours under these circumstances, expecting and indeed wishing every moment to be my last.

I have already told the reader, that there were two strong staples fixed upon the side of my box, which had no window, and into which the servant, who used to carry me on horseback, would put a leathern belt, and buckle it about his waist. Being in this disconsolate state, I heard, or at least thought I heard some kind of grating noise on that side of my box where the staples were fixed; and soon after I began to fancy that the box was pulled, or towed along in the sea; for, I now and then felt a sort of tugging, which made the waves rise near the tops of my windows, leaving me almost in the dark. This gave me some faint hopes of relief, although I were not able to imagine how it could be brought about. I ventured to unscrew one of my chairs, which were always fastned to the floor; and having made a hard shift to screw it down again directly under the slipping - board that I had lately opened; I mounted on the chair, and putting my mouth as near as I could to the hole, I called for help in a loud voice, and in all the languages I understood. I then fastned my hand-kerchief to a stick I usually carried, and thrusting it up the hole, waved it several times in the air; that if any boat or ship were near, the seamen might conjecture some unhappy mortal to be shut up in the box.

I found no effect from all I could do, but plainly perceived my closet to be moved along; and in the space of an hour, or better, that side of the box where the staples were, and had no window, struck against something that was hard. I apprehended it to be a rock, and found my self tossed more than ever. I plainly heard a noise upon the cover of my closet, like that of a cable, and the grating of it as it passed through the ring. I then found my self hoisted up by degrees, at least three foot higher than I was before. Whereupon, I again thrust up my stick and handkerchief, calling for help until I was almost hoarse. In return to which, I heard a great shout repeated three times, giving me such transports of joy as are not to be conceived but by those who feel them. I now heard a trampling over my head; and somebody calling through the hole with a loud voice in the English tongue: 'If there be any body below, let them speak.' I answered, I was an Englishman, drawn by ill fortune into the greatest calamity that ever any creature underwent; and begged, by all that was moving, to be delivered out of the dungeon I was in. The voice replied, I was safe, for my box was fastned to their ship; and the carpenter should immediately come, and saw an hole in the cover, large enough to pull me out. I answered, that was needless, and would take up too much time; for there was no more to be done, but let one of the crew put his finger into the ring, and take the box out of the sea into the ship, and so into the captain's cabbin. Some of them upon hearing me talk so wildly, thought I was mad; others laughed; for indeed it never came into my head, that I was now got among people of my own stature and strength. The carpenter came, and in a few minutes sawed a passage about four foot square; then let down a

small ladder, upon which I mounted, and from thence was
taken into the ship in a very weak condition.

The sailors were all in amazement, and asked me a thousand questions, which I had no inclination to answer. I
was equally confounded at the sight of so many pigmies;
for such I took them to be, after having so long accustomed
mine eyes to the monstrous objects I had left. But, the
captain, Mr. Thomas Wilcocks, an honest worthy Shrop-
shire man, observing I was ready to faint, took me into his
cabbin, gave me a cordial to comfort me, and made me *turn
in* upon his own bed; advising me to take a little rest, of
which I had great need. Before I went to sleep, I gave him
to understand, that I had some valuable furniture in my
box, too good to be lost; a fine hammock, an handsome
field-bed, two chairs, a table and a cabinet: that, my closet
was hung on all sides, or rather quilted with silk and cotton:
that, if he would let one of the crew bring my closet into
his cabbin, I would open it before him, and shew him my
goods. The captain hearing me utter these absurdities,
concluded I was raving: however, (I suppose to pacify
me) he promised to give order as I desired; and going upon
deck, sent some of his men down into my closet, from
whence (as I afterwards found) they drew up all my goods,
and stripped off the quilting; but the chairs, cabinet and
bed-sted being screwed to the floor, were much damaged by
the ignorance of the seamen, who tore them up by force.
Then they knocked off some of the boards for the use of
the ship; and when they had got all they had a mind for,
let the hulk drop into the sea, which, by reason of many
breaches made in the bottom and sides, sunk to *rights*.
And indeed I was glad not to have been a spectator of the
havock they made; because I am confident it would have
sensibly touched me, by bringing former passages into my
mind, which I had rather forget.

I slept some hours, but perpetually disturbed with

dreams of the place I had left, and the dangers I had escaped. However, upon waking I found my self much recovered. It was now about eight a clock at night, and the captain ordered supper immediately, thinking I had already fasted too long. He entertained me with great kindness, observing me not to look wildly, or talk inconsistently; and when we were left alone, desired I would give him a relation of my travels, and by what accident I came to be set adrift in that monstrous wooden chest. He said, that about twelve a clock at noon, as he was looking through his glass, he spied it at a distance, and thought it was a sail, which he had a mind to make; being not much out of his course, in hopes of buying some biscuit, his own beginning to fall short. That, upon coming nearer, and finding his error, he sent out his long-boat to discover what I was. That, his men came back in a fright, swearing they had seen a swimming house: that, he laughed at their folly, and went himself in the boat, ordering his men to take a strong cable along with them: that, the weather being calm, he rowed round me several times, observed my windows, and the wire lattices that defended them. That he discovered two staples upon one side, which was all of boards, without any passage for light. He then commanded his men to row up to that side; and fastning a cable to one of the staples, ordered his men to tow my chest (as he called it) towards the ship. When it was there, he gave directions to fasten another cable to the ring fixed in the cover, and to raise up my chest with pullies, which all the sailors were not able to do above two or three foot. He said, they saw my stick and handkerchief thrust out of the hole, and concluded, that some unhappy man must be shut up in the cavity. I asked whether he or the crew had seen any prodigious birds in the air about the time he first discovered me: to which he answered, that discoursing this matter with the sailors while I was asleep, one of them said, he had *observed* three eagles flying towards the north; but remarked nothing of their being larger than the usual size; which I suppose must be imputed to the great height they were at: and he could not guess the reason of my question. I then asked the captain how far he reckoned we might be from land; he said, by the best computation he could make, we were at least an hundred leagues. I assured him, that he must be mistaken by almost half; for I had not left the country from whence I came, above two hours before I dropt into the sea. Whereupon he began again to think that my brain was disturbed, of which he gave me a hint, and advised me to go to bed in a cabin he had provided. I assured him I was well refreshed with his good entertainment and company, and as much in my senses as ever I was in my life. He then grew serious, and desired to ask me freely, whether I were not troubled in mind, by the consciousness of some enormous crime, for which I was punished at the command of some prince, by exposing me in that chest; as great criminals in other countries have been forced to sea in a leaky vessel, without provisions: for, although he should be sorry to have taken so ill a man into his ship, yet he would engage his word to set me safe on shoar in the first port where we arrived. He added, that his suspicions were much increased by some very absurd speeches I had delivered at first to the sailors, and afterwards to himself, in relation to my closet or chest, as well as by my odd looks and behaviour while I was at supper.

I begged his patience to hear me tell my story; which I faithfully did from the last time I left England, to the moment he first discovered me. And, as truth always forceth its way into rational minds; so, this honest worthy gentleman, who had some tincture of learning, and very good sense, was immediately convinced of my candor and veracity. But, further to confirm all I had said, I entreated him to give order that my cabinet should be brought, of which I kept the key in my pocket. (For he had already informed me how the seamen disposed of my closet.) I opened it in his presence, and shewed him the small collection of rarities I made in the country from whence I had been so strangely delivered. There was the comb I had contrived out of the stumps of the king's beard; and another of the same materials, but fixed into a paring of her Majesty's thumb‑nail, which served for the back. There was a collection of needles and pins from a foot to half a yard long. Four wasp-stings, like joyners tacks: some combings of the queen's hair: a gold ring which one day she made me a present of in a most obliging manner, taking it from her little finger, and throwing it over my head like a collar. I desired the captain would please to accept this ring in return of his civilities; which he absolutely refused. I shewed him a corn, that I had cut off with my own hand, from a maid of honour's toe; it was about the bigness of a Kentish pippin, and grown so hard, that when I returned to England, I got it hollowed into a cup, and set in silver. Lastly, I desired him to see the breeches I had then on, which were made of a mouse's skin.

I could force nothing on him but a footman's tooth, which I observed him to examine with great curiosity, and found he had a fancy for it. He received it with abundance of thanks, more than such a trifle could deserve. It was drawn by an unskilful surgeon in a mistake from one of Glumdalclitch's men, who was afflicted with the tooth-ach; but it was as sound as any in his head. I got it cleaned, and put it into my cabinet. It was about a foot long, and four inches in diameter.

The captain was very well satisfied with this plain relation I had given him; and said, he hoped when we returned to England, I would oblige the world by putting it in paper, and making it publick. My answer was, that I thought we were already overstocked with books of travels: that, nothing could now pass which was not extraordinary; wherein I doubted, some authors less consulted truth than their own vanity or interest, or the diversion of ignorant readers. That, my story could contain little beside common events, without those ornamental descriptions of strange plants, trees, birds and other animals; or the barbarous customs and idolatry of savage people, with which most writers abound. However, I thanked him for his good opinion, and promised to take the matter into my thoughts.

He said, he wondered at one thing very much; which was, to hear me speak so loud; asking me whether the king or queen of that country were thick of hearing. I told him it was what I had been used to for above two years past; and, that I admired as much at the voices of him and his men, who seemed to me only to whisper, and yet I could hear them well enough. But, when I spoke in that country, it was like a man talking in the street, to another looking out from the top of a steeple, unless when I was placed upon a table, or held in any person's hand. I told him, I had likewise observed another thing; that when I first got into the ship, and the sailors stood all about me, I thought they were the most little, contemptible creatures I had ever beheld. For, indeed, while I was in that prince's country, I could never endure to look in a glass after mine eyes had been accustomed to such prodigious objects; because, the comparison gave me so despicable a conceit of my self. The captain said, that while we were at supper, he observed me to look at every thing with a sort of wonder; and, that I often seemed hardly able to contain my laughter; which he knew not well how to take, but imputed it to some disorder in my brain. I answered, it was very true; and I wondered how I could forbear, when I saw his dishes of the size of a silver three-pence, a leg of pork hardly a mouthful, a cup not so big as a nutshel: and so I went on, describing the rest of his houshold stuff and provisions after the same manner. For, although the queen had ordered a little equipage of all things necessary for me, while I was in her service; yet, my ideas were wholly taken up with what I saw on every side of me; and I winked at my own littleness, as people do at their own faults. The captain understood my raillery very well, and merrily replied with the old English proverb, that he doubted, mine eyes were bigger than my belly; for he did not observe my stomach so good, although I had fasted all day: and, continuing in his mirth, protested he would have gladly given an hundred pounds to have seen my closet in the eagle's bill, and afterwards in its fall from so great an height into the sea; which would certainly have been a most astonishing object, worthy to have the description of it transmitted to future ages: and, the comparison of Phaeton was so obvious, that he could not forbear applying it, although I did not much admire the conceit.

The captain having been at Tonquin, was in his return to England, driven north eastward to the latitude of 44 degrees, and of longitude 143. But, meeting a trade wind, two days after I came on board him, we sailed southward a long time, and coasting New-Holland, kept our course west - south - west, and then south - south - west, until we doubled the Cape of Good-hope. Our voyage was very prosperous, but I shall not trouble the reader with a journal of it. The captain called in at one or two ports, and sent in his long-boat for provisions and fresh water; but, I never went out of the ship until we came into the Downs, which was on the 3d day of June 1706, about nine months after my escape. I offered to leave my goods in security for payment of my freight; but, the captain protested he would not receive one farthing. We took kind leave of each other; and, I made him promise he would come to see me at my house in Redriff. I hired a horse and guide for five shillings, which I borrowed of the captain.

As I was on the road; observing the littleness of the houses, the trees, the cattle, and the people, I began to think my self in Lilliput. I was afraid of trampling on every traveller I met; and often called aloud to have them stand out of the way; so, that I had like to have gotten one or two broken heads for my impertinence.

When I came to mine own house, for which I was forced to enquire, one of the servants opening the door, I bent down to go in (like a goose under a gate) for fear of striking my head. My wife ran out to embrace me, but I stooped lower than her knees, thinking she could otherwise never be able to reach my mouth. My daughter kneeled to ask me blessing, but I could not see her until she arose; having been so long used to stand with my head and eyes erect to above sixty foot; and, then I went to take her up with one hand, by the waist. I looked down upon the servants, and one or two friends who were in the house, as if they had been pigmies, and I a giant. I told my wife, she had been too thrifty; for I found she had starved herself and her daughter to nothing. In short, I behaved my self so unaccountably, that they were all of the captain's opinion, when he first saw me; and, concluded I had lost my wits. This I mention as an instance of the great power of habit and prejudice.

In a little time, I and my family and friends, came to a right understanding: but, my wife protested I should never go to sea any more; although, my evil destiny so ordered, that she had not power to hinder me; as the reader may know hereafter. In the mean time, I here conclude the second part of my unfortunate voyages.

THE END OF THE SECOND PART

PART III

A VOYAGE TO LAPUTA, BALNIBARBI, LUGG-NAGG, GLUBBDUBDRIB, AND JAPAN

Parts Unknown

LAND OF
St James Bay
Robbin I
IESSO
SalmonB
C Patient
Straits of the Vries
C Canal
Companys
Land
Stats I

Sea of Corea
Sande I
Torpia
Nivala
Yedo
Gunnso
JAPON
Sacca
Toy Pt
Red Pt
Rosho Pt
Barnevelts
Tonsa
Bungo I
Dimeris Strait
I Tanaxima
Ongeluchig I
South I
Stato
Glangurin
Maldoneda
LUGN AGG
Hubtlepudal
Clamrynig
I Deserta
Glubdubbdribb
Urac
Tunal

Liapula
BALNIBARBI
Lagado
Discovered A.D 1701

CHAPTER I

The author sets out on his third voyage. Is taken by pyrates. The malice of a Dutchman. His arrival at an island. He is received into Laputa.

I HAD not been at home above ten days, when Captain William Robinson, a Cornish man, commander of the *Hopewell*, a stout ship of three hundred tuns, came to my house. I had formerly been surgeon of another ship where he was master, and a fourth part owner, in a voyage to the Levant. He had always treated me more like a brother than an inferior officer; and, hearing of my arrival, made me a visit, as I apprehended, only out of friendship, for nothing passed more than what is usual after long absence. But, repeating his visits often, expressing his joy to find me in good health, asking whether I were now settled for life, adding that he intended a voyage to the East Indies, in two months; at last he plainly invited me, although with some apologies, to be surgeon of the ship. That, I should have another surgeon under me, besides our two mates: that my salary should be double to the usual pay: and, that having experienced my knowledge in sea-affairs, to be at least equal to his, he would enter into any engagement to follow my advice, as much as if I had share in the command.

He said so many other obliging things, and I knew him to be so honest a man, that I could not reject his proposal; the thirst I had of seeing the world, notwithstanding my past misfortunes, continuing as violent as ever: the only difficulty that remained, was to persuade my wife, whose consent, however, I at last obtained, by the prospect of advantage she proposed to her children.

We set out the 5th day of August, 1706, and arrived at Fort St. George, the 11th of April 1707.   We stayed there three weeks to refresh our crew, many of whom were sick. From thence, we went to Tonquin, where the captain resolved to continue some time; because, many of the goods he intended to buy were not ready, nor could he expect to be dispatched in several months.   Therefore, in hopes to defray some of the charges he must be at, he bought a sloop, loaded it with several sorts of goods, wherewith the Tonquinese usually trade to the neighbouring islands; and putting fourteen men on board, whereof three were of the country, he appointed me master of the sloop, and gave me power to traffick, while he transacted his affairs at Tonquin.

We had not sailed above three days, when a great storm arising, we were driven five days to the north-north-east, and then to the east; after which we had fair weather, but still with a pretty strong gale from the west.   Upon the 10th day we were chased by two pyrates, who soon overtook us; for, my sloop was so deep loaden, that she sailed very slow; neither were we in a condition to defend our selves.

We were boarded about the same time by both the pyrates, who entered furiously at the head of their men; but, finding us all prostrate upon our faces, (for so I gave order) they pinioned us with strong ropes, and setting a guard upon us, went to search the sloop.

I observed among them a Dutchman, who seemed to be of some authority, although he were not commander of either ship.   He knew us by our countenances to be Englishmen, and jabbering to us in his own language, swore we should be tyed back to back, and thrown into the sea.   I spoke Dutch tolerably well; I told him who we were, and begged him in consideration of our being Christians and Protestants, of neighbouring countries, in strict alliance, that he would move the captains to take some pity on us.

This inflamed his rage; he repeated his threatnings, and turning to his companions, spoke with great vehemence, in the Japanese language, as I suppose; often using the word 'Christianos.'

The largest of the two pyrate ships was commanded by a Japanese captain, who spoke a little Dutch, but very imperfectly. He came up to me, and after several questions, which I answered in great humility, he said we should not die. I made the captain a very low bow, and then, turning to the Dutchman, said, I was sorry to find more mercy in a heathen, than in a brother Christian. But, I had soon reason to repent those foolish words; for, that malicious reprobate, having often endeavoured, in vain, to persuade both the captains, that I might be thrown into the sea, (which they would not yield to after the promise made me, that I should not die) however, prevailed so far as to have a punishment inflicted on me, worse in all human appearance than death itself. My men were sent, by an equal division, into both the pyrate-ships, and, my sloop new manned. As to my self, it was determined, that I should be set a-drift, in a small canoe, with paddles and a sail, and four days provisions; which last, the Japanese captain, was so kind to double out of his own stores, and would permit no man to search me. I got down into the canoe, while the Dutchman standing upon the deck, loaded me with all the curses, and injurious terms, his language could afford.

About an hour before we saw the pyrates, I had taken an observation, and found we were in the latitude of 46 N. and of longitude 183. When I was at some distance from the pyrates, I discovered by my pocket-glass several islands to the south-east. I set up my sail, the wind being fair, with a design to reach the nearest of those islands; which I made a shift to do in about three hours. It was all rocky; however, I got many birds eggs; and striking fire, I kindled some

heath and dry sea weed, by which I roasted my eggs.   I
eat no other supper, being resolved to spare my provisions
as much as I could.   I passed the night under the shelter
of a rock, strowing some heath under me, and slept pretty
well.

The next day I sailed to another island, and thence to a
third, and fourth; sometimes using my sail, and sometimes
my paddles.   But, not to trouble the reader with a particular account of my distresses; let it suffice, that on the 5th
day, I arrived at the last island in my sight, which lay
south-south-east to the former.

This island was at a greater distance than I expected, and
I did not reach it in less than five hours.   I encompassed
it almost round, before I could find a convenient place to
land in, which was a small creek, about three times the
wideness of my canoe.   I found the island to be all rocky,
only a little intermingled with tufts of grass, and sweet
smelling herbs.   I took out my small provisions, and after
having refreshed my self, I secured the remainder in a cave,
whereof there were great numbers.   I gathered plenty of
eggs upon the rocks, and got a quantity of dry sea-weed,
and parched grass, which I designed to kindle the next
day, and roast my eggs as well as I could.   (For I had about
me my flint, steel, match, and burning-glass.)   I lay all
night in the cave where I had lodged my provisions.   My
bed was the same dry grass and sea-weed which I intended
for fuel.   I slept very little; for the disquiets of my mind
prevailed over my weariness, and kept me awake.   I considered how impossible it was to preserve my life, in so
desolate a place; and how miserable my end must be.   Yet,
I found my self so listless and desponding, that I had not
the heart to rise; and before I could get spirits enough to
creep out of my cave, the day was far advanced.   I walked
a while among the rocks; the sky was perfectly clear, and
the sun so hot, that I was forced to turn my face from it:

when all on a sudden it became obscured, as I thought, in a manner very different from what happens by the interposition of a cloud. I turned back, and perceived a vast opake body between me and the sun, moving forwards towards the island: it seemed to be about two miles high, and hid the sun six or seven minutes, but I did not observe the air to be much colder, or the sky more darkned, than if I had stood under the shade of a mountain. As it approached nearer over the place where I was, it appeared to be a firm substance, the bottom flat, smooth, and shining very bright from the reflexion of the sea below. I stood upon a height about two hundred yards from the shoar, and saw this vast body descending almost to a parallel with me, at less than an English mile distance. I took out my pocket-perspective, and could plainly discover numbers of people moving up and down the sides of it, which appeared to be sloping, but what those people were doing, I was not able to distinguish.

The natural love of life gave me some inward motions of joy; and I was ready to entertain a hope, that this adventure might some way or other help to deliver me from the desolate place and condition I was in. But, at the same time, the reader can hardly conceive my astonishment, to behold an island in the air, inhabited by men, who were able (as it should seem) to raise, or sink, or put it into a progressive motion, as they pleased. But not being, at that time, in a disposition to philosophise upon this phænomenon, I rather chose to observe what course the island would take; because it seemed for a while to stand still. Yet soon after it advanced nearer; and I could see the sides of it, encompassed with several gradations of galleries and stairs, at certain intervals, to descend from one to the other. In the lowest gallery, I beheld some people fishing with long angling rods, and others looking on. I waved my cap, (for my hat was long since worn out,) and my handkerchief towards the island; and upon its nearer approach, I called and shouted with the utmost strength of my voice; and then looking circumspectly, I beheld a crowd gathered to that side which was most in my view. I found by their pointing towards me, and to each other, that they plainly discovered me, although they made no return to my shouting: but, I could see four or five men running in great haste up the stairs to the top of the island, who then disappeared. I happened rightly to conjecture, that these were sent for orders to some person in authority upon this occasion.

The number of people increased; and in less than half an hour, the island was moved and raised in such a manner, that the lowest gallery appeared in a parallel of less than an hundred yards distance from the height where I stood. I then put my self into the most supplicating postures, and spoke in the humblest accent, but received no answer. Those who stood nearest over-against me, seemed to be persons of distinction, as I supposed, by their habit. They conferred earnestly with each other, looking often upon me. At length, one of them called out in a clear, polite, smooth dialect, not unlike in sound to the Italian; and therefore I returned an answer in that language, hoping at least, that the cadence might be more agreeable to his ears. Although neither of us understood the other, yet my meaning was easily known, for the people saw the distress I was in.

They made signs for me to come down from the rock, and go towards the shoar, which I accordingly did; and the flying island being raised to a convenient height, the verge directly over me, a chain was let down from the lowest gallery, with a seat fastned to the bottom, to which I fixed my self, and was drawn up by pullies.

CHAPTER II

The humours and dispositions of the Laputans described.
An account of their learning. Of the king, and his court.
The author's reception there. The inhabitants subject to
fears and disquietudes. An account of the women.

AT my alighting, I was surrounded by a crowd of people,
but those who stood nearest, seemed to be of better quality.
They beheld me with all the marks and circumstances of
wonder; neither indeed was I much in their debt; having
never until then seen a race of mortals so singular in their
shapes, habits, and countenances. Their heads were all
reclined either to the right, or to the left; one of their eyes
turned inward, and the other directly up to the zenith.
Their outward garments were adorned with the figures of
suns, moons, and stars, interwoven with those of fiddles,
flutes, harps, trumpets, guittars, harpsicords, and many
more instruments of musick, unknown to us in Europe.   I
observed here and there many in the habit of servants,
with a blown bladder fastned like a flail to the end of a short
stick, which they carried in their hands.   In each bladder
was a small quantity of dried pease, or little pebbles, (as I
was afterwards informed.)   With these bladders they now
and then flapped the mouths and ears of those who stood
near them, of which practice I could not then conceive the
meaning.   It seems, the minds of these people are so taken
up with intense speculations, that they neither can speak,
or attend to the discourses of others, without being rouzed
by some external taction upon the organs of speech and
hearing; for which reason, those persons who are able to
afford it, always keep a flapper, (the original is *climenole*)
in their family, as one of their domesticks; nor ever walk
abroad, or make visits, without him.   And the business of
this officer is, when two or more persons are in company,

gently to strike with his bladder the mouth of him who is to speak, and the right ear of him, or them, to whom the speaker addresseth himself. This flapper is likewise employed diligently to attend his master in his walks, and upon occasion to give him a soft flap on his eyes; because he is always so wrapped up in cogitation, that he is in manifest danger of falling down every precipice, and bouncing his head against every post; and in the streets, of jostling others, or being jostled himself into the kennel.

It was necessary to give the reader this information, without which he would be at the same loss with me, to understand the proceedings of these people, as they conducted me up the stairs, to the top of the island, and from thence to the royal palace. While we were ascending, they forgot several times what they were about, and left me to my self, until their memories were again rouzed by their flappers; for they appeared altogether unmoved by the sight of my foreign habit and countenance, and by the shouts of the vulgar, whose thoughts and minds were more disengaged.

At last we entered the palace, and proceeded into the chamber of presence; where I saw the king seated on his throne, attended on each side by persons of prime quality. Before the throne, was a large table filled with globes and spheres, and mathematical instruments of all kinds. His Majesty took not the least notice of us, although our entrance were not without sufficient noise, by the concourse of all persons belonging to the court. But, he was then deep in a problem, and we attended, at least, an hour, before he could solve it. There stood by him, on each side, a young page, with flaps in their hands; and when they saw he was at leisure, one of them gently struck his mouth, and the other his right ear; at which he started like one awaked on the sudden, and looking towards me, and the company I was in, recollected the occasion of our coming, whereof

he had been informed before. He spoke some words;
whereupon, immediately, a young man with a flap came
up to my side, and slapt me gently on the right ear; but I
made signs as well as I could, that I had no occasion for
such an instrument; which, as I afterwards found, gave his
Majesty and the whole court a very mean opinion of my
understanding. The king, as far as I could conjecture,
asked me several questions, and I addressed my self to him
in all the languages I had. When it was found, that I
could neither understand nor be understood, I was conducted, by his order, to an apartment in his palace, (this
prince being distinguished above all his predecessors for his
hospitality to strangers,) where two servants were appointed
to attend me. My dinner was brought, and four persons
of quality, whom I remembered to have seen very near the
king's person, did me the honour to dine with me. We had
two courses, of three dishes each. In the first course, there
was a shoulder of mutton, cut into an æquilateral triangle;
a piece of beef into a rhomboides; and a pudding into a
cycloid. The second course was two ducks, trussed up into
the form of fiddles; sausages, and puddings, resembling
flutes and hautboys, and a breast of veal in the shape of a
harp. The servants cut our bread into cones, cylinders,
parallelograms, and several other mathematical figures.

While we were at dinner, I made bold to ask the names
of several things in their language; and those noble persons,
by the assistance of their flappers, delighted to give me
answers, hoping to raise my admiration of their great
abilities, if I could be brought to converse with them. I
was soon able to call for bread, and drink, or whatever else
I wanted.

After dinner, my company withdrew, and a person was
sent to me by the king's order, attended by a flapper. He
brought with him, pen, ink, and paper, and three or four
books; giving me to understand by signs, that he was sent

to teach me the language. We sat together four hours, in which time, I wrote down a great number of words in columns, with the translations over-against them. I likewise made a shift to learn several short sentences. For, my tutor would order one of my servants to fetch something, to turn about, to make a bow, to sit, or stand, or walk, and the like. Then I took down the sentence in writing. He shewed me also, in one of his books, the figures of the sun, moon, and stars, the zodiack, the tropics, and polar circles, together with the denominations of many figures of planes and solids. He gave me the names and descriptions of all the musical instruments, and the general terms of art in playing on each of them. After he had left me, I placed all my words, with their interpretations, in alphabetical order. And thus, in a few days, by the help of a very faithful memory, I got some insight into their language.

The word, which I interpret the 'Flying' or 'Floating Island,' is in the original 'Laputa'; whereof I could never learn the true etymology. 'Lap' in the old obsolete language signifieth 'high,' and 'untuh' a 'governor'; from which they say by corruption was derived 'Laputa' from 'Lapuntah.' But I do not approve of this derivation, which seems to be a little strained. I ventured to offer to the learned among them, a conjecture of my own, that 'Laputa' was *quasi* 'Lap outed'; 'lap' signifying properly the dancing of the sun beams in the sea; and 'outed' a wing, which however I shall not obtrude, but submit to the judicious reader.

Those to whom the king had entrusted me, observing how ill I was clad, ordered a taylor to come next morning, and take my measure for a suit of cloaths. This operator did his office after a different manner from those of his trade in Europe. He first took my altitude by a quadrant, and then with rule and compasses, described the dimensions and out-lines of my whole body; all which he entered upon paper, and in six days brought my cloths very ill made, and quite out of shape, by happening to mistake a figure in the calculation. But my comfort was, that I observed such accidents very frequent, and little regarded.

During my confinement for want of cloaths, and by an indisposition that held me some days longer, I much enlarged my dictionary; and when I went next to court, was able to understand many things the king spoke, and to return him some kind of answers. His Majesty had given orders, that the island should move north-east and by east, to the vertical point over Lagado, the metropolis of the whole kingdom, below upon the firm earth. It was about ninety leagues distant, and our voyage lasted four days and an half. I was not in the least sensible of the progressive motion made in the air by the island. On the second morning, about eleven o'clock, the king himself in person, attended by his nobility, courtiers, and officers, having prepared all their musical instruments, played on them for three hours without intermission; so that I was quite stunned with the noise; neither could I possibly guess the meaning, until my tutor informed me. He said, that the people of their island had their ears adapted to hear the musick of the spheres, which always played at certain periods; and the court was now prepared to bear their part in whatever instrument they most excelled.

In our journey towards Lagado, the capital city, his Majesty ordered that the island should stop over certain towns and villages, from whence he might receive the petitions of his subjects. And to this purpose, several packthreads were let down with small weights at the bottom. On these packthreads the people strung their petitions, which mounted up directly like the scraps of paper fastned by school-boys at the end of the string that holds their kite. Sometimes we received wine and victuals from below, which were drawn up by pullies.

The knowledge I had in mathematicks gave me great assistance in acquiring their phraseology, which depended much upon that science and musick; and in the latter I was not unskilled. Their ideas are perpetually conversant in lines and figures. If they would, for example, praise the beauty of a woman, or any other animal, they describe it by rhombs, circles, parallelograms, ellipses, and other geometrical terms; or else by words of art drawn from musick, needless here to repeat. I observed in the king's kitchen all sorts of mathematical and musical instruments, after the figures of which they cut up the joynts that were served to his Majesty's table.

Their houses are very ill built, the walls bevil, without one right angle in any apartment; and this defect ariseth from the contempt they bear for practical geometry; which they despise as vulgar and mechanick, those instructions they give being too refined for the intellectuals of their workmen; which occasions perpetual mistakes. And, although they are dextrous enough upon a piece of paper in the management of the rule, the pencil, and the divider, yet in the common actions and behaviour of life, I have not seen a more clumsy, awkward, and unhandy people, nor so slow and perplexed in their conceptions upon all other subjects, except those of mathematicks and musick. They are very bad reasoners, and vehemently given to opposition, unless when they happen to be of the right opinion, which is seldom their case. Imagination, fancy, and invention, they are wholly strangers to, nor have any words in their language by which those ideas can be expressed; the whole compass of their thoughts and mind, being shut up within the two forementioned sciences.

Most of them, and especially those who deal in the astronomical part, have great faith in judicial astrology, although they are ashamed to own it publickly. But, what I chiefly admired, and thought altogether unaccountable,

was the strong disposition I observed in them towards
news and politicks; perpetually enquiring into publick
affairs, giving their judgments in matters of State; and
passionately disputing every inch of a party opinion. I
have indeed observed the same disposition among most of
the mathematicians I have known in Europe; although I
could never discover the least analogy between the two
sciences; unless those people suppose, that because the
smallest circle hath as many degrees as the largest, therefore the regulation and management of the world require
no more abilities than the handling and turning of a globe.
But, I rather take this quality to spring from a very common infirmity of human nature, inclining us to be more
curious and conceited in matters where we have least concern, and for which we are least adapted either by study
or nature.

These people are under continual disquietudes, never
enjoying a minute's peace of mind; and their disturbances
proceed from causes which very little affect the rest of
mortals. Their apprehensions arise from several changes
they dread in the celestial bodies. For instance; that the
earth by the continual approaches of the sun towards it,
must in course of time be absorbed or swallowed up. That,
the face of the sun will by degrees be encrusted with its own
effluvia, and give no more light to the world. That, the
earth very narrowly escaped a brush from the tail of the
last comet, which would have infallibly reduced it to ashes;
and that the next, which they have calculated for one and
thirty years hence, will probably destroy us. For, if in its
perihelion it should approach within a certain degree of
the sun, (as by their calculations they have reason to dread)
it will conceive a degree of heat ten thousand times more
intense than that of red hot glowing iron; and in its absence
from the sun, carry a blazing tail ten hundred thousand and
fourteen miles long; through which, if the earth should pass

at the distance of one hundred thousand miles from the nucleus, or main body of the comet, it must in its passage be set on fire, and reduced to ashes. That, the sun daily spending its rays without any nutriment to supply them, will at last be wholly consumed and annihilated; which must be attended with the destruction of this earth, and of all the planets that receive their light from it.

They are so perpetually alarmed with the apprehensions of these, and the like impending dangers, that they can neither sleep quietly in their beds, nor have any relish for the common pleasures or amusements of life. When they meet an acquaintance in the morning, the first question is about the sun's health; how he looked at his setting and rising, and what hopes they have to avoid the stroak of the approaching comet. This conversation they are apt to run into with the same temper that boys discover, in delighting to hear terrible stories of sprites and hobgoblins, which they greedily listen to, and dare not go to bed for fear.

The women of the island have abundance of vivacity; they contemn their husbands, and are exceedingly fond of strangers, whereof there is always a considerable number from the continent below, attending at court, either upon affairs of the several towns and corporations, or their own particular occasions; but are much despised, because they want the same endowments. Among these the ladies chuse their gallants: but the vexation is, that they act with too much ease and security; for the husband is always so wrapped in speculation, that the mistress and lover may proceed to the greatest familiarities before his face, if he be but provided with paper and implements, and without his flapper at his side.

The wives and daughters lament their confinement to the island, although I think it the most delicious spot of ground in the world; and although they live here in the greatest plenty and magnificence, and are allowed to do whatever they please: they long to see the world, and take the diversions of the metropolis, which they are not allowed to do without a particular licence from the king; and this is not easy to be obtained, because the people of quality have found by frequent experience, how hard it is to persuade their women to return from below.   I was told, that a great court lady, who had several children, is married to the Prime Minister, the richest subject in the kingdom, a very graceful person, extremely fond of her, and lives in the finest palace of the island; went down to Lagado, on the pretence of health, there hid herself for several months, until the king sent a warrant to search for her; and she was found in an obscure eating-house all in rags, having pawned her clothes to maintain an old deformed footman, who beat her every day, and in whose company she was taken much against her will.   And, although her husband received her with all possible kindness; and without the least reproach; she soon after contrived to steal down again with all her jewels, to the same gallant, and hath not been heard of since.

This may perhaps pass with the reader, rather for an European or English story, than for one of a country so remote.   But he may please to consider, that the caprices of womankind are not limited by any climate or nation; and that they are much more uniform than can be easily imagined.

In about a month's time I had made a tolerable proficiency in their language, and was able to answer most of the king's questions, when I had the honour to attend him. His Majesty discovered not the least curiosity to enquire into the laws, government, history, religion, or manners of the countries where I had been; but confined his questions to the state of mathematicks, and received the account I gave him, with great contempt and indifference, although often rouzed by his flapper on each side.

CHAPTER III

A phænomenon solved by modern philosophy and astronomy.
The Laputans great improvements in the latter. The
king's method of suppressing insurrections.

I DESIRED leave of this prince to see the curiosities of the
island; which he was graciously pleased to grant, and
ordered my tutor to attend me. I chiefly wanted to know
to what cause in art or in nature, it owed its several motions;
whereof I will now give a philosophical account to the
reader.

The flying, or floating island, is exactly circular; its
diameter seven thousand eight hundred and thirty seven
yards, or about four miles and an half, and consequently
contains ten thousand acres. It is three hundred yards
thick. The bottom, or under surface, which appears to
those who view it from below, is one even regular plate of
adamant, shooting up to the height of about two hundred
yards. Above it lye the several minerals in their usual
order; and over all is a coat of rich mould ten or twelve foot
deep. The declivity of the upper surface, from the circumference to the center, is the natural cause why all the dews
and rains which fall upon the island, are conveyed in small
rivulets towards the middle, where they are emptied into
four large basons, each of about half a mile in circuit, and
two hundred yards distant from the center. From these
basons the water is continually exhaled by the sun in
the day-time, which effectually prevents their overflowing.
Besides, as it is in the power of the monarch to raise the
island above the region of clouds and vapours, he can prevent the falling of dews and rains whenever he pleaseth.
For the highest clouds cannot rise above two miles, as
naturalists agree, at least they were never known to do so
in that country.

At the center of the island there is a chasm about fifty yards in diameter, from whence the astronomers descend into a large dome, which is therefore called 'Flandona Gagnole,' or the 'Astronomers Cave'; situated at the depth of an hundred yards beneath the upper surface of the adamant. In this cave are twenty lamps continually burning, which from the reflection of the adamant cast a strong light into every part. The place is stored with great variety of sextants, quadrants, telescopes, astrolabes, and other astronomical instruments. But the greatest curiosity, upon which the fate of the island depends, is a load-stone of a prodigious size, in shape resembling a weaver's shuttle. It is in length six yards, and in the thickest part at least three yards over. This magnet is sustained by a very strong axle of adamant, passing through its middle, upon which it plays, and is poized so exactly, that the weakest hand can turn it. It is hooped round with an hollow cylinder of adamant, four foot deep, as many thick, and twelve yards in diameter, placed horizontally, and supported by eight adamantine feet, each six yards high. In the middle of the concave side there is a groove twelve inches deep, in which the extremities of the axle are lodged, and turned round as there is occasion.

This stone cannot be moved from its place by any force, because the hoop and its feet are one continued piece with that body of adamant which constitutes the bottom of the island.

By means of this load-stone, the island is made to rise and fall, and move from one place to another. For, with respect to that part of the earth over which the monarch presides, the stone is endued at one of its sides with an attractive power, and at the other with a repulsive. Upon placing the magnet erect with its attracting end towards the earth, the island descends; but when the repelling extremity points downwards, the island mounts directly upwards. When the position of the stone is oblique, the motion of the island is so to. For in this magnet the forces always act in lines parallel to its direction.

By this oblique motion, the island is conveyed to different parts of the monarch's dominions. To explain the manner of its progress, let *AB* represent a line drawn cross the dominions of Balnibarbi; let the line *cd* represent the loadstone, of which let *d* be the repelling end, and *c* the attracting end, the island being over *C*; let the stone be placed in the position *cd* with its repelling end downwards; then the island will be driven upwards obliquely towards *D*. When it is arrived at *D*, let the stone be turned upon its axle until its attracting end points towards *E*, and then the island will be carried obliquely towards E; where, if the stone be again turned upon its axle until it stands in the position EF, with its repelling point downwards, the island will rise obliquely towards F, where, by directing the attracting end towards G, the island may be carried to G, and from G to H, by turning the stone, so as to make its repelling extremity point directly downwards. And thus by changing the situation of the stone as often as there is occasion, the island is made to rise and fall by turns in an oblique direction; and by those alternate risings and fallings (the obliquity being not considerable) is conveyed from one part of the dominions to the other.

But it must be observed, that this island cannot move beyond the extent of the dominions below; nor can it rise above the height of four miles. For which the astronomers (who have written large systems concerning the stone) assign the following reason: that the magnetick virtue doth not extend beyond the distance of four miles, and that the mineral which acts upon the stone in the bowels of the earth, and in the sea about six leagues distant from the shoar, is not diffused through the whole globe, but terminated with the limits of the king's dominions: and it was easy from the great advantage of such a superior situation, for a prince to bring under his obedience whatever country lay within the attraction of that magnet.

When the stone is put parallel to the plane of the horizon, the island standeth still; for in that case, the extremities of it being at equal distance from the earth, act with equal force, the one in drawing downwards, the other in pushing upwards; and consequently no motion can ensue.

This load-stone is under the care of certain astronomers, who from time to time give it such positions as the monarch directs. They spend the greatest part of their lives in observing the celestial bodies, which they do by the assistance of glasses, far excelling ours in goodness. For, although their largest telescopes do not exceed three feet, they magnify much more than those of a hundred with us, and shew the stars with greater clearness. This advantage hath enabled them to extend their discoveries much farther than our astronomers in Europe. They have made a catalogue of ten thousand fixed stars, whereas the largest of ours do not contain above one third part of that number. They have likewise discovered two lesser stars, or satellites, which revolve about Mars; whereof the innermost is distant from the center of the primary planet exactly three of his diameters, and the outermost five; the former revolves in the space of ten hours, and the latter in twenty one and an half; so that the squares of their periodical times, are very near in the same proportion with the cubes of their distance from the center of Mars; which evidently shews them to be governed by the same law of gravitation, that influences the other heavenly bodies.

They have observed ninety-three different comets, and settled their periods with great exactness. If this be true, (and they affirm it with great confidence) it is much to be wished that their observations were made publick; whereby the theory of comets, which at present is very lame and defective, might be brought to the same perfection with other parts of astronomy.

The king would be the most absolute prince in the universe, if he could but prevail on a ministry to join with him; but these having their estates below on the continent, and considering that the office of a favourite hath a very uncertain tenure, would never consent to the enslaving their country.

If any town should engage in rebellion or mutiny, fall into violent factions, or refuse to pay the usual tribute; the king hath two methods of reducing them to obedience. The first and the mildest course is by keeping the island hovering over such a town, and the lands about it; whereby he

can deprive them of the benefit of the sun and the rain, and
consequently afflict the inhabitants with dearth and diseases. And if the crime deserve it, they are at the same
time pelted from above with great stones, against which
they have no defence, but by creeping into cellars or caves,
while the roofs of their houses are beaten to pieces. But,
if they still continue obstinate, or offer to raise insurrections;
he proceeds to the last remedy, by letting the island drop
directly upon their heads, which makes a universal destruction both of houses and men. However, this is an extremity
to which the prince is seldom driven, neither indeed is he
willing to put it in execution; nor dare his ministers advise
him to an action, which as it would render them odious
to the people, so it would be a great damage to their own
estates that lie all below; for the island is the king's
demesne.

But there is still indeed a more weighty reason, why
the kings of this country have been always averse from
executing so terrible an action, unless upon the utmost
necessity. For, if the town intended to be destroyed should
have in it any tall rocks, as it generally falls out in the
larger cities; a situation probably chosen at first with a
view to prevent such a catastrophe: or, if it abound in high
spires or pillars of stone, a sudden fall might endanger the
bottom or under surface of the island, which although it
consist as I have said, of one entire adamant two hundred
yards thick, might happen to crack by too great a choque,
or burst by approaching too near the fires from the houses
below; as the backs both of iron and stone will often do in
our chimnies. Of all this the people are well apprized, and
understand how far to carry their obstinacy, where their
liberty or property is concerned. And the king, when he
is highest provoked, and most determined to press a city
to rubbish, orders the island to descend with great gentleness, out of a pretence of tenderness to his people, but

indeed for fear of breaking the adamantine bottom; in which case it is the opinion of all their philosophers, that the load-stone could no longer hold it up, and the whole mass would fall to the ground.

By a fundamental law of this realm, neither the king nor either of his two elder sons, are permitted to leave the island; nor the queen until she is past child-bearing.

CHAPTER IV

The author leaves Laputa, is conveyed to Balnibarbi, arrives at the metropolis. A description of the metropolis and the country adjoining. The author hospitably received by a great lord. His conversation with that lord.

ALTHOUGH I cannot say, that I was ill treated in this island, yet I must confess, I thought my self too much neglected, not without some degree of contempt. For, neither prince nor people appeared to be curious in any part of know-ledge, except mathematicks and musick; wherein I was far their inferior, and upon that account very little regarded.

On the other side, after having seen all the curiosities of the island, I was very desirous to leave it, being heartily weary of those people. They were indeed, excellent in two sciences for which I have great esteem, and wherein I am not unversed: but, at the same time, so abstracted and involved in speculation, that I never met with such dis-agreeable companions. I conversed only with women, tradesmen, flappers, and court-pages, during two months of my abode there; by which at last I rendered my self extremely contemptible; yet, these were the only people from whom I could ever receive a reasonable answer.

I had obtained by hard study a good degree of knowledge in their language: I was weary of being confined to an
island where I received so little countenance; and resolved
to leave it with the first opportunity.

There was a great lord at court, nearly related to the
king, and for that reason alone used with respect. He was
universally reckoned the most ignorant and stupid person
among them. He had performed many eminent services
for the Crown; had great natural and acquired parts,
adorned with integrity and honour; but, so ill an ear for
musick, that his detractors reported he had been often
known to beat time in the wrong place; neither could his
tutors without extreme difficulty, teach him to demonstrate
the most easy proposition in the mathematicks. He was
pleased to shew me many marks of favour; often did me
the honour of a visit; desired to be informed in the affairs
of Europe; the laws and customs, the manners and learning
of the several countries where I had travelled. He listened
to me with great attention, and made very wise observations on all I spoke: he had two flappers attending him
for state, but never made use of them except at court, and
in visits of ceremony; and, would always command them
to withdraw, when we were alone together.

I intreated this illustrious person, to intercede in my
behalf with his Majesty, for leave to depart; which he
accordingly did, as he was pleased to tell me, with regret:
for, indeed he had made me several offers very advantageous; which however I refused with expressions of the
highest acknowledgment.

On the 16th day of February, I took leave of his Majesty
and the court: the king made me a present to the value of
about two hundred pounds English; and my protector his
kinsman as much more, together with a letter of recommendation to a friend of his in Lagado, the metropolis:
the island being then hovering over a mountain about two

miles from it, I was let down from the lowest gallery, in the same manner as I had been taken up.

The continent, as far as it is subject to the monarch of the flying island, passeth under the general name of Balnibarbi; and the metropolis, as I said before, is called Lagado. I felt some little satisfaction in finding my self on firm ground. I walked to the city without any concern, being clad like one of the natives, and sufficiently instructed to converse with them. I soon found out the person's house to whom I was recommended; presented my letter, from his friend the grandee in the island; and was received with much kindness. This great lord, whose name was Munodi, ordered me an apartment in his own house; where I continued during my stay, and was entertained in a most hospitable manner.

The next morning after my arrival, he took me in his chariot to see the town, which is about half the bigness of London; but the houses very strangely built, and most of them out of repair. The people in the streets walked fast, looked wild, their eyes fixed, and were generally in rags. We passed through one of the town gates, and went about three miles into the country, where I saw many labourers working with several sorts of tools in the ground, but was not able to conjecture what they were about; neither did I observe any expectation either of corn or grass, although the soil appeared to be excellent. I could not forbear admiring at these odd appearances both in town and country; and, I made bold to desire my conductor, that he would be pleased to explain to me, what could be meant by so many busy heads, hands, and faces, both in the streets and the fields, because I did not discover any good effects they produced; but, on the contrary, I never knew a soil so unhappily cultivated, houses so ill contrived and so ruinous, or a people whose countenances and habit, expressed so much misery and want.

This Lord Munodi was a person of the first rank, and had been some years governor of Lagado; but by a cabal of ministers was discharged for insufficiency. However, the king treated him with tenderness, as a well-meaning man, but of a low contemptible understanding.

When I gave that free censure of the country and its inhabitants, he made no further answer than by telling me, that I had not been long enough among them to form a judgment; and that the different nations of the world had different customs; with other common topicks to the same purpose. But, when we returned to his palace, he asked me how I liked the building, what absurdities I observed, and what quarrel I had with the dress and looks of his domesticks. This he might safely do; because every thing about him, was magnificent, regular, and polite. I answered, that his excellency's prudence, quality, and fortune, had exempted him from those defects which folly and beggary had produced in others. He said, if I would go with him to his country house, about twenty miles distant, where his estate lay, there would be more leisure for this kind of conversation. I told his excellency, that I was entirely at his disposal; and accordingly we set out next morning.

During our journey, he made me observe the several methods used by farmers, in managing their lands; which to me, were wholly unaccountable: for, except in some very few places, I could not discover one ear of corn, or blade of grass. But, in three hours travelling, the scene was wholly altered; we came into a most beautiful country; farmers houses at small distances, neatly built, the fields enclosed, containing vine-yards, corn-grounds and meadows: neither do I remember to have seen a more delightful prospect.

His excellency observed my countenance to clear up; he told me with a sigh, that there his estate began, and would continue the same until we should come to his house: that, his countrymen ridiculed and despised him for managing his affairs no better, and for setting so ill an example to the kingdom; which, however was followed by very few; such as were old and wilful, and weak like himself.

We came at length to the house, which was indeed a noble structure, built according to the best rules of ancient architecture. The fountains, gardens, walks, avenues, and groves, were all disposed with exact judgment and taste. I gave due praises to every thing I saw, whereof his excellency took not the least notice until after supper; when, there being no third companion, he told me with a very melancholy air, that he doubted he must throw down his houses in town and country, to rebuild them after the present mode; destroy all his plantations, and cast others into such a form, as modern usage required; and give the same directions to all his tenants, unless he would submit to incur the censure of pride, singularity, affectation, ignorance, caprice; and perhaps, increase his Majesty's displeasure.

That, the admiration I appeared to be under, would cease or diminish, when he had informed me of some particulars, which probably I never heard of at court; the people there being too much taken up in their own speculations, to have regard to what passed here below.

The sum of his discourse was to this effect. That, about forty years ago, certain persons went up to Laputa, either upon business or diversion; and after five months continuance, came back with a very little smattering in mathematicks, but full of volatile spirits, acquired in that airy region. That, these persons upon their return, began to dislike the management of every thing below; and fell into schemes of putting all arts, sciences, languages, and

mechanicks upon a new foot.   To this end, they procured
a royal patent, for erecting an academy of projectors in
Lagado: and, the humour prevailed so strongly among the
people, that there is not a town of any consequence in the
kingdom, without such an academy.   In these colleges, the
professors contrive new rules and methods of agriculture
and building, and new instruments and tools for all trades
and manufactures; whereby, as they undertake, one man
shall do the work of ten: a palace may be built in a week,
of materials so durable, as to last for ever without repairing.
All the fruits of the earth shall come to maturity, at whatever season we think fit to chuse, and encrease an hundred
fold more than they do at present; with innumerable other
happy proposals.   The only inconvenience is, that none of
these projects are yet brought to perfection; and, in the
mean time, the whole country lies miserably waste; the
houses in ruins, and the people without food or cloaths: by
all which, instead of being discouraged, they are fifty times
more violently bent upon prosecuting their schemes; driven
equally on by hope and despair: that, as for himself, being
not of an enterprizing spirit, he was content to go on in
the old forms; to live in the houses his ancestors had built,
and act as they did in every part of life without innovation:
that, some few other persons of quality and gentry had done
the same; but were looked on with an eye of contempt and
ill-will; as enemies to art; ignorant, and ill commonwealths-
men; preferring their own ease and sloth before the general
improvement of their country.

His lordship added, that he would not by any further
particulars prevent the pleasure I should certainly take in
viewing the grand academy, whither he was resolved I
should go.   He only desired me to observe a ruined building
upon the side of a mountain about three miles distant, of
which he gave me this account.   That, he had a very convenient mill within half a mile of his house, turned by a

current from a large river, and sufficient for his own family, as well as a great number of his tenants. That, about seven years ago, a club of those projectors came to him with proposals to destroy this mill, and build another on the side of that mountain, on the long ridge whereof, a long canal must be cut for a repository of water, to be conveyed up by pipes and engines to supply the mill: because the wind and air upon a height agitated the water, and thereby, made it fitter for motion: and, because the water descending down a declivity, would turn the mill with half the current of a river, whose course is more upon a level. He said, that being then not very well with the court, and pressed by many of his friends, he complied with the proposal; and after employing an hundred men for two years, the work miscarried, the projectors went off, laying the blame entirely upon him; railing at him ever since, and putting others upon the same experiment, with equal assurance of success, as well as equal disappointment.

In a few days we came back to town; and his Excellency, considering the bad character he had in the academy, would not go with me himself; but recommended me to a friend of his, to bear me company thither. My lord was pleased to represent me as a great admirer of projects, and a person of much curiosity and easy belief; which, indeed was not without truth; for, I had my self, been a sort of projector in my younger days.

CHAPTER V

The author permitted to see the grand academy of Lagado. The academy largely described. The arts wherein the professors employ themselves.

THIS academy is not an entire single building, but a continuation of several houses on both sides of a street; which growing waste, was purchased and applied to that use.

I was received very kindly by the warden, and went for many days to the academy. Every room hath in it one or more projectors; and, I believe, I could not be in fewer than five hundred rooms.

The first man I saw, was of a meagre aspect, with sooty hands and face; his hair and beard long, ragged and singed in several places. His cloaths, shirt, and skin, were all of the same colour: he had been eight years upon a project for extracting sun-beams out of cucumbers; which were to be put into vials, hermetically sealed, and let out to warm the air, in raw inclement summers. He told me, he did not doubt, in eight years more, that he should be able to supply the governor's gardens with sun-shine at a reasonable rate; but, he complained that his stock was low, and intreated me to give him something as an encouragement to ingenuity, especially since this had been a very dear season for cucumbers: I made him a small present, for my lord had furnished me with money on purpose; because he knew their practice of begging from all who go to see them.

I went into another chamber, but was ready to hasten back; being almost overcome with a horrible stink: my conductor pressed me forward, conjuring me in a whisper to give no offence, which would be highly resented; and therefore, I durst not so much as stop my nose. The projector of this cell, was the most ancient student of the academy: his face and beard were of a pale yellow; his hands and cloaths dawbed over with filth. When I was presented to him, he gave me a very close embrace, (a compliment I could well have excused:) his employment from his first coming into the academy; was an operation to reduce human excrement to its original food; by separating the several parts; removing the tincture which it receives from the gall; making the odour exhale; and scumming off the saliva. He had a weekly allowance from the society, of a vessel filled with human ordure, about the bigness of a Bristol barrel.

I saw another at work to calcine ice into gun-powder; who likewise shewed me a treatise he had written, concerning the malleability of fire; which he intended to publish.

There was a most ingenious architect, who had contrived a new method for building houses, by beginning at the roof, and working downwards to the foundation; which he justified to me, by the like practice of those two prudent insects, the bee and the spider.

There was a man born blind, who had several apprentices in his own condition: their employment was to mix colours for painters, which their master taught them to distinguish by feeling and smelling: it was indeed my misfortune to find them at that time, not very perfect in their lessons; and the professor himself happened to be generally mistaken. This artist is much encouraged and esteemed by the whole fraternity.

In another apartment, I was highly pleased with a projector, who had found a device of plowing the ground with hogs, to save the charges of plows, cattle, and labour. The method is this: In an acre of ground you bury at six inches distance, and eight deep, a quantity of acorns, dates, chestnuts, and other masts or vegetables, whereof these animals are fondest; then you drive six hundred or more of them into the field, where in a few days they will root up the whole ground in search of their food, and make it fit for sowing, at the same time manuring it with their dung. It is true, upon experiment, they found the charge and trouble very great, and they had little or no crop. However, it is not doubted, that this invention may be capable of great improvement.

I went into another room, where the walls and cieling were all hung round with cobwebs, except a narrow passage for the artist to go in and out. At my entrance, he called aloud to me not to disturb his webs. He lamented the fatal mistake the world had been so long in of using silk-worms, while we had such plenty of domestick insects, who infinitely excelled the former; because, they understood how to weave as well as spin. And he proposed farther, that by employing spiders, the charge of dying silks would be wholly saved; whereof I was fully convinced, when he shewed me a vast number of flies most beautifully coloured, wherewith he fed his spiders; assuring us, that the webs would take a tincture from them; and as he had them of all hues, he hoped to fit every body's fancy, as soon as he could find proper food for the flies, of certain gums, oyls, and other glutinous matter, to give a strength and consistence to the threads.

There was an astronomer who had undertaken to place a sun-dial upon the great weather-cock on the town-house, by adjusting the annual and diurnal motions of the earth and sun, so as to answer and coincide with all accidental turnings of the wind.

I was complaining of a small fit of the cholick; upon which my conductor led me into a room, where a great physician resided, who was famous for curing that disease by contrary operations from the same instrument. He had a large pair of bellows, with a long slender muzzle of ivory: this he conveyed eight inches up the anus, and drawing in the wind, he affirmed he could make the guts as lank as a dried bladder. But when the disease was more stubborn and violent, he let in the muzzle while the bellows was full of wind, which he discharged into the body of the patient; then withdrew the instrument to replenish it, clapping his thumb strongly against the orifice of the fundament; and this being repeated three or four times, the adventitious wind would rush out, bringng the noxious along with it (like water put into a pump) and the patient recovers. I saw him try both experiments upon a dog; but could not discern any effect from the former. After the latter, the animal was ready to burst, and made so violent a discharge, as was very offensive to me and my companions. The dog died on the spot, and we left the doctor endeavouring to recover him by the same operation.

I visited many other apartments, but shall not trouble my reader with all the curiosities I observed, being studious of brevity.

I had hitherto seen only one side of the academy, the other being appropriated to the advancers of speculative learning; of whom I shall say something when I have mentioned one illustrious person more, who is called among them, 'The universal artist.' He told us, he had been thirty years employing his thoughts for the improvement of human life. He had two large rooms full of wonderful curiosities, and fifty men at work: some were condensing air into a dry tangible substance, by extracting the nitre, and letting the aqueous or fluid particles percolate: others softening marble for pillows and pincushions; others petrifying the hoofs of a living horse, to preserve them from foundering. The artist himself, was at that time busy upon two great designs: the first, to sow land with chaff; wherein he affirmed the true seminal virtue to be contained, as he demonstrated by several experiments which I was not skilful enough to comprehend. The other was, by a certain composition of gums, minerals, and vegetables outwardly applied, to prevent the growth of wool upon two young lambs; and he hoped in a reasonable time to propagate the breed of naked sheep all over the kingdom.

We crossed a walk to the other part of the academy, where, as I have already said, the projectors in speculative learning resided.

The first professor I saw was in a very large room, with forty pupils about him. After salutation, observing me to look earnestly upon a frame, which took up the greatest part of both the length and breadth of the room; he said, perhaps I might wonder to see him employed in a project for improving speculative knowledge by practical and mechanical operations. But the world would soon be sensible of its usefulness; and he flattered himself, that a more noble exalted thought never sprang in any other man's head. Every one knew how laborious the usual

method is of attaining to arts and sciences; whereas by
his contrivance, the most ignorant person at a reasonable
charge, and with a little bodily labour, may write books in
philosophy, poetry, politicks, law, mathematicks and theology, without the least assistance from genius or study.
He then led me to the frame, about the sides whereof all
his pupils stood in ranks. It was twenty foot square,
placed in the middle of the room. The superficies was
composed of several bits of wood, about the bigness of a
dye, but some larger than others. They were all linked
together by slender wires. These bits of wood were covered
on every square with paper pasted on them; and, on these
papers were written all the words of their language in their
several moods, tenses, and declensions, but without any
order. The professor then desired me to observe, for he
was going to set his engine at work. The pupils at his
command took each of them hold of an iron handle, whereof
there were forty fixed round the edges of the frame; and
giving them a sudden turn, the whole disposition of the
words was entirely changed. He then commanded six and
thirty of the lads to read the several lines softly as they
appeared upon the frame; and where they found three or
four words together that might make part of a sentence,
they dictated to the four remaining boys who were scribes.
This work was repeated three or four times, and at every
turn the engine was so contrived, that the words shifted
into new places, as the square bits of wood moved upside
down.

Six hours a-day the young students were employed in
this labour; and the professor shewed me several volumes in
large folio already collected, of broken sentences, which he
intended to piece together; and out of those rich materials
to give the world a compleat body of all arts and sciences;
which, however might be still improved, and much ex-
pedited, if the publick would raise a fund for making and

employing five hundred such frames in Lagado, and oblige the managers to contribute in common their several collections.

He assured me, that this invention had employed all his thoughts from his youth; that he had emptied the whole vocabulary into his frame, and made the strictest computation of the general proportion there is in books between the numbers of particles, nouns, and verbs, and other parts of speech.

I made my humblest acknowledgments to this illustrious person for his great communicativeness; and promised, if ever I had the good fortune to return to my native country, that I would do him justice, as the sole inventor of this wonderful machine; the form and contrivance of which I desired leave to delineate upon paper as in the figure here annexed.   I told him, although it were the custom of our learned in Europe to steal inventions from each other, who had thereby at least this advantage, that it became a controversy which was the right owner; yet I would take such caution, that he should have the honour entire without a rival.

We next went to the school of languages, where three professors sat in consultation upon improving that of their own country.

The first project was to shorten discourse by cutting polysyllables into one, and leaving out verbs and participles; because in reality all things imaginable are but nouns.

The other, was a scheme for entirely abolishing all words whatsoever: and this was urged as a great advantage in point of health as well as brevity.   For, it is plain, that every word we speak is in some degree a diminution of our lungs by corrosion; and consequently contributes to the shortning of our lives.   An expedient was therefore offered, that since words are only names for *things*, it would be more convenient for all men to carry about them, such *things* as were necessary to express the particular business they are to discourse on. And this invention would certainly have taken place, to the great ease as well as health of the subject, if the women in conjunction with the vulgar and illiterate had not threatned to raise a rebellion, unless they might be allowed the liberty to speak with their tongues, after the manner of their forefathers: such constant irreconcileable enemies to science are the common people. However, many of the most learned and wise adhere to the new scheme of expressing themselves by *things*; which hath only this inconvenience attending it; that if a man's business be very great, and of various kinds, he must be obliged in proportion to carry a greater bundle of *things* upon his back, unless he can afford one or two strong servants to attend him. I have often beheld two of those sages almost sinking under the weight of their packs, like pedlars among us; who, when they met in the streets would lay down their loads, open their sacks, and hold conversation for an hour together; then put up their implements, help each other to resume their burthens, and take their leave.

But, for short conversations, a man may carry implements in his pockets and under his arms, enough to supply him, and in his house he cannot be at a loss; therefore the room where company meet who practise this art, is full of all things ready at hand, requisite to furnish matter for this kind of artificial converse.

Another great advantage proposed by this invention, was, that it would serve as an universal language to be understood in all civilized nations, whose goods and utensils are generally of the same kind, or nearly resembling, so that their uses might easily be comprehended. And thus, embassadors would be qualified to treat with foreign princes or ministers of State, to whose tongues they were utter strangers.

I was at the mathematical school, where the master

taught his pupils after a method scarce imaginable to us in Europe. The proposition and demonstration were fairly written on a thin wafer, with ink composed of a cephalick tincture. This the student was to swallow upon a fasting stomach, and for three days following eat nothing but bread and water. As the water digested, the tincture mounted to his brain, bearing the proposition along with 't. But the success hath not hitherto been answerable, partly by some error in the *quantum* or composition, and partly by the perverseness of lads; to whom this bolus is so nauseous, that they generally steal aside, and discharge it upwards before it can operate; neither have they been yet persuaded to use so long an abstinence as the prescription requires.

CHAPTER VI

A further account of the academy. The author proposeth some improvements, which are honourably received.

IN the school of political projectors, I was but ill entertained; the professors appearing in my judgment wholly out of their senses; which is a scene that never fails to make me melancholy. These unhappy people were proposing schemes for persuading monarchs to chuse favourites upon the score of their wisdom, capacity, and virtue; of teaching ministers to consult the publick good; of rewarding merit, great abilities, and eminent services; of instructing princes to know their true interest, by placing it on the same foundation with that of their people: of chusing for employments persons qualified to exercise them; with many other wild impossible chimæras, that never entered before into the heart of man to conceive; and confirmed in me the old observation, that there is nothing so extravagant and irrational which some philosophers have not maintained for truth.

But, however I shall so far do justice to this part of the academy, as to acknowledge, that all of them were not so visionary.   There was a most ingenious doctor who seemed to be perfectly versed in the whole nature and system of government.   This illustrious person had very usefully employed his studies in finding out effectual remedies for all diseases and corruptions, to which the several kinds of publick administration are subject by the vices or infirmities of those who govern, as well as by the licentiousness of those who are to obey.   For instance: whereas all writers and reasoners have agreed, that there is a strict universal resemblance between the natural and the political body; can there be any thing more evident, than that the health of both must be preserved, and the diseases cured by the same prescriptions?   It is allowed, that senates and great councils are often troubled with redundant, ebulliant, and other peccant humours; with many diseases of the head, and more of the heart; with strong convulsions, with grievous contractions of the nerves and sinews in both hands, but especially the right: with spleen, flatus, vertigoes and deliriums; with scrophulous tumours full of fœtid purulent matter; with sowre frothy ructations; with canine appetites and crudeness of digestion; besides many others needless to mention.   This doctor therefore proposed, that upon the meeting of a senate, certain physicians should attend at the three first days of their sitting, and at the close of each day's debate, feel the pulses of every senator; after which, having maturely considered, and consulted upon the nature of the several maladies, and the methods of cure; they should on the fourth day return to the senate-house, attended by their apothecaries stored with proper medicines; and before the members sat, administer to each of them lenitives, aperitives, abstersives, corrosives, restrin-

gents, palliatives, laxatives, cephalalgicks, ictericks, apo-
phlegmaticks, acousticks, as their several cases required;
and, according as these medicines should operate, repeat,
alter, or omit them at the next meeting.

This project could not be of any great expence to the
publick; and might, in my poor opinion, be of much use
for the dispatch of business in those countries, where senates
have any share in the legislative power; beget unanimity,
shorten debates, open a few mouths which are now closed,
and close many more, which are now open; curb the petu-
lancy of the young, and correct the positiveness of the old;
rouse the stupid, and damp the pert.

Again; because it is a general complaint, that the
favourites of princes are troubled with short and weak
memories; the same doctor proposed, that whoever attended
a First Minister, after having told his business with the
utmost brevity, and in the plainest words; should at his
departure, give the said minister, a tweak by the nose, or a
kick in the belly, or tread on his corns, or lug him thrice by
both ears, or run a pin into his breech, or pinch his arm
black and blue; to prevent forgetfulness: and, at every levee
day, repeat the same operation, until the business were
done, or absolutely refused.

He likewise directed, that every senator in the great
council of a nation, after he had delivered his opinion, and
argued in the defence of it, should be obliged to give his
vote directly contrary; because if that were done, the
result would infallibly terminate in the good of the
publick.

When parties in a State are violent, he offered a wonderful contrivance to reconcile them: the method is this. You
take an hundred leaders of each party; you dispose them
into couples of such whose heads are nearest of a size; then
let two nice operators saw off the occiput of each couple at
the same time, in such a manner, that the brain may be

equally divided. Let the occiputs thus cut off be inter-
changed, applying each to the head of his opposite party-
man. It seems indeed to be a work that requireth some
exactness; but the professor assured us, that if it were
dextrously performed, the cure would be infallible. For,
he argued thus; that the two half brains being left to
debate the matter between themselves within the space of
one scull, would soon come to a good understanding, and
produce that moderation as well as regularity of thinking,
so much to be wished for in the heads of those, who imagine
they came into the world only to watch and govern its
motion: and as to the difference of brains in quantity or
quality, among those who are directors in faction; the
doctor assured us from his own knowledge, that it was a
perfect trifle.

I heard a very warm debate between two professors,
about the most commodious and effectual ways and means
of raising money without grieving the subject. The first
affirmed, the justest method would be to lay a certain tax
upon vices and folly; and the sum fixed upon every man,
to be rated after the fairest manner, by a jury of his neighbours. The second was of an opinion directly contrary;
to tax those qualities of body and mind for which men
chiefly value themselves; the rate to be more or less according to the degrees of excelling; the decision whereof should
be left entirely to their own breast. The highest tax was
upon men, who are the greatest favourites of the other sex;
and the assessments according to the number and natures
of the favours they have received; for which they are
allowed to be their own vouchers. Wit, valour, and polite-
ness were likewise proposed to be largely taxed, and collected in the same manner, by every person giving his own
word for the quantum of what he possessed. But, as to
honour, justice, wisdom and learning, they should not be
taxed at all; because, they are qualifications of so singular

a kind, that no man will either allow them in his neighbour, or value them in himself.

The women were proposed to be taxed according to their beauty and skill in dressing; wherein they had the same privilege with the men, to be determined by their own judgment. But constancy, chastity, good sense, and good nature were not rated, because they would not bear the charge of collecting.

To keep senators in the interest of the Crown, it was proposed that the members should raffle for employments; every man first taking an oath, and giving security that he would vote for the court, whether he won or no; after which the losers had in their turn the liberty of raffling upon the next vacancy. Thus, hope and expectation would be kept alive; none would complain of broken promises, but impute their disappointments wholly to fortune, whose shoulders are broader and stronger than those of a ministry.

Another professor shewed me a large paper of instructions for discovering plots and conspiracies against the Government. He advised great statesmen to examine into the diet of all suspected persons; their times of eating; upon which side they lay in bed; with which hand they wiped their posteriors; to take a strict view of their excrements, and from the colour, the odour, the taste, the consistence, the crudeness, or maturity of digestion, form a judgment of their thoughts and designs: because, men are never so serious, thoughtful, and intent, as when they are at stool; which he found by frequent experiment: for in such conjectures, when he used merely as a trial to consider which was the best way of murdering the king, his ordure would have a tincture of green; but quite different when he thought only of raising an insurrection, or burning the metropolis.

The whole discourse was written with great acuteness, containing many observations both curious and useful for politicians; but, as I conceived, not altogether compleat. This I ventured to tell the author, and offered, if he pleased, to supply him with some additions. He received my proposition with more compliance than is usual among writers, especially those of the projecting species; professing he would be glad to receive farther information.

I told him, that in the kingdom of Tribnia by the natives called Langden, where I had long sojourned, the bulk of the people consisted wholly of discoverers, witnesses, informers, accusers, prosecutors, evidences, swearers; together with their several subservient and subaltern instruments; all under the colours, the conduct, and pay of ministers and their deputies. The plots in that kingdom are usually the workmanship of those persons who desire to raise their own characters of profound politicians; to restore new vigour to a crazy administration; to stifle or divert general discontents; to fill their coffers with forfeitures; and raise or sink the opinion of publick credit, as either shall best answer their private advantage. It is first agreed and settled among them, what suspected persons shall be accused of a plot: then, effectual care is taken to secure all their letters and other papers, and put the owners in chains. These papers are delivered to a set of artists very dextrous in finding out the mysterious meanings of words, syllables and letters. For instance, they can decypher a close-stool, to signify a privy-council; a flock of geese, a senate; a lame dog, an invader; the plague, a standing army; a buzard, a minister; the gout, a high priest; a gibbet, a Secretary of State; a chamber-pot, a committee of grandees; a sieve, a court lady; a broom, a revolution; a mouse-trap, an employment; a bottomless pit, the treasury; a sink, a c——t; a cap and bells, a favourite; a broken reed, a court of justice; an empty tun, a general; a running sore, the Administration.

When this method fails, they have two others more effectual; which, the learned among them call acrosticks, and anagrams.   First, they can decypher all initial letters into political meanings: thus, *N*, shall signify a plot; *B*, a regiment of horse; *L*, a fleet at sea.   Or, secondly, by transposing the letters of the alphabet, in any suspected paper, they can lay open the deepest designs of a discontented party.   So, for example, if I should say in a letter to a friend, 'Our brother Tom hath just got the piles'; a man of skill in this art would discover how the same letters which compose that sentence, may be analysed into the following words; 'Resist,——a plot is brought home—the tour.' And, this is the anagrammatick method.

The professor made me great acknowledgments for communicating these observations, and promised to make honourable mention of me in his treatise.

I saw nothing in this country that could invite me to a longer continuance; and began to think of returning home to England.

CHAPTER VII

The author leaves Lagado, arrives at Maldonada.   No ship ready.   He takes a short voyage to Glubbdubdrib.   His reception by the governor.

THE continent of which this kingdom is a part, extends itself, as I have reason to believe, eastward to that unknown tract of America, westward of California, and north to the Pacifick Ocean, which is not above an hundred and fifty miles from Lagado; where there is a good port, and much commerce with the great island of Luggnagg, situated to the north-west about 29 degrees north latitude, and 140 longitude.   This island of Luggnagg stands south eastwards of Japan, about an hundred leagues distant.   There is a strict alliance between the Japanese emperor, and the King of Luggnagg, which affords frequent opportunities of sailing from one island to the other. I determined therefore to direct my course this way, in order to my return to Europe. I hired two mules with a guide to shew me the way, and carry my small baggage. I took leave of my noble protector, who had shewn me so much favour, and made me a generous present at my departure.

My journey was without any accident or adventure worth relating. When I arrived at the port of Maldonada, (for so it is called) there was no ship in the harbour bound for Luggnagg, nor like to be in some time. The town is about as large as Portsmouth. I soon fell into some acquaintance, and was very hospitably received. A gentleman of distinction said to me, that since the ships bound for Luggnagg, could not be ready in less than a month, it might be no disagreeable amusement for me to take a trip to the little island of Glubbdubdrib, about five leagues off to the southwest. He offered himself and a friend to accompany me, and that I should be provided with a small convenient barque for the voyage.

'Glubbdubdrib,' as nearly as I can interpret the word, signifies the Island of Sorcerers or Magicians. It is about one third as large as the Isle of Wight, and extreamly fruitful: it is governed by the head of a certain tribe, who are all magicians. This tribe marries only among each other; and the eldest in succession is prince or governor. He hath a noble palace, and a park of about three thousand acres, surrounded by a wall of hewn stone twenty foot high. In this park are several small inclosures for cattle, corn and gardening.

The governor and his family are served and attended by domesticks of a kind somewhat unusual. By his skill in

necromancy, he hath power of calling whom he pleaseth
from the dead, and commanding their service for twenty
four hours, but no longer; nor can he call the same persons
up again in less than three months, except upon very
extraordinary occasions.

When we arrived at the island, which was about eleven
in the morning, one of the gentlemen who accompanied
me, went to the governor, and desired admittance for a
stranger, who came on purpose to have the honour of
attending on his Highness. This was immediately granted,
and we all three entered the gate of the palace between two
rows of guards, armed and dressed after a very antick
manner, and something in their countenances that made
my flesh creep with a horror I cannot express. We passed
through several apartments between servants of the same
sort, ranked on each side as before, until we came to
the chamber of presence, where after three profound obey-
sances, and a few general questions, we were permitted to
sit on three stools near the lowest step of his Highness's
throne. He understood the language of Balnibarbi, although it were different from that of his island. He desired
me to give him some account of my travels; and to let me
see that I should be treated without ceremony, he dismissed
all his attendants with a turn of his finger, at which to my
great astonishment they vanished in an instant, like visions
in a dream, when we awake on a sudden. I could not
recover my self in some time, until the governor assured me
that I should receive no hurt; and observing my two companions to be under no concern, who had been often entertained in the same manner, I began to take courage; and
related to his Highness a short history of my several adventures, yet not without some hesitation, and frequently
looking behind me to the place where I had seen those
domestick spectres. I had the honour to dine with the
governor, where a new set of ghosts served up the meat,

and waited at table. I now observed my self to be less terrified than I had been in the morning. I stayed until sun-set, but humbly desired his Highness to excuse me for not accepting his invitation of lodging in the palace. My two friends and I lay at a private house in the town adjoining, which is the capital of this little island; and the next morning we returned to pay our duty to the governor, as he was pleased to command us.

After this manner we continued in the island for ten days, most part of every day with the governor, and at night in our lodging. I soon grew so familiarized to the sight of spirits, that after the third or fourth time they gave me no emotion at all; or if I had any apprehensions left, my curiosity prevailed over them. For his Highness the governor ordered me to call up whatever persons I would chuse to name, and in whatever numbers among all the dead from the beginning of the world to the present time, and command them to answer any questions I should think fit to ask; with this condition, that my questions must be confined within the compass of the times they lived in. And one thing I might depend upon, that they would certainly tell me truth; for lying was a talent of no use in the lower world.

I made my humble acknowledgments to his Highness for so great a favour. We were in a chamber, from whence there was a fair prospect into the park. And because my first inclination was to be entertained with scenes of pomp and magnificence, I desired to see Alexander the Great, at the head of his army just after the battle of Arbela; which upon a motion of the governor's finger immediately appeared in a large field under the window, where we stood. Alexander was called up into the room: it was with great difficulty that I understood his Greek, and had but little of my own. He assured me upon his honour, that he was not poisoned, but dyed of a fever by excessive drinking.

Next I saw Hannibal passing the Alps, who told me he had not a drop of vinegar in his camp.

I saw Cæsar and Pompey at the head of their troops just ready to engage. I saw the former in his last great triumph. I desired that the Senate of Rome might appear before me in one large chamber, and a modern representative, in counterview, in another. The first seemed to be an assembly of heroes and demi-gods; the other, a knot of pedlars, pick-pockets, highwaymen, and bullies.

The governor, at my request, gave the sign for Cæsar and Brutus to advance towards us. I was struck with a profound veneration at the sight of Brutus; and could easily discover the most consummate virtue, the greatest intrepidity, and firmness of mind, the truest love of his country, and general benevolence for mankind in every lineament of his countenance. I observed with much pleasure, that these two persons were in good intelligence with each other; and Cæsar freely confessed to me, that the greatest actions of his own life were not equal by many degrees to the glory of taking it away. I had the honour to have much conversation with Brutus; and was told, that his ancestor Junius, Socrates, Epaminondas, Cato the Younger, Sir Thomas More, and himself, were perpetually together: a sextumvirate to which all the ages of the world cannot add a seventh.

It would be tedious to trouble the reader with relating what vast numbers of illustrious persons were called up, to gratify that insatiable desire I had to see the world in every period of antiquity placed before me. I chiefly fed mine eyes with beholding the destroyers of tyrants and usurpers, and the restorers of liberty to oppressed and injured nations. But, it is impossible to express the satisfaction I received in my own mind, after such a manner as to make it a suitable entertainment to the reader.

CHAPTER VIII

A further account of Glubbdubdrib.   Antient and modern
history corrected.

HAVING a desire to see those antients, who were most renowned for wit and learning, I set apart one day on purpose.   I proposed that Homer and Aristotle might appear
at the head of all their commentators; but these were so
numerous, that some hundreds were forced to attend in the
court and outward rooms of the palace.   I knew, and could
distinguish those two heroes at first sight, not only from the
crowd, but from each other.   Homer was the taller and
comelier person of the two, walked very erect for one
of his age, and his eyes were the most quick and
piercing I ever beheld.   Aristotle stooped much, and
made use of a staff.   His visage was meager, his hair
lank and thin, and his voice hollow.   I soon discovered,
that both of them were perfect strangers to the rest of the
company, and had never seen or heard of them before.
And I had a whisper from a ghost, who shall be nameless,
that these commentators always kept in the most distant
quarters from their principals in the lower world, through a
consciousness of shame and guilt, because they had so
horribly misrepresented the meaning of those authors to
posterity.   I introduced Didymus and Eustathius to
Homer, and prevailed on him to treat them better than
perhaps they deserved; for he soon found they wanted a
genius to enter into the spirit of a poet.   But Aristotle was
out of all patience with the account I gave him of Scotus and
Ramus, as I presented them to him; and he asked them
whether the rest of the tribe were as great dunces as
themselves.

I then desired the governor to call up Descartes and
Gassendi, with whom I prevailed to explain their systems

to Aristotle. This great philosopher freely acknowledged his own mistakes in natural philosophy, because he proceeded in many things upon conjecture, as all men must do; and he found, that Gassendi, who had made the doctrine of Epicurus as palatable as he could, and the *vortices* of Descartes, were equally exploded. He predicted the same fate to *attraction*, whereof the present learned are such zealous asserters. He said, that new systems of nature were but new fashions, which would vary in every age; and even those who pretend to demonstrate them from mathematical principles, would flourish but a short period of time, and be out of vogue when that was determined.

I spent five days in conversing with many others of the antient learned. I saw most of the first Roman emperors. I prevailed on the governor to call up Eliogabalus's cooks to dress us a dinner; but they could not shew us much of their skill, for want of materials. A helot of Agesilaus made us a dish of Spartan broth, but I was not able to get down a second spoonful.

The two gentlemen who conducted me to the island were pressed by their private affairs to return in three days, which I employed in seeing some of the modern dead, who had made the greatest figure for two or three hundred years past in our own and other countries of Europe; and having been always a great admirer of old illustrious families, I desired the governor would call up a dozen or two of kings with their ancestors in order, for eight or nine generations. But my disappointment was grievous and unexpected. For, instead of a long train with royal diadems, I saw in one family two fidlers, three spruce courtiers, and an Italian prelate. In another, a barber, an abbot, and two cardinals. I have too great a veneration for crowned heads to dwell any longer on so nice a subject: but as to counts, marquesses, dukes, earls, and the like, I was not so scrupulous. And I confess, it was not without some pleasure that I found my self able to trace the particular features, by which certain families are distinguished up to their originals. I could plainly discover from whence one family derives a long chin; why a second hath abounded with knaves for two generations, and fools for two more; why a third happened to be crack-brained; and a fourth, to be sharpers. Whence it came, what Polydore Virgil says of a certain great house, 'Nec vir fortis, nec fœmina casta.' How cruelty, falshood, and cowardice grew to be characteristicks, by which certain families are distinguished as much as by their coat of arms. Who first brought the pox into a noble house, which hath lineally descended in scrophulous tumours to their posterity. Neither could I wonder at all this, when I saw such an interruption of lineages by pages, lacqueys, valets, coachmen, gamesters, fidlers, players, captains, and pick-pockets.

I was chiefly disgusted with modern history. For having strictly examined all the persons of greatest name in the courts of princes for an hundred years past, I found how the world had been misled by prostitute writers, to ascribe the greatest exploits in war to cowards, the wisest counsel to fools, sincerity to flatterers, Roman virtue to betrayers of their country, piety to atheists, chastity to sodomites, truth to informers. How many innocent and excellent persons had been condemned to death or banishment, by the practising of great ministers upon the corruption of judges, and the malice of factions. How many villains had been exalted to the highest places of trust, power, dignity, and profit: how great a share in the motions and events of courts, councils, and senates might be challenged by bawds, whores, pimps, parasites, and buffoons: how low an opinion I had of human wisdom and integrity, when I was truly informed of the springs and motives of great enterprizes and revolutions in the world, and of the contemptible accidents to which they owed their success.

Here I discovered the roguery and ignorance of those
who pretend to write *anecdotes*, or secret history; who send
so many kings to their graves with a cup of poison; will
repeat the discourse between a prince and chief minister,
where no witness was by; unlock the thoughts and cabinets
of ambassadors and Secretaries of State; and have the
perpetual misfortune to be mistaken. Here I discovered
the true causes of many great events that have surprized
the world: how a whore can govern the back-stairs, the
back-stairs a council, and the council a senate. A general
confessed in my presence, that he got a victory purely by
the force of cowardice and ill conduct: and an admiral,
that for want of proper intelligence, he beat the enemy to
whom he intended to betray the fleet. Three kings protested to me, that in their whole reigns they did never once
prefer any person of merit, unless by mistake or treachery
of some minister in whom they confided: neither would
they do it, if they were to live again; and they shewed with
great strength of reason, that the royal throne could not
be supported without corruption; because, that positive,
confident, restive temper, which virtue infused into man,
was a perpetual clog to publick business.

I had the curiosity to enquire in a particular manner, by
what method great numbers had procured to themselves
high titles of honour, and prodigious estates; and I confined
my enquiry to a very modern period: however, without
grating upon present times, because I would be sure to give
no offence, even to foreigners. (For I hope the reader need
not be told, that I do not in the least intend my own
country, in what I say upon this occasion.) A great
number of persons concerned were called up, and upon a
very slight examination, discovered such a scene of infamy,
that I cannot reflect upon it without some seriousness.
Perjury, oppression, subornation, fraud, pandarism, and
the like *infirmities* were amongst the most excuseable arts

they had to mention; and for these I gave, as it was reasonable, due allowance. But, when some confessed, they owed their greatness and wealth to sodomy or incest; others to the prostituting of their own wives and daughters; others to the betraying their country or their prince; some to poisoning, more to the perverting of justice in order to destroy the innocent: I hope, I may be pardoned, if these discoveries inclined me a little to abate of that profound veneration, which I am naturally apt to pay to persons of high rank, who ought to be treated with the utmost respect due to their sublime dignity, by us their inferiors.

I had often read of some great services done to princes and States, and desired to see the persons by whom those services were performed. Upon enquiry, I was told, that their names were to be found on no record, except a few of them whom history hath represented as the vilest rogues and traitors. As to the rest, I had never once heard of them. They all appeared with dejected looks, and in the meanest habit; most of them telling me they died in poverty and disgrace, and the rest on a scaffold or a gibbet.

Among others, there was one person whose case appeared a little singular. He had a youth about eighteen years old standing by his side. He told me, he had for many years been commander of a ship; and in the sea fight at Actium, had the good fortune to break through the enemy's great line of battle, sink three of their capital ships, and take a fourth, which was the sole cause of Antony's flight, and of the victory that ensued: that, the youth standing by him, his only son, was killed in the action. He added, that upon the confidence of some merit, the war being at an end, he went to Rome, and sollicited at the court of Augustus, to be preferred to a greater ship, whose commander had been killed; but without any regard to his pretensions, it was given to a boy who had never seen the sea, the son of a *libertina*, who waited on one of the emperor's mistresses.

Returning back to his own vessel, he was charged with neglect of duty, and the ship given to a favourite page of Publicola the vice-admiral; whereupon he retired to a poor farm, at a great distance from Rome, and there ended his life.   I was so curious to know the truth of this story, that I desired Agrippa might be called, who was admiral in that fight.   He appeared, and confirmed the whole account, but with much more advantage to the captain; whose modesty had extenuated or concealed a great part of his merit.

I was surprized to find corruption grown so high and so quick in that empire, by the force of luxury so lately introduced; which made me less wonder at many parallel cases in other countries, where vices of all kinds have reigned so much longer, and where the whole praise as well as pillage, hath been engrossed by the chief commander; who, perhaps, had the least title to either.

As every person called up, made exactly the same appearance he had done in the world, it gave me melancholy reflections to observe how much the race of human kind was degenerate among us, within these hundred years past. How the pox under all its consequences and denominations had altered every lineament of an English countenance, shortened the size of bodies, unbraced the nerves, relaxed the sinews and muscles, introduced a sallow complexion, and rendered the flesh loose and *rancid*.

I descended so low as to desire that some English yoemen of the old stamp, might be summoned to appear; once so famous for the simplicity of their manners, diet, and dress; for justice in their dealings; for their true spirit of liberty; for their valour and love of their country.   Neither could I be wholly unmoved after comparing the living with the dead, when I considered how all these pure native virtues were prostituted for a piece of money by their grand-children; who in selling their votes, and managing at elections, have acquired every vice and corruption that can possibly be learned in court.

CHAPTER IX

The author's return to Maldonada.   Sails to the kingdom of
    Luggnagg.   The author confined.   He is sent for to court.
    The manner of his admittance.   The king's great lenity to
    his subjects.

THE day of our departure being come, I took leave of his
Highness the Governor of Glubbdubdribb, and returned
with my two companions to Maldonada, where, after a
fortnight's waiting, a ship was ready to sail for Luggnagg.
The two gentlemen, and some others, were so generous and
kind, as to furnish me with provisions, and see me on board.
I was a month in this voyage.   We had one violent storm,
and were under a necessity of steering westward to get into
the trade-wind, which holds for above sixty leagues.   On
the 21st of April, 1708, we sailed in the river of Clumegnig,
which is a sea-port town, at the south-east point of Luggnagg.   We cast anchor within a league of the town, and
made a signal for a pilot.   Two of them came on board in
less than half an hour, by whom we were guided between
certain shoals and rocks, which are very dangerous in the
passage, to a large basin, where a fleet may ride in safety
within a cable's length of the town wall.

Some of our sailors, whether out of treachery, or in-
advertence, had informed the pilots that I was a stranger,
and a great traveller, whereof these gave notice to a custom-
house officer, by whom I was examined very strictly upon
my landing. ⁻ This officer spoke to me in the language of
Balnibarbi, which by the force of much commerce is
generally understood in that town, especially by seamen,
and those employed in the customs.   I gave him a short
account of some particulars, and made my story as plausible
and consistent as I could; but I thought it necessary to
disguise my country, and call my self an Hollander; because

my intentions were for Japan, and I knew the Dutch were the only Europeans permitted to enter into that kingdom. I therefore told the officer, that having been shipwrecked on the coast of Balnibarbi, and cast on a rock, I was received up into Laputa, or the flying island (of which he had often heard) and was now endeavouring to get to Japan, from whence I might find a convenience of returning to my own country. The officer said, I must be confined until he could receive orders from court, for which he would write immediately, and hoped to receive an answer in a fortnight. I was carried to a convenient lodging, with a centry placed at the door; however, I had the liberty of a large garden, and was treated with humanity enough, being maintained all the time at the king's charge. I was invited by several persons, chiefly out of curiosity, because it was reported I came from countries very remote, of which they had never heard.

I hired a young man who came in the same ship to be an interpreter; he was a native of Luggnagg, but had lived some years at Maldonada, and was a perfect master of both languages. By his assistance, I was able to hold a conversation with those that came to visit me; but this consisted only of their questions and my answers.

The dispatch came from court about the time we expected. It contained a warrant for conducting me and my retinue to Traldragdubb or Trildrogdrib, (for it is pronounced both ways as near as I can remember) by a party of ten horse. All my retinue was that poor lad for an interpreter, whom I persuaded into my service. At my humble request, we had each of us a mule to ride on. A messenger was dispatched half a day's journey before us, to give the king notice of my approach, and to desire that his Majesty would please to appoint a day and hour, when it would be his gracious pleasure that I might have the honour to *lick the dust before his footstool*. This is the court style, and I found it to be more than matter of form: for, upon my admittance two days after my arrival, I was commanded to crawl upon my belly, and lick the floor as I advanced; but on account of my being a stranger, care was taken to have it so clean, that the dust was not offensive. However, this was a peculiar grace, not allowed to any, but persons of the highest rank, when they desire an admittance: nay, sometimes the floor is strewed with dust on purpose, when the person to be admitted happens to have powerful enemies at court: and I have seen a great lord with his mouth so crammed, that when he had crept to the proper distance from the throne, he was not able to speak a word. Neither is there any remedy, because it is capital for those who receive an audience, to spit or wipe their mouths in his Majesty's presence. There is indeed another custom, which I cannot altogether approve of. When the king hath a mind to put any of his nobles to death in a gentle indulgent manner; he commands to have the floor strowed with a certain brown powder, of a deadly composition, which being licked up, infallibly kills him in twenty-four hours. But in justice to this prince's great clemency, and the care he hath of his subjects lives, (wherein it were much to be wished that the monarchs of Europe would imitate him) it must be mentioned for his honour, that strict orders are given to have the infected parts of the floor well washed after every such execution; which, if his domesticks neglect, they are in danger of incurring his royal displeasure. I my self heard him give directions, that one of his pages should be whipt, whose turn it was to give notice about washing the floor after an execution, but maliciously had omitted it; by which neglect, a young lord, of great hopes, coming to an audience, was unfortunately poisoned, although the king, at that time, had no design against his life. But this good prince was so gracious, as to forgive the page his whipping, upon promise that he would do so no more, without special orders.

To return from this digression; when I had crept within four yards of the throne, I raised my self gently upon my knees, and then striking my forehead seven times against the ground, I pronounced the following words, as they had been taught me the night before, 'Ickpling gloffthrobb squutserumm blhiop mlashnalt zwin tnodbalkguffh slhiophad gurdlubh asht.' This is the compliment established by the laws of the land for all persons admitted to the king's presence. It may be rendered into English thus: 'May your cœlestial Majesty out-live the sun, eleven moons and an half.' To this the king returned some answer, which although I could not understand, yet I replied as I had been directed; 'Fluft drin yalerick dwuldum prastrad mirplush,' which properly signifies, 'My tongue is in the mouth of my friend'; and by this expression was meant, that I desired leave to bring my interpreter; whereupon the young man already mentioned, was accordingly introduced; by whose intervention I answered as many questions as his Majesty could put in above an hour. I spoke in the Balnibarbian tongue, and my interpreter delivered my meaning in that of Luggnagg.

The king was much delighted with my company, and ordered his *Bliffmarklub*, or High Chamberlain, to appoint a lodging in the court for me, and my interpreter, with a daily allowance for my table, and a large purse of gold for my common expences.

I stayed three months in this country out of perfect obedience to his Majesty, who was pleased highly to favour me, and made me very honourable offers. But I thought it more consistent with prudence and justice to pass the remainder of my days with my wife and family.

CHAPTER X

The Luggnaggians commended. A particular description of the Struldbruggs, with many conversations between the author and some eminent persons upon that subject.

THE Luggnaggians are a polite and generous people, and although they are not without some share of that pride which is peculiar to all eastern countries, yet they shew themselves courteous to strangers, especially such who are countenanced by the court. I had many acquaintance among persons of the best fashion; and being always attended by my interpreter, the conversation we had was not disagreeable.

One day in much good company, I was asked by a person of quality, whether I had seen any of their Struldbruggs, or Immortals. I said I had not; and desired he would explain to me what he meant by such an appellation, applyed to a mortal creature. He told me, that sometimes, although very rarely, a child happened to be born in a family with a red circular spot in the forehead, directly over the left eye-brow, which was an infallible mark that it should never dye. The spot, as he described it, was about the compass of a silver threepence, but in the course of time grew larger, and changed its colour; for at twelve years old it became green, so continued until five and twenty, then turned to a deep blue; at five and forty it grew coal-black, and as large as an English shilling; but never admitted any farther alteration. He said these births were so rare, that he did not believe there could be above eleven hundred Struldbruggs of both sexes in the whole kingdom, of which he computed about fifty in the metropolis, and among the rest a young girl born about three years ago. That, these productions were not peculiar to any family, but a meer effect of chance; and the children of the Struldbruggs themselves, were equally mortal with the rest of the people.

I freely own my self to have been struck with inexpressible delight upon hearing this account: and the person who gave it me happening to understand the Balnibarbian language, which I spoke very well, I could not forbear breaking out into expressions perhaps a little too extravagant. I cryed out as in a rapture; 'Happy nation, where every child hath at least a chance for being immortal! Happy people who enjoy so many living examples of antient virtue, and have masters ready to instruct them in the wisdom of all former ages! But, happiest beyond all comparison are those excellent Struldbruggs, who being born exempt from that universal calamity of human nature, have their minds free and disingaged, without the weight and depression of spirits caused by the continual apprehension of death.' I discovered my admiration that I had not observed any of these illustrious persons at court; the black spot on the forehead, being so remarkable a distinction, that I could not have easily overlooked it: and it was impossible that his Majesty, a most judicious prince, should not provide himself with a good number of such wise and able counsellors. Yet, perhaps, the virtue of those reverend sages was too strict for the corrupt and libertine manners of a court. And we often find by experience, that young men are too opinionative and volatile to be guided by the sober dictates of their seniors. However, since the king was pleased to allow me access to his royal person, I was resolved upon the very first occasion to deliver my opinion to him on this matter freely, and at large by the help of my interpreter; and whether he would please to take my advice or no, yet in one thing I was determined, that his Majesty having frequently offered me an establishment in this country, I would, with great thankfulness accept the favour, and pass my life here in the conversation of those superior beings the Struldbruggs, if they would please to admit me.

The gentleman to whom I addressed my discourse,

because (as I have already observed) he spoke the language of Balnibarbi, said to me with a sort of a smile, which usually ariseth from pity to the ignorant, that he was glad of any occasion to keep me among them, and desired my permission to explain to the company what I had spoke. He did so; and they talked together for some time in their own language, whereof I understood not a syllable, neither could I observe by their countenances what impression my discourse had made on them. After a short silence, the same person told me, that his friends and mine (so he thought fit to express himself) were very much pleased with the judicious remarks I had made on the great happiness and advantages of immortal life; and they were desirous to know in a particular manner, what scheme of living I should have formed to my self, if it had fallen to my lot to have been born a Struldbrugg.

I answered, it was easy to be eloquent on so copious and delightful a subject, especially to me, who have been often apt to amuse my self with visions of what I should do if I were a king, a general, or a great lord: and upon this very case, I had frequently run over the whole system how I should employ my self, and pass the time if I were sure to live for ever.

That, if it had been my good fortune to come into the world a Struldbrugg; as soon as I could discover my own happiness, by understanding the difference between life and death, I would first resolve by all arts and methods whatsoever, to procure my self riches: in the pursuit of which, by thrift and management, I might reasonably expect in about two hundred years, to be the wealthiest man in the kingdom. In the second place, I would from my earliest youth, apply my self to the study of arts and sciences, by which I should arrive in time to excel all others in learning. Lastly, I would carefully record every action and event of consequence that happened in the publick, impartially draw the characters of the several successions of princes, and great ministers of State; with my own observations on every point. I would exactly set down the several changes in customs, languages, fashions, dress, dyet and diversions. By all which acquirements, I should be a living treasury of knowledge and wisdom, and certainly become the oracle of the nation.

I would never marry after threescore, but live in an hospitable manner, yet still on the saving side. I would entertain my self in forming and directing the minds of hopeful young men, by convincing them from my own remembrance, experience and observation, fortified by numerous examples of the usefulness of virtue in publick and private life. But, my choice and constant companions, should be a set of my own immortal brotherhood; among whom I would elect a dozen from the most ancient down to my own contemporaries. Where any of these wanted fortunes, I would provide them with convenient lodges round my own estate, and have some of them always at my table, only mingling a few of the most valuable among you mortals; whom length of time would harden me to lose with little or no reluctance, and treat your posterity after the same manner: just as a man diverts himself with the annual succession of pinks and tulips in his garden, without regretting the loss of those which withered the preceding year.

These Struldbruggs and I would mutually communicate our observations and memorials through the course of time; remark the several gradations by which corruption steals into the world, and oppose it in every step, by giving perpetual warning and instruction to mankind; which, added to the strong influence of our own example, would probably prevent that continual degeneracy of human nature, so justly complained of in all ages.

Add to all this, the pleasure of seeing the various

revolutions of states and empires; the changes in the lower
and upper world; antient cities in ruins, and obscure villages
become the seats of kings.   Famous rivers lessening into
shallow brooks; the ocean leaving one coast dry, and over-
whelming another: the discovery of many countries yet
unknown.   Barbarity over-running the politest nations,
and the most barbarous becoming civilized.   I should then
see the discovery of the *longitude*, the *perpetual motion*, the
universal medicine, and many other great inventions brought
to the utmost perfection.

What wonderful discoveries should we make in astronomy, by outliving and confirming our own predictions;
by observing the progress and returns of comets, with the
changes of motion in the sun, moon and stars.

I enlarged upon many other topicks, which the natural
desire of endless life and sublunary happiness could easily
furnish me with.   When I had ended, and the sum of my
discourse had been interpreted as before, to the rest of the
company, there was a good deal of talk among them in the
language of the country, not without some laughter at my
expence.   At last, the same gentleman who had been my
interpreter, said, he was desired by the rest, to set me right
in a few mistakes, which I had fallen into through the
common imbecility of human nature, and upon that allowance was less answerable for them.   That, this breed of
Struldbruggs was peculiar to their country, for there were
no such people either in Balnibarbi or Japan, where he had
the honour to be ambassador from his Majesty, and found
the natives in both those kingdoms, very hard to believe
that the fact was possible; and it appeared from my astonishment when he first mentioned the matter to me, that
I received it as a thing wholly new, and scarcely to be
credited.   That, in the two kingdoms above-mentioned,
where during his residence he had conversed very much,
he observed long life to be the universal desire and wish of

mankind. That, whoever had one foot in the grave, was sure to hold back the other as strongly as he could. That, the oldest had still hopes of living one day longer, and looked on death as the greatest evil, from which nature always prompted him to retreat; only in this island of Luggnagg, the appetite for living was not so eager, from the continual example of the Struldbruggs before their eyes.

That, the system of living contrived by me was unreasonable and unjust, because it supposed a perpetuity of youth, health, and vigour, which no man could be so foolish to hope, however extravagant he might be in his wishes. That, the question therefore was not whether a man would chuse to be always in the prime of youth, attended with prosperity and health; but how he would pass a perpetual life under all the usual disadvantages which old age brings along with it. For, although few men will avow their desires of being immortal upon such hard conditions, yet in the two kingdoms beforementioned of Balnibarbi and Japan, he observed that every man desired to put off death for some time longer, let it approach ever so late; and he rarely heard of any man who died willingly, except he were excited by the extremity of grief or torture. And he appealed to me whether in those countries I had travelled as well as my own, I had not observed the same general disposition.

After this preface, he gave me a particular account of the Struldbruggs among them. He said they commonly acted like mortals, until about thirty years old, after which by degrees they grew melancholy and dejected, increasing in both until they came to fourscore. This he learned from their own confession; for otherwise, there not being above two or three of that species born in an age, they were too few to form a general observation by. When they came to fourscore years, which is reckoned the extremity of living in this country, they had not only all the follies and infirmities of other old men, but many more which arose from the dreadful prospect of never dying. They were not only opinionative, peevish, covetous, morose, vain, talkative; but uncapable of friendship, and dead to all natural affection, which never descended below their grand-children. Envy and impotent desires, are their prevailing passions. But those objects against which their envy seems principally directed, are the vices of the younger sort, and the deaths of the old. By reflecting on the former, they find themselves cut off from all possibility of pleasure; and whenever they see a funeral, they lament and repine that others are gone to a harbour of rest, to which they themselves never can hope to arrive. They have no remembrance of any thing but what they learned and observed in their youth and middle age, and even that is very imperfect: and for the truth or particulars of any fact, it is safer to depend on common traditions, than upon their best recollections. The least miserable among them, appear to be those who turn to dotage, and entirely lose their memories; these meet with more pity and assistance, because they want many bad qualities which abound in others.

If a Struldbrugg happen to marry one of his own kind, the marriage is dissolved of course by the courtesy of the kingdom, as soon as the younger of the two comes to be fourscore. For the law thinks it a reasonable indulgence, that those who are condemned without any fault of their own, to a perpetual continuance in the world, should not have their misery doubled by the load of a wife.

As soon as they have compleated the term of eighty years, they are looked on as dead in law; their heirs immediately succeed to their estates, only a small pittance is reserved for their support; and the poor ones are maintained at the publick charge. After that period, they are held incapable of any employment of trust or profit; they cannot purchase lands, or take leases; neither are they allowed to be witnesses in any cause, either civil or criminal, not even for the decision of meers and bounds.

At ninety they lose their teeth and hair; they have at that age no distinction of taste, but eat and drink what ever they can get, without relish or appetite. The diseases they were subject to, still continue without encreasing or diminishing. In talking, they forget the common appellation of things, and the names of persons, even of those, who are their nearest friends and relations. For the same reason, they never can amuse themselves with reading, because their memory will not serve to carry them from the beginning of a sentence to the end; and by this defect, they are deprived of the only entertainment whereof they might otherwise be capable.

The language of this country being always upon the flux, the Struldbruggs of one age, do not understand those of another; neither are they able after two hundred years, to hold any conversation (farther than by a few general words) with their neighbours the mortals; and thus they lye under the disadvantage of living like foreigners in their own country.

This was the account given me of the Struldbruggs, as near as I can remember. I afterwards saw five or six of different ages, the youngest not above two hundred years old, who were brought to me at several times by some of my friends; but although they were told that I was a great traveller, and had seen all the world, they had not the least curiosity to ask me a question; only desired I would give them *slumskudask*, or a token of remembrance; which is a modest way of begging, to avoid the law that strictly forbids it, because they are provided for by the publick, although, indeed, with a very scanty allowance.

They are despised and hated by all sorts of people: when one of them is born, it is reckoned ominous, and their birth is recorded very particularly; so that you may know their

I 60

age by consulting the registry, which however, hath not
been kept above a thousand years past, or at least, hath
been destroyed by time or publick disturbances.   But the
usual way of computing how old they are, is, by asking them
what kings or great persons they can remember, and then
consulting history; for infallibly, the last prince in their
mind, did not begin his reign after they were fourscore
years old.

They were the most mortifying sight I ever beheld; and
the women more horrible than the men.   Besides the usual
deformities in extreme old age, they acquired an additional
ghastliness in proportion to their number of years, which is
not to be described; and among half a dozen I soon distinguished which was the eldest, although there were not
above a century or two between them.

The reader will easily believe, that from what I had heard
and seen, my keen appetite for perpetuity of life was much
abated.   I grew heartily ashamed of the pleasing visions
I had formed; and thought no tyrant could invent a death,
into which I would not run with pleasure from such a life.
The king heard of all that had passed between me and my
friends upon this occasion, and rallied me very pleasantly;
wishing I would send a couple of Struldbruggs to my own
country, to arm our people against the fear of death; but
this it seems is forbidden by the fundamental laws of the
kingdom; or else, I should have been well content with the
trouble and expence of transporting them.

I could not but agree, that the laws of this kingdom
relating to the Struldbruggs, were founded upon the
strongest reasons, and such as any other country would be
under the necessity of enacting in the like circumstances.
Otherwise, as avarice is the necessary consequent of old age,
those immortals would in time, become proprietors of the
whole nation, and engross the civil power; which, for want
of abilities to manage, must end in the ruin of the publick.

CHAPTER XI

The author leaves Luggnagg and sails to Japan. From thence he returns in a Dutch ship to Amsterdam, and from Amsterdam to England.

I THOUGHT this account of the Struldbruggs might be some entertainment to the reader, because it seems to be a little out of the common way; at least, I do not remember to have met the like in any book of travels that hath come to my hands: and, if I am deceived, my excuse must be, that it is necessary for travellers who describe the same country, very often to agree in dwelling on the same particulars, without deserving the censure of having borrowed or transcribed from those who wrote before them.

There is indeed a perpetual commerce between this kingdom and the great empire of Japan; and it is very probable, that the Japanese authors may have given some account of the Struldbruggs; but my stay in Japan was so short, and I was so entirely a stranger to the language, that I was not qualified to make any enquiries. But I hope the Dutch, upon this notice, will be curious and able enough to supply my defects.

His Majesty having often pressed me to accept some employment in his court, and finding me absolutely determined to return to my native country; was pleased to give me his licence to depart; and honoured me with a letter of recommendation under his own hand, to the Emperor of Japan. He likewise presented me with four hundred forty-four large pieces of gold (this nation delighting in even numbers) and a red diamond, which I sold in England, for eleven hundred pounds.

On the 6th day of May, 1709, I took a solemn leave of his Majesty, and all my friends. This prince was so gracious, as to order a guard to conduct me to Glanguen-stald, which is a royal port to the south-west part of the island. In six days I found a vessel ready to carry me to Japan; and spent fifteen days in the voyage. We landed at a small port-town called Xamoschi, situated on the south-east part of Japan. The town lies on the western part, where there is a narrow streight, leading northward into a long arm of the sea, upon the north-west part of which, Yedo the metropolis stands. At landing I shewed the custom-house officers my letter from the King of Luggnagg to his Imperial Majesty: they knew the seal perfectly well; it was as broad as the palm of my hand. The impression was, 'A King lifting up a Lame Beggar from the Earth.' The magistrates of the town hearing of my letter, received me as a publick minister; they provided me with carriages and servants, and bore my charges to Yedo, where I was ad-mitted to an audience, and delivered my letter; which was opened with great ceremony, and explained to the emperor by an interpreter, who gave me notice of his Majesty's order, that I should signify my request; and whatever it were, it should be granted for the sake of his royal brother of Luggnagg. This interpreter was a person employed to transact affairs with the Hollanders: he soon conjectured by my countenance, that I was an European, and therefore repeated his Majesty's commands in Low-Dutch, which he spoke perfectly well. I answered (as I had before deter-mined) that I was a Dutch merchant, shipwrecked in a very remote country, from whence I travelled by sea and land to Luggnagg, and then took shipping for Japan, where I knew my countrymen often traded; and, with some of these, I hoped to get an opportunity of returning into Europe: I therefore most humbly intreated his royal favour, to give order, that I should be conducted in safety to Nanga-sac. To this I added another petition, that for the sake of my patron the King of Luggnagg, his Majesty would condescend to excuse my performing the ceremony imposed on my countrymen, of *trampling upon the crucifix*; because I had been thrown into his kingdom by my misfortunes, without any intention of trading. When this latter petition was interpreted to the emperor, he seemed a little surprized; and said, he believed I was the first of my countrymen who ever made any scruple in this point; and that he began to doubt, whether I were a real Hollander or no; but rather suspected I must be a Christian. However, for the reasons I had offered, but chiefly to gratify the King of Luggnagg, by an uncommon mark of his favour, he would comply with the *singularity* of my humour; but, the affair must be managed with dexterity, and his officers should be commanded to let me pass, as it were, by forgetfulness. For he assured me, that if the secret should be discovered by my countrymen, the Dutch, they would cut my throat in the voyage. I returned my thanks, by the interpreter, for so unusual a favour; and some troops being at that time on their march to Nangasac, the commanding officer had orders to convey me safe thither, with particular instructions about the business of the *crucifix*.

On the 9th day of June, 1709, I arrived at Nangasac, after a very long and troublesome journey. I soon fell into company of some Dutch sailors belonging to the *Amboyna* of Amsterdam, a stout ship of 450 tons. I had lived long in Holland, pursuing my studies at Leyden, and I spoke Dutch well: the seamen soon knew from whence I came last; they were curious to enquire into my voyages and course of life. I made up a story as short and probable as I could, but concealed the greatest part. I knew many persons in Holland; I was able to invent names for my parents, whom I pretended to be obscure people in the province of Guelderland. I would have given the captain (one Theodorus Vangrult) what he pleased to ask for my voyage to Holland; but, understanding I was a surgeon, he was contented to take half the usual rate, on condition that I would serve him in the way of my calling. Before we took shipping, I was often asked by some of the crew, whether I had performed the ceremony abovementioned? I evaded the question by general answers, that I had satisfied the emperor and court in all particulars. However, a malicious rogue of a skipper went to an officer, and pointing to me, told him, I had not yet *trampled upon the crucifix*: but the other, who had received instructions to let me pass, gave the rascal twenty strokes on the shoulders with a bamboo; after which I was no more troubled with such questions.

Nothing happened worth mentioning in this voyage. We sailed with a fair wind to the Cape of Good Hope, where we staid only to take in fresh water. On the 16th of April we arrived safe at Amsterdam, having lost only three men by sickness in the voyage, and a fourth who fell from the fore-mast into the sea, not far from the coast of Guinea. From Amsterdam, I soon after set sail for England, in a small vessel belonging to that city.

On the 10th of April, 1710, we put in at the Downs. I landed the next morning, and saw once more my native country, after an absence of five years and six months compleat. I went strait to Redriff, whither I arrived the same day at two in the afternoon, and found my wife and family in good health.

THE END OF THE THIRD PART

PART IV

A VOYAGE TO THE COUNTRY
OF THE HOUYHNHNMS

CHAPTER I

The author sets out as a captain of a ship. His men conspire against him, confine him a long time to his cabbin, set him on shore in an unknown land. He travels up into the country. The Yahoos, a strange sort of animal described. The author meets two Houyhnhnms.

I CONTINUED at home with my wife and children about five months in a very happy condition, if I could have learned the lesson of knowing when I was well. I left my poor wife big with child, and accepted an advantageous offer made me to be captain of the *Adventure*, a stout merchant-man of 350 tuns: for I understood navigation well, and being grown weary of a surgeon's employment at sea, which however I could exercise upon occasion, I took a skilful young man of that calling, one Robert Purefoy, into my ship. We set sail from Portsmouth upon the 7th day of September, 1710; on the 14th we met with Captain Pocock of Bristol, at Tenariff, who was going to the Bay of Campeachy to cut logwood. On the 16th, he was parted from us by a storm: I heard since my return, that his ship foundered, and none escaped, but one cabbin-boy. He was an honest man, and a good sailor, but a little too positive in his own opinions; which was the cause of his destruction, as it hath been of several others. For, if he had followed my advice, he might at this time have been safe at home with his family, as well as my self.

I had several men died in my ship of calentures, so that I was forced to get recruits out of Barbadoes, and the Lee-ward Islands, where I touched by the direction of the merchants who employed me; which I had soon too much cause to repent; for I found afterwards that most of them had been buccaneers. I had fifty hands on board; and my orders were, that I should trade with the Indians in the South-sea, and make what discoveries I could. These rogues whom I had picked up, debauched my other men, and they all formed a conspiracy to seize the ship and secure me; which they did one morning, rushing into my cabbin, and binding me hand and foot, threatning to throw me overboard, if I offered to stir. I told them, I was their prisoner, and would submit. This they made me swear to do, and then unbound me, only fastening one of my legs with a chain near my bed; and placed a centry at my door with his piece charged, who was commanded to shoot me dead, if I attempted my liberty. They sent me down victuals and drink, and took the government of the ship to themselves. Their design was to turn pirates, and plunder the Spaniards; which they could not do, until they got more men. But first, they resolved to sell the goods in the ship, and then go to Madagascar for recruits; several among them having died since my confinement. They sailed many weeks, and traded with the Indians; but I knew not what course they took, being kept close prisoner in my cabbin, and expecting nothing less than to be murdered, as they often threatned me.

Upon the 9th day of May, 1711, one James Welch came down to my cabbin; and said, he had orders from the captain to set me ashore. I expostulated with him, but in vain; neither would he so much as tell me, who their new captain was. They forced me into the long-boat, letting me put on my best suit of cloaths, which were as good as new, and a small bundle of linnen, but no arms except my hanger; and they were so civil as not to search my pockets; into which I conveyed what money I had, with some other little necessaries. They rowed about a league; and then set me down on a strand. I desired them to tell me what country it was: they all swore, they knew no more than my self, but said, that the captain (as they called him) was resolved, after they had sold the lading, to get rid of me in the first place where they discovered land. They pushed off immediately, advising me to make haste, for fear of being overtaken by the tide; and bade me farewell.

In this desolate condition, I advanced forward, and soon got upon firm ground, where I sat down on a bank to rest my self, and consider what I had best to do. When I was a little refreshed, I went up into the country, resolving to deliver my self to the first savages I should meet; and purchase my life from them by some bracelets, glass rings, and other toys, which sailors usually provide themselves with in those voyages, and whereof I had some about me: the land was divided by long rows of trees, not regularly planted, but naturally growing; there was great plenty of grass, and several fields of oats. I walked very circumspectly for fear of being surprized, or suddenly shot with an arrow from behind, or on either side. I fell into a beaten road, where I saw many tracts of human feet, and some of cows, but most of horses. At last, I beheld several animals in a field, and one or two of the same kind sitting in trees. Their shape was very singular, and deformed, which a little discomposed me, so that I lay down behind a thicket to observe them better. Some of them coming forward near the place where I lay, gave me an opportunity of distinctly marking their form. Their heads and breasts were covered with a thick hair, some frizzled and others lank; they had beards like goats, and a long ridge of hair down their backs, and the fore parts of their legs and feet; but the rest of their bodies were bare, so that I might see their skins, which were of a brown buff colour. They had no tails, nor any hair at all on their buttocks, except about the *anus*; which, I presume, nature had placed there to defend them as they sat on the ground, for this posture they used, as well as lying down, and often stood on their hind feet. They climbed high trees as nimbly as a squirrel, for they had strong extended claws before and behind, terminating on sharp points, hooked. They would often spring, and bound, and leap with prodigious agility. The females were not so large as the males; they had long lank hair on their heads, and only a sort of down on the rest of their bodies, except about the *anus*, and *pudenda*. Their dugs hung between their fore feet, and often reached almost to the ground as they walked. The hair of both sexes was of several colours, brown, red, black and yellow. Upon the whole, I never beheld in all my travels so disagreeable an animal, or one against which I naturally conceived so strong an antipathy. So, that thinking I had seen enough, full of contempt and aversion, I got up and pursued the beaten road, hoping it might direct me to the cabbin of some Indian. I had not gone far, when I met one of these creatures full in my way, and coming up directly to me. The ugly monster, when he saw me, distorted several ways every feature of his visage, and stared, as at an object he had never seen before; then, approaching nearer, lifted up his fore paw, whether out of curiosity or mischief, I could not tell: but I drew my hanger, and gave him a good blow with the flat side of it; for I durst not strike him with the edge, fearing the inhabitants might be provoked against me, if they should come to know, that I had killed or maimed any of their cattle. When the beast felt the smart, he drew back, and roared so loud, that a herd, of at least forty, came flocking about me from the next field, howling and making odious faces; but I ran to the body of a tree, and leaning my back against it, kept them off, by waving my hanger. Several of this cursed brood getting hold of the branches behind, leaped up into the tree; from whence they began to discharge their excrements on my head: however, I escaped pretty well, by sticking close to the stem of the tree, but was almost stifled with the filth; which fell about me on every side.

In the midst of this distress, I observed them all to run away on a sudden as fast as they could; at which I ventured to leave the tree, and pursue the road, wondering what it was that could put them into this fright. But looking on my left hand, I saw a horse walking softly in the field; which my persecutors having sooner discovered, was the cause of their flight. The horse started a little when he came near me, but soon recovering himself, looked full in my face with manifest tokens of wonder: he viewed my hands and feet, walking round me several times. I would have pursued my journey, but he placed himself directly in the way; yet looking with a very mild aspect, never offering the least violence. We stood gazing at each other for some time; at last, I took the boldness to reach my hand towards his neck, with a design to stroak it; using the common style and whistle of jockies when they are going to handle a strange horse. But, this animal seeming to receive my civilities with disdain, shook his head, and bent his brows, softly raising up his left fore foot to remove my hand. Then he neighed three or four times, but in so different a cadence, that I almost began to think he was speaking to himself in some language of his own.

While he and I were thus employed, another horse came up; who applying himself to the first in a very formal manner; they gently struck each others right hoof before, neighing several times by turns, and varying the sound, which seemed to be almost articulate. They went some paces off, as if it were to confer together, walking side by side, backward and forward, like persons deliberating upon some affair of weight; but often turning their eyes towards me, as it were to watch that I might not escape. I was amazed to see such actions and behaviour in brute beasts; and concluded with my self, that if the inhabitants of this country were endued with a proportionable degree of reason, they must needs be the wisest people upon earth. This thought gave me so much comfort, that I resolved to go forward until I could discover some house or village, or meet with any of the natives; leaving the two horses to discourse together as they pleased. But the first, who was a dapple-grey, observing me to steal off, neighed after me in so expressive a tone, that I fancied my self to understand what he meant; whereupon I turned back, and came near him, to expect his farther commands; but concealing my fear as much as I could; for I began to be in some pain, how this adventure might terminate; and the reader will easily believe, I did not much like my present situation.

The two horses came up close to me, looking with great earnestness upon my face and hands. The grey steed rubbed my hat all round with his right fore hoof, and discomposed it so much, that I was forced to adjust it better, by taking it off, and settling it again; whereat both he and his companion, (who was a brown bay) appeared to be much surprized; the latter felt the lappet of my coat, and finding it to hang loose about me, they both looked with new signs of wonder. He stroked my right hand, seeming to admire the softness, and colour; but he squeezed it so hard between his hoof and his pastern, that I was forced to roar; after which they both touched me with all possible tenderness. They were under great perplexity about my shoes and stockings, which they felt very often, neighing to each other, and using various gestures, not unlike those of a philosopher, when he would attempt to solve some new and difficult phænomenon.

Upon the whole, the behaviour of these animals was so orderly and rational, so acute and judicious, that I at last concluded, they must needs be magicians, who had thus metamorphosed themselves upon some design; and seeing a stranger in the way, were resolved to divert themselves with him; or perhaps were really amazed at the sight of a man so very different in habit, feature and complexion from those who might probably live in so remote a climate. Upon the strength of this reasoning, I ventured to address them in the following manner: 'Gentlemen, if you be conjurers, as I have good cause to believe, you can understand any language; therefore I make bold to let your worships know, that I am a poor distressed Englishman, driven by his misfortunes upon your coast; and I entreat one of you to let me ride upon his back, as if he were a real horse, to some house or village, where I can be relieved. In return of which favour, I will make you a present of this knife and bracelet' (taking them out of my pocket.) The two creatures stood silent while I spoke, seeming to listen with great attention; and when I had ended, they neighed frequently towards each other, as if they were engaged in serious conversation. I plainly observed, that their language expressed the passions very well, and the words might with little pains be resolved into an alphabet more easily than the Chinese.

I could frequently distinguish the word 'Yahoo,' which was repeated by each of them several times; and although it were impossible for me to conjecture what it meant, yet while the two horses were busy in conversation, I endeavoured to practise this word upon my tongue; and as soon as they were silent, I boldly pronounced 'Yahoo' in a loud voice, imitating, at the same time, as near as I could, the neighing of a horse; at which they were both visibly surprized, and the grey repeated the same word twice, as if he meant to teach me the right accent, wherein I spoke after him as well as I could, and found my self percievably to improve every time, although very far from any degree of perfection. Then the bay tried me with a second word, much harder to be pronounced; but reducing it to the English orthography, may be spelt thus, 'Houyhnhnm.' I

did not succeed in this so well as the former, but after two
or three farther trials, I had better fortune; and they both
appeared amazed at my capacity.

After some farther discourse, which I then conjectured
might relate to me, the two friends took their leaves, with
the same compliment of striking each other's hoof; and the
grey made me signs that I should walk before him; wherein,
I thought it prudent to comply, until I could find a better
director.   When I offered to slacken my pace, he would
cry 'Hhuun, hhuun'; I guessed his meaning, and gave him
to understand, as well as I could, that I was weary, and not
able to walk faster; upon which, he would stand a while
to let me rest.

CHAPTER II

The author conducted by a Houyhnhnm to his house.   The
house described.   The author's reception.   The food of the
Houyhnhnms.   The author in distress for want of meat, is
at last relieved.   His manner of feeding in that country.

HAVING travelled about three miles, we came to a long
kind of building, made of timber, stuck in the ground; and
wattled a-cross; the roof was low, and covered with straw.
I now began to be a little comforted; and took out some
toys, which travellers usually carry for presents to the
savage Indians of America and other parts, in hopes the
people of the house would be thereby encouraged to receive
me kindly.   The horse made me a sign to go in first; it was
a large room with a smooth clay floor, and a rack and manger extending the whole length on one side.   There were
three nags, and two mares, not eating, but some of them
sitting down upon their hams, which I very much wondered
at; but wondered more, to see the rest employed in domes-

tick business: the last seemed but ordinary cattle; however, this confirmed my first opinion, that a people who could so far civilize brute animals, must needs excel in wisdom all the nations of the world. The grey came in just after, and thereby prevented any ill treatment, which the others might have given me. He neighed to them several times in a style of authority, and received answers.

Beyond this room there were three others, reaching the length of the house, to which you passed through three doors, opposite to each other, in the manner of a vista: we went through the second room towards the third; here the grey walked in first, beckoning me to attend: I waited in the second room, and got ready my presents for the master and mistress of the house: they were two knives, three bracelets of false pearl, a small looking-glass, and a bead-necklace. The horse neighed three or four times, and I waited to hear some answers in a human voice, but I heard no other returns than in the same dialect, only one or two a little shriller than his. I began to think that this house must belong to some person of great note among them; because there appeared so much ceremony before I could gain admittance. But, that a man of quality should be served all by horses, was beyond my comprehension. I feared my brain was disturbed by my sufferings and mis-fortunes: I roused my self, and looked about me in the room where I was left alone; this was furnished as the first, only after a more elegant manner. I rubbed mine eyes often, but the same objects still occurred. I pinched my arms and sides, to awake my self, hoping I might be in a dream. I then absolutely concluded, that all these appear-ances could be nothing else but necromancy and magick. But I had no time to pursue these reflections; for the grey horse came to the door, and made me a sign to follow him into the third room; where I saw a very comely mare, together with a colt and fole, sitting on their haunches, upon mats of straw, not unartfully made, and perfectly neat and clean.

The mare, soon after my entrance, rose from her mat, and coming up close, after having nicely observed my hands and face, gave me a most contemptuous look; then turning to the horse, I heard the word 'Yahoo' often repeated betwixt them; the meaning of which word I could not then comprehend, although it were the first I had learned to pronounce; but I was soon better informed, to my everlasting mortification: for the horse beckoning to me with his head, and repeating the word 'Hhuun, hhuun,' as he did upon the road, which I understood was to attend him, led me out into a kind of court, where was another building at some distance from the house. Here we entered, and I saw three of those detestable creatures, which I first met after my landing, feeding upon roots, and the flesh of some animals, which I afterwards found to be that of asses and dogs, and now and then a cow dead by accident or disease. They were all tyed by the neck with strong wyths, fastened to a beam; they held their food between the claws of their fore feet, and tore it with their teeth.

The master horse ordered a sorrel nag, one of his servants, to untie the largest of these animals, and take him into a yard. The beast and I were brought close together; and our countenances diligently compared, both by master and servant, who thereupon repeated several times the word 'Yahoo.' My horror and astonishment are not to be described, when I observed, in this abominable animal, a perfect human figure; the face of it, indeed, was flat and broad, the nose depressed, the lips large, and the mouth wide: but these differences are common to all savage nations, where the lineaments of the countenance are distorted by the natives suffering their infants to lie grovelling on the earth, or by carrying them on their backs, nuzzling with their face against the mother's shoulders. The fore-feet of the Yahoo differed from my hands in nothing else, but the length of the nails, the coarseness and brownness of the palms, and the hairiness on the backs. There was the same resemblance between our feet, with the same differences, which I knew very well, although the horses did not, because of my shoes and stockings; the same in every part of our bodies, except as to hairiness and colour, which I have already described.

The great difficulty that seemed to stick with the two horses, was, to see the rest of my body so very different from that of a Yahoo, for which I was obliged to my cloaths, whereof they had no conception: the sorrel nag offered me a root, which he held (after their manner, as we shall describe in its proper place) between his hoof and pastern; I took it in my hand, and having smelt it, returned it to him again as civilly as I could. He brought out of the Yahoo's kennel a piece of ass's flesh, but it smelt so offensively that I turned from it with loathing; he then threw it to the Yahoo, by whom it was greedily devoured. He afterwards shewed me a wisp of hay, and a fettlock full of oats; but I shook my head, to signify, that neither of these were food for me. And indeed, I now apprehended, that I must absolutely starve, if I did not get to some of my own species: for as to those filthy Yahoos, although there were few greater lovers of mankind, at that time, than my self; yet I confess I never saw any sensitive being so detestable on all accounts; and the more I came near them, the more hateful they grew, while I stayed in that country. This the master horse observed by my behaviour, and therefore sent the Yahoo back to his kennel. He then put his fore-hoof to his mouth, at which I was much surprized, although he did it with ease, and with a motion that appeared perfectly natural; and made other signs to know what I would eat; but I could not return him such an answer as he was able to apprehend; and if he had understood me, I did not see how it was possible to contrive any way for finding my self nourishment. While we were thus engaged, I observed a cow passing by; whereupon I pointed to her, and expressed a desire to let me go and milk her. This had its effect; for he led me back into the house, and ordered a mare-servant to open a room, where a good store of milk lay in earthen and wooden vessels, after a very orderly and cleanly manner. She gave me a large bowl full, of which I drank very heartily, and found my self well refreshed.

About noon I saw coming towards the house a kind of vehicle, drawn like a sledge by four Yahoos. There was in it an old steed, who seemed to be of quality; he alighted with his hind-feet forward, having by accident got a hurt in his left fore-foot. He came to dine with our horse, who received him with great civility. They dined in the best room, and had oats boiled in milk for the second course; which the old horse eat warm, but the rest cold. Their mangers were placed circular in the middle of the room, and divided into several partitions, round which they sat on their haunches upon bosses of straw. In the middle was a large rack, with angles answering to every partition of the manger. So that each horse and mare eat their own hay, and their own mash of oats and milk, with much decency and regularity. The behaviour of the young colt and fole appeared very modest; and that of the master and mistress extremely chearful and complaisant to their guest. The grey ordered me to stand by him; and much discourse passed between him and his friend concerning me, as I found by the strangers often looking on me, and the frequent repetition of the word 'Yahoo.'

I happened to wear my gloves, which the master grey observing, seemed perplexed; discovering signs of wonder what I had done to my fore feet; he put his hoof three or four times to them, as if he would signify, that I should reduce them to their former shape, which I presently did, pulling off both my gloves, and putting them into my pocket. This occasioned farther talk, and I saw the company was pleased with my behaviour, whereof I soon found the good effects. I was ordered to speak the few words I understood; and while they were at dinner, the master taught me the names for oats, milk, fire, water, and some others; which I could readily pronounce after him; having from my youth a great facility in learning languages.

When dinner was done, the master horse took me aside, and by signs and words made me understand the concern he was in, that I had nothing to eat. Oats in their tongue, are called 'hlunnh.' This word I pronounced two or three times; for although I had refused them at first, yet upon second thoughts, I considered that I could contrive to make of them a kind of bread, which might be sufficient with milk to keep me alive, until I could make my escape to some other country, and to creatures of my own species. The horse immediately ordered a white mare-servant of his family to bring me a good quantity of oats in a sort of wooden tray. These I heated before the fire as well as I could, and rubbed them until the husks came off, which I made a shift to winnow from the grain; I ground and beat them between two stones, then took water, and made them into a paste or cake, which I toasted at the fire, and eat warm with milk. It was at first a very insipid diet, although common enough in many parts of Europe, but grew tolerable by time; and having been often reduced to hard fare in my life, this was not the first experiment I had made how easily nature is satisfied. And I cannot but observe, that I never had one hour's sickness, while I stayed in this island. It is true, I sometimes made a shift to catch a rabbit, or a bird, by springes made of Yahoos hairs; and I often gathered wholesome herbs, which I boiled, or eat as salades with my bread; and now and then, for a rarity, I made a little butter, and drank the whey. I was at first at a great loss for salt; but custom soon reconciled the want of it; and I am confident, that the frequent use of salt among us, is an effect of luxury, and was first introduced only as a provocative to drink; except where it is necessary for preserving of flesh in long voyages, or in places remote from great markets. For we observe no animal to be fond of it but man: and as to my self, when I left this country, it was a great while before I could endure the taste of it in any thing that I eat.

This is enough to say upon the subject of my diet, where-with other travellers fill their books, as if the readers were personally concerned, whether we fare well or ill. How-ever, it was necessary to mention this matter, lest the world should think it impossible that I could find sustenance for three years in such a country, and among such inhabitants.

When it grew towards evening, the master horse ordered a place for me to lodge in; it was but six yards from the house, and separated from the stable of the Yahoos. Here I got some straw, and covering my self with my own cloaths, slept very sound. But I was in a short time better accom-modated, as the reader shall know hereafter, when I come to treat more particularly about my way of living.

CHAPTER III

The author studies to learn the language, the Houyhnhnm his master assists in teaching him. The language described. Several Houynhhnms of quality come out of curiosity to see the author. He gives his master a short account of his voyage.

MY principal endeavour was to learn the language, which my master (for so I shall henceforth call him) and his children, and every servant of his house were desirous to teach me. For they looked upon it as a prodigy, that a brute animal should discover such marks of a rational creature. I pointed to every thing, and enquired the name of it, which I wrote down in my journal book when I was alone, and corrected my bad accent, by desiring those of the family to pronounce it often. In this employment, a sorrel nag, one of the under servants, was very ready to assist me.

In speaking, they pronounce through the nose and throat, and their language approacheth nearest to the High-Dutch or German, of any I know in Europe; but is much more graceful and significant. The Emperor Charles V. made almost the same observation, when he said, that if he were to speak to his horse, it should be in High-Dutch.

The curiosity and impatience of my master were so great, that he spent many hours of his leisure to instruct me. He was convinced (as he afterwards told me) that I must be a Yahoo, but my teachableness, civility and cleanliness, astonished him; which were qualities altogether so opposite to those animals. He was most perplexed about my cloaths, reasoning sometimes with himself, whether they were a part of my body; for I never pulled them off until the family were asleep, and got them on before they waked in the morning. My master was eager to learn from whence I came; how I acquired those appearances of reason, which I discovered in all my actions; and to know my story from my own mouth, which he hoped he should soon do by the great proficiency I made in learning and pronouncing their words and sentences. To help my memory, I formed all I learned into the English alphabet, and writ the words down with the translations. This last, after some time, I ventured to do in my master's presence. It cost me much trouble to explain to him what I was doing; for the inhabitants have not the least idea of books or literature.

In about ten weeks time I was able to understand most

of his questions; and in three months could give him some tolerable answers. He was extremely curious to know from what part of the country I came, and how I was taught to imitate a rational creature; because the Yahoos, (whom he saw I exactly resembled in my head, hands and face, that were only visible,) with some appearance of cunning, and the strongest disposition to mischief, were observed to be the most unteachable of all brutes. I answered; that I came over the sea, from a far place, with many others of my own kind, in a great hollow vessel made of the bodies of trees: that, my companions forced me to land on this coast, and then left me to shift for my self. It was with some difficulty, and by the help of many signs, that I brought him to understand me. He replyed, that I must needs be mistaken, or that I *said the thing which was not.* (For they have no word in their language to express lying or falshood.) He knew it was impossible that there could be a country beyond the sea, or that a parcel of brutes could move a wooden vessel whither they pleased upon water. He was sure no Houyhnhnm alive could make such a vessel, or would trust Yahoos to manage it.

The word 'Houyhnhnm,' in their tongue, signifies a horse; and its etymology, 'the perfection of nature.' I told my master, that I was at a loss for expression, but would improve as fast as I could; and hoped in a short time I should be able to tell him wonders: he was pleased to direct his own mare, his colt and fole, and the servants of the family to take all opportunities of instructing me; and every day for two or three hours, he was at the same pains himself: several horses and mares of quality in the neighbourhood came often to our house, upon the report spread of a wonderful Yahoo, that could speak like a Houyhnhnm, and seemed in his words and actions to discover some glimmerings of reason. These delighted to converse with me;

they put many questions, and received such answers, as I was able to return. By all which advantages, I made so great a progress, that in five months from my arrival, I understood whatever was spoke, and could express my self tolerably well.

The Houyhnhnms who came to visit my master, out of a design of seeing and talking with me, could hardly believe me to be a right Yahoo, because my body had a different covering from others of my kind. They were astonished to observe me without the usual hair or skin, except on my head, face and hands: but I discovered that secret to my master, upon an accident, which happened about a fortnight before.

I have already told the reader, that every night when the family were gone to bed, it was my custom to strip and cover myself with my cloaths: it happened one morning early, that my master sent for me, by the sorrel nag, who was his valet; when he came, I was fast asleep, my cloaths fallen off on one side, and my shirt above my waiste. I awaked at the noise he made, and observed him to deliver his message in some disorder; after which he went to my master, and in a great fright gave him a very confused account of what he had seen: this I presently discovered; for going as soon as I was dressed, to pay my attendance upon his honour, he asked me the meaning of what his servant had reported; that I was not the same thing when I slept as I appeared to be at other times; that his valet assured him, some part of me was white, some yellow, at least not so white, and some brown.

I had hitherto concealed the secret of my dress, in order to distinguish my self as much as possible, from that cursed race of Yahoos; but now I found it in vain to do so any longer. Besides, I considered that my cloaths and shoes would soon wear out, which already were in a declining condition, and must be supplied by some contrivance from the hides of Yahoos, or other brutes; whereby the whole secret would be known. I therefore told my master, that in the country from whence I came, those of my kind always covered their bodies with the hairs of certain animals prepared by art, as well for decency, as to avoid inclemencies of air both hot and cold; of which, as to my own person, I would give him immediate conviction, if he pleased to command me; only desiring his excuse, if I did not expose those parts that nature taught us to conceal. He said, my discourse was all very strange, but especially the last part; for he could not understand why nature should teach us to conceal what nature had given. That neither himself, nor family, were ashamed of any parts of their bodies; but however I might do as I pleased. Whereupon, I first unbottoned my coat, and pulled it off. I did the same with my waistecoat; I drew off my shoes, stockings, and breeches. I let my shirt down to my waiste, and drew up the bottom, fastening it like a girdle about my middle to hide my nakedness.

My master observed the whole performance with great signs of curiosity and admiration. He took up all my cloaths in his pastern, one piece after another, and examined them diligently; he then stroaked my body very gently, and looked round me several times; after which he said, it was plain I must be a perfect Yahoo; but that I differed very much from the rest of my species, in the whiteness, and smoothness of my skin, my want of hair in several parts of my body, the shape and shortness of my claws behind and before, and my affectation of walking continually on my two hinder feet. He desired to see no more; and gave me leave to put on my cloaths again, for I was shuddering with cold.

I expressed my uneasiness at his giving me so often the appellation of Yahoo, an odious animal, for which I had so utter an hatred and contempt. I begged he would forbear applying that word to me, and take the same order in his family, and among his friends whom he suffered to see me. I requested likewise, that the secret of my having a false covering to my body might be known to none but himself, at least as long as my present cloathing should last: for, as to what the sorrel nag, his valet, had observed, his honour might command him to conceal it.

All this my master very graciously consented to; and thus the secret was kept until my cloaths began to wear out, which I was forced to supply by several contrivances, that shall hereafter be mentioned. In the mean time, he desired I would go on with my utmost diligence to learn their language, because he was more astonished at my capacity for speech and reason, than at the figure of my body, whether it were covered or no; adding, that he waited with some impatience to hear the wonders which I promised to tell him.

From thenceforward he doubled the pains he had been at to instruct me; he brought me into all company, and made them treat me with civility, because, as he told them privately, this would put me into good humour, and make me more diverting.

Every day when I waited on him, beside the trouble he was at in teaching, he would ask me several questions concerning my self, which I answered as well as I could; and by those means he had already received some general ideas, although very imperfect. It would be tedious to relate the several steps, by which I advanced to a more regular conversation: but the first account I gave of my self in any order and length, was to this purpose:

That, I came from a very far country, as I already had attempted to tell him, with about fifty more of my own species; that, we travelled upon the seas, in a great hollow vessel made of wood, and larger than his honour's house. I described the ship to him in the best terms I could; and explained by the help of my handkerchief displayed, how it was driven forward by the wind. That, upon a quarrel among us, I was set on shoar on this coast, where I walked forward without knowing whither, until he delivered me from the persecution of those execrable Yahoos. He asked me, who made the ship, and how it was possible that the Houyhnhnms of my country would leave it to the management of brutes? My answer was, that I durst proceed no farther in my relation, unless he would give me his word and honour that he would not be offended; and then I would tell him the wonders I had so often promised. He agreed; and I went on by assuring him, that the ship was made by creatures like my self, who in all the countries I had travelled, as well as in my own, were the only governing, rational animals; and that upon my arrival hither, I was as much astonished to see the Houyhnhnms act like rational beings, as he or his friends could be in finding some marks of reason in a creature he was pleased to call a Yahoo; to which I owned my resemblance in every part, but could not account for their degenerate and brutal nature. I said farther, that if good fortune ever restored me to my native country, to relate my travels hither, as I resolved to do; every body would believe that I *said the thing which was not*; that I invented the story out of my own head: and with all possible respect to himself, his family, and friends, and under his promise of not being offended, our countrymen would hardly think it probable, that a Houyhnhnm should be the presiding creature of a nation, and a Yahoo the brute.

CHAPTER IV

The Houyhnhnms notion of truth and falshood. The author's discourse disapproved by his master. The author gives a more particular account of himself, and the accidents of his voyage.

My master heard me with great appearances of uneasiness in his countenance; because *doubting* or *not believing*, are so little known in this country, that the inhabitants cannot tell how to behave themselves under such circumstances. And I remember in frequent discourses with my master concerning the nature of manhood, in other parts of the world; having occasion to talk of *lying* and *false representation*, it was with much difficulty that he comprehended what I meant; although he had otherwise a most acute judgment. For he argued thus; that the use of speech was to make us understand one another, and to receive information of facts; now if any one *said the thing which was not*, these ends were defeated; because I cannot properly be said to understand him; and I am so far from receiving information, that he leaves me worse than in ignorance; for I am led to believe a thing *black*, when it is *white*; and *short*, when it is *long*. And these were all the notions he had concerning that faculty of *lying*, so perfectly well understood, and so universally practised among human creatures.

To return from this digression; when I asserted that the Yahoos were the only governing animals in my country; which my master said was altogether past his conception, he desired to know, whether we had Houyhnhnms among us, and what was their employment: I told him, we had great numbers; that in summer they grazed in the fields, and in winter were kept in houses, with hay and oats, where Yahoo-servants were employed to rub their skins smooth, comb their manes, pick their feet, serve them with food, and make their beds. 'I understand you well,' said my master; 'it is now very plain from all you have spoken, that whatever share of reason the Yahoos pretend to, the Houyhnhnms are your masters; I heartily wish our Yahoos would be so tractable.' I begged his honour would please to excuse me from proceeding any farther, because I was very certain that the account he expected from me would be highly displeasing. But he insisted in commanding me to let him know the best and the worst: I told him he should be obeyed. I owned, that the Houyhnhnms among us, whom we called 'horses,' were the most generous and comely animal we had; that they excelled in strength and swiftness; and when they belonged to persons of quality, employed in travelling, racing, and drawing chariots, they were treated with much kindness and care, until they fell into diseases, or became foundered in the feet; but then they were sold, and used to all kind of drudgery until they died; after which, their skins were stripped and sold for what they were worth, and their bodies left to be devoured by dogs and birds of prey. But the common race of horses had not so good fortune, being kept by farmers and carriers, and other mean people, who put them to greater labour, and feed them worse. I described as well as I could, our way of riding; the shape and use of a bridle, a saddle, a spur, and a whip; of harness and wheels. I added, that we fastened plates of a certain hard substance called iron at the bottom of their feet, to preserve their hoofs from being broken by the stony ways on which we often travelled.

My master, after some expressions of great indignation, wondered how we dared to venture upon a Houyhnhnm's back; for he was sure, that the meanest servant in his house would be able to shake off the strongest Yahoo; or by lying down, and rolling upon his back, squeeze the brute to death. I answered, that our horses were trained up from three or four years old to the several uses we intended them for;

that, if any of them proved intolerably vicious, they were employed for carriages; that, they were severely beaten while they were young for any mischievous tricks: that, the males, designed for the common use of riding or draught, were generally *castrated* about two years after their birth, to take down their spirits, and make them more tame and gentle: that, they were indeed sensible of rewards and punishments; but his honour would please to consider, that they had not the least tincture of reason any more than the Yahoos in this country.

It put me to the pains of many circumlocutions to give my master a right idea of what I spoke; for their language doth not abound in variety of words, because their wants and passions are fewer than among us. But it is impossible to express his noble resentment at our savage treatment of the Houyhnhnm race; particularly after I had explained the manner and use of *castrating* horses among us, to hinder them from propagating their kind, and to render them more servile. He said, if it were possible there could be any country where Yahoos alone were endued with reason, they certainly must be the governing animal, because reason will in time always prevail against brutal strength, But, considering the frame of our bodies, and especially of mine, he thought no creature of equal bulk was so ill contrived, for employing that reason in the common offices of life; whereupon he desired to know whether those among whom I lived, resembled me or the Yahoos of his country. I assured him, that I was as well shaped as most of my age; but the younger and the females were much more soft and tender, and the skins of the latter generally as white as milk. He said, I differed indeed from other Yahoos, being much more cleanly, and not altogether so deformed; but in point of real advantage, he thought I differed for the worse: that my nails were of no use either to my fore or hinder feet: as to my fore feet, he could not properly call them by that

name, for he never observed me to walk upon them; that,
they were too soft to bear the ground; that, I generally
went with them uncovered, neither was the covering I
sometimes wore on them, of the same shape, or so strong
as that on my feet behind: that I could not walk with any
security; for if either of my hinder feet slipped, I must
inevitably fall.   He then began to find fault with other
parts of my body; the flatness of my face, the prominence
of my nose, mine eyes placed directly in front, so that I
could not look on either side without turning my head:
that I was not able to feed my self, without lirting one of
my fore feet to my mouth: and therefore nature had placed
those joints to answer that necessity.   He knew not what
could be the use of those several clefts and divisions in my
feet behind; that these were too soft to bear the hardness
and sharpness of stones without a covering made from the
skin of some other brute; that, my whole body wanted a
fence against heat and cold, which I was forced to put on
and off every day with tediousness and trouble.   And lastly,
that he observed every animal in this country naturally
to abhor the Yahoos, whom the weaker avoided, and the
stronger drove from them.   So that supposing us to have
the gift of reason, he could not see how it were possible to
cure that natural antipathy which every creature discovered
against us; nor consequently, how we could tame and
render them serviceable.   However, he would (as he said)
debate the matter no farther, because he was more desirous
to know my own story, the country, where I was born, and
the several actions and events of my life before I came
hither.

I assured him, how extreamly desirous I was that he
should be satisfied in every point; but I doubted much,
whether it would be possible for me to explain my self on
several subjects whereof his honour could have no conception, because I saw nothing in his country to which I

could resemble them. That however, I would do my best, and strive to express my self by similitudes, humbly desiring his assistance when I wanted proper words; which he was pleased to promise me.

I said, my birth was of honest parents, in an island called England, which was remote from this country, as many days journey as the strongest of his honour's servants could travel in the annual course of the sun. That, I was bred a surgeon, whose trade is to cure wounds and hurts in the body, got by accident or violence. That, my country was governed by a female man, whom we called 'queen.' That, I left it to get riches, whereby I might maintain my self and family when I should return. That, in my last voyage, I was commander of the ship, and had about fifty Yahoos under me, many of which died at sea, and I was forced to supply them by others picked out from several nations. That, our ship was twice in danger of being sunk; the first time by a great storm, and the second, by striking against a rock. Here my master interposed, by asking me, how I could persuade strangers out of different countries to venture with me, after the losses I had sustained, and the hazards I had run. I said, they were fellows of desperate fortunes, forced to fly from the places of their birth, on account of their poverty or their crimes. Some were undone by law suits; others spent all they had in drinking, whoring, and gaming; others fled for treason; many for murder, theft, poysoning, robbery, perjury, forgery, coining false money; for committing rapes or sodomy; for flying from their colours, or deserting the enemy; and most of them had broken prison. None of these durst return to their native countries for fear of being hanged, or of starving in a jail; and therefore were under a necessity of seeking a livelihood in other places.

During this discourse, my master was pleased often to interrupt me. I had made use of many circumlocutions,

K 60

in describing to him the nature of the several crimes, for which most of our crew had been forced to fly their country. This labour took up several days conversation before he was able to comprehend me. He was wholly at a loss to know what could be the use or necessity of practising those vices. To clear up which, I endeavoured to give him some ideas of the desire of power and riches; of the terrible effects of lust, intemperance, malice, and envy. All this I was forced to define and describe by putting of cases, and making suppositions. After which, like one whose imagination was struck with something never seen or heard of before, he would lift up his eyes with amazement and indignation. Power, government, war, law, punishment, and a thousand other things, had no terms, wherein that language could express them; which made the difficulty almost insuperable to give my master any conception of what I meant; but being of an excellent understanding, much improved by contemplation and converse, he at last arrived at a competent knowledge of what human nature in our parts of the world is capable to perform; and desired I would give him some particular account of that land, which we call Europe, especially of my own country.

CHAPTER V

The author, at his master's commands, informs him of the state of England. The causes of war among the princes of Europe. The author begins to explain the English constitution.

THE reader may please to observe, that the following extract of many conversations I had with my master, contains a summary of the most material points, which were discoursed at several times for above two years; his honour often desiring fuller satisfaction, as I farther improved in the Houyhnhnm tongue. I laid before him, as well as I could, the whole state of Europe; I discoursed of trade and manufactures, of arts and sciences; and the answers I gave to all the questions he made, as they arose upon several subjects, were a fund of conversation not to be exhausted. But, I shall here only set down the substance of what passed between us concerning my own country, reducing it into order as well as I can, without any regard to time or other circumstances, while I strictly adhere to truth. My only concern is, that I shall hardly be able to do justice to my master's arguments and expressions, which must needs suffer by my want of capacity, as well as by a translation into our barbarous English.

In obedience therefore to his honour's commands, I related to him the *revolution* under the Prince of Orange; the long war with France entered into by the said prince, and renewed by his successor the present queen; wherein the greatest powers of Christendom were engaged, and which still continued: I computed at his request, that about a million of Yahoos might have been killed in the whole progress of it; and perhaps a hundred or more cities taken, and five times as many ships burnt or sunk.

He asked me what were the usual causes or motives, that made one country go to war with another. I answered they were innumerable; but I should only mention a few of the chief. Sometimes the ambition of princes, who never think they have land or people enough to govern: sometimes the corruption of ministers, who engage their master in a war, in order to stifle or divert the clamour of the subjects against their evil administration. Difference in opinions hath cost many millions of lives: for instance, whether *flesh* be *bread*, or *bread* be *flesh*: whether the juice of a certain *berry* be *blood* or *wine*: whether *whistling* be a vice or a virtue: whether it be better to *kiss a post*, or throw it into the fire: what is the best colour for a *coat*, whether *black*, *white*, *red*, or *grey*; and whether it should be *long* or *short*, *narrow* or *wide*, *dirty* or *clean*; with many more. Neither are any wars so furious and bloody, or of so long continuance, as those occasioned by difference in opinion, especially if it be in things indifferent.

Sometimes the quarrel between two princes is to decide which of them shall dispossess a third of his dominions, where neither of them pretend to any right. Sometimes one prince quarrelleth with another, for fear the other should quarrel with him. Sometimes a war is entered upon, because the enemy is too *strong*, and sometimes because he is too *weak*. Sometimes our neighbours *want* the *things* which we *have*, or *have* the things which we want; and we both fight, until they take ours, or give us theirs. It is a very justifiable cause of war, to invade a country after the people have been wasted by famine, destroyed by pestilence, or embroiled by factions amongst themselves. It is justifiable to enter into a war against our nearest ally, when one of his towns lie convenient for us, or a territory of land, that would render our dominions round and compact. If a prince send forces into a nation, where the people are poor and ignorant, he may lawfully put half of them to death, and make slaves of the rest, in order to civilize and reduce them from their barbarous way of living. It is a very kingly, honourable, and frequent practice, when one prince desires the assistance of another to secure him against an invasion, that the assistant, when he hath driven out the invader, should seize on the dominions himself, and kill, imprison, or banish the prince he came to relieve. Alliance by blood or marriage, is a sufficient cause of war between princes; and the nearer the kindred is, the greater is their disposition to quarrel: *poor* nations are *hungry*, and *rich* nations are *proud*; and pride and hunger will ever be at variance. For these reasons, the trade of a *soldier* is held the most honourable of all others: because a *soldier* is a Yahoo hired to kill in cold blood as many of his own species, who have never offended him, as possibly he can.

There is likewise a kind of beggarly princes in Europe, not able to make war by themselves, who hire out their troops to richer nations for so much a day to each man; of which they keep three fourths to themselves, and it is the best part of their maintenance; such are those in many northern parts of Europe.

'What you have told me' (said my master) 'upon the subject of war, doth indeed discover most admirably the effects of that reason you pretend to: however, it is happy that the *shame* is greater than the *danger*; and that nature hath left you utterly uncapable of doing much mischief: for your mouths lying flat with your faces, you can hardly bite each other to any purpose, unless by consent. Then, as to the claws upon your feet before and behind, they are so short and tender, that one of our Yahoos would drive a dozen of yours before him. And therefore, in recounting the numbers of those who have been kiiled in battle, I cannot but think, that you have *said the thing which is not.*'

I could not forbear shaking my head and smiling a little at his ignorance. And, being no stranger to the art of war, I gave him a description of cannons, culverines, muskets, carabines, pistols, bullets, powder, swords, bayonets, sieges, retreats, attacks, undermines, countermines, bombardments, sea-fights; ships sunk with a thousand men; twenty thousand killed on each side; dying groans, limbs flying in the air: smoak, noise, confusion, trampling to death under horses feet: flight, pursuit, victory: fields strewed with carcases left for food to dogs, and wolves, and birds of prey; plundering, stripping, ravishing, burning and destroying. And, to set forth the valour of my own dear countrymen, I assured him, that I had seen them blow up a hundred enemies at once in a siege, and as many in a ship;

and beheld the dead bodies drop down in pieces from the clouds, to the great diversion of all the spectators.

I was going on to more particulars, when my master commanded me silence. He said, whoever understood the nature of Yahoos might easily believe it possible for so vile an animal, to be capable of every action I had named, if their strength and cunning equalled their malice. But, as my discourse had increased the abhorrence of the whole species, so he found it gave him a disturbance in his mind, to which he was wholly a stranger before. He thought his ears being used to such abominable words, might by degrees admit them with less detestation. That, although he hated the Yahoos of this country, yet he no more blamed them for their odious qualities, than he did a *gnnayh* (a bird of prey) for its cruelty, or a sharp stone for cutting his hoof. But, when a creature pretending to reason, could be capable of such enormities, he dreaded, lest the corruption of that faculty, might be worse than brutality itself. He seemed therefore confident, that instead of reason, we were only possessed of some quality fitted to increase our natural vices; as the reflection from a troubled stream, returns the image of an ill-shapen body, not only *large*, but more *distorted*.

He added, that he had heard too much upon the subject of war, both in this, and some former discourses. There was another point which a little perplexed him at present. I had said, that some of our crew left their country on account of being ruined by law: that, I had already explained the meaning of the word; but he was at a loss how it should come to pass, that the law which was intended for *every* man's preservation, should be any man's ruin. Therefore he desired to be farther satisfied what I meant by law, and the dispensers thereof, according to the present practice in my own country: because he thought, nature and reason were sufficient guides for a reasonable animal, as we pretended to be, in shewing us what we ought to do, and what to avoid.

I assured his honour, that law was a science wherein I had not much conversed, further than by employing advocates, in vain, upon some injustices that had been done me. However, I would give him all the satisfaction I was able.

I said there was a society of men among us, bred up from their youth in the art of proving by words multiplied for the purpose, that *white* is *black*, and *black* is *white*, according as they are paid. To this society all the rest of the people are slaves.

For example, if my neighbour hath a mind to my cow, he hireth a lawyer to prove that he ought to have my cow from me. I must then hire another to defend my right; it being against all rules of law that any man should be allowed to speak for himself. Now in this case, I who am the true owner, lie under two great disadvantages. First, my lawyer being practised almost from his cradle in defending falshood; is quite out of his element when he would be an advocate for justice, which as an office unnatural, he always attempts with great aukwardness, if not with illwill. The second disadvantage is, that my lawyer must proceed with great caution: or else, he will be reprimanded by the judges, and abhorred by his brethren, as one who would lessen the practice of the law. And therefore, I have but two methods to preserve my cow. The first is, to gain over my adversary's lawyer with a double fee; who will then betray his client, by insinuating that he hath justice on his side. The second way is, for my lawyer to make my cause appear as unjust as he can; by allowing the cow to belong to my adversary; and this, if it be skilfully done, will certainly bespeak the favour of the bench.

Now, your honour is to know, that these judges are persons appointed to decide all controversies of property, as well as for the tryal of criminals; and picked out from the most dextrous lawyers, who are grown old or lazy: and having been byassed all their lives against truth and equity, lie under such a fatal necessity of favouring fraud, perjury and oppression; that I have known some of them to have refused a large bribe from the side where justice lay, rather than injure the faculty, by doing any thing unbecoming their nature or their office.

It is a maxim among these lawyers, that whatever hath been done before, may legally be done again: and therefore they take special care to record all the decisions formerly made against common justice, and the general reason of mankind. These, under the name of *precedents*, they produce as authorities to justify the most iniquitous opinions; and the judges never fail of directing accordingly.

In pleading, they studiously avoid entering into the *merits* of the cause; but are loud, violent and tedious in dwelling upon all *circumstances* which are not to the purpose. For instance, in the case already mentioned: they never desire to know what claim or title my adversary hath to my cow; but whether the said cow were red or black; her horns long or short; whether the field I graze her in be round or square; whether she were milked at home or abroad; what diseases she is subject to, and the like. After which, they consult *precedents*, adjourn the cause, from time to time, and in ten, twenty, or thirty years come to an issue.

It is likewise to be observed, that this society hath a peculiar cant and jargon of their own, that no other mortal can understand, and wherein all their laws are written, which they take special care to multiply; whereby they have wholly confounded the very essence of truth and falshood, of right and wrong; so that it will take thirty years to decide whether the field, left me by my ancestors for six generations, belong to me, or to a stranger three hundred miles off.

In the tryal of persons accused for crimes against the

State, the method is much more short and commendable: the judge first sends to sound the disposition of those in power; after which he can easily hang or save the criminal, strictly preserving all the forms of law.

Here my master interposing, said it was a pity, that creatures endowed with such prodigious abilities of mind as these lawyers, by the description I gave of them must certainly be, were not rather encouraged to be instructors of others in wisdom and knowledge. In answer to which, I assured his honour, that in all points out of their own trade, they were usually the most ignorant and stupid generation among us, the most despicable in common conversation, avowed enemies to all knowledge and learning; and equally disposed to pervert the general reason of mankind, in every other subject of discourse, as in that of their own profession.

CHAPTER VI

A continuation of the state of England, under Queen Anne.
The character of a First Minister in the courts of Europe.

MY master was yet wholly at a loss to understand what motives could incite this race of lawyers to perplex, disquiet, and weary themselves by engaging in a confederacy of injustice, merely for the sake of injuring their fellow-animals; neither could he comprehend what I meant in saying they did it for *hire*. Whereupon I was at much pains to describe to him the use of *money*, the materials it was made of, and the value of the metals: that, when a Yahoo had got a great store of this precious substance, he was able to purchase whatever he had a mind to; the finest cloathing, the noblest houses, great tracts of land, the most costly meats and drinks; and have his choice of the most
*K 60

beautiful females. Therefore since *money* alone, was able
to perform all these feats, our Yahoos thought, they could
never have enough of it to spend or to save, as they found
themselves inclined from their natural bent either to pro-
fusion or avarice. That, the rich man enjoyed the fruit
of the poor man's labour, and the latter were a thousand
to one in proportion to the former. That, the bulk of our
people was forced to live miserably, by labouring every day
for small wages, to make a few live plentifully. I enlarged
my self much on these and many other particulars to the
same purpose: but his honour was still to seek: for he went
upon a supposition, that all animals had a title to their
share in the productions of the earth; and especially those
who presided over the rest. Therefore he desired I would
let him know what these costly meats were, and how any
of us happened to want them. Whereupon I enumerated
as many sorts as came into my head, with the various
methods of dressing them, which could not be done without
sending vessels by sea to every part of the world, as well for
liquors to drink, as for sauces, and innumerable other conveniencies. I assured him, that this whole globe of earth
must be at least three times gone round, before one of our
better female Yahoos could get her breakfast, or a cup to
put it in. He said, that must needs be a miserable country
which cannot furnish food for its own inhabitants. But
what he chiefly wondered at, was how such vast tracts of
ground as I described, should be wholly without *fresh-
water*, and the people put to the necessity of sending over
the sea for drink. I replied, that England (the dear place
of my nativity) was computed to produce three times the
quantity of food, more than its inhabitants are able to consume, as well as liquors extracted from grain, or pressed out
of the fruit of certain trees, which made excellent drink;
and the same proportion in every other convenience of life.
But, in order to feed the luxury and intemperance of the

males, and the vanity of the females, we sent away the greatest part of our necessary things to other countries, from whence in return we brought the materials of diseases, folly, and vice, to spend among our selves. Hence it follows of necessity, that vast numbers of our people are compelled to seek their livelihood by begging, robbing, stealing, cheating, pimping, forswearing, flattering, suborning, forging, gaming, lying, fawning, hectoring, voting, scribling, stargazing, poysoning, whoring, canting, libelling, free-thinking, and the like occupations: every one of which terms, I was at much pains to make him understand.

That, *wine* was not imported among us from foreign countries, to supply the want of water or other drinks, but because it was a sort of liquid which made us merry, by putting us out of our senses; diverted all melancholy thoughts, begat wild extravagant imaginations in the brain, raised our hopes, and banished our fears; suspended every office of reason for a time, and deprived us of the use of our limbs, until we fell into a profound sleep; although it must be confessed, that we always awaked sick and dispirited; and that the use of this liquor filled us with diseases, which made our lives uncomfortable and short.

But beside all this, the bulk of our people supported themselves by furnishing the necessities or conveniencies of life to the rich, and to each other. For instance, when I am at home and dressed as I ought to be, I carry on my body the workmanship of an hundred tradesmen; the building and furniture of my house employ as many more; and five times the number to adorn my wife.

I was going on to tell him of another sort of people, who get their livelihood by attending the sick; having upon some occasions informed his honour that many of my crew had died of diseases: but here it was with the utmost difficulty that I brought him to apprehend what I meant. He could easily conceive, that a Houyhnhnm grew weak and heavy

a few days before his death; or by some accident might hurt
a limb. But that nature, who worketh all things to perfection, should suffer any pains to breed in our bodies, he
thought impossible; and desired to know the reason of so
unaccountable an evil. I told him, we fed on a thousand
things which operated contrary to each other: that, we eat
when we were not hungry, and drank without the provocation of thirst: that, we sat whole nights drinking strong
liquors without eating a bit; which disposed us to sloth,
enflamed our bodies, and precipitated or prevented digestion. That, prostitute female Yahoos acquired a certain
malady, which bred rottenness in the bones of those, who
fell into their embraces: that, this and many other diseases,
were propagated from father to son; so that great numbers
come into the world with complicated maladies upon them:
that, it would be endless to give him a catalogue of all
diseases incident to human bodies; for they could not be
fewer than five or six hundred, spread over every limb, and
joint: in short, every part, external and intestine, having
diseases appropriated to each. To remedy which, there
was a sort of people bred up among us, in the profession or
pretence of curing the sick. And, because I had some skill
in the faculty, I would in gratitude to his honour, let him
know the whole mystery and method by which they
proceed.

Their fundamental is, that all diseases arise from *repletion*;
from whence they conclude, that a great *evacuation* of the
body is necessary, either through the natural passage, or
upwards at the mouth. Their next business is, from herbs,
minerals, gums, oyls, shells, salts, juices, sea-weed, excrements, barks of trees, serpents, toads, frogs, spiders, dead
mens flesh and bones, beasts and fishes, to form a composition for smell and taste the most abominable, nauseous
and detestable, that they can possibly contrive, which the
stomach immediately rejects with loathing: and this they

call a *vomit*.   Or else from the same store-house, with some
other poysonous additions, they command us to take in at
the orifice *above* or *below* (just as the physician then happens
to be disposed) a medicine equally annoying and disgustful
to the bowels; which relaxing the belly, drives down all
before it: and this they call a *purge*, or a *clyster*.   For
nature (as the physicians alledge) having intended the
superior anterior orifice only for the *intromission* of solids
and liquids, and the inferior posterior for ejection; these
artists ingeniously considering that in all diseases nature
is forced out of her seat; therefore to replace her in it, the
body must be treated in a manner directly contrary, by
interchanging the use of each orifice; forcing solids and
liquids in at the *anus*, and making evacuations at the
mouth.

But, besides real diseases, we are subject to many that
are only imaginary, for which the physicians have invented
imaginary cures; these have their several names, and so
have the drugs that are proper for them; and with these our
female Yahoos are always infested.

One great excellency in this tribe is their skill at *progno-
sticks*, wherein they seldom fail; their predictions in real
diseases, when they rise to any degree of malignity, generally
portending *death*, which is always in their power, when
recovery is not: and therefore, upon any unexpected signs
of amendment, after they have pronounced their sentence,
rather than be accused as false prophets, they know how to
approve their sagacity to the world by a seasonable dose.

They are likewise of special use to husbands and wives,
who are grown weary of their mates; to eldest sons, to great
ministers of State, and often to princes.

I had formerly upon occasion discoursed with my master
upon the nature of *government* in general, and particularly
of our own *excellent constitution*, deservedly the wonder and
envy of the whole world.   But having here accidentally

mentioned a *minister of State*; he commanded me some time after to inform him, what species of Yahoo I particularly meant by that appellation.

I told him, that a *First* or *Chief Minister of State*, whom I intended to describe, was a creature wholly exempt from joy and grief, love and hatred, pity and anger; at least makes use of no other passions but a violent desire of wealth, power, and titles: that, he applies his words to all uses, except to the indication of his mind: that, he never tells a *truth*, but with an intent that you should take it for a *lye*; nor a *lye*, but with a design that you should take it for a *truth*; that those he speaks worst of behind their backs, are in the surest way to preferment; and whenever he begins to praise you to others or to your self, you are from that day forlorn. The worst mark you can receive is a *promise*, especially when it is confirmed with an oath; after which every wise man retires, and gives over all hopes.

There are three methods by which a man may rise to be Chief Minister: the first is, by knowing how with prudence to dispose of a wife, a daughter, or a sister: the second, by betraying or undermining his predecessor: and the third is, by a *furious zeal* in publick assemblies against the corruptions of the court. But a wise prince would rather chuse to employ those who practise the last of these methods; because such zealots prove always the most obsequious and subservient to the will and passions of their master. That, these *ministers* having all employments at their disposal, preserve themselves in power by bribing the majority of a Senate, or Great Council; and at last by an expedient called an Act of Indemnity (whereof I described the nature to him) they secure themselves from after-reckonings, and retire from the publick, laden with the spoils of the nation.

The palace of a Chief Minister, is a seminary to breed up others in his own trade: the pages, lacquies, and porter, by imitating their master, become ministers of State in their several districts, and learn to excel in the three principal *ingredients*, of *insolence, lying,* and *bribery*. Accordingly, they have a *subaltern* court paid to them by persons of the best rank; and sometimes by the force of dexterity and impudence, arrive through several gradations to be successors to their lord.

He is usually governed by a decayed wench, or favourite footman, who are the tunnels through which all graces are conveyed, and may properly be called, *in the last resort*, the governors of the kingdom.

One day, my master, having heard me mention the *nobility* of my country, was pleased to make me a compliment which I could not pretend to deserve: that, he was sure, I must have been born of some noble family, because I far exceeded in shape, colour, and cleanliness, all the Yahoos of his nation, although I seemed to fail in strength, and agility, which must be imputed to my different way of living from those other brutes; and besides, I was not only endowed with the faculty of speech, but likewise with some rudiments of reason, to a degree, that with all his acquaintance I passed for a prodigy.

He made me observe, that among the Houyhnhnms, the White, the Sorrel, and the Iron-Grey, were not so exactly shaped as the Bay, the Dapple Grey, and the Black; nor born with equal talents of mind, or a capacity to improve them; and therefore continued always in the condition of servants, without ever aspiring to match out of their own race, which in that country would be reckoned monstrous and unnatural.

I made his honour my most humble acknowledgments for the good opinion he was pleased to conceive of me; but assured him at the same time, that my birth was of the lower sort, having been born of plain, honest parents, who were just able to give me a tolerable education: that, *nobility* among us was altogether a different thing from the idea he

had of it: that, our young *noblemen* are bred from their
childhood in idleness and luxury: that, as soon as years
will permit, they consume their vigour, and contract odious
diseases among lewd females; and when their fortunes are
almost ruined, they marry some woman of mean birth,
disagreeable person, and unsound constitution, merely for
the sake of money, whom they hate and despise: that, the
production of such marriages are generally scrophulous,
rickety, or deformed children; by which means the family
seldom continues above three generations, unless the wife
take care to provide a healthy father among her neighbours,
or domesticks, in order to improve and continue the breed:
that, a weak diseased body, a meager countenance, and
sallow complexion, are the true marks of *noble blood*; and a
healthy robust appearance is so disgraceful in a man of
quality, that the world concludes his real father to have
been a groom or a coachman. The imperfections of his
mind run parallel with those of his body; being a composition of spleen, dulness, ignorance, caprice, sensuality,
and pride.

Without the consent of this illustrious body, no law can
be enacted, repealed, or altered: and these nobles have
likewise the decision of all our possessions without appeal.

CHAPTER VII

The author's great love of his native country. His master's
   observations upon the constitution and administration of
   England, as described by the author, with parallel cases
   and comparisons. His master's observations upon humane
   nature.

THE reader may be disposed to wonder how I could prevail
on my self to give so free a representation of my own
species, among a race of mortals who were already too apt

to conceive the vilest opinion of humane kind, from that entire congruity betwixt me and their Yahoos. But I must freely confess, that the many virtues of those excellent *quadrupeds* placed in opposite view to humane corruptions, had so far opened mine eyes, and enlarged my understanding, that I began to view the actions and passions of man in a very different light; and to think the honour of my own kind not worth managing; which, besides, it was impossible for me to do before a person of so acute a judgment as my master, who daily convinced me of a thousand faults in my self, whereof I had not the least perception before, and which with us would never be numbered, even among human infirmities. I had likewise learned from his example an utter detestation of all falsehood or disguise; and truth appeared so amiable to me, that I determined upon sacrificing every thing to it.

Let me deal so candidly with the reader, as to confess, that there was yet a much stronger motive for the freedom I took in my representation of things. I had not been a year in this country, before I contracted such a love and veneration for the inhabitants, that I entered on a firm resolution never to return to human kind, but to pass the rest of my life among these admirable Houyhnhnms in the contemplation and practice of every virtue; where I could have no example or incitement to vice. But it was decreed by fortune, my perpetual enemy, that so great a felicity should not fall to my share. However, it is now some comfort to reflect, that in what I said of my countrymen, I *extenuated* their faults as much as I durst before so strict an examiner; and upon every article, gave as *favourable* a turn as the matter would bear. For, indeed, who is there alive that will not be swayed by his byass and partiality to the place of his birth?

I have related the substance of several conversations I had with my master, during the greatest part of the time I had the honour to be in his service; but have indeed for brevity sake omitted much more than is here set down.

When I had answered all his questions, and his curiosity seemed to be fully satisfied; he sent for me one morning early, and commanding me to sit down at some distance, (an honour which he had never before conferred upon me) he said, he had been very seriously considering my whole story, as far as it related both to my self and my country: that, he looked upon us as a sort of animals to whose share, by what accident he could not conjecture, some small pittance of *reason* had fallen, whereof we made no other use than by its assistance to aggravate our *natural* corruptions, and to acquire new ones which nature had not given us: that, we disarmed our selves of the few abilities she had bestowed; had been very successful in multiplying our original wants, and seemed to spend our whole lives in vain endeavours to supply them by our own inventions: that, as to my self, it was manifest I had neither the strength or agility of a common Yahoo: that, I walked infirmly on my hinder feet; had found out a contrivance to make my claws of no use or defence, and to remove the hair from my chin, which was intended as a shelter from the sun and the weather. Lastly, that I could neither run with speed, nor climb trees like my *brethren* (as he called them) the Yahoos in this country.

That, our institutions of government and law were plainly owing to our gross defects in *reason*, and by consequence, in *virtue*; because *reason* alone is sufficient to govern a *rational* creature; which was therefore a character we had no pretence to challenge, even from the account I had given of my own people; although he manifestly perceived, that in order to favour them, I had concealed many particulars, and often *said the thing which was not*.

He was the more confirmed in this opinion, because he observed, that as I agreed in every feature of my body with other Yahoos, except where it was to my real disadvantage in point of strength, speed and activity, the shortness of my claws, and some other particulars where nature had no part; so, from the representation I had given him of our lives, our manners, and our actions, he found as near a resemblance in the disposition of our minds. He said, the Yahoos were known to hate one another more than they did any different species of animals; and the reason usually assigned, was, the odiousness of their own shapes, which all could see in the rest, but not in themselves. He had therefore begun to think it not unwise in us to *cover* our bodies, and by that invention, conceal many of our deformities from each other, which would else be hardly supportable. But, he now found he had been mistaken; and that the dissentions of those brutes in his country were owing to the same cause with ours, as I had described them. For, if (said he) you throw among five Yahoos as much food as would be sufficient for fifty, they will, instead of eating peaceably, fall together by the ears, each single one impatient to *have all to itself*; and therefore a servant was usually employed to stand by while they were feeding abroad, and those kept at home were tied at a distance from each other: that, if a cow died of age or accident, before a Houyhnhnm could secure it for his own Yahoos, those in the neighbourhood would come in herds to seize it, and then would ensue such a battle as I had described, with terrible wounds made by their claws on both sides, although they seldom were able to kill one another, for want of such convenient instruments of death as we had invented. At other times the like battles have been fought between the Yahoos of several neighbourhoods without any visible cause: those of one district watching all opportunities to surprize the next before they are prepared. But, if they find their project hath miscarried, they return home, and for want of enemies, engage in what I call a *civil war* among themselves.

That, in some fields of his country, there are certain *shining stones* of several colours, whereof the Yahoos are violently fond; and when part of these *stones* are fixed in the earth, as it sometimes happeneth, they will dig with their claws for whole days to get them out, and carry them away, and hide them by heaps in their kennels; but still looking round with great caution, for fear their comrades should find out their treasure. My master said, he could never discover the reason of this unnatural appetite, or how these *stones* could be of any use to a Yahoo; but now he believed it might proceed from the same principle of *avarice*, which I had ascribed to mankind: that, he had once, by way of experiment, privately removed a heap of these *stones* from the place where one of his Yahoos had buried it: whereupon, the sordid animal missing his treasure, by his loud lamenting brought the whole herd to the place, there miserably howled, then fell to biting and tearing the rest; began to pine away, would neither eat nor sleep, nor work, until he ordered a servant privately to convey the *stones* into the same hole, and hide them as before; which when his Yahoo had found, he presently recovered his spirits and good humour; but took care to remove them to a better hiding place; and hath ever since been a very serviceable brute.

My master farther assured me, which I also observed my self; that in the fields where these *shining stones* abound, the fiercest and most frequent battles are fought, occasioned by perpetual inroads of the neighbouring Yahoos.

He said, it was common when two Yahoos discovered such a *stone* in a field, and were contending which of them should be the proprietor, a third would take the advantage, and carry it away from them both; which my master would needs contend to have some resemblance with our *suits at law*; wherein I thought it for our credit not to undeceive him; since the decision he mentioned was much more equitable than many decrees among us: because the plaintiff and defendant there lost nothing beside the *stone* they contended for; whereas our *courts of equity*, would never have dismissed the cause while either of them had any thing left.

My master continuing his discourse, said, there was nothing that rendered the Yahoos more odious, than their undistinguished appetite to devour every thing that came in their way, whether herbs, roots, berries, corrupted flesh of animals; or all mingled together: and, it was peculiar in their temper, that they were fonder of what they could get by rapine or stealth at a greater distance, than much better food provided for them at home: if their prey held out, they would eat until they were ready to burst, after which nature had pointed out to them a certain *root* that gave them a general evacuation.

There was also another kind of *root* very *juicy*, but something rare and difficult to be found; which the Yahoos fought for with much eagerness, and would suck it with great delight: it produced the same effects that wine hath upon us. It would make them sometimes hug, and sometimes tear one another; they would howl and grin, and chatter, and roul, and tumble, and then fall asleep in the mud.

᠆I did indeed observe, that the Yahoos were the only animals in this country subject to any diseases; which, however, were much fewer than horses have among us, and contracted not by any ill treatment they meet with, but by the nastiness and greediness of that sordid brute. Neither has their language any more than a general appellation for those maladies; which is borrowed from the name of the beast, and called 'Hnea Yahoo,' or the Yahoo's-evil; and the cure prescribed is a mixture of *their own dung* and *urine*, forcibly put down the Yahoo's throat. This I have since often known to have been taken with success: and do here freely recommend it to my countrymen, for the publick good, as an admirable specifick against all diseases produced by repletion.

As to learning, government, arts, manufactures, and the like; my master confessed he could find little or no resemblance between the Yahoos of that country, and those in ours. For, he only meant to observe what parity there was in our natures. He had heard indeed some curious Houyhnhnms observe, that in most herds there was a sort of ruling Yahoo, (as among us there is generally some leading or principal stag in a park) who was always more *deformed* in body, and *mischievous in disposition*, than any of the rest. That, this *leader* had usually a favourite as *like himself* as he could get, whose employment was to *lick his master's feet and posteriors, and drive the female Yahoos to his kennel*; for which he was now and then rewarded with a piece of ass's flesh. This *favourite* is hated by the whole herd; and therefore to protect himself, keeps always *near the person of his leader*. He usually continues in office until a worse can be found; but the very moment he is discarded, his successor, at the head of all the Yahoos in that district, young and old, male and female, come in a body, and discharge their excrements upon him from head to foot. But how far this might be applicable to our *courts* and *favourites*, and *ministers of State*, my master said I could best determine.

I durst make no return to this malicious insinuation, which debased humane understanding below the sagacity of a common *hound*, who hath judgment enough to distinguish and follow the cry of the *ablest dog in the pack*, without being ever mistaken.

My master told me, there were some qualities remarkable in the Yahoos, which he had not observed me to mention, or at least very slightly, in the accounts I had given him of humane kind. He said, those animals, like other brutes, had their females in common; but in this they differed, that the she-Yahoo would admit the male, while she was pregnant; and that the hees would quarrel and fight with the females as fiercely as with each other. Both which practices were such degrees of infamous brutality, that no other sensitive creature ever arrived at.

Another thing he wondered at in the Yahoos, was their strange disposition to nastiness and dirt; whereas there appears to be a natural love of cleanliness in all other animals. As to the two former accusations, I was glad to let them pass without any reply, because I had not a word to offer upon them in defence of my species, which otherwise I certainly had done from my own inclinations. But I could have easily vindicated human kind from the imputation of singularity upon the last article, if there had been any *swine* in that country, (as unluckily for me there were not) which although it may be a *sweeter quadruped* than a Yahoo, cannot I humbly conceive in justice pretend to more cleanliness; and so his honour himself must have owned, if he had seen their filthy way of feeding, and their custom of wallowing and sleeping in the mud.

My master likewise mentioned another quality, which his servants had discovered in several Yahoos, and to him was wholly unaccountable. He said, a fancy would sometimes take a Yahoo, to retire into a corner, to lie down and howl, and groan, and spurn away all that came near him, although he were young and fat, and wanted neither food nor water; nor did the servants imagine what could possibly ail him. And the only remedy they found, was to set him to hard work, after which he would infallibly come to himself. To this I was silent out of partiality to my own kind; yet here I could plainly discover the true seeds of *spleen*, which only seizeth on the *lazy*, the *luxurious*, and the *rich*; who, if they were forced to undergo the *same regimen*, I would undertake for the cure.

His honour had farther observed, that a female-Yahoo

would often stand behind a bank or a bush, to gaze on the young males passing by, and then appear, and hide, using many antick gestures and grimaces; at which time it was observed, that she had a most *offensive smell*; and when any of the males advanced, would slowly retire, looking often back, and with a counterfeit shew of fear, run off into some convenient place where she knew the male would follow her.

At other times, if a female stranger came among them, three or four of her own sex would get about her, and stare and chatter, and grin, and smell her all over; and then turn off with gestures that seemed to express contempt and disdain.

Perhaps my master might refine a little in these speculations, which he had drawn from what he observed himself, or had been told him by others: however, I could not reflect without some amazement, and much sorrow, that the rudiments of *lewdness, coquetry, censure,* and *scandal,* should have place by instinct in womankind.

I expected every moment, that my master would accuse the Yahoos of those unnatural appetites in both sexes, so common among us. But nature it seems hath not been so expert a school-mistress; and these politer pleasures are entirely the productions of art and reason, on our side of the globe.

CHAPTER VIII

The author relateth several particulars of the Yahoos. The great virtues of the Houyhnhnms. The education and exercise of their youth. Their general assembly.

As I ought to have understood human nature much better than I supposed it possible for my master to do, so it was easy to apply the character he gave of the Yahoos to myself and my countrymen; and I believed I could yet make farther discoveries from my own observation. I therefore often begged his honour to let me go among the herds of Yahoos in the neighbourhood; to which he always very graciously consented, being perfectly convinced that the hatred I bore those brutes would never suffer me to be corrupted by them; and his honour ordered one of his servants, a strong sorrel nag, very honest and good-natured, to be my guard; without whose protection I durst not undertake such adventures. For I have already told the reader how much I was pestered by those odious animals upon my first arrival. I afterwards failed very narrowly three or four times of falling into their clutches, when I happened to stray at any distance without my hanger. And I have reason to believe, they had some imagination that I was of their own species, which I often assisted myself, by stripping up my sleeves, and shewing my naked arms and breast in their sight, when my protector was with me: at which times they would approach as near as they durst, and imitate my actions after the manner of monkeys, but ever with great signs of hatred; as a tame *jack daw* with cap and stockings, is always persecuted by the wild ones, when he happens to be got among them.

They are prodigiously nimble from their infancy; however, I once caught a young male of three years old, and endeavoured by all marks of tenderness to make it quiet; but the little imp fell a squalling, and scratching, and biting with such violence, that I was forced to let it go; and it was high time, for a whole troop of old ones came about us at the noise; but finding the cub was safe, (for away it ran) and my sorrel nag being by, they durst not venture near us. I observed the young animal's flesh to smell very rank, and the stink was somewhat between a *weasel* and a *fox*, but much more disagreeable. I forgot another circumstance, (and perhaps I might have the readers pardon, if it were wholly omitted) that while I held the odious vermin in my hands, it voided its filthy excrements of a yellow liquid substance, all over my cloaths; but by good fortune there was a small brook hard by, where I washed myself as clean as I could; although I durst not come into my master's presence, until I were sufficiently aired.

By what I could discover, the Yahoos appear to be the most unteachable of all animals, their capacities never reaching higher than to draw or carry burthens. Yet I am of opinion, this defect ariseth chiefly from a perverse, restive disposition. For they are cunning, malicious, treacherous and revengeful. They are strong and hardy, but of a cowardly spirit, and by consequence insolent, abject, and cruel. It is observed, that the *red-haired* of both sexes are more libidinous and mischievous than the rest, whom yet they much exceed in strength and activity.

The Houyhnhnms keep the Yahoos for present use in huts not far from the house; but the rest are sent abroad to certain fields, where they dig up roots, eat several kinds of herbs, and search about for carrion, or sometimes catch *weasels* and *luhimuhs* (a sort of *wild rat*) which they greedily devour. Nature hath taught them to dig deep holes with their nails on the side of a rising ground, wherein they lie by themselves; only the kennels of the females are larger, sufficient to hold two or three cubs.

They swim from their infancy like frogs, and are able to continue long under water, where they often take fish, which the females carry home to their young. And upon this occasion, I hope the reader will pardon my relating an odd adventure.

Being one day abroad with my protector the sorrel nag, and the weather exceeding hot, I entreated him to let me bathe in a river that was near. He consented, and I immediately stripped myself stark naked, and went down softly into the stream. It happened that a young female Yahoo standing behind a bank, saw the whole proceeding; and inflamed by desire, as the nag and I conjectured, came running with all speed, and leaped into the water within five yards of the place where I bathed. I was never in my life so terribly frighted; the nag was grazing at some distance, not suspecting any harm; she embraced me after a most fulsome manner; I roared as loud as I could, and the nag came galloping towards me, whereupon she quitted her grasp, with the utmost reluctancy, and leaped upon the opposite bank, where she stood gazing and howling all the time I was putting on my cloaths.

This was matter of diversion to my master and his family, as well as of mortification to my self. For now I could no longer deny, that I was a real Yahoo, in every limb and feature, since the females had a natural propensity to me as one of their own species: neither was the hair of this brute of a red colour (which might have been some excuse for an appetite a little irregular) but black as sloe, and her countenance did not make an appearance altogether so hideous as the rest of the kind; for, I think, she could not be above eleven years old.

Having already lived three years in this country, the reader I suppose will expect, that I should, like other travellers, give him some account of the manners and customs of its inhabitants, which it was indeed my principal study to learn.

As these noble Houyhnhnms are endowed by nature with a general disposition to all virtues, and have no conceptions or ideas of what is evil in a rational creature; so their grand maxim is, to cultivate *reason*, and to be wholly governed by it. Neither is *reason* among them a point problematical as with us, where men can argue with plausibility on both sides of the question; but strikes you with immediate conviction; as it must needs do where it is not mingled, obscured, or discoloured by passion and interest. I remember it was with extreme difficulty that I could bring my master to understand the meaning of the word *opinion*, or how a point could be disputable; because *reason* taught us to affirm or deny, only where we are certain; and beyond our knowledge, we cannot do either.   So that controversies, wranglings, disputes, and positiveness in false or dubious propositions, are evils unknown among the Houyhnhnms. In the like manner, when I used to explain to him our several systems of *natural philosophy*, he would laugh that a creature pretending to *reason*, should value it self upon the knowledge of other peoples conjectures, and in things, where that knowledge, if it were certain, could be of no use. Wherein he agreed entirely with the sentiments of Socrates, as Plato delivers them; which I mention as the highest honour I can do that prince of philosophers.   I have often since reflected what destruction such a doctrine would make in the libraries of Europe; and how many paths to fame would be then shut up in the learned world.

Friendship and *benevolence* are the two principal virtues among the Houyhnhnms; and these not confined to particular objects, but universal to the whole race: for, a stranger from the remotest part, is equally treated with the nearest neighbour, and wherever he goes, looks upon himself as at home.   They preserve *decency* and *civility* in the highest degrees, but are altogether ignorant of *ceremony*.   They have no fondness for their colts or foles; but the care they take in educating them proceedeth entirely from the dictates of *reason*.   And, I observed my master to shew the same affection to his neighbour's issue, that he had for his own.   They will have it that *nature* teaches them to love the whole species, and it is *reason* only that maketh a distinction of persons, where there is a superior degree of virtue.

When the matron Houyhnhnms have produced one of each sex, they no longer accompany with their consorts, except they lose one of their issue by some casualty, which very seldom happens: but in such a case they meet again; or when the like accident befals a person, whose wife is past bearing, some other couple bestows on him one of their own colts, and then go together a second time, until the mother be pregnant. This caution is necessary to prevent the country from being overburthened with numbers. But the race of inferior Houyhnhnms bred up to be servants, is not so strictly limited upon this article; these are allowed to produce three of each sex, to be domesticks in the noble families.

In their marriages, they are exactly careful to chuse such colours as will not make any disagreeable mixture in the breed. *Strength* is chiefly valued in the male, and *comeliness* in the female; not upon the account of *love*, but to preserve the race from degenerating: for, where a female happens to excel in *strength*, a consort is chosen with regard to *comeliness*. Courtship, love, presents, joyntures, settlements, have no place in their thoughts; or terms whereby to express them in their language. The young couple meet and are joined, merely because it is the determination of their parents and friends: it is what they see done every day; and they look upon it as one of the necessary actions in a reasonable being. But, the violation of marriage, or any other unchastity, was never heard of: and the married pair pass their lives with the same friendship, and mutual benevolence that they bear to all others of the same species, who come in their way; without jealousy, fondness, quarrelling, or discontent.

In educating the youth of both sexes, their method is admirable, and highly deserveth our imitation. These are not suffered to taste a grain of *oats*, except upon certain days, until eighteen years old; nor *milk*, but very rarely; and in summer, they graze two hours in the morning, and as many in the evening, which their parents likewise observe; but the servants are not allowed above half that time; and a great part of the grass is brought home, which they eat at the most convenient hours, when they can be best spared from work.

Temperance, industry, exercise, and *cleanliness,* are the lessons equally enjoyned to the young ones of both sexes: and my master thought it monstrous in us to give the females a different kind of education from the males, except in some articles of domestick management; whereby, as he truly observed, one half of our natives were good for nothing but bringing children into the world: and to trust the care of their children to such useless animals, he said was yet a greater instance of brutality.

But, the Houyhnhnms train up their youth to strength, speed, and hardiness, by exercising them in running races up and down steep hills, or over hard stony grounds; and when they are all in a sweat, they are ordered to leap over head and ears into a pond or river. Four times a year the youth of certain districts meet to shew their proficiency in running, and leaping, and other feats of strength or agility; where the victor is rewarded with a song, made in his or her praise. On this festival, the servants drive a herd of Yahoos into the field, laden with hay, and oats, and milk for a repast to the Houyhnhnms; after which, these brutes are immediately driven back again, for fear of being noisome to the assembly.

Every fourth year, at the *vernal equinox,* there is a representative council of the whole nation, which meets in a plain about twenty miles from our house, and continueth about five or six days. Here they inquire into the state and condition of the several districts; whether they abound, or be deficient in hay, or oats, or cows, or Yahoos? And wherever there is any want (which is but seldom) it is immediately supplied by unanimous consent and contribution. Here likewise the regulation of children is settled: as for instance, if a Houyhnhnm hath two males, he changeth one of them with another who hath two females: and when a child hath been lost by any casualty, where the mother is past breeding, it is determined what family shall breed another to supply the loss.

CHAPTER IX

A grand debate at the general assembly of the Houyhnhnms; and how it was determined. The learning of the Houyhnhnms. Their buildings. Their manner of burials. The defectiveness of their language.

ONE of these grand assemblies was held in my time, about three months before my departure, whither my master went as the representative of our district. In this council was resumed their old debate, and indeed, the only debate that ever happened in their country; whereof my master, after his return, gave me a very particular account.

The question to be debated was, whether the Yahoos should be exterminated from the face of the earth. One of the *members* for the affirmative offered several arguments of great strength and weight; alledging, that, as the Yahoos were the most filthy, noisome, and deformed animal which nature ever produced, so they were the most restive and indocible, mischievous and malicious: they would privately suck the teats of the Houyhnhnms cows; kill and devour their cats, trample down their oats and grass, if they were not continually watched; and commit a thousand other extravagancies. ⟨ He took notice of a general tradition, that Yahoos had not been always in their country: but, that many ages ago, two of these brutes appeared together upon a mountain; whether produced by the heat of the sun upon corrupted mud and slime, or from the ooze and froth of the sea, was never known. That, these Yahoos engendered, and their brood in a short time grew so numerous, as to overrun and infest the whole nation. That, the Houyhnhnms, to get rid of this evil, made a general hunting, and at last inclosed the whole herd; and destroying the older, every Houyhnhnm kept two young ones in a kennel, and brought them to such a degree of tameness, as an animal so savage by nature, can be capable of acquiring; using them for draught and carriage. That, there seemed to be much truth in this tradition, and that those creatures could not be *ylnhniamshy* (or *aborigines* of the land) because of the violent hatred the Houyhnhnms, as well as all other animals bore them; which although their evil disposition sufficiently deserved, could never have arrived at so high a degree, if they had been *aborigines*, or else they would have long since been rooted out. That, the inhabitants taking a fancy to use the service of the Yahoos, had very imprudently neglected to cultivate the breed of *asses*, which were a comely animal, easily kept, more tame and orderly, without any offensive smell, strong enough for labour, although they yield to the other in agility of body; and if their braying be no agreeable sound, it is far preferable to the horrible howlings of the Yahoos.

Several others declared their sentiments to the same purpose; when my master proposed an expedient to the assembly, whereof he had indeed borrowed the hint from me. He approved of the tradition mentioned by the *honourable member*, who spoke before; and affirmed, that the two Yahoos said to be first seen among them, had been driven thither over the sea: that, coming to land, and being forsaken by their companions, they retired to the mountains, and degenerating by degrees, became in process of time, much more savage than those of their own species in the country from whence these two originals came. The reason of his assertion was, that he had now in his possession, a certain wonderful Yahoo (meaning my self) which most of them had heard of, and many of them had seen. He then related to them, how he first found me: that, my body was all covered with an artificial composure of the skins and hairs of other animals: that, I spoke in a language of my own, and had thoroughly learned theirs: that, I had related to him the accidents which brought me thither: that, when he saw me without my covering, I was an exact Yahoo in every part, only of a whiter colour, less hairy, and with shorter claws. He added, how I had endeavoured to persuade him, that in my own and other countries, the Yahoos acted as the governing, rational animal, and held the Houyhnhnms in servitude: that, he observed in me, all the qualities of a Yahoo, only a little more civilized by some tincture of reason; which however, was in a degree as far inferior to the Houyhnhnm race, as the Yahoos of their country were to me: that, among other things, I mentioned a custom we had of *castrating* Houyhnhnms when they were young, in order to render them tame; that the operation was easy and safe: that, it was no shame to learn wisdom from brutes, as industry is taught by the ant, and building by the swallow: (for so I translate the word 'lyhannh,' although it be a much larger fowl) that, this invention might be practised upon the younger Yahoos here, which, besides rendering them tractable and fitter for use, would in an age, put an end to the whole species, without destroying life: that, in the mean time, the Houyhnhnms should be *exhorted* to cultivate the breed of asses, which, as they are in all respects more valuable brutes, so they have this advantage, to be fit for service at five years old, which the others are not until twelve.

This was all my master thought fit to tell me at that time, of what passed in the Grand Council But he was pleased to conceal one particular, which related personally to my self, whereof I soon felt the unhappy effect, as the reader will know in its proper place, and from whence I date all the succeeding misfortunes of my life.

The Houyhnhnms have no letters, and consequently, their knowledge is all traditional. But, there happening few events of any moment among a people so well united, naturally disposed to every virtue, wholly governed by reason, and cut off from all commerce with other nations; the historical part is easily preserved without burthening their memories. I have already observed, that they are subject to no diseases, and therefore can have no need of physicians. However, they have excellent medicines composed of herbs, to cure accidental bruises and cuts in the pastern or frog of the foot by sharp stones, as well as other maims and hurts in the several parts of the body.

They calculate the year by the revolution of the sun and the moon, but use no subdivisions into weeks. They are well enough acquainted with the motions of those two luminaries, and understand the nature of *eclipses*; and this is the utmost progress of their *astronomy*.

In *poetry*, they must be allowed to excel all other mortals; wherein the justness of their similes, and the minuteness, as well as exactness of their descriptions, are indeed, inimitable. Their verses abound very much in both of these; and usually contain either some exalted notions of friendship and benevolence, or the praises of those who were victors in races, and other bodily exercises. Their buildings, although very rude and simple, are not inconvenient, but well contrived to defend them from all injuries of cold and heat. They have a kind of tree, which at forty years old loosens in the root, and falls with the first storm; it grows very strait, and being pointed like stakes with a sharp stone, (for the Houyhnhnms know not the use of iron) they stick them erect in the ground about ten inches asunder, and then weave in oat straw, or sometimes wattles betwixt them. The roof is made after the same manner, and so are the doors.

The Houyhnhnms use the hollow part between the pastern and the hoof of their fore-feet, as we do our hands, and this with greater dexterity, than I could at first imagine. I have seen a white mare of our family thread a needle (which I lent her on purpose) with that joint. They milk their cows, reap their oats, and do all the work which requires hands, in the same manner. They have a kind of hard flints, which by grinding against other stones, they form into instruments, that serve instead of wedges, axes, and hammers. With tools made of these flints, they likewise cut their hay, and reap their oats, which there groweth naturally in several fields: the Yahoos draw home the sheaves in carriages, and the servants tread them in certain covered hutts, to get out the grain, which is kept in stores. They make a rude kind of earthen and wooden vessels, and bake the former in the sun.

If they can avoid casualties, they die only of old age, and are buried in the obscurest places that can be found, their friends and relations expressing neither joy nor grief at their departure; nor does the dying person discover the least regret that he is leaving the world, any more than if he were upon returning home from a visit to one of his neighbours. I remember, my master having once made an appointment with a friend and his family, to come to his house upon some affair of importance; on the day fixed, the mistress and her two children came very late; she made two excuses, first for her husband, who, as she said happened that very morning to *lhduwhn*. The word is strongly expressed in their language, but not easily rendered into English; it signifies, *to retire to his first mother*. Her excuse for not coming sooner, was, that her husband dying late in the morning, she was a good while consulting her servants about a convenient place where his body should be laid; and I observed, she behaved her self at our house, as chearfully as the rest: she died about three months after.

They live generally to seventy or seventy-five years, very seldom to fourscore: some weeks before their death, they feel a gradual decay, but without pain.   During this time, they are much visited by their friends, because they cannot go abroad with their usual ease and satisfaction.   However, about ten days before their death, which they seldom fail in computing, they return the visits that have been made them by those who are nearest in the neighbourhood, being carried in a convenient sledge drawn by Yahoos; which vehicle they use, not only upon this occasion, but when they grow old, upon long journies, or when they are lamed by any accident.   And therefore, when the dying Houyhnhnms return those visits, they take a solemn leave of their friends, as if they were going to some remote part of the country, where they designed to pass the rest of their lives.

I know not whether it may be worth observing, that the Houyhnhnms have no word in their language to express any thing that is *evil*, except what they borrow from the deformities or ill-qualities of the Yahoos.   Thus they denote the folly of a servant, an omission of a child, a stone that cuts their feet, a continuance of foul or unseasonable weather, and the like, by adding to each, the epithet of Yahoo.   For instance, *hhnum Yahoo, whnaholm Yahoo, ynlhmnawihlma Yahoo*, and an ill contrived house, *ynholm-hnmrohlnw Yahoo*.

I could with great pleasure enlarge farther upon the manners and virtues of this excellent people; but intending in a short time to publish a volume by it self expressly upon that subject, I refer the reader thither.   And in the mean time. proceed to relate my own sad catastrophe.

CHAPTER X

The author's œconomy and happy life among the Houyhnhnms. His great improvement in virtue, by conversing
with them. Their conversations. The author hath notice
given him by his master, that he must depart from the
country. He falls into a swoon for grief, but submits. He
contrives and finishes a canoo, by the help of a fellow-
servant; and puts to sea at a venture.

I HAD settled my little œconomy to my own heart's content.
My master had ordered a room to be made for me after
their manner, about six yards from the house; the sides and
floors of which I plaistered with clay, and covered with
rush-mats of my own contriving. I had beaten hemp,
which there grows wild, and made of it a sort of ticking:
this I filled with the feathers of several birds I had taken
with springes made of Yahoos hairs; and were excellent
food. I had worked two chairs with my knife, the sorrel
nag helping me in the grosser and more laborious part.
When my cloaths were worn to rags, I made my self others
with the skins of rabbets, and of a certain beautiful animal
about the same size, called *nnuhnoh*, the skin of which is
covered with a fine down. Of these I likewise made very
tolerable stockings. I soaled my shoes with wood, which
I cut from a tree, and fitted to the upper leather, and when
this was worn out, I supplied it with the skins of Yahoos,
dried in the sun. I often got honey out of hollow trees,
which I mingled with water, or eat it with my bread. No
man could more verify the truth of these two maxims:
that, nature is very easily satisfied; and, *that necessity is the
mother of invention.* I enjoyed perfect health of body, and
tranquility of mind; I did not feel the treachery or incon-
stancy of a friend, nor the injuries of a secret or open
enemy. I had no occasion of bribing, flattering or
pimping, to procure the favour of any great man, or of his

minion. I wanted no fence against fraud or oppression: here was neither physician to destroy my body, nor lawyer to ruin my fortune: no informer to watch my words and actions, or forge accusations against me for hire: here were no gibers, censurers, backbiters, pickpockets, highwaymen, house-breakers, attorneys, bawds, buffoons, gamesters, politicians, wits, spleneticks, tedious talkers, controvertists, ravishers, murderers, robbers, virtuosoes; no leaders or followers of party and faction; no encouragers to vice, by seducement or examples: no dungeon, axes, gibbets, whipping-posts, or pillories: no cheating shop-keepers or mechanicks: no pride, vanity or affectation: no fops, bullies, drunkards, strolling whores, or poxes: no ranting, lewd expensive wives: no stupid, proud pedants: no importunate, over-bearing, quarrelsome, noisy, roaring, empty, conceited, swearing companions: no scoundrels raised from the dust upon the merit of their vices; or nobility thrown into it, on account of their virtues: no lords, fiddlers, judges, or dancing-masters.

I had the favour of being admitted to several Houyhnhnms, who came to visit or dine with my master; where his honour graciously suffered me to wait in the room, and listen to their discourse. Both he and his company would often condescend to ask me questions, and receive my answers. I had also, sometimes the honour of attending my master in his visits to others. I never presumed to speak, except in answer to a question; and then I did it with inward regret, because it was a loss of so much time for improving my self: but, I was infinitely delighted with the station of an humble auditor in such conversations, where nothing passed but what was useful, expressed in the fewest and most significant words: where (as I have already said) the greatest *decency* was observed, without the least degree of ceremony; where no person spoke without being pleased himself, and pleasing his companions:

where there was no interruption, tediousness, heat, or difference of sentiments. They have a notion, that when people are met together, a short silence doth much improve conversation: this I found to be true; for during those little intermissions of talk, new ideas would arise in their minds, which very much enlivened the discourse. Their subjects are generally on friendship and benevolence; on order and œconomy; sometimes upon the visible operations of nature, or ancient traditions; upon the bounds and limits of virtue; upon the unerring rules of reason; or upon some determinations, to be taken at the next great assembly; and often upon the various excellencies of *poetry*. I may add, without vanity, that my presence often gave them sufficient matter for discourse, because it afforded my master an occasion of letting his friends into the history of me and my country, upon which they were all pleased to descant in a manner not very advantageous to human kind; and for that reason, I shall not repeat what they said: only I may be allowed to observe, that his honour, to my great admiration, appeared to understand the nature of Yahoos much better than my self. He went through all our vices and follies, and discovered many which I had never mentioned to him; by only supposing what qualities a Yahoo of their country, with a small proportion of reason, might be capable of exerting: and concluded, with too much probability, how vile as well as miserable such a creature must be.

I freely confess, that all the little knowledge I have of any value, was acquired by the lectures I received from my master, and from hearing the discourses of him and his friends; to which I should be prouder to listen, than to dictate to the greatest and wisest assembly in Europe. I admired the strength, comeliness and speed of the inhabitants; and such a constellation of virtues in such amiable persons, produced in me the highest veneration. At first, indeed, I did not feel that natural awe, which the Yahoos

and all other animals, bear towards them; but it grew upon
me by degrees, much sooner than I imagined, and was
mingled with a respectful love and gratitude, that they
would condescend to distinguish me from the rest of
my species.

When I thought of my family, my friends, my countrymen, or human race in general, I considered them as they
really were, Yahoos in shape and disposition, perhaps a
little more civilized, and qualified with the gift of speech;
but making no other use of reason, than to improve and
multiply those vices, whereof their brethren in this country,
had only the share that nature allotted them.   When I
happened to behold the reflection of my own form in a lake
or fountain, I turned away my face in horror and detestation of myself; and could better endure the sight of a
common Yahoo, than of my own person.   By conversing
with the Houyhnhnms, and looking upon them with delight,
I fell to imitate their gait and gesture, which is now grown
into a habit; and my friends often tell me in a blunt way,
that *I trot like a horse*; which, however, I take for a great
compliment: neither shall I disown, that in speaking I am
apt to fall into the voice and manner of the Houyhnhnms,
and hear my self ridiculed on that account without the
least mortification.

In the midst of this happiness, when I looked upon my
self to be fully settled for life, my master sent for me one
morning a little earlier than his usual hour.   I observed
by his countenance, that he was in some perplexity, and at
a loss how to begin what he had to speak.   After a short
silence, he told me, he did not know how I would take what
he was going to say: that, in the last general assembly, when
the affair of the Yahoos was entered upon, the representatives had taken offence at his keeping a Yahoo (meaning
my self) in his family more like a Houyhnhnm than a brute
animal: that, he was known frequently to converse with

me, as if he could receive some advantage or pleasure in my company: that, such a practice was not agreeable to reason or nature, or a thing ever heard of before among them. The assembly did therefore *exhort* him, either to employ me like the rest of my species, or command me to swim back to the place from whence I came: that, the first of these expedients was utterly rejected by all the Houyhnhnms, who had ever seen me at his house or their own: for, they alledged, that because I had some rudiments of reason, added to the natural pravity of those animals, it was to be feared, I might be able to seduce them into the woody and mountainous parts of the country, and bring them in troops by night to destroy the Houyhnhnms cattle, as being naturally of the ravenous kind, and averse from labour.

My master added, that he was daily pressed by the Houyhnhnms of the neighbourhood to have the assembly's *exhortation* executed, which he could not put off much longer. He doubted, it would be impossible for me to swim to another country; and therefore wished I would contrive some sort of vehicle resembling those I had described to him, that might carry me on the sea; in which work I should have the assistance of his own servants, as well as those of his neighbours. He concluded, that for his own part he could have been content to keep me in his service as long as I lived; because he found I had cured myself of some bad habits and dispositions, by endeavouring, as far as my inferior nature was capable, to imitate the Houyhnhnms.

I should here observe to the reader, that a decree of the general assembly in this country, is expressed by the word 'hnhloayn,' which signifies an *exhortation*; as near as I can render it: for they have no conception how a rational creature can be *compelled*, but only advised, or *exhorted*; because no person can disobey reason, without giving up his claim to be a rational creature.

I was struck with the utmost grief and despair at my

master's discourse; and being unable to support the agonies I was under, I fell into a swoon at his feet: when I came to myself, he told me, that he concluded I had been dead. (For these people are subject to no such imbecillities of nature.) ₁ I answered, in a faint voice, that death would have been too great a happiness: that, although I could not blame the assembly's *exhortation*, or the urgency of his friends; yet in my weak and corrupt judgment, I thought it might consist with reason to have been less rigorous: that, I could not swim a league, and probably the nearest land to theirs might be distant above an hundred: that, many materials, necessary for making a small vessel to carry me off, were wholly wanting in this country; which, however, I would attempt in obedience and gratitude to his honour, although I concluded the thing to be impossible, and therefore looked on my self as already devoted to destruction: that, the certain prospect of an unnatural death, was the least of my evils: for, supposing I should escape with life by some strange adventure, how could I think with temper, of passing my days among Yahoos, and relapsing into my old corruptions, for want of examples to lead and keep me within the paths of virtue: that, I knew too well upon what solid reasons all the determinations of the wise Houyhnhnms were founded, not to be shaken by arguments of mine, a miserable Yahoo; and therefore, after presenting him with my humble thanks for the offer of his servants assistance in making a vessel, and desiring a reasonable time for so difficult a work, I told him, I would endeavour to preserve a wretched being; and, if ever I returned to England, was not without hopes of being useful to my own species, by celebrating the praises of the renowned Houyhnhnms, and proposing their virtues to the imitation of mankind.

'My master in a few words made me a very gracious reply, allowed me the space of two *months* to finish my boat; and ordered the sorrel nag, my fellow-servant, (for so at this distance I may presume to call him) to follow my instructions, because I told my master, that his help would be sufficient, and I knew he had a tenderness for me.

In his company my first business was to go to that part of the coast, where my rebellious crew had ordered me to be set on shore. I got upon a height, and looking on every side into the sea, fancied I saw a small island, towards the north-east: I took out my pocket-glass, and could then clearly distinguish it about five leagues off, as I computed; but it appeared to the sorrel nag to be only a blue cloud: for, as he had no conception of any country beside his own, so he could not be as expert in distinguishing remote objects at sea, as we who so much converse in that element.

After I had discovered this island, I considered no farther; but resolved, it should, if possible, be the first place of my banishment, leaving the consequence to fortune.

I returned home, and consulting with the sorrel nag, we went into a copse at some distance, where I with my knife, and he with a sharp flint fastened very artificially, after their manner, to a wooden handle, cut down several oak wattles about the thickness of a walking staff, and some larger pieces. But I shall not trouble the reader with a particular description of my own mechanicks: let it suffice to say, that in six weeks time, with the help of the sorrel nag, who performed the parts that required most labour, I finished a sort of Indian canoo, but much larger, covering it with the skins of Yahoos well stitched together, with hempen threads of my own making. My sail was likewise composed of the skins of the same animal; but I made use of the youngest I could get, the older being too tough and thick; and I likewise provided my self with four paddles. I laid in a stock of boiled flesh, of rabbets and fowls; and took with me two vessels, one filled with milk, and the other with water.

I tried my canoo in a large pond near my master's house, and then corrected in it what was amiss; stopping all the chinks with Yahoos tallow, until I found it stanch, and able to bear me, and my freight. And when it was as compleat as I could possibly make it, I had it drawn on a carriage very gently by Yahoos, to the sea-side, under the conduct of the sorrel nag, and another servant.

When all was ready, and the day came for my departure, I took leave of my master and lady, and the whole family, mine eyes flowing with tears, and my heart quite sunk with grief. But his honour, out of curiosity, and perhaps (if I may speak it without vanity) partly out of kindness, was determined to see me in my canoo; and got several of his neighbouring friends to accompany him. I was forced to wait above an hour for the tide, and then observing the wind very fortunately bearing towards the island, to which I intended to steer my course, I took a second leave of my master: but, as I was going to prostrate my self to kiss his hoof, he did me the honour to raise it gently to my mouth. I am not ignorant how much I have been censured for mentioning this last particular. Detractors are pleased to think it improbable, that so illustrious a person should descend to give so great a mark of distinction to a creature so inferior as I. Neither have I forgot, how apt some travellers are to boast of extraordinary favours they have received. But, if these censurers were better acquainted with the noble and courteous disposition of the Houy-hnhnms, they would soon change their opinion.

I paid my respects to the rest of the Houyhnhnms in his honour's company; then getting into my canoo, I pushed off from shore.

CHAPTER XI

The author's dangerous voyage.   He arrives at New-Holland,
hoping to settle there.   Is wounded with an arrow by one
of the natives.   Is seized and carried by force into a Portugueze ship.   The great civilities of the captain.   The author
arrives at England.

I BEGAN this desperate voyage on February 15, 171⅘, at
nine o'clock in the morning.   The wind was very favourable; however, I made use at first only of my paddles; but
considering I should soon be weary, and that the wind
might probably chop about, I ventured to set up my little
sail; and thus, with the help of the tide, I went at the rate
of a league and a half an hour, as near as I could guess.
My master and his friends continued on the shoar, until I
was almost out of sight; and I often heard the sorrel nag
(who always loved me) crying out, 'Hnuy illa nyha maiah
Yahoo' (Take care of thy self, gentle Yahoo).

My design was, if possible, to discover some small island
uninhabited, yet sufficient by my labour to furnish me with
necessaries of life, which I would have thought a greater
happiness than to be first minister in the politest court of
Europe; so horrible was the idea I conceived of returning
to live in the society and under the government of Yahoos.
For, in such a solitude as I desired, I could at least enjoy
my own thoughts, and reflect with delight on the virtues
of those inimitable Houyhnhnms, without any opportunity
of degenerating into the vices and corruptions of my own
species.

The reader may remember what I related when my crew
conspired against me, and confined me to my cabbin.   How
I continued there several weeks, without knowing what
course we took; and when I was put ashore in the long-boat,
how the sailors told me with oaths, whether true or false,

that they knew not in what part of the world we were. However, I did then believe us to be about ten degrees southward of the Cape of Good Hope, or about 45 degrees southern latitude, as I gathered from some general words I overheard among them, being I supposed to the south-east in their intended voyage to Madagascar. And although this were but little better than conjecture, yet I resolved to steer my course eastward, hoping to reach the south-west coast of New-Holland, and perhaps some such island as I desired, lying westward of it. The wind was full west, and by six in the evening I computed I had gone eastward at least eighteen leagues; when I spied a very small island about half a league off, which I soon reached. It was nothing but a rock with one creek, naturally arched by the force of tempests. Here I put in my canoo, and climbing a part of the rock, I could plainly discover land to the east, extending from south to north. I lay all night in my canoo; and repeating my voyage early in the morning, I arrived in seven hours to the south-east point of New-Holland. This confirmed me in the opinion I have long entertained, that the *maps* and *charts* place this country at least three degrees more to the east than it really is; which thought I communicated many years ago to my worthy friend Mr. Herman Moll, and gave him my reasons for it, although he hath rather chosen to follow other authors.

I saw no inhabitants in the place where I landed; and being unarmed, I was afraid of venturing far into the country. I found some shell-fish on the shore, and eat them raw, not daring to kindle a fire, for fear of being discovered by the natives. I continued three days feeding on oysters and limpits, to save my own provisions; and I fortunately found a brook of excellent water, which gave me great relief.

On the fourth day, venturing out early a little too far, I saw twenty or thirty natives upon a height, not above five hundred yards from me. They were stark naked, men, women, and children, round a fire, as I could discover by the smoke. One of them spied me, and gave notice to the rest; five of them advanced towards me, leaving the women and children at the fire. I made what haste I could to the shore, and getting into my canoo, shoved off: the savages observing me retreat, ran after me; and before I could get far enough into the sea, discharged an arrow, which wounded me deeply on the inside of my left knee (I shall carry the mark to my grave.) I apprehended the arrow might be poisoned; and paddling out of the reach of their darts (being a calm day) I made a shift to suck the wound, and dress it as well as I could.

I was at a loss what to do, for I durst not return to the same landing-place, but stood to the north, and was forced to paddle; for the wind, although very gentle, was against me, blowing north-west. As I was looking about for a secure landing place, I saw a sail to the north north-east, which appearing every minute more visible, I was in some doubt, whether I should wait for them or no; but at last my detestation of the Yahoo race prevailed; and turning my canoo, I sailed and paddled together to the south, and got into the same creek from whence I set out in the morning; choosing rather to trust my self among these *barbarians*, than live with European Yahoos. I drew up my canoo as close as I could to the shore, and hid my self behind a stone by the little brook, which, as I have already said, was excellent water.

The ship came within half a league of this creek, and sent out her long-boat with vessels to take in fresh water (for the place it seems was very well known) but I did not observe it until the boat was almost on shore; and it was too late to seek another hiding-place. The seamen at their landing observed my canoo, and rummaging it all over, easily conjectured that the owner could not be far off. Four of them well armed, searched every cranny and lurking-hole, until at last they found me flat on my face behind the stone. They gazed a while in admiration at my strange uncouth dress; my coat made of skins, my wooden-soaled shoes, and my furred stockings; from whence, however, they concluded I was not a native of the place, who all go naked. One of the seamen in Portuguese bid me rise, and asked who I was. I understood that language very well, and getting upon my feet, said, I was a poor Yahoo, banished from the Houyhnhnms, and desired they would please to let me depart. They admired to hear me answer them in their own tongue, and saw by my complexion I must be an European; but were at a loss to know what I meant by Yahoos and Houyhnhnms; and at the same time fell a laughing at my strange tone in speaking, which resembled the neighing of a horse. I trembled all the while betwixt fear and hatred: I again desired leave to depart, and was gently moving to my canoo; but they laid hold on me, desiring to know what country I was of? Whence I came? With many other questions. I told them I was born in England, from whence I came about five years ago, and then their country and ours was at peace. I therefore hoped they would not treat me as an enemy, since I meant them no harm, but was a poor Yahoo, seeking some desolate place where to pass the remainder of my unfortunate life.

When they began to talk, I thought I never heard or saw any thing so unnatural; for it appeared to me as monstrous as if a dog or a cow should speak in England, or a Yahoo in Houyhnhnm-land. The honest Portugueze were equally amazed at my strange dress, and the odd manner of delivering my words, which however they understood very well. They spoke to me with great humanity, and said they were sure their captain would carry me *gratis* to Lisbon, from whence I might return to my own country: that, two of the seamen would go back to the ship, to inform the captain of what they had seen, and receive his orders;

in the mean time, unless I would give my solemn oath not
to fly, they would secure me by force. I thought it best
to comply with their proposal. They were very curious
to know my story, but I gave them very little satisfaction;
and they all conjectured, that my misfortunes had impaired
my reason. In two hours the boat, which went loaden with
vessels of water, returned with the captain's commands to
fetch me on board. I fell on my knees to preserve my
liberty; but all was in vain, and the men having tied me
with cords, heaved me into the boat, from whence I was
taken into the ship, and from thence into the captain's
cabbin.

His name was Pedro de Mendez; he was a very courteous
and generous person; he entreated me to give some account
of my self, and desired to know what I would eat or drink;
said, I should be used as well as himself, and spoke so many
obliging things, that I wondered to find such civilities from
a Yahoo. However, I remained silent and sullen; I was
ready to faint at the very smell of him and his men. At last
I desired something to eat out of my own canoo; but he
ordered me a chicken and some excellent wine, and then
directed that I should be put to bed in a very clean cabbin.
I would not undress my self, but lay on the bed-cloaths;
and in half an hour stole out, when I thought the crew was
at dinner; and getting to the side of the ship, was going to
leap into the sea, and swim for my life, rather than continue
among Yahoos: but one of the seamen prevented me, and
having informed the captain, I was chained to my cabbin.

After dinner Don Pedro came to me, and desired to know
my reason for so desperate an attempt; assured me he only
meant to do me all the service he was able; and spoke so
very movingly, that at last I descended to treat him like
an animal which had some little portion of reason. I gave
him a very short relation of my voyage; of the conspiracy
against me by my own men; of the country where they set

me on shoar; and of my five years residence there. All which he looked upon as if it were a dream or a vision; whereat I took great offence: for I had quite forgot the faculty of lying, so peculiar to Yahoos in all countries where they preside, and consequently the disposition of suspecting truth in others of their own species. I asked him, whether it were the custom of his country to *say the thing that was not*? I assured him I had almost forgot what he meant by falshood; and if I had lived a thousand years in Houyhn-hnmland, I should never have heard a lie from the meanest servant: that, I was altogether indifferent whether he believed me or no; but however, in return for his favours, I would give so much allowance to the corruption of his nature, as to answer any objection he would please to make; and he might easily discover the truth.

The captain, a wise man, after many endeavours to catch me tripping in some part of my story, at last began to have a better opinion of my veracity. But he added, that since I professed so inviolable an attachment to truth, I must give him my word of honour to bear him company in this voyage without attempting any thing against my life; or else he would continue me a prisoner until we arrived at Lisbon. I gave him the promise he required; but at the same time protested, that I would suffer the greatest hardships rather than return to live among Yahoos.

Our voyage passed without any considerable accident. In gratitude to the captain I sometimes sate with him at his earnest request, and strove to conceal my antipathy against human kind, although it often broke out; which he suffered to pass without observation. But the greatest part of the day, I confined my self to my cabbin, to avoid seeing any of the crew. The captain had often intreated me to strip myself of my savage dress, and offered to lend me the best suit of cloaths he had. This I would not be prevailed on to accept, abhorring to cover myself with any thing that had been on the back of a Yahoo. I only desired he would lend me two clean shirts, which having been washed since he wore them, I believed would not so much defile me. These I changed every second day, and washed them my self.

We arrived at Lisbon, Nov. 5, 1715. At our landing, the captain forced me to cover my self with his cloak, to prevent the rabble from crouding about me. I was conveyed to his own house; and at my earnest request, he led me up to the highest room backwards. I conjured him to conceal from all persons what I had told him of the Houyhnhnms; because the least hint of such a story would not only draw numbers of people to see me, but probably put me in danger of being imprisoned, or burnt by the *Inquisition*. The captain persuaded me to accept a suit of cloaths newly made; but I would not suffer the taylor to take my measure; however, Don Pedro being almost of my size, they fitted me well enough. He accoutred me with other necessaries all new, which I aired for twenty four hours before I would use them.

The captain had no wife, nor above three servants, none of which were suffered to attend at meals; and his whole deportment was so obliging, added to very good *human* understanding, that I really began to tolerate his company. He gained so far upon me, that I ventured to look out of the back window. By degrees I was brought into another room, from whence I peeped into the street, but drew my head back in a fright. In a week's time he seduced me down to the door. I found my terror gradually lessened, but my hatred and contempt seemed to increase. I was at last bold enough to walk the street in his company, but kept my nose well stopped with rue, or sometimes with tobacco.

In ten days, Don Pedro, to whom I had given some account of my domestick affairs, put it upon me as a point of honour and conscience, that I ought to return to my native country, and live at home with my wife and children. He told me, there was an English ship in the port just ready to sail, and he would furnish me with all things necessary. It would be tedious to repeat his arguments, and my contradictions.   He said, it was altogether impossible to find such a solitary island as I had desired to live in; but I might command in my own house, and pass my time in a manner as recluse as I pleased.

I complied at last, finding I could not do better.   I left Lisbon the 24th day of November, in an English merchantman, but who was the master I never inquired.   Don Pedro accompanied me to the ship, and lent me twenty pounds.   He took kind leave of me, and embraced me at parting; which I bore as well as I could.   During this last voyage I had no commerce with the master, or any of his men; but pretending I was sick kept close in my cabbin. On the fifth of December, 1715, we cast anchor in the Downs about nine in the morning, and at three in the afternoon I got safe to my house at Redriff.

My wife and family received me with great surprize and joy, because they concluded me certainly dead; but I must freely confess, the sight of them filled me only with hatred, disgust and contempt; and the more, by reflecting on the near alliance I had to them.   For, although since my unfortunate exile from the Houyhnhnm country, I had compelled my self to tolerate the sight of Yahoos, and to converse with Don Pedro de Mendez; yet my memory and imaginations were perpetually filled with the virtues and ideas of those exalted Houyhnhnms.   And when I began to consider, that by copulating with one of the Yahoo-species, I had become a parent of more; it struck me with the utmost shame, confusion, and horror.

As soon as I entered the house, my wife took me in her arms, and kissed me; at which, having not been used to the touch of that odious animal for so many years, I fell in a swoon for almost an hour.   At the time I am writing, it is five years since my last return to England: during the first year I could not endure my wife or children in my presence, the very smell of them was intolerable; much less could I suffer them to eat in the same room.   To this hour they dare not presume to touch my bread, or drink out of the same cup; neither was I ever able to let one of them take me by the hand.   The first money I laid out was to buy two young stone-horses, which I keep in a good stable, and next to them the groom is my greatest favourite; for I feel my spirits revived by the smell he contracts in the stable. My horses understand me tolerably well; I converse with them at least four hours every day.   They are strangers to bridle or saddle; they live in great amity with me, and friendship to each other.

CHAPTER XII

The author's veracity.   His design in publishing this work. His censure of those travellers who swerve from the truth. The author clears himself from any sinister ends in writing. An objection answered.   The method of planting colonies. His native country commended.   The right of the Crown to those countries described by the author, is justified.   The difficulty of conquering them.   The author taketh his last leave of the reader; proposeth his manner of living for the future; gives good advice, and concludeth.

THUS, gentle reader, I have given thee a faithful history of my travels for sixteen years and above seven months; wherein I have not been so studious of ornament as of truth. I could perhaps, like others, have astonished thee with strange improbable tales; but, I rather chose to relate plain matter of fact in the simplest manner and style; because my principal design was to inform, and not to amuse thee.

It is easy for us who travel into remote countries, which are seldom visited by Englishmen or other Europeans, to form descriptions of wonderful animals both at sea and land. Whereas, a traveller's chief aim should be to make men wiser and better, and to improve their minds by the bad, as well as good example of what they deliver concerning foreign places.

I could heartily wish a law were enacted, that every traveller, before he were permitted to publish his voyages, should be obliged to make oath before the Lord High Chancellor, that all he intended to print was absolutely true to the best of his knowledge; for, then the world would no longer be deceived as it usually is, while some writers, to make their works pass the better upon the publick, impose the grossest falsities on the unwary reader. I have perused several books of travels with great delight in my younger days; but having since gone over most part of the globe, and been able to contradict many fabulous accounts from my own observation; it hath given me a great disgust against this part of reading, and some indignation to see the credulity of mankind so impudently abused. Therefore, since my acquaintance were pleased to think my poor endeavours might not be unacceptable to my country; I imposed on my self as a maxim, never to be swerved from, that I would *strictly adhere to truth*; neither indeed, can I be ever under the least temptation to vary from it, while I retain in my mind the lectures and example of my noble master, and the other illustrious Houyhnhnms, of whom I had so long the honour to be an humble hearer.

———Nec si miserum Fortuna Sinonem
Finxit, vanum etiam, mendacemque improba finget.

I know very well, how little reputation is to be got by writings which require neither genius nor learning, nor indeed any other talent, except a good memory, or an exact *journal*. I know likewise, that writers of travels, like dictionary-makers, are sunk into oblivion by the weight and bulk of those who come last, and therefore lie uppermost. And, it is highly probable, that such travellers who shall hereafter visit the countries described in this work of mine, may by detecting my errors, (if there be any) and adding many new discoveries of their own, jostle me out of vogue, and stand in my place; making the world forget that ever I was an author. This indeed would be too great a mortification if I wrote for fame: but, as my sole intention was the PUBLICK GOOD; I cannot be altogether disappointed. For, who can read the virtues I have mentioned in the glorious Houyhnhnms, without being ashamed of his own vices, when he considers himself as the reasoning, governing animal of his country? I shall say nothing of those remote nations where Yahoos preside; amongst which the least corrupted are the Brobdingnagians, whose wise maxims in morality and government, it would be our happiness to observe. But I forbear descanting further, and rather leave the judicious reader to his own remarks and applications.

I am not a little pleased that this work of mine can possibly meet with no censurers: for what objections can be made against a writer who relates only plain facts that happened in such distant countries, where we have not the least interest with respect either to trade or negociations? I have carefully avoided every fault with which common writers of travels are often too justly charged. Besides, I meddle not the least with any *party*, but write without passion, prejudice, or ill-will against any man or number of men whatsoever. I write for the noblest end, to inform and instruct mankind, over whom I may, without breach of modesty, pretend to some superiority, from the advantages I received by conversing so long among the most accomplished Houyhnhnms. I write without any view towards profit or praise. I never suffer a word to pass that may look like reflection, or possibly give the least offence even to those who are most ready to take it. So that, I hope, I may with justice pronounce my self an author perfectly blameless; against whom the tribes of answerers, considerers, observers, reflecters, detecters, remarkers, will never be able to find matter for exercising their talents.

I confess, it was whispered to me, that I was bound in duty as a subject of England, to have given in a memorial to a Secretary of State, at my first coming over; because, whatever lands are discovered by a subject, belong to the Crown. But I doubt, whether our conquests in the countries I treat of, would be as easy as those of Ferdinando Cortez, over the naked Americans. The Lilliputians I think, are hardly worth the charge of a fleet and army to reduce them; and I question whether it might be prudent or safe to attempt the Brobdingnagians: or, whether an English army would be much at their ease with the flying island over their heads. The Houyhnhnms, indeed, appear not to be so well prepared for war, a science to which they are perfect strangers, and especially against missive weapons. However, supposing my self to be a minister of State, I could never give my advice for invading them. Their prudence, unanimity, unacquaintedness with fear, and their love of their country, would amply supply all defects in the military art. Imagine twenty thousand of them breaking into the midst of an European army, confounding the ranks, overturning the carriages, battering the warriors faces into mummy, by terrible yerks from their hinder hoofs: for they would well deserve the character given to Augustus; 'Recalcitrat undique tutus.' But instead of proposals for conquering that magnanimous nation, I rather wish they were in a capacity or disposition to send a sufficient number of their inhabitants for civilizing Europe; by teaching us the first principles of honour, justice, truth, temperance, publick spirit, fortitude, chastity, friendship, benevolence, and fidelity. The *names* of all which virtues are still retained among us in most languages, and are to be met with in modern as well as ancient authors; which I am able to assert from my own small reading.

But, I had another reason which made me less forward to enlarge his Majesty's dominions by my discoveries: to say the truth, I had conceived a few scruples with relation to the distributive justice of princes upon those occasions. For instance, a crew of pyrates are driven by a storm they know not whither; at length a boy discovers land from the top-mast; they go on shore to rob and plunder; they see an harmless people, are entertained with kindness, they give the country a new name, they take formal possession of it for the king, they set up a rotten plank or a stone for a memorial, they murder two or three dozen of the natives, bring away a couple more by force for a sample, return home, and get their pardon. Here commenceth a new dominion acquired with a title by *divine right*. Ships are sent with the first opportunity; the natives driven out or destroyed, their princes tortured to discover their gold; a free licence given to all acts of inhumanity and lust; the earth reeking with the blood of its inhabitants: and this execrable crew of butchers employed in so pious an expedition, is a *modern colony* sent to convert and civilize an idolatrous and barbarous people.

But this description, I confess, doth by no means affect the British nation, who may be an example to the whole world for their wisdom, care, and justice in planting colonies; the liberal endowments for the advancement of religion and learning; their choice of devout and able pastors to propagate Christianity; their caution in stocking their provinces with people of sober lives and conversations from this the mother kingdom; their strict regard to the distribution of justice, in supplying the civil administration through all their colonies with officers of the greatest abilities, utter strangers to corruption: and to crown all, by sending the most vigilant and virtuous governors, who have no other views than the happiness of the people over whom they preside, and the honour of the king their master.

But, as those countries which I have described do not appear to have a desire of being conquered, and enslaved, murdered or driven out by colonies; nor abound either in gold, silver, sugar or tobacco; I did humbly conceive they were by no means proper objects of our zeal, or valour, or our interest.   However, if those whom it may concern, think fit to be of another opinion, I am ready to depose, when I shall be lawfully called, that no European did ever visit these countries before me.   I mean, if the inhabitants ought to be believed.

But, as to the formality of taking possession in my sovereign's name, it never came once into my thoughts; and if it had, yet as my affairs then stood, I should perhaps in point of prudence and self-preservation, have put it off to a better opportunity.

Having thus answered the *only* objection that can be raised against me as a traveller; I here take a final leave of my courteous readers, and return to enjoy my own speculations in my little garden at Redriff; to apply those excellent lessons of virtue which I learned among the Houyhnhnms; to instruct the Yahoos of my own family as far as I shall find them docible animals; to behold my figure often in a glass, and thus, if possible, habituate my self, by time, to tolerate the sight of a human creature: to lament the brutality of Houyhnhnms in my own country, but always treat their persons with respect, for the sake of my noble master, his family, his friends, and the whole Houyhnhnm race, whom these of ours have the honour to resemble in all their lineaments, however their intellectuals came to degenerate.

I began last week to permit my wife to sit at dinner with me, at the farthest end of a long table; and to answer (but with the utmost brevity) the few questions I asked her. Yet the smell of a Yahoo continuing very offensive, I always keep my nose well stopped with rue, lavender, or tobacco-leaves. And although it be hard for a man late in life to remove old habits; I am not altogether out of hopes in some time to suffer a neighbour Yahoo in my company, without the apprehensions I am yet under of his teeth or his claws.

My reconcilement to the Yahoo-kind in general might not be so difficult, if they would be content with those vices and follies only which nature hath entitled them to. I am not in the least provoked at the sight of a lawyer, a pick-pocket, a colonel, a fool, a lord, a gamester, a politician, a whoremonger, a physician, an evidence, a suborner, an attorney, a traytor, or the like: this is all according to the due course of things: but, when I behold a lump of de-formity, and diseases both in body and mind, smitten with *pride*, it immediately breaks all the measures of my patience; neither shall I be ever able to comprehend how such an animal and such a vice could tally together. The wise and virtuous Houyhnhnms, who abound in all excellencies that can adorn a rational creature, have no name for this vice in their language, which hath no terms to express any thing that is evil, except those whereby they describe the de-testable qualities of their Yahoos; among which they were not able to distinguish this of pride, for want of thoroughly understanding humane nature, as it sheweth it self in other countries, where that animal presides. But I, who had more experience, could plainly observe some rudiments of it among the wild Yahoos.

But the Houyhnhnms, who live under the government of reason, are, no more proud of the good qualities they possess, than I should be for not wanting a leg or an arm, which no man in his wits would boast of, although he must be miserable without them. I dwell the longer upon this subject from the desire I have to make the society of an English Yahoo by any means not insupportable; and therefore, I here intreat those who have any tincture of this absurd vice, that they will not presume to appear in my sight.

FINIS

ABOUT THE INTRODUCER

PAT ROGERS is DeBartolo Professor in the Liberal Arts at the University of South Florida. He has edited the complete poems of Jonathan Swift and is the author of *Literature and Popular Culture in Eighteenth-Century England*, *The Augustan Vision*, and books on Pope, Defoe, Johnson and Fielding.

EVERYMAN'S LIBRARY, founded in 1906 and
relaunched in 1991, aims to offer the most
complete library in the English language
of the world's classics. Each volume
is printed in a classic typeface
on acid-free, cream-wove
paper with a sewn
full cloth bind-
ing.